DORRIT WILLUMSEN is a central figure among Scandinavian writers with a writing career starting in 1965 and a great number of prizes to her name, notably The Danish Academy's Grand Prize (1981). In her own words, she is a 'war child', born in 1940 in Copenhagen, and much of her fiction and memoirs concern themselves with the war years and the decades leading up to the postwar economic boom in Denmark. However, she is also a master of historical fiction, including the popular novels *Marie* about Madame Tussaud and *Klædt i purpur* (Dressed in Purple) portraying the Byzantine Empress Theodora. *Bang*, Willumsen's exceptional biographical novel about the Danish canonical writer Herman Bang, earned her The Nordic Council Literature Prize in 1997.

MARINA ALLEMANO holds a Ph.D. in Comparative Literature and has taught Scandinavian Studies at the University of Alberta, Canada. She has previously translated Suzanne Brøgger's *A Fighting Pig's Too Tough to Eat and Other Prose Texts* (1997) and Hanne Marie Svendsen's novel *Under the Sun* (2006). Monographs dealing with the same writers, as well as Dorrit Willumsen, were published in Danish: *Suzanne Brøgger. En introduktion* (2004), *HAV-FRUE. Hanne Marie Svendsens forfatterskab* (2010) and *Prinsesse Sukkergodt med barberblad. Læsninger i Dorrit Willumsens forfatterskab* (2015).

Some other books by Norvik Press:

Benny Andersen: *The Contract Killer* (Translated by Paul Russell Garrett)

Jógvan Isaksen: *Walpurgis Tide* (Translated by John Keithsson)

Jørgen-Frantz Jacobsen: *Barbara* (Translated by George Johnston)

Klaus Rifbjerg: *Terminal Innocence* (translated by Paul Larkin)

Hanne Marie Svendsen: *Under the Sun* (Translated by Marina Allemano)

Kirsten Thorup: *The God of Chance* (Translated by Janet Garton)

Dan Turèll: *Murder in the Dark* (Translated by Mark Mussari)

For our complete back catalogue, please visit
www.norvikpress.com

Bang

A Novel about the Danish Writer

by

Dorrit Willumsen

Translated from the Danish by
Marina Allemano

Norvik Press
2017

Originally published in Danish as *Bang* © Dorrit Willumsen &
Gyldendal, Copenhagen 1996. Published by agreement with the
Gyldendal Group Agency.

This translation © Marina Allemano 2017.

The translator's moral right to be identified as the translator of the
work has been asserted.

A catalogue record for this book is available from the British Library.
ISBN: 978-1-909408-34-0

Norvik Press
Department of Scandinavian Studies
University College London
Gower Street
London WC1E 6BT
United Kingdom

Website: www.norvikpress.com
E-mail address: norvik.press@ucl.ac.uk

Managing editors: Elettra Carbone, Sarah Death, Janet Garton,
C. Claire Thomson.

Cover image: Ameen Fahmy, 2016, unsplash.com

Cover design: Essi Viitanen

Printed in the UK by Lightning Source UK Ltd.

This publication has been made possible by the generous support
of the Danish Arts Foundation.

DANISH ARTS FOUNDATION

Contents

Translator's Preface 7
1..17
2..39
3..66
4..86
5..115
6..132
7..153
8..170
9..187
10..201
11..214
12..236
13..260
14..291
15..311
16..331
17..360
Coda...375
Acknowledgements...381
Notes..383
Postscript..389

Translator's Preface

After having written an article in 1991 about her literary hero Herman Bang (1857-1912) for the daily paper *Jyllands-Posten*, with a subsequent reprinting of the piece in the volume *Heltehistorier* (Stories of Heroes), Dorrit Willumsen (born 1940) was approached by the then editor at Gyldendal publishers, Kurt Fromberg, to write a new biography of the canonical Danish writer.

Dorrit Willumsen – an established and prolific writer in her own right with several historical novels and plays to her credit – accepted the offer and embarked on her research in the Royal Library in Copenhagen. In addition to studying previous biographies and Bang's literary and journalistic output in depth, she spent months reading the thousands of letters in Bang's original, scrawled handwriting.

However, the conventional approach and style expected in biographical 'life and times' narratives did not suit her literary temperament, and in consultation with her new editor, Johannes Riis, she abandoned her first draft and launched into a fictional biography that not only pays allegiance to the historical facts of Bang's life but also reflects her talent as an imaginative writer. The result is *Bang. En roman om Herman Bang* (1996), a novel that earned the author the prestigious Nordic Council Literature Prize in 1997.

Dorrit Willumsen's Herman Bang is a man in motion. The framework of the novel takes place over seventeen days in January, 912, on board a train from New York en route to San Francisco from where the traveller intends to sail to Japan as part of his planned World Reading Tour. The tour, however, is abruptly cut short when the already ailing writer is found unconscious in his train compartment. Herman Bang dies in Ogden, Utah, on 29 January 1912, at the age of fifty-four.

Through Bang's memories that are narrated in flashbacks, the reader follows him on his erratic journey through life from his birthplace on the island of Als to his final days on the American train. Bang moves constantly from dwelling to dwelling, from town to town, from city to city, from country to country – from Copenhagen to Berlin to Vienna to Prague, through the Nordic region, Russia, Germany, Austria, France and the USA. As a literary writer, journalist, actor and theatre director he pursues his ambitions unwaveringly in spite of a weak constitution, financial problems and a law that forbids homosexual activities. He is fuelled by a will to strength, if not to power.

In Denmark, Herman Bang is especially loved for his stories about the so-called *Stille Eksistenser* (Quiet Lives), a number of inconspicuous characters – often women – who lack agency or strength to change their circumstances. Katinka in his novel *Ved Vejen* (By the Road) is one of those tragic heroines whom life and passion have passed by, and it is to the credit of both Bang and Willumsen that the reader of the present biographical novel is deeply affected by Katinka's story and Bang's creation of her character while he himself was living a troubled life in Vienna and Prague. In 2006, *Ved Vejen* was given a well-deserved place in the official Danish Cultural Canon.

The style in Dorrit Willumsen's novel mimics in part Herman Bang's own narrative style which he by 1890 had identified as being impressionist. 'The Impressionist,' Bang writes in an open letter addressed to his colleague Erik Skram, 'consciously avoids elucidation and reflection and the mulling over of things … . He believes that the object of his account is to present people in action.' Hence, less telling and more showing. Bang continues: 'Like all art, impressionist narratives set out to present human emotions and thoughts. But they shy away from all direct explanations and only show mankind's emotional life in a series of mirrors – through it actions.'[1] Interestingly, five years later Bang met the French painter Claude Monet in Norway, the very artist whose painting 'Impression Soleil Levant' (1872) gave its name to the impressionist movement in France, and after they had been introduced to each other, Monet read Bang's novel *Tine* in a French translation and declared that it was the only impressionist novel he knew of.

Like Herman Bang, Dorrit Willumsen has an eye for sensory details and dynamic scenes as well as an intuitive understanding of emotional lives. Yet the novel about Bang is far from being derivative. Willumsen is known for her black humour and occasional razor-edged touch that inspired a Danish critic to nickname her 'Princess Sugar With Razor Blade.'[2] In her depiction of moments in Bang's life, she effectively conjures up images that stay with the reader for a long time. For instance, near the beginning of the novel where the protagonist remembers his early childhood years, the narrator describes a surreal dinner scene where the child's mismatched and eccentric parents give an odd performance that presages dark days ahead:

> Just before the dessert, father takes her hand and places it on a perfectly clean plate and parades her around the table so everyone can see that her hand is as white as porcelain.
>
> She lowers her head a little as if she is embarrassed. But laughs nevertheless. You can see the blue veins just under the delicate skin on the back of her hand. And everyone is sitting there, smiling, with their forks and knives, saying that it is fantastic. That a married woman can have such a hand.
>
> No, she is definitely not made for menial work.
>
> And all the knives and forks cut against the white porcelain. And what if one of the guests were suddenly to turn around and nick that hand. Just like snipping off the head of a white flower.
>
> Those hands, they are so delicious you could eat them.

The source of this scene is based on an anecdote mentioned in Harry Jacobsen's biography of Bang,[3] but Willumsen admits that letting the young child imagine that a guest could snip off his mother's hand is her own invention,[4] by which she grants her biographical subject an early fantasy life that is in keeping with what is known about his unusual childhood and the literary genius that he later became - and also in keeping with her own style as a writer.

Accordingly, the biographical novel is a many-layered representation of a man's life in terms of facts and fiction. Willumsen writes in her memoir that 'many have written about Herman Bang: writers, personal friends, old schoolmates, journalists and actors with whom he had worked. He made a strong and very diverse impression on the people who met him. There is probably no final truth about Herman Bang. But many stories and truths.'[5]

The task of the translator is to capture the words, the tone and the meaning of the original work in another language, and in the case of Dorrit Willumsen's novel, the translator is also indirectly dealing with the voices that resonate through the many preceding interpretations and impressions.

The myriad of letters quoted in Willumsen's text have proven to be an extra challenge for the translator in that Bang's informal style reflects epistolary conventions of his time as well as his particular whimsical and often emotional language. It is my hope that the translation has done right by both Dorrit Willumsen's and Herman Bang's creative language and their respective idioms.

Finally thank you to Dorrit Willumsen who kindly answered all my questions about Herman Bang's life and work. Also many thanks to my editors Claire Thomson and Janet Garton for their painstaking efforts with the manuscript.

Marina Allemano
Edmonton, Alberta, Canada
August 2017

Endnotes

1 Herman Bang, '"Impressionisme." En lille replik,' *Tilskueren.*
Maanedsskrift for Litteratur, Kunst, Samfundsspørgsmaal og
almenfattelige videnskabelige Skildringer August 1890: 692-694.
2 Marina Allemano, *Prinsesse Sukkergodt med barberblad*
(Copenhagen: Gyldendal, 2015), 24.
3 Harry Jacobsen, *Den unge Herman Bang* (Copenhagen:
H. Hagerup, 1954), 21.
4 Dorrit Willumsen, letter to Marina Allemano, 13 October 2014.
5 Dorrit Willumsen, *Pligten til lykke. Erindringer* (Copenhagen:
Gyldendal, 2011), 194-5.

Dorrit Willumsen: selected works

1940 Dorrit Willumsen was born in Copenhagen on 31 August.
1965 *Knagen. Noveller* (The Hook. Short Stories).
1966 *Stranden. Roman* (The Beach. Novel).
1968 *Da. Roman* (Then. Novel).
1970 *The krydderi acryl salær græshopper. Roman* (Tea Spices
Acrylic Salary Grasshoppers. Novel).
1973 *Modellen Coppelia. Noveller og digte* (The Model Coppelia.
Short Stories and Poems).
1974 *En værtindes smil. Roman og novellette* (A Hostess' Smile.
Novel and Novella).
1976 *Kontakter. Digte* (Contacts. Poems).
1976 *Neonhaven. Roman* (The Neon Garden. Novel).
1978 *Hvis det virkelig var en film. Noveller* (If It Really Were a
Film. Short Stories).
1978 *Den stærkeste II* (The Stronger II. Play).
1980 *Manden som påskud. Roman* (Man as an Excuse. Novel).
1981 *Programmeret til kærlighed. Roman* (Programmed for Love.
Novel).
1983 *Umage par. Digte* (Odd Couples. Poems).
1983 *Marie. En roman om Madame Tussauds liv* (Marie. A
Novel about the Life of Madame Tussaud).
1985 *Caroline. Skuespil i 2 akter* (Caroline. Play in Two Acts).
1986 *Suk hjerte. Roman* (Your Heart May Ache. Novel)

1988   *Glemslens forår. Noveller* (The Spring of Oblivion. Short
        Stories)
1990   *Klædt i purpur. Roman* (Dressed in Purple. Novel).
1991   *Margrete den 1.* (Queen Margrete I. Play).
1992   *Klædt i purpur. Skuespil i 2 akter* (Dressed in Purple. Play
        in Two Acts).
1996   *Bang. En roman om Herman Bang* (Bang. A Novel about
        the Danish Writer).
2000   *Koras stemme. Roman* (Kora's Voice. Novel).
2001   *Tøs. Et hundeliv. Roman* (Lass. A Dog's Life. Novel).
2003   *Bruden fra Gent. Roman* (The Bride from Ghent. Novel).
2005   *Den dag jeg blev Honey Hotwing. Noveller* (The Day I
        Became Honey Hotwing. Short Stories).
2005   *Min søn – digteren. Monolog* (My Son – The Poet.
        Monologue about Hans Christian Andersen).
2008   *Dage med Slave. Roman* (Days with a Slave. Novel).
2009   *Det søde med det sure. Erindringer* (Taking the Smooth
        with the Rough, Memoir).
2011   *Pligten til lykke. Erindringer* (Duty to Happiness. Memoir).
2013   *Guldbryllup. Digte* (with Jess Ørnsbo) (Golden Wedding
        Annivesary. Poems).
2015   *Nær og fjern. Roman* (Near and Far. Novel).

Other English Translations of Works by Dorrit Willumsen

1982   *If It Really Were a Film.* Trans. Ann-Marie Rasmussen.
        Curbstone Press. Trans. of the anthology of short
        stories *Hvis det virkelig var en film.*
1986   *Marie. A Novel about the Life of Madame Tussaud.* Trans.
        Patricia Crampton. The Bodley Head. Transl. of *Marie. En
        roman om Madame Tussauds liv.*

Life and Works of Herman Bang

1857   Born in Asserballe on the island of Als on 20 April.
1863   The family moves to Horsens.
1871   Mother Thora Bang dies.

1872 The family moves to Tersløse. Herman attends the boarding school Sorø Akademi.

1875 Father Frederik L. Bang dies. Herman graduates from high school.

1875 Herman Bang moves to Copenhagen and is supported by his famous grandfather Oluf Lundt Bang, Royal Physician.

1877 Oluf Lundt Bang dies.

1879 *Realisme og Realister* (Realism and Realists. Critical essays).

1880 *Haabløse Slægter* (Hopeless Generations. Novel).

1883 *Fædra* (Phaedra. Novel).

1885 *Excentriske Noveller* (Eccentric Stories): 'Fratelli Bedini', 'Charlot Dupont', 'Franz Pander'.

1886 *Stille Eksistenser* (Quiet Lives): *Ved Vejen* (By the Road), 'Min gamle Kammerat' (My Old Friend), 'Enkens Søn' (The Widow's Son) and 'Son Altesse' (aka 'Hendes Højhed', [Her Highness]).

1887 *Stuk* (Stucco. Novel).

1889 *Tine* (Tine. Novel).

1890 *Under Aaget* (Carrying the Yoke): 'Irene Holm', 'En dejlig Dag' (A Lovely Day), 'Frøken Caja' (Miss Caja).

1890 'Les Quatre diables' (The Four Devils. Novella).

1896 *Ludvigsbakke* (Ludvigsbakke. Novel).

1898 *Det hvide Hus* (The White House. Memoir).

1901 *Det graa Hus* (The Grey House. Memoir).

1902 *Sommerglæder* (Joys of Summer. Novel).

1907 *Sælsomme Fortællinger* (Strange Tales): 'Barchan er død' (Barchan Is Dead), 'Men du skal mindes mig' (But You Shall Remember Me), 'Stærkest' (Strongest).

1904 *Mikaël* (Novel).

1906 *De uden Fædreland* (Those Without a Country. Novel).

1909 Herman Bang dictates 'Gedanken zum Sexualitätsproblem' to Dr. Max Wasbutzki in Berlin.

1912 Herman Bang dies in Ogden, Utah, on 29 January.

1922 Publ. of 'Gedanken zum Sexualitätsproblem' (Bonn).

1927 Publ of. 'Mine Tanker om det sexuelle Problem' (My Thoughts About the Sexual Problem) in the Danish weekly *K.T. Smart*.

English Translations of Works by Herman Bang

1927   *Denied a Country*. Trans. Arthur G. Chater and Marie Busch. Knopf. Trans. of *De uden Fædreland*.

1928   *Four Devils*. Trans. Guy Fowler. Grosset and Dunlap. Trans. of 'Les Quatre diables.'

1928   *Ida Brandt*. Trans. Arthur G. Chater. Knopf. Trans. of *Ludvigsbakke*.

1928   'Irene Holm' and 'In Rosenborg Park.' *Denmark's Best Stories: An Introduction to Danish Fiction*. Ed. Hanna Astrup Larsen. The American-Scandinavian Foundation and W.W. Norton. Trans. of 'Irene Holm' and 'Gennem Rosenborg Have.'

1984   *Tina*. Trans. Paul Christophersen. Athlone Press. Trans. of *Tine*.

1990   *Katinka*. Trans. Tiina Nunnally. Fjord Press. Trans. of *Ved Vejen*.

2012   *Ida Brandt*. Trans. W. Glyn Jones. Dedalus Books. Trans. of *Ludvigsbakke*.

2014   *As Trains Pass By*. Trans. W. Glyn Jones. Dedalus Books. Trans. of *Ved Vejen*.

1.

The night between the 22nd and 23rd of January, 1912, he checked in at Hotel Astor near Times Square, two days late because of the storm but otherwise entirely according to plan. And New York was appalling.

Cars roamed through the streets, howling like wolves. Powdered, cliff-like buildings were bathed in a strange pink light. They sparkled in the glow of the street lamps and the advertisements' vulgar phoniness. The city was just the place for seizures and fainting spells.

When he finally got to his room and tried turning on the light, a propeller on the ceiling began to spin. An ice-cold wind scattered the notes for his travel article, and while he was crawling on his hands and knees, trying to gather them up, the telephone rang. And he, who practically never spoke on the phone, was forced to lift the receiver to make the ringing stop and then listen to a voice he didn't understand. It was of no use hanging up, for the dreadful ringing and the same unpleasant voice came back until he finally discovered that by following the cable he could unplug it from the wall.

Then he managed to open the curtains, and the strange light seeped into the room. He put the papers under the pillow and placed himself on top of it. He had to gather himself before finally locating the switch on a wall lamp so he could make his way to the door and turn off that hideous contraption in the ceiling. But by now the room was already so cold that his attempts at warming up his hands under the scalding hot water tap were in vain. In New York he could have given up on the tour.

Sleeping was not possible. The sounds of the city percolated through him. Footsteps, doors, bells. Switches that went on and off. On and off. Distant ringing like thousands of insects stepping amongst fine wires on tiny metal feet. And he forced himself to think about his reading tomorrow. And he forced himself not to think about his reading tomorrow. But would they leave the money in cash by his mirror, or would they say that the money would be forwarded in a month's time?

When the light turned bluish, he got up and looked out on the city and took a double dose of sleeping draught. But it didn't help. It wasn't until late in the afternoon that he became so exhausted that the descending strokes in his travel piece grew increasingly longer and thicker until the pen dropped out of his hand.

And then, suddenly, they were in his room ready to collect him. A delightful young man and a pretty young lady.

He insisted on seeing a barber before the reading. And it was awful. Not even the barber understood him.

'Make me beautiful,' he said. 'And hide my little bald patch. Colour it black. Teindre en noir,' he said. The barber himself was a lovely shade of black. But the fool just kept on cutting and cutting.

And he didn't colour the patch black. No, he can positively feel that it is white. A grinning moon white as a corpse.

But the actual reading was a success. They wept over his novel *Tine* and wrung their tears from their sodden handkerchiefs.

Naturally, he didn't receive any money. But the hotel room filled up with flowers which he had to leave behind. He only took a single daisy and stuck it in his buttonhole.

In New York he could have given up on the tour. From New York he could have returned on the steamer.

Admittedly, he didn't have enough cash to pay for a ticket. But if he could have found a pawnbroker. The diamond ring and the golden cigarette case with his monogram set in small blue sapphires. Gifts from actors and friends on his fiftieth birthday. It would have been especially painful to part with those things that had given him much pleasure every day for four, nearly five years. And he would never be able to admit that he had sold them. He would have to say that he had been robbed. Well, the situation never arose. How do you find a pawnbroker if you cannot even make yourself understood to a barber?

*

The train moves fast. Much too fast. And suddenly: a meadow white with flowers. Camomile, daisies or dandelion globes. He puts on his glasses, and everything disappears in a fog. He feels dizzy and must close his eyes.

White flowers and a slight, young woman dressed in white. Under her dark chignon her neck is so delicate and slender. She bends down and picks one of the white seed heads. She blows, and all the downy tufts burst into the air. And a young boy runs in front of her, catching the dancing fluffy seeds. He falls and picks his own dandelions and blows and blows until his face turns red from the effort and tears well in his eyes.

The young woman bends down towards him. 'Now, tomorrow will be a fine day,' she says and lifts him up.

*

She stands at the top of the stairs, dressed in white, and her hair, almost black, gathered in a soft bun. The sitting room behind her is white. The door is open, and you can see all her green plants. The entire house is white, the stairs too.

Facing the sun, she laughs while the children slide down the banisters.

They are much too wild and badly behaved, those children.

'One of these days, one of you will break your neck,' she says. Her voice is still clear and bright.

'If you break your neck, will you then fly around like a dead chicken?' Herman asks.

*

She is the loveliest of mothers, and the children cling too much to her skirts. When she walks through the grove, they flock around her like a brood of chicks. When she reads out loud to them, they follow her and all her movements. She is both hero and heroine. She can make her voice sound very frail as if it might break at any moment. But then she suddenly gets up and flings the dark red tablecloth with all the golden fringes around her like a knight's cape. And she stands fearless and furious right under the lamp.

'Aren't the children ever going to bed?' asks the father, sounding like he is tired of both the children and the woman wrapped in the tablecloth.

When father is away, all the dolls come out and are put on the table. They are models that she has cut out of fashion journals. They are so thin that they sometimes break in two. They have small heads with almond-shaped eyes and long, long legs. Some of them tuck their hands into fur muffs. Others hold a fan under their chin.

Mother guides them across the table and lets them speak in different voices. 'Dearest,' they say. And one of them is weeping: 'My heart is nearly bursting with love.' 'But dear me, you unhappy soul.' 'And then I said: "Let's have a nice hot cup of tea."'

All the servant girls come into the sitting room and look at the dolls. And especially at mother, the pastor's wife.

'The pastor!' Hanne suddenly cries out.

'The pastor! The pastor!' The girls scurry out in all directions. With a single movement mother sweeps all the dolls into the drawer.

Father looks at mother who is sitting tall and straight. And at the children, standing wide-eyed. It is as if he can see the shadows of all the dolls on the table.

*

They are happy as only a few can claim to be, the pastor and his wife. That a husband can be so much in love with his own wife. That is quite unheard of.

They stroll arm in arm along the tree-lined driveway. 'Thora, my love, you make me so happy!' Father repeats it over and over again. No one can come between them. He kisses her hands.

When do children become happy?

Children should be seen and not heard. And only when you

are able to eat with your elbows tucked in close to your body and without spilling your food are you allowed to sit at the table when there is company.

Mother eats more elegantly than anyone else, she has the most beautiful hands in the world. They are pure white, and the nails are like small, pale pink cockle shells. She buffs them on a small leather pillow. If one of those nails were to break, the world would collapse.

Just before the dessert, father takes her hand and places it on a perfectly clean plate and parades her around the table so everyone can see that her hand is as white as porcelain.

She lowers her head a little as if she is embarrassed. But laughs nevertheless. You can see the blue veins just under the delicate skin on the back of her hand. And everyone is sitting there, smiling, with their forks and knives, saying that it is fantastic. That a married woman can have such a hand.

No, she is definitely not made for menial work.

And all the knives and forks cut against the white porcelain. And what if one of the guests were suddenly to turn around and nick that hand. Just like snipping off the head of a white flower.

Those hands, they are so delicious you could eat them.

Herman drinks some water. He has to cool down to stop himself from laughing or crying.

*

It is so ugly, so ugly to cry. And especially not a thing for a mother to do.

Mother is all in black. She swallows up all the shadows. She bends her head so her face becomes a shadow too.

Mother is too delicate and beautiful to be crying out loud. Her face must never turn red and look distorted. Her nose mustn't be running. Her mouth mustn't open up and spit out ugly sounds.

Her tears are internal. Grief makes her cold and fragile. And her movements are slow and small. She can't even get up from her chair.

The children come to her. They lie down on the floor by her feet and stroke the deep black folds on her skirt. She pushes their hands away as if their warm, gentle caresses cause her pain.

They have never seen her like this.

'The missus' father has died,' says Hanne. 'You should leave your mother alone.'

Father is standing in the doorway. He looks at the woman turned to stone. Then he turns on his heel and goes back to his sermon.

*

In the pond tadpoles swim in and out between Herman's fingers. His ship is sailing to the end of the world. But he cannot stop himself from looking at his reflection in the water. He forgets about the ship that Oluf, his older brother, has made from a cardboard box and a stick for a mast. For it is as if his face is lying at the bottom, and the tadpoles and the movements of his fingers are making it all creased. And he feels a tickle in his tummy, and maybe he is about to be transformed.

It is impossible not to look in the mirror. It is not as if he is pleased about what he sees. His hair could be longer and the collar cleaner. And the neck should never be grimy.

His eyes are large and dark brown. But the right one is looking in the wrong direction. They are not allowed to tease him about it, says mother. And it will probably correct itself.

When he covers his good eye with his hand, everything disappears. His face is just a mist on the mirror. It frightens him and he pulls his hand away and everything comes back again. His own face, too, that looks so frightened that he bursts out laughing. And he pulls his eyes to see himself as a Chinaman. He tries to look like someone who wants to kiss. Or someone who is about to cry. Or as if he had suddenly caught sight of the big dark man behind his back. Small boys are forbidden to play with mirrors. For girls it is not as bad.

Mother gazes in the mirror for long spells at a time. Especially when she combs her hair. And it is a joy to watch her putting up her hair. It is so heavy and dark and shiny that it is hard to comprehend how she can carry it all on her small head and thin, delicate neck. It is loveliest when her hair fans out as if she were an elf maiden or a princess. Unfortunately she braids it and sticks hairpins in it. The parting in the middle is so white and smooth that you can see how delicate and dainty she is from head to toe. No one can look away when mother is putting up her hair in front of the mirror.

Nini only looks at herself in the mirror a little bit. And perhaps Tine never does. For she can twist her braid around her head in a flash while sitting on the swing with William, the spoiled child, on her lap.

William is too well-behaved and much too small to look at himself in the mirror. But he, Herman, cannot help himself. Even in a window or a polished cabinet he can suddenly catch his own reflection. And that is dangerous. For behind the pond is the grove, and behind the grove is the wood, and in the wood lives the big dark man who snatches away children who look in the mirror and ask too many questions and cry because they have to go to bed.

And he cries, and he looks in the mirror, and he protests, and he asks questions, and he never wants to go to bed. For in the darkness the man comes to grab him, especially him, the boy who is so impossible and difficult.

And it is no use crying, hitting, scratching or kicking. Not even a packet of sewing needles under the pillow would help. For he is so big, so big and strong, the black man. And he carries all the naughty children out into the big, dark wood. And then father and mother will be free. They just put a lump of sugar on the windowsill. And then the stork will bring a new child that is truly sweet and well-behaved.

*

The path leading to the parish clerk's house is getting wider and wider. Father rides that way. Mother walks down there a couple of days a week with the children. The parish clerk's family are such nice people. Their chairs are softer than any others, their blackberries are sweeter and their waffles so hot that you'll burn your fingertips. Tine carries them in without burning herself. The nicest of them all is Tine.

Many a time she has helped him get up when he fell down and has rocked him in her arms like in a small boat. Her skin smells of sunshine, and her hair is perfectly fair from the sun. Tine is a ray of sunshine with white stockings and braids tied in bows. Besides, she is as strong as a farmhand. But luckily you cannot see it.

The servant girls tease her and say she has puppy fat. They are clearly envious. For Tine doesn't have to be in service. She can come and go as she likes and do needlework and eat rusks and play.

And she can have visitors herself.

The servant girls at the parsonage have visitors, especially at night. They live in the low yellow building with bars on the windows like in a prison where the smell of sleep and yellow everlasting flowers fills the air.

Tine says: 'My little tot. My dumpling. My squirrel.' She swings William around and then Herman. And he insists that she mustn't let go of him. Never. 'The two of us, Tine. We will always be together.'

'But, surely, I am going to get married. I want a husband and four big boys.'

'Like me. – I am strong and brave and one metre and five tall.'

She laughs and shakes her head. Perhaps not exactly like him.

She pulls a leaf off a plantain weed. Three white ribs. That means three boyfriends.

Nini holds up a buttercup to Tine's chin. The sun is shining. Three yellow spots show right above Tine's dimple. And that is surely a sign that she will have three boys.

They pick daisies. He loves me, he loves me not. He loves me.

'Who do you love, Tine. Who, Tine?'

She blushes and doesn't know.

It is nice to know someone who has puppy fat and whose face sometimes turns red, and who can swing and sew and bake and sing and swirl around and run without getting tired.

*

Saturday is like thin ice. Sunday morning is all ice and agony.

All Saturday you have to be quiet. Not a sound in the house. You are not allowed to disturb the pastor, for he is pacing up and down in his study, rehearsing his sermon.

When he finally opens the door, his face is all gloomy. And the horse is saddled up, and the pastor goes for a ride to clear his head.

The pastor is a real man. He swims in the fjord even in the winter. And when it is all frozen solid, he glides across the ice on his beautiful silvery skates while holding out his coat tails to gain speed. The pastor does figures of eight and outside edges on his Copenhagen skates. You have never seen such a daft pastor, and when he galops along on his horse who would have thought that he sometimes has to tie rags around his aching head in the house, and that the children's voices pierce his ears right through to his brain.

But Sunday mornings sting the most. Herman has seen it himself. He has seen his father cross the yard wearing his thick blue bathrobe. Father knocks on Hanne's window. It almost sounds like thunder. For it is the time beween night and dawn when only the pastor is awake, and also those children who cannot sleep.

Hanne groans a bit inside and comes out, her eyes puffy from sleep. She has pulled a jersey over her nightgown and thrown a shawl around her head. She is dragging her big yellow clogs across the courtyard, and her entire body exudes sleep. She pauses by the well. She pumps and pumps a whole bucket full of icy Sunday water and hauls it into the scullery.

And there is the pastor, white and bright like Christ on the cross, apart from the pastor's loin cloth that is monogrammed with F. & T. Bang in satin stitch.

'What are we waiting for, Hanne?' The pastor is impatient.

'Yes, pastor Bang.' The cold makes her voice sound clearer than usual.

Then she steps out of her clogs and climbs on to the stool with her bucket, and with her last bit of strength and with a vacant look in her eyes, she pours the ice-cold water over the pastor, who suddenly flails about and shakes like a wet dog.

'Thank you, Hanne,' he says very politely.

But over in the church when he stands in the tall, carved pulpit and raises both his voice and his arms, then it is father, the master, the pastor who is in charge.

Afterwards, from sheer relief, he will enjoy a glass of red wine with dinner.

And mother keeps saying that he was wonderful.

'Really?' he asks. 'Do you really mean that?'

She smiles and nods.

And sometimes the parish clerk and two other pastors come to play cards and drink port and punch.

It sometimes happens that they stay until dawn.

But by then father, the master, the pastor is a beaten man with an aching body and so many rags tied around his sore head that you can hardly recognize him.

*

Hanne, the maid, lifts Herman up. He notices the smell of lavender from her collar and the warm, slightly oily smell from her hair. She stands him in the tall chair, and first he sways a bit as if he is about to fall. Then he grabs the back of the chair and closes his eyes for a moment.

'Just like the pastor,' Hanne doubles up with laughter. 'It is like seeing the pastor himself.'

And he spreads out his arms and raises his eyes towards the ceiling, or heaven, and begins to chant. He does exactly like father does over in the church. He chants and sings from his belly, and the sound fills up the entire room.

Mother enters and for a moment she looks serious. But then she can't hold back her laughter either.

'The new year is a Christ child,' he says. And he continues to repeat it like father does while raising his arms as if he himself is carrying the blessed child, or the new year, in his hands.

He nearly falls over backwards. The servant girls are doubled up with laughter. They are all watching him. Hanne, Sofie, Ane and Marie. And mother and Oluf and Nini and Christella and William. He says it over and over again. And they laugh.

Then, suddenly, he sees their faces freeze.

A shadow approaches from behind, grabs him and pulls him down. Father shakes him until his head dangles like a loose button.

'Are you making fun of Jesus and your father?'

And he is put in the corner, staring at the wall while tears run down his cheeks and neck, soaking his collar. For it feels much to sad and salty to try to catch them with your tongue. And besides, you mustn't stick your tongue out. He has to think things over and repent and ask for forgiveness.

'You are spoiling that boy, all of you,' he hears his father say.

Mother says something in her small thin voice.

All the girls have left.

He closes his eyes, and his stomach feels queasy just like when Hanne lifted him up. It felt like an invisible ladder. White like mother's nightgown. And tall. Just as tall as the one in the circus where the beautiful lady climbed way up high while balancing a pretty coffee cup on a knife she held in her mouth.

But his ladder is even taller. It grows out of the tent and all the way to heaven, and it becomes flexible and light so you can swing on it like in a hammock. You can get up much higher than you can blow a dandelion seed.

'Have you now had a look inside yourself?' asks father. 'What did you see?'

He tells him about the ladder that reached the sky. Higher than a dandelion seed can fly.

'You can't even tell the truth. There is no ladder.'

But father has said so himself over in the church. One of the bleak Sundays where Hanne's ice-cold water made the words spring from his mouth. And father himself has done tricks, standing way up under the ceiling.

Mother says that Herman is just a little boy with a vivid imagination. But his tears are brave. Nothing can stop them. Neither cold water, darkness nor the world's thickest handkerchief.

*

'Look at me, mother, look at me!' He jumps on her bed. And he is a troll, an angel and a Chinaman.

But she looks mostly at William for he is the youngest and so good and pretty. William never asks questions, he just sits there and looks straight ahead with his big blue eyes and lets them kiss his forehead and his hair and his small, fat, dimply hands.

'Look at me, mother, look at me!' Herman can't sit still.

Sometimes she looks at him with a gentle, surprised look.

'Yes, look at the boy,' she says. And he shouts with joy.

Or she says: 'Walk properly on your feet.' And he forces his feet to turn outward like a duckling.

'Stand straight,' says his father. 'A boy should stand tall and straight.'

He looks at his father's tall slender back and thinks about water buckets and skates. He tries to stand as straight as a poker. But as soon as he sits down, he slumps. His head is large and heavy.

'Nini – Nini!' His voice sounds like the call of a young bird when he tries to catch up with his older sister.

She turns around – 'Nina – won't you ever learn it?'

'Nini!'

'Stop dragging your feet.'

'Nini – Nini! – Wait for me!'

Finally she stops. Christella is waiting at the pond. The girls are washing the dolls' hands and stockings ceremoniously.

'Can I play too?' He tries to pretend that he is little and sweet like William.

Nini shrugs her shoulders indulgently and stretches tall as if she weren't already tall enough. She who, alas, grows out of all her dresses.

'I am playing with Christella.'

'Nini, I can be your baby, your dog, your squirrel.'

Christella sizes him up, and he does his best jumping up and down.

Christella: 'Maybe we could use a squirrel.'

Nini: 'If we allow you to be our squirrel, you will have to sit up in a tree and keep quiet.'

Herman: 'I promise, Nini. I promise.'

Nini: 'Promises are one thing, but keeping them is another. Why aren't you playing with Oluf?'

Herman: 'He doesn't want to.'

Nini: 'Then play with William.'

Herman: 'I don't want to.'

Nini: 'Don't want to is not an answer.'

Herman: 'But it is true. I don't want to.'

Nini: 'Come, then, impossible child – if you must be our squirrel.'

Herman: 'You have to feed me nuts and raisins, Nini. And in the mornings I'll come and tickle your toes.'

Nini: 'I'm not so sure now – '

Christella: 'Oh, let him – '

Nini: 'Get up in the tree, then, and sit still.'

Herman: 'Lift me up, Nini. I have to be lifted up.'

Nini: 'Who has ever heard of a squirrel that has to be lifted?'

*

A thick warm smell of the barn, and in the corner the swallow's nest. Lars has broken a window with his clog so the birds can fly in and out and keep the barn free of flies. A swallow is a blessing. Swallows build nests with saliva and clay and feed on mosquitoes and flies. The belly of the swallow is so unbelievably white, it is hard to comprehend.

And suddenly in the middle of the hay he notices the little grey-striped cat with her litter. Oluf has just taught him to count to ten. He counts eight. Eight kittens that she is looking after all by herself. He tells her how clever she is and strokes her forehead that is softer than anything in the world. The tiny kittens are the most beautiful he has seen. One is reddish, the first ginger cat on the farm, one is grey-striped like the kitty herself, one is all black, one white with a black mask around her eyes, one looks like the smoke from Ane's stove, one is white with paws the colour of cream, and then there are two tiny tigers. She is clever. How clever she is. The very ordinary little cat in the barn.

She must be proud, he says. And he lifts up the kittens. They scratch only a little bit through his shirt. He drops three of them. They roll around in the hay, and it's no use to tell the cat that she shouldn't pick them up with her mouth.

He carries an armful of kittens, and in the kitchen he finds the milk pitcher and a small bowl. He pours, and the milkdrops hang like small pearls in the kittens' fur. They sneeze a bit, and he praises them when they begin to lap it up. He tells them that he will fetch their sisters and brothers and their mother.

Then Ane is suddenly there, standing in front of him as big as a mountain. A screaming mountain of flesh. For what is this filth he has brought into the kitchen? And the cream top that was meant for the sauce!

'Lars!' She shouts. 'Lars!' And he bites her leg as hard as he can when she pushes the little kittens away with the mop.

But it is no use trying to bite Lars. Herman can only scream for his mother.

When she finally comes, Ane has lifted him up on the kitchen table and filled his mouth with sugar candy and prunes and raisins and almonds. Everything she can think of to make him stop screaming. But he just spits it all out. In truth, he is as naughty as a child can possibly be.

But the missus shouldn't worry about this, Ane says. And especially not in her condition. It was just some kittens that the boy had dragged in. And Lars will drown them. After all, there are enough cats around here. And one cat has nine lives.

The life of a cat is no blessing. Cats are neither brought by the stork nor by God. Cats come from cats and are drowned in ice-cold water.

He cries and cries, and he sneaks out of his bed and into the kitchen to see if there might still be one hiding.

Hanne and Ane don't hear him. They have enough to do, pouring the piping hot coffee into saucers and lapping it up.

Hanne: 'And now the missus is expecting again.'

Ane: 'You can't even see it. – You can barely see that she is getting bigger.'

Hanne: 'She laces herself up. – She laces herself up very tightly. It is like a cage around the child. I reckon that the little one can barely breathe.'

Ane: 'She still looks like a young girl. So pretty and vain she is.'

Hanne: 'I am afraid that things will turn out like they did with Herman.'

Ane: 'How?'

Hanne: 'But didn't you know that the labour lasted a full twenty-four hours? And the kid was so weak that they thought he was dead. They dipped him in ice water to make him cry. That kind of thin marks you for the rest of your life.'

Ane: 'Yes, there has always been something wrong with that boy. But the missus is fond of him anyway.'

Hanne: 'Yes – . But it is really little William who is the apple of her eye. And I agree, he is surely as pretty as an angel. And he never makes a fuss at bedtime.'

Ane: 'No, not like Herman. He bawls for no reason. And he is a mischievous one, as well.'

Hanne: 'And then he gets funny ideas in his head. – But hopefully he will grow more handsome with age. And be less wimpy.'

Ane: 'But the pastor, he is quite a character too.'

Hanne: 'But wimpy he isn't.'

Ane: 'No, you would know about that. You with your bucket. – And then he has a way with words.'

Hanne: 'Do you mean that?'

Ane: 'Yes, I always fall asleep when I'm listening to him. Not everyone's head can hold that many words.'

Hanne: 'No – . But if it weren't for the pastor's father – '

Ane: 'Yes, it's anyone's guess what would become of the pastor and the missus in that case. I have certainly noticed how the finances improve when the Royal Physician comes to visit.'

Hanne: 'Yes, that's what I've been thinking too. And one's thoughts are one's own.'

Ane: 'Without him we wouldn't have a penny to our name.'

Hanne: 'Without him the two of us wouldn't be sitting here drinking coffee. – But for all that, the pastor is a kind man.'

Ane: 'And to those God gives a vocation, he also gives brains.'[1]

Hanne: 'Do you really think so? Oh, no, Herman has slipped out here again. Watch out, little pitchers have big ears.'

Still, they don't really believe that he, being so small, understands all this grown-up talk.

*

Father's father is a Royal Physician and very very posh. He has been at the bedside of princes and princesses and has trimmed their orns and ingrown toenails. He has listened to their hearts and the throbbing of their pulses and sometimes ordered them to step out in the cold snow. And he has helped to bring their children into the world.

He is hale and hearty and old and very rich. But it doesn't show.

He has a wife in Copenhagen who is much too elegant to travel to the countryside. She eats with a silver fork and is so grand and delicate that she is barely able to lift her food to her mouth. But it doesn't matter for she has servants in uniforms with gold braids and a lady companion who keeps her company and reads the entire newspaper to her.

Grandfather has a coat of arms with a crescent moon on a sky-blue ground. Unfortunately he cannot bring it with him. It is hanging in a palace. Oh, to go there and see the moon lying on its sky-blue bed.

Mother says: 'But surely, Herman, you have been to Copenhagen when you were a little boy.'

But he doesn't remember all the dolled-up children that she is telling him about. Boys dressed in velvet blouses and girls wearing pantalets trimmed with lace. And he doesn't remember that she was very sad because she was afraid to spend money on a photograph of herself. He only remembers a room with many lights and a tall, thin drinking glass that would shatter into ten thousand pieces if it should strike his teeth.

'Don't bite on it,' mother said.

He stuck his tongue into her glass. And he felt a tingle on his tongue and in his nose. It's embarrassing to think that he was so small that all of Copenhagen was nothing but a tickle in his nose.

When grandfather visits, they always ride in a closed carriage. Grandfather doesn't care for the sun, and besides he is too posh to suffer any gawking.

When they drive home from a visit, you can sometimes see the stars.

'Father,' asks Herman. 'Does the Great Bear ride in an open or a closed carriage?'[2]

Perhaps father doesn't hear him.

'Closed,' he says to himself. 'Of course the Great Bear, like God, rides in a closed carriage.'

Mother laughs: 'Listen to the boy, father-in-law! Fools can ask more questions than the wise can answer.'

Grandfather gives his hand a little squeeze: 'And it appears that he can provide his own answers.'

So, what is he then? Wise or foolish?

*

Easter is a heavy season. Two days with cold water and an obligation to feel sad. They are not allowed to speak in loud voices, for father is wearing rags around his head. And they can't play. It would be improper and mean after mother has told them about God's son on the cross. They have to think about soldiers and nails and vinegar and tears.

But the following day they get to paint eggs in red and blue. And the day after that mother hides the eggs among the anemones in the wood. And Oluf and Nini and Christella and Herman and William go hunting for the eggs, and sometimes mother too. For the red and sky-blue eggs are much too difficult to find. The children get moss on their knees, twigs in their stockings and runny noses. And the colours are as light and bright as if they are ready to fly away on a whim. They can eat supper without the lamp being lit. And the starling, the swallow and the stork will soon be coming.

Whoever sees the stork first gets to go on a trip. The children compete to be the first. They sing about the stork and throw their caps high up in the air, and the bird takes off and glides majestically over the familar fields.

It is the long, long dizzying summer itself with its bruised knees and tadpoles that are impossible to catch. Light summer nights and mosquitoes make it impossible to sleep. The birds don't sleep either. He sneaks out of bed and draws with his finger on the misty windowpane.

The shadows smell of lilacs and elder blossoms, and when he slips into the arbour, the cold settles between his shoulder blades and won't let go.

Summer time and Tine who swings so high up that you can see her white stockings. Or they play a game of tag or some other chase game. Mother runs until she drops. Tine is the fastest and runs farther than everyone else.

He rocks back and forth on top of the hayloads, high under the sky, and is covered in earwigs and perhaps fleas too. And large hands catch him and swing him around so he has to close his eyes.

In the mornings the cobwebs in the hedges glitter like silver. And the early berries make you purse your lips.

So many strawberries to thread on straws like beads on a string. So many raspberries to crush with a spoon in the cream. And apples, pears and plums to preserve, and the grapes that burst like glass on your tongue but are disappointingly sour.

The first touch of fall and the bitter sharp light that makes mother shiver. When father bathes in the fjord, his fingers turn blue and probably his toes as well. But the children don't notice them. They are already looking forward to Christmas.

At Christmas mother changes into a busy angel with wings of white apron frills. The boxes from grandfather arrive, and she is the only one who may open them and divvy up the gifts. Sometimes it makes her nervous. She racks her brain, trying to find things for the servant girls and the farmhands too. So she steals cigars from her husband to make the farmhands' gift table look fuller, and she rips silk ribbons off her collar to add some decorations.

The children, too, surpass each other in their generosity. For at Christmas you think about the poor who have almost nothing. All the things that you no longer play with yourself, they will be grateful to have. The one-armed doll, the hoop, the spinning top and the cart that only has three wheels. William looks surprised when Herman gives away his fancy sword. And actually, Herman regrets it too when the new owner turns out to be a bigger boy with big red ears and green snot hanging from his nose. Of course, you cannot expect the poor to use handkerchiefs, but the boy could have blown his nose or at least sniffed up the snot, because it was Christmas after all.

Fortunately he doesn't have to spend too much time instructing the boy in the use of weaponry. For mother, the pastor's wife, sprinkles a thick layer of cinnamon sugar on the rice pudding, and all the children stare at this extravagant woman and the big platters and the pitchers with fruit juice. And outside the mothers press their noses against the window.

Afterwards the pastor's wife and the pastor's children have to hurry home. For after they have celebrated the poor folks' Christmas, the roast goose is waiting for them at home. And after dinner and all the hymns, the presents are passsed around, and after the presents they sing the merry Christmas carols. On Christmas Eve the children fall asleep on the floor, and the servant girls carry them to bed. Nobody is crying, nobody is scolding. They are all heavy and peaceful and dizzy from the food and the sweets and the lights.

Every year the number of stars and candles on the tree grows. Mother's tree is the most beautiful of them all. And it was at its absolutely most beautiful the time when the entire tree was ablaze and everyone was screaming, running out to get buckets and rags.

She was the only one who stayed completely calm, fascinated and flushed from the heat of the flames.

It was her Christmas. Her silver and gold and fiery Christmas.

Only her birthday is better. The white feast when the roses trail around the posts of the arbour. Her long nightdress is white, and the whipped cream, the sugar glaze and Tine's apron, everything is pure white. And the children pull her in all directions, they all want her to open their particular presents first.

She reaches for William's first. The smaller children always come first. William is growing much quicker than Herman. Maybe there is hope of him one day being the smallest and first in line after all.

The servant girls and the farmhands come over to congratulate her. Some hands are red, others have deep cracks where the dirt has settled in for good. Lars, the farm foreman, always has splinters and thorns in his hands. But he doesn't feel them. Sometimes he pares the skin with a small knife.

Mother smiles, and her hand disappears in all those large rough hands. It is a miracle that it can stand up to all that.

Afterwards she walks down to the pond. Her hair is still loose. She looks at her own reflection in the water while rinsing her fingers very thoroughly so her hands again will be clean and cool and as ⸴hite as an un-used dinner plate.

Only then does she look at her presents. Father has kept himself at a distance during this noisy time. From him there is a book with a letter inside.

A wrinkle as thin as a needle forms on her forehead when she reads his letter. She seems more sad than happy. And in that instance the two of them are not a father and a mother. But a hero and a heroine in a fairy tale. And between them is a mystery that will never be solved.

*

Herman is lying under the table listening to the world falling apart and watching his mother's feet, small and restless and skipping, and his father's, that are at first large and still and then suddenly stomping.

'This is a miserable calling,' father says. 'I have applied to the Church of Our Saviour in Horsens.'

'We know what we have,' mother says. 'But we don't know what we will get. Our home and all our good friends are here.'

'Friends. We don't have any friends here at all. They cheat us through and through. They steal from us left, right and centre.' His voice sounds like when he speaks about the devil, and his hand makes the table shake. 'We don't have a single friend!'

'But the parish clerk and Fangel and – '

'Pastors and parish clerks don't count. – I refuse to be made a fool of. I refuse to be reprimanded as if I were a schoolboy.'

'Don't take that letter from the bishop so seriously.' It sounds to Herman as if her eyes are getting misty.

'It is a reprimand, and there's no getting away from it!' Now the table shakes again. 'It appears that I don't have the right aptitude for handling the business end of my vocation. I don't understand how to ask for payment. I have studied to become a minister. But I neither am or will be a debt collector. I come from a family where money is not something you speak about, but something you have.'

'But Fritz, we are not in need of anything.' Her voice is pleading. And under the table, Herman establishes that her shoes are worn down and that her stocking has been mended.

'In need,' says father. 'No, but that's because he's constantly giving us money. I am a man in the prime of his life, and I am still supported by my father.'

'Fritz, he gives from the bottom of his good heart. But of course, it is true that we always go to him for help.'

'There! You said it yourself. We always go to him. And you have to admit that I do attend to my calling. Sick calls. Holy Communion for the dying. Home christenings. Have I ever said no? I ride out in all kinds of weather. And then – when I come to collect the debt, not least on behalf of the bishop, then the harvest has failed. Then the sow has died, or she has eaten all her piglets. And the cows are not yielding milk. And the husband is sick, and the wife is not what she once was. And they are given deferment after deferment, and deferment once again. In the end I might as well tear up the bills. And then they laugh behind my back. May they go to hell!'

'But Fritz!'

'I want to move to a city. I am a city person.'

'I can't travel right now just before the birth.'

'Naturally, we'll stay until the baby is born.'

*

Then the day arrives when mother and Nini and Christella and William and Herman are standing on top of a tall hill, overlooking their green island. Oluf is in school, and Aage is at home in his cradle. There will be no more dreams of Herman being the smallest. He has started to suck his fingers, and sometimes he nibbles at his nails, which taste a bit like nuts. Mother says that his fingers are becoming misshapen, and Hanne threatens to spread mustard on his nails. But he continues to suck, and if they should dip his fingers in the mustard pot, he will just wash his hands in the pond, and then the fish can eat the mustard.

That day on top of the hill, mother doesn't even notice that he has all five fingers stuck in his mouth. She is pointing at the landscape in front of them. Over there is the mill. And here Tine lives. And all the fruit trees are in blossom. Gravenstein, James Grieve, Reine-Claude nd Kirke's Blue in the garden behind their white house. And they can spot the church. And the sea – far away in the distance.

Her voice trembles. Her finger too. And then she throws herself down on the grass, weeping like a child. Just like when they say that Herman is acting up. That's how she sobs and gasps for air. Her face turns red and puffy. Dirt and grass streak down her cheeks.

'Mother, stop it,' says Nini and begins crying herself. Christella and William snivel.

But mother is still lying in the grass, bawling. And it is so ugly, so ugly to be crying and not at all something a mother should do. Because of that she covers her eyes and cheeks with her hands.

Herman slowly walks over to her and lifts her hands off her face. Then he presses his lips against hers so tightly that their teeth grate against each other. And tears and grass and dirt form a steady stream until finally she is once again big enough to get up by herself.

2.

The island of Als is his paradise lost. When he closes his eyes, he is back in the white house, the surrounding garden and the grove. And he will never again experience a sight as beautiful as the island's blossoming fruit trees.

But it is America that he is supposed to be writing about. That's what the newspapers and magazines are expecting back home. He looks for his glasses.

'It is very odd, Bang, that you have been able to see without glasses for so many years.' That's what the eye doctor had said.

And that was indeed an insult, pure and simple. As if everything that Herman Bang has written has not been seen. That's the whole point! Besides, he wouldn't have acquired glasses had it not been for this journey.

Outside there are mountains. But they don't impress him. He has seen mountains before. In Tyrol he even climbed one just so he could watch the newspaper with his first article in print flutter away into the valley, all the while he was declaring boldly that literature and science would never again reach this height. And in the mountains near Prague, he walked with his beloved. The fragrance of the acacia trees was in the air, and he believed that everything would remain the same forever. That he would be living in the golden city with the scent of flowers in his lungs, holding a warm hand in his.

He puts down his glasses and notices that it is a figure eight he has been wearing on his nose. His unlucky number. Two circles mirroring each other. The masculine and the feminine. A sign that gives you nervous headaches, nervous digestion and intense energy. That number has followed him ever since he boarded the steamer and they showed him to cabin number eight. He sat down on the berth and looked at his ticket, realizing that the food was not included in the price and that every single meal would be an embarrassing act of calculation.

There might still be some good mail coming his way. But it is as if both the publishers and his friends have forgotten him. He writes one article after another and postcards and letters. But no answers come back. Perhaps they are actually relieved that he is now halfway across the world. Or they are offended because he didn't host a farewell dinner for them.

The readings were his party and his way of saying farewell. For everyone loves him when he gives a reading. He doesn't do it for less than three hundred kroner. After all, he travels with a valet and stays in hotels. And there are so many extras. The clothes alone. The shirts have to be new and with collar stiffeners that support his head a little so he will seem confident and fearless the moment he makes his entry. The shirt enhances his posture, the narrow trousers accentuate his legs, and the socks and the vest must be of silk.

A reading turns the entire day into a ritual. First the coffee and the cigarettes. At nine o'clock he takes a bath. A quarter past nine the doctor arrives. He would not want to do without the dionine injections. It is a mild pain, cold and distinct, alternately in the right and left shoulder. He is so thin now that it is difficult not to hit the bone. But already at half past nine when he is at the barber, he feels the invigorating and nerve-calming effect of the dionine.[3]

His hair must appear thick, shiny and black as a Spaniard's. He has overheard people whispering that it is incredible that a man of his age doesn't have a single grey hair. But the day he stops dying his hair and no longer has the energy to rub walnut oil on his face, both his hair and his face will be white. It would look very striking but also a little frightening. No one would recognize him. He would just be an old man, lonely and poor.

But as long as he is performing, he will be Herman Bang, handsome, lively and eccentric and a steady customer at the doctor's, the barber's and the photographer's.

In Denmark he demands certain props. A table, half a bottle of red wine that he will merely sip, and an easy chair that he will sit in for approximately half a minute. In addition he needs a folding screen for the sake of intimacy, a lamp that he carefully tests so that he is able to adjust the light during the performance, a stand for his hat, a potted fan palm and flowers. Especially flowers.

It was hurtful that time when he could see the roses in full bloom right outside the lecture hall. And no one in the audience had thought of giving him flowers.

'A small bouquet would have been delightful,' he said. 'Now, permit me to step out and help myself to a few flowers.'

No one responded. They were no doubt embarrassed, and he took his time picking and arranging his roses.

But as soon as he began reading, he had the audience in the palm of his hand. That's how it is every time. Actually, he doesn't really read at all. The book is just a pretext. As he gets older, he is, if truth be told, not able to distinguish the letters without a magnifying glass. But he performs his characters. He knows their movements, their voices, their sighs and silences and downcast eyes. He transforms himself right in front of the audience like the born actor and director he is.

Sometimes there is a ball afterwards, and he asks the ladies to dance, showing great tolerance. Even the little girl who disturbed him by constantly asking her mother how arms could turn blue. Even her he danced with. For when he has done a reading and received his applause, he is in high spirits and feels at ease.

Later the loneliness sets in at the hotel. It is not part of the valet's duties to attend the readings or stay awake. No, the celebrated Herman Bang steps out of his shoes, takes off his shirt soaked in sweat, looks at his face and wipes off the flattering lines above the eyelashes. Then he mixes some chloral with a little red wine, and if it isn't enough to make him go to sleep, he tries morphine.

The wine he usually has sent from Copenhagen. But on his last tour he had to make do with the wine from the local grocers.

That was due to Nini, once again. He can easily imagine how she must have been carrying on about him at Dreyer's, the wine merchant, in front of all the customers.

'My brother will never learn that you must cut your coat according to your cloth.' That is probably what she said, her voice full of indignation. And then she would have swept out of the shop, surly and testy under her big ostrich feathers.

He took his time answering her letter. Every time he picked up the pen, he felt the humiliation burning. He had done business with Dreyer for five years and always paid his bill at the beginning of the month.

Finally he pulled himself together:

'Nini, dear Nini.

Thank you for your letters. I haven't written because I am constantly travelling and also – because I find it necessary to write about a matter that is highly embarrassing.

Dreyer wrote to me that he hadn't sent ten bottles of wine over here because a lady had been in his shop inquiring whether the bill had been paid – "for if it hadn't, he was not to deliver the order." Dear Nini, you have no idea how much trouble you cause me when you do that kind of thing.'

*

No, you can't accuse Nini of being a fun-loving person. But maybe she was right after all. He had gotten used to the grocers' cheap plonk. And later on, she had told him at least thirty times that travelling around the world was complete madness and certainly no cause for celebration.

Right now he tends to agree with her. The train ride through America is just as awful as that time when they drove away from their childhood home on Als and from Tine who was running alongside the carriage with tears streaming down her face. Mother was pale and silent, sitting with Aage on her lap. The two servant girls that came along from Als were of no help. Ane was sobbing, saying that she was born and bred there and had never been off the island. When they approached the ferry, Hanne covered her face with her shawl so as not to see it. She would do anything for the missus, she whimpered. For her sake she would walk through fire and water. Herman himself sat between Oluf and Nini and was thinking about the jam in the big jars and about the piano and the bookcase that had already been shipped across the water. The piano had looked so strangely alive, all wrapped up in blankets and rope.

Actually, he had been looking forward to sailing across. But he completely forgot about it when Hanne leaned over the rail after first having noted the direction of the wind. Already in the harbour she had stuck her head out, retching. Soon after, he had begun retching himself, but he wasn't tall enough to reach above the rail, and so he soiled his shoe.

'Look at the boy,' mother sighed.

So much for that boat trip.

Everything was still moving after they disembarked, and he practically fell into the carriage.

Horsens town wasn't at all what he had expected. There were neither lights nor beautifully dressed ladies and gentlemen, and people just stared at their carriage without waving. Travelling was like disappearing. Like a ball that rolls under a bush and isn't found until next spring, ugly and full of holes.

Father was waiting in front of the house. Their furniture stood helter-skelter in the living room and dining room, and the windows were tiny.

'Mother,' he asked, 'how poor have we become?'

'Poor – ' she said. 'But Herman, think of the children in the orphanage.'

He had never thought they would sink this low.

*

The arrival of summer doesn't make the living room any brighter. The summer heat is stifling, and father takes mother's hand and places it on his forehead.

'Run outside and play,' says mother.

But the other children in the neighbourhood have sized Nini and Herman up and found them odd. Oluf they look up to because he is big. William they tolerate because he is small. And Christella everyone is fond of.

Only in the attic can you be by yourself. Herman stirs up the dust, and in the narrow band of sunlight the dancing dust motes look like gold. He imagines that the smell of heat and dust must be like it is in old castles where spiders amuse themselves among the shields and where knights in silver armour and unhappy princesses in their golden slippers haunt the rooms.

The attic is not a healthy place, says mother. He has to be a big boy and get some fresh air in his lungs.

Children shouldn't sit still, says the doctor. Especially not little Herman. He should be running around building up an appetite. He should be eating lots of rye bread so he can grow and become big and strong. And be a good boy and take his cod-liver oil – in the summer, too.

He is not at all a good boy. Hanne pinches his nose until he opens his mouth and she is able to force the disgusting white oil on the big spoon down his throat. She practically pours it into him. Afterwards he is rewarded with a small spoonful of jam. And he wishes she would get seasick right there in the middle of the kitchen floor. Protesting to the doctor is impossible, for he is a friend of the family.

It is for the very same reason that he is obliged to bow and smile and say he is pleased the day the detestable headmaster from the grammar school showers his face with saliva only to announce that they will meet after the summer holidays, refreshed and cheerful. After all, both little Herman and William are lucky to be admitted to his school.

It is not something Herman is looking forward to at all. If anything, it feels like a shock. And he doesn't understand why it is necessary. If he could just go with mother to the orphanage, he could attend school there.

But mother only teaches Bible stories and spelling. Herman and William have to study mathematics and Latin. And the girls laugh and say that he is tied to his mother's apron strings. But once he starts going to school, he will be singing a different tune.

And reality is even worse than he imagined. The cane that stings, the yardsticks that sing and the never-ending multiplication tables, dates and hymns. It really exists, all that. But he hadn't eve thought that he would be bored and afraid at the same time. Or that he would be relieved to hear that he is one of the good and hard-working students while at the same time finding himself to be stupid and lazy.

Small and quick is better than big and lazy, they say. And he has got brains although you cannot see it. The only boy who is brighter than little Herman is Julius Schiøtt who is a redhead. He is top of the class and Herman comes second.

'Just try it, see if you can top him,' says father. 'The day you are top of the class, we will go to the theatre.' But unfortunately Herman has no knack for mathematics while Julius is good at everything.

He and Julius become friends. Which in any case is most practical since they have to share the desk in the front row as well as stand next to each other and be the first to go up the stairs.

It would be a catastrophe if Herman were to be third or fourth. Having to move away from the first row would be worse than dying. From the second row he would not be able to see what the teacher writes on the blackboard. And then he would sink deeper and deeper and would have to move further and further away from the front – all the way to the back row where the lost souls sit. The stupid and lazy children that are called up before the headmaster to feel the cane.

Just thinking about it makes his heart flutter against his ribs like a bird in a cage. And the day the reports are given out, it feels like his heart has lodged so high in his throat that he could step out in the hallway and spit it out in the washbasin. Afterwards he would wipe his mouth with the white towel that only the teacher is allowed to use. And then he would drop dead.

But he keeps his place. He will always be second. William is sinking but not so deep that he is called up before the headmaster. After all, nothing that bad would happen to the pastor's son.

Fear becomes a habit, the multiplication tables and the memorized lists become a habit and the oppressive, grey mornings become a habit. Even those winter mornings when the windows are frozen over as if the entire house were enclosed in a large white egg. Mother and father are still sleeping under their big eiderdowns, cozy and warm. But the children must venture outside with hats and mittens and scarves covering their faces – and with Ane's packed lunches that have been thrown together in a hurry.

Sometimes he throws the food away, and he dreams of how he could succeed in spitting out the cod-liver oil. He is looking forward to getting the measles or some other children's disease. The faintness, the slight pain in the joints and the fever that throbs in your head. Finally mother's fingers on your wrist and her small frown once she finds your pulse. And his relief when she insists that he better stay in bed. Children's diseases, they are a blessing from God. Having a fever is almost as good as Christmas.

No, not quite. For in the days before Christmas all the shops light up. It is almost like the streets become wider. Sometimes he goes window shopping with mother. They are two greedy souls who fantasize about owning all that money can buy.

All the beautifully bound books with leather spines and gilt edges. Those they argue about.

The black velvet blouse and the sailor doll with his hat on at a jaunty angle become Herman's possessions.

Mother wants the Japanese shawl with cherry blossoms and cranes embroidered in gold. Herman wants it too. They share it but agree that mother can have the French woollen shawl as well even though it is probably more expensive and more classy with its blue interlaced pattern and ten thousand fringes for her fingers to play with.

In front of the jeweller's shop they argue again, this time about rings and bracelets and whether the large diamonds or the blue sapphires are the more beautiful. And all of a sudden they look at each other and burst into laughter.

*

Father comes home, and he is happy. His face is flushed, the veins in his forehead bulge as if he is incapable of containing all that joy.

'Thora, my love!' he shouts while still out in the yard. He has a parcel under his arm, and Herman has to help him cover mother's eyes while father unwraps it and puts the French shawl round her shoulders.

'Fritz,' she says, and her fingers are already entangled in the fringes. 'Fritz, it is lovely. But it must have been expensive. Much too expensive.'

Father laughs overexcitedly. 'Do you know where I have been today?'

'In the shops – And in the church – '

'At the town hall. I checked the whole register of taxpayers. After all, a pastor must familiarize himself with everything. We are rich, Thora. We are among the top twenty-five taxpayers in Horsens. Do you know whose name is just above ours on the list?'

'No – maybe the headmaster?'

'Wrong. He is further down the list.'

'The doctor.'

'No, you will never guess who. Holst. Squire Holst himself – the biggest landowner for miles around. We are almost as rich as Holst. – We are going to invite him, Thora. We will have a dinner party for him and the headmaster and the doctor.'

At the dinner party mother wears the shawl, father dons his patent-leather shoes and Oluf, Nini, Christella, Herman and William are so squeaky clean that their ears are still red by the time the dessert is served.

Father is right. They must really have become rich. There are flowers and candles on the table. The wine is served from crystal decanters, and father has hired both a waiter and an occasional cook who spends her time ordering Ane and Hanne around as if they were two schoolgirls.

Squire Holst kisses mother's hand. Luckily, her hands are made to be kissed. He invites them to his estate Rodvigsballe in the summer.

' – But the children?' Mother looks at her brood with a helpless expression.

'Yes. Of course the children, too.'

Herman feels joy rising all the way up to his face.

After the guests have left, father puts his arm around mother's waist, and the two of them dance around the table. The shawl swings behind her and sweeps a glass onto the floor. Father's long dancer's legs move like drum sticks. And the patent-leather shoes sparkle. They turn the house upside down, those two. Until mother has to sit down on a chair.

Ane brings some water and mumbles something about the missus' condition. But father's condition is much worse. The entire next day his head is wrapped in cold rags, and only towards the evening is he able to speak a little.

*

Perhaps it is because of the shawl that they finally get to go to the theatre. Herman has been pestering his father countless times. All his schoolmates have been there. But father, the pastor, doesn't want his children's taste to be sullied. *Horsens Teater* is and will always be third class. And then it is somewhat awkward attending the theatre with a boy who cries on the slightest provocation.

He promises to hold back his tears in the theatre. He promises to be a very big boy.

Of course, it is a bit disappointing that he will only be allowed to see a 'harmless play.' There are literally infants in the theatre. They sit on the nursemaids' laps, cooing and laughing when held up to see better.

But Herman does cry. He cries when they argue, when they fight, when they kiss, when they turn their backs on each other, when they misunderstand each other, when they are being cheated, when they hate, when they love, when they cry. And finally when they are united under the beautiful rose-coloured lights and will live happily ever after. Of course he applauds as well. He claps until his hands smart and turn red without noticing that his nice black velvet blouse is sopping wet.

'Such a baby,' says Nini.

Christella wipes his face with a handkerchief. And he knows that he is a disgrace to the whole family. But he has never experienced anything that wonderful before. All he can think about is going to the theatre again. Even after Hanne has pulled his blouse off and put him to bed, saying that this blouse will never be a blouse again, and wasn't that just what she had expected. And anyway, he is too small for that kind of thing.

They call him a sissy and a crybaby. But one day when he is at th graveyard and sees a mother laying flowers on her little son's grave, he neither cries nor sucks his fingers. He walks right up to her and says: 'Dear madam, all the little boys in Horsens grieve with you.'

That day they praise him and say that he has behaved well like a pastor's son and that one day he will surely be a good pastor himself.

But he knows exactly what he wants to be. He would like to be on stage dressed in silk and velvet with the world's most beautiful lady by his side. He would fight and suffer without making his blouse wet. But the words that come out of his mouth would make everyone in the audience cry or laugh.

'Herman is stage-struck,' his siblings say, and the servant girls look at him with an indulgent smile. But no one smiles or giggles the day Horsens' finest ladies come visiting and mother suggests to them that they start an amateur theatre to benefit the orphanage.

At first the ladies seem hesitant. But then they get excited and begin to talk about roles and costumes.

The following day mother has tea with three actresses who are not quite as young and beautiful as they seem on stage.

Once you are in the limelight, you are neither small nor wimpy nor ugly.

*

When Horsens' ladies and gentlemen have finished their rehearsal, they eat sausages and drink wine. The ladies get red spots on their cheeks, and the gentlemen's laughter gets louder, and everyone agrees that it is more fun to act than to embroider cross stitch or bake pound cake for the bazaar.

When mother comes home late, father shuts himself in in his study. The pastor detests amateur theatre. He has seen the stars, Johanne Luise Heiberg and Anna Nielsen, in the great tragedies and knows how things are done.

But the day they rehearse at the pastor's, he can't stay away after all. Suddenly he sweeps the hero off to the side and acts the entire role without a script.

The women watch with their eyes wide, and the original owner of the role retreats mortified.

'The pastor is the town's most elegant man,' Herman overhears a woman whispering. And father, the pastor, draws attention to himself with his patent-leather shoes and his long dancer's legs.

'Mother – are you not going to play a part?' Herman asks.

'No,' she answers.

But in the kitchen Ane says that if the missus just wanted to, she could outdo all the ladies in Horsens. Yes, – the men too for that matter.

'Yes – even in her condition,' says Hanne.

They are expecting a new little brother or sister. The children leave sweets on the window sill for the stork.

But how will the stork find its way around in Horsens?

*

Father, the pastor, is a hero. He rides out in all kinds of weather in his vestments. Snow collects in his ruffed collar and settles like islands on his shoulders. He is a real man who rides out to where the bullets are flying.

He rides southward in order to speak with the Danish soldiers. He has seen the entrenchments. From time to time the horse nearly plunges into one of the trenches. But it doesn't affect him. Back in the day when he was young, he enlisted in the army. But after he had waited for two weeks without being sent into action, he crumbled and was sent home.

The pastor is the bravest man in town. One day a bullet went right through his sleeve. He brought it home with him. He got off the horse to look for it without thinking that he might get hit. For father, the pastor, wants to be enlightened about human behaviour, the better to carry out his calling. And an ordinary bullet couldn't destroy an ambition like that.

Perhaps father, the pastor, rides out because he cannot bear to listen to Aage's coughing. It is hard to fathom how much havoc whooping cough can wreak on such a small body. Everything mother tries to give him, even his medicine, tuns into coughs. He is getting smaller and smaller. Only the hyacinth-blue veins in his temples are growing. When he coughs it is as if the delicate crov of his head is trembling, and with his hands and feet he attempts to grab on to something as though he were in free fall somewhere between heaven and earth.

Father rides out. Mother sits by the cradle. Windows and doors are kept shut. Aage's little soul must not get cold and fly out the window.

*

One night there is a sound of moaning and whimpering like two big dogs cooped up in a dark room. They howl and wail. It isn't Thyra, for Thyra is either out with father or sleeping by the stove. It isn't the dogs in the yard. It is a lament coming from the larger living room. Herman leaps out of bed and runs into the living room. The cold under his feet hits him, and his heart beats in time with all the windows and doors that are left wide open.

It is Ane and Hanne who are wailing. And mother has her head stuck out the window, not caring about proper behaviour and without noticing that the wind is messing up her hair and the rain is beating down on her face.

'Mother – ' he pulls her nightdress to get her away from the window. And Oluf, Nini, Christella and William come running, just as afraid as him.

From the street the sound of a bugle is heard like a huge sob that has broken loose and penetrated every nook and cranny. And then the clacking of heavy boots and running and shouting in the darkness.

'It's the Danes fleeing,' says mother. The rain is dripping from her hair on to her shoulders.

'Father – ' says Nini. 'Where is father?'

'Als, our Als is lost,' Hanne cries. Ane is sobbing.

And it is this island with the garden and the grove and the big white house that is falling and falling and breaking into a thousand bits and pieces.

Father comes home and stands in the middle of the floor. His hands are shaking, his knuckles are all bloodied, and his face is dirty nd wet. The white collar has collapsed, and there is no sign of his legs waltzing and quick-stepping. The vestment hangs on his frame like a sack. Father begins talking about the shame as if he were a small child who has fallen down, miserable and covered in tears and scratches and dirt.

'There are still Danish warships in the fjord,' he says. 'The Germans will probably burn down and plunder all of Horsens.'

Herman crawls under the table. Christella follows him.

'How will it burn?' she asks and holds his hand.

'Like a Christmas tree,' he answers. 'Like the one with too many candles.'

*

Windows and doors are open and let in all kinds of trouble. Of course no one in Horsens will be burnt. But a German officer with his two manservants and two horses is actually going to reside at the pastor's.

He is tall and blond and smiling. But when he requests to pay his respects to the lady of the house, father replies that his wife has never yet received a German. And when he wants to stroke Nini's pretty, rounded forehead and her blonde hair, she shakes off his caresses.

Father says that she did well. That's the way one should respond, like ice. They have to be frozen out. They have to feel that they are getting a bucket full of ice-cold water poured over their heads. Herman is thinking about doing exactly that. But he isn't tall enough. He tries to stand up straight and turn to ice from the inside out while staring at the captain and his horses and his servants with a steady and manly gaze. Unfortunately they only laugh at him.

*

But Aage turns to ice. He is lying very still. His small, bluish fists are clenched as if he wants to fight his misfortune. He has turned into a little, wrinkly old man, a distant and foreign creature who no longer tries to reach for anything.

The word 'death' hangs suspended in the air, and it make

everyone cry again. Mother's tears flow like rain in May. Father's are like a hailstorm. For father is the one who cries the loudest in the whole church when the curate delivers the funeral oration by Aage's small coffin and says that God has called him home.

Mother moves slowly, weighed down by a new child.

Herman is so dizzy that he must hang on to the curate's cassock to prevent himself from falling when he throws a little white carnation into the grave.

'Nerves,' says the doctor and pats him on his pale cheeks. 'And perhaps a bit anaemic. – You do take your cod-liver oil, don't you?'

And anaemia sounds so terrible to Herman that he feels heavy black curtains closing down in front of his eyes.

'Yes,' mother whispers and hugs him gently. 'It runs in the family, I believe.'

Two days later the stork brings the new baby. It is not an Aage like they had wished for but an Ingeborg, a hot-headed, bawling child who wants to eat every three hours. A pale creature that keeps mother in bed and drives father out of the bedroom.

At first he sleeps on the sofa in the living room to get some rest. But after the Germans move out, he has Ane and Hanne bring the eiderdowns and pillows and most of the things from the study into the vacant rooms.

For days on end he shuts himself in with his sermons and financial records.

Father is a raincloud with damp rags tied around his head.

'Is your father a Bedouin?' asks Julius.

'It is better if you don't bring any friends home,' says mother.

The childhood home is no longer white. And all the doors have to be kept closed.

*

Father, the pastor, is no longer a father. He has become a kind of weather. Either forebodingly silent or roaring.

Sometimes his fingertips are blue, and he reaches for his wineglass with both hands when the children raise their voices. He rubs his forehead, and mother sends a reproachful look to the child who has uttered but a single little word.

'Why can't we ever have some peace and quiet in this house!' he shouts. 'It is impossible to do any work. Impossible to think. These children have never learned proper manners.' He gets up and goes to his study, slamming the door shut behind him.

Or he laughs. Suddenly he may begin laughing so hard that he nearly suffocates in his own laughter. No one dares to thump him on the back. And he just laughs and laughs and laughs.

'Fritz,' says mother. 'What is it, Fritz?'

'Can't you see how funny it is?'

She runs her hand over her forehead and hair where the first white flecks by the temples are like flakes of ashes.

'I can see it all – the whole universe,' he says proudly. 'There is a man and a woman, and there is shame. No one has yet been able to subdue the beast in woman. But man can destroy without feeling guilt.'

'Fritz,' she says very gently as if she were kissing his pain away. 'Don't you think we should visit your father in Copenhagen?'

'My father. – I wonder, is it my father that you are married to? The one who has seen through the ways of the universe is much too grand to have a father. He is an idiot – my father!'

'He is a doctor,' she says softly with this recently acquired bashful look of hers.

'Doctor. – No, he is a lecherous old goat. Don't you think I have seen the two of you sitting together, whispering. You two are of a piece. And he gives you envelopes and wallets. And where does it all go?'

'The children, Fritz.'

'No, it burns up. In your hands money goes up in smoke all by itself. Everything simply disappears. But man has the right to destroy.' He laughs and sweeps the plate with rhubarb soup onto the floor.

Christella wants to do the same. But he snatches the plate away from her.

'Only man, I said! Really, these children don't know anything.'

Christella begins to cry.

'But father,' says Oluf and tries to look grown-up and calm.

'Father – '

'Stop that "father" business. It is nothing to be proud of. When finally I was able to see through the universe, I also saw all the faults in my own family.'

'Children, you can leave the table,' says mother. 'Go and see Ane. Fritz, you are not yourself.'

'No,' he says and collapses in the chair. 'I looked in the mirror. And I didn't see a Hvide or a Ryg or a descendant from a regicide. Do you know what I saw? A barber. A common barber – jowly and with large bony hands. His feet are wide and his back crooked from bending over the customers, soaping their greasy chins. And "How do you do, sir?" And "Perhaps we should trim it a bit more in the back?" I saw that I look like a simple barber. For that specialist in childbirths – the Royal Physician – the one with all the money and the medals – he insisted on fathering me with a tubercular daughter of a barber in the humble street of Kattesundet.'

'But that is nothing to be ashamed of, Fritz.'

'No, of course, you frequented that barber riff-raff yourself. Birds of a feather flock together.'

'But Fritz, you know that my father was a postmaster.'

'Yes – And your mother a Jewess. And in the family there were also a keeper of a billiard hall and a tenor – a debauched tenor.'

'Mother,' Herman whispers. 'Is it true what he says?'

'Don't say "he,"' she reproves. '"Father." Of course it is always true what father says.'

Father says nothing. He is slumped over in his chair like a sick bird on its perch. And none of the children have left the table.

'You put poison in the food,' he says. 'That's why all the children have turned out so odd.'

Her face goes red and she covers her eyes as if she wants to blot out everything.

The following morning the dog and the saddle horse are kept inside. The heavy horses are hitched up to the closed carriage.

Dressed in sky-blue and with his long dancer's legs, father, the pastor, goes off with their mother who has become a small woman in black.

*

For four days the children look at the parents' empty chairs at the table. Hanne serves the food that mother has planned for them to eat.

It is as if they suddenly discover each other and feel united through the one word that none of them wants to say. 'Crazy. Crazy. Father must be crazy.' Herman is about to repeat it several times. But the buzzing, sizzling word is not permitted to pass his lips. For Christella and Ingeborg are small and must be kept in the dark as long as possible. And if he were to say it, Nini would give him the cold shoulder. Nini is grown-up now and corrects the youngsters' behaviour while Oluf just shakes his head and says that he wants to get away.

'How away?' Herman asks.

'To sea,' he says.

'Oh.' Herman has lost a good deal of his inquisitiveness at school because all the teachers do is ask questions about things they already know. And it tires him to the point where he would put rags around his head if it wasn't for the fact that he would look like father.

Nini and Oluf have their father's colouring. They are tall and blond and very calm. If it wasn't for the two empty seats, you would have thought that they were the parents.

Christella and Herman are short and dark-haired. And sometimes she runs after him the same way he used to run after Nini. But luckily Christella is an easy child although not quite as good as William who can spend hours stroking the dog or rubbing it behind its ears, and all the while just staring into space.

But Ingeborg's silence is troubling. She is as pale as a white candle, her teeth are small and pointed and her hair a mass of light-brown locks that can't be contained in braids.

She rips the heads off flowers. Even in other people's gardens. Regardless of what she has been told, she squeezes the flowers in her small sweaty hand. She gets stung by bees and wasps. But she cannot help herself. She picks off the petals and finds aphids, ladybugs, spiders and even earwigs. And she lets them crawl on the palm of her hands and up her arms.

Only if you take the bugs away from her or try to untangle her hair will she let out a fiery red screech like a bird, her mouth wide open.

Nini attempts to do both but has to give it up. Ingeborg sleeps with a spider on her eiderdown, and she doesn't miss her parents.

*

Mother returns home. Suddenly one morning she is sitting in the living room still wearing her travelling clothes, smiling a smile that is vulnerable and at the same time much too big for her face.

The children come rushing in.

She has forgotten to buy presents, she says. Or no, she didn't have time.

'Where is father?' asks Nini.

'Father,' she says. 'He stayed in Copenhagen. He has important business to do.'

'Business – ' Oluf repeats.

'Mother,' Nini says with a small, brittle voice. 'Father is ill. Poor father.'

Crazy – Herman thinks to himself.

The smile disappears from mother's face and she looks at her children. Her voice is faint and flutters like a sparrow trapped in a small box.

'Children,' she says. 'Dearest children. Don't tell anyone. Your father is in hospital. Don't talk about it to anyone. Keep it a secret. People have so many preconceived ideas. Some diseases are not only tragic, they are also shameful. It is God's will. But it is very difficult, so very difficult.'

Herman is holding Christella's hand and notices that she is trying to catch a tear with her tongue. Ingeborg is teaching her spider to dance.

'What are we supposed to say?' Nini asks.

'That father has important business to do in Copenhagen. And afterwards he will be going to a health spa. There he will take the baths to get well. Don't mention the last part.'

'Do you get sick from bathing at home?' William asks meekly.

'Is it contagious?' whispers Herman.

But mother doesn't answer. She shakes off the dust on her travelling clothes and says that they will be busy. Tomorrow they are all going on a vacation to Rodvigsballe. Their invitation from long ago is still outstanding. Father is unfortunately tied up with some business of his. 'Don't forget now,' she says. 'And you will have to help Ane and Hanne by packing your things yourselves.'

Nini stands very close to their mother and whispers: 'Who admitted him?'

'Grandfather.'

'Where to?'

'Saint Hans Mental Hospital.' Mother's voice is merely a faint puff of air. She leans against her tall, blonde daughter.

But the next day she is surrounded by the children in the large closed carriage, and when it finally comes to a halt in the courtyard, Squire Holst himself comes down the stairs and helps her to climb out.

The first couple of days the children follow their mother like a flock of young birds. And she chatters and laughs and holds their hands tightly as if she in this way can keep the sadness and fear at a distance. But little by little the children scatter over the big lawns. They befriend the Squire's children: Rikke and Peter. And other summer guests with children arrive. They play blind man's buff and hide and seek and battledore and shuttlecock and ringtoss. They are on holiday. They sleep under white, fresh-smelling linen, and their skin absorbs the rays of the sun.

Mother should have been married to a squire, Herman thinks. She ought to be served many fine dishes every day and to be strolling across the green lawns in a lace-trimmed dress under a small bobbing parasol. She should have been rich. Or she should have been married to a forester at least, to a man with a beautiful deep voice and a laugh that would make her feel safe. And Herman himself should have been a fearless boy who could easily climb trees and pull a squirrel by its tail ever so carefully.

Mother wipes her brow. Small drops of perspiration sparkle at her temples. She neither runs nor dances. Her belly makes her summer dress bulge out in a bow and lifts it up above her small feet.

The lack of news makes her miserable.

Letters make her sad.

The birds' warbling is a laughter that won't stop.

A fly buzzes the word 'crazy.'

Summer clouds form white crosses and white floating beds.

Cows look at her with deep compassion.

The fragrance of the white clover is nausea.

The jasmine is fainting fits.

A moth that settles on her hand makes her scream.

Hence she tries to laugh.

Herman bites his lip hard and seeks the shade. He has turned twelve and no longer believes in the stork.

She should have been married to somebody else.

And he shouldn't have been born, ever. Neither he nor father, the pastor.

*

The first yellow leaves lie scattered on the streets of Horsens when father comes home. His stooped figure looks small. His voice has dried up and his gaze is directed towards his own feet. The patent-leather shoes and his dancer's legs are gone. His frame droops like a withered flower. But little by little his back straightens out like a tentacle on a sea urchin. And the day he once again stands in the pulpit and tells the congregation about God's will, the ruff of his clerical collar frames his face like the crown of a narcissus.

The little newborn is christened Sofie. She is so delicate and sweet, babbling away.

'The dearest of them all,' Hanne says.

'One would hope she is also the last,' Ane says. 'Things are going downhill for the missus.'

'But surely, she has always had someone to do the hard labour.'

'Not to do the worst part. The part with the pastor.'

Mother is so terribly tired and she pushes her soup bowl away.

'But the missus has to eat,' Ane says. 'Otherwise the missus will never get better.'

Ane prepares her rusks thick with butter and piles the jam on in big mounds. Mother looks at it with her tired smile and takes the tray with her outside in the sun, or she simply falls asleep sitting bolt upright. When she wakes up, she runs her hand over her forehead with a sudden movement.

Otherwise she is becoming more and more beautiful. Her face is even thinner than before. Her eyes seem larger with a slightly surprised look. Suddenly droplets appear in her long curved lashes. Her hands with their protruding blue veins rest in her lap, and regardless of how long she sits in the sun, she remains pale.

A certain languor is stealing over her, making her movements imperceptible and her voice feeble and timid. And her hair. Never before has it been so plentiful. She isn't able to contain it with combs and nets or to gather it in a bun. Time and again it comes loose, goes flying in all directions, shiny, dark and now suddenly with white streaks.

Once in a while she pulls out one of the long white hairs and stares at it for a long time. She has turned forty and borne eight children. That must be it. Of course that's all it is.

'Fresh air and port wine keep me going,' she writes to her father-in-law.

But one day she begins coughing.

She coughs so much that the children wake up during the night and stare into the darkness, frightened.

She coughs at the table and presses her handkerchief against her mouth to muffle the sound. Father gives her a disapproving look. She reaches for the water and doubles up again, coughing and coughing, staring dejectedly at her handkerchief.

Father takes it from her and unfolds it.

She is spitting out poppies of blood.

'Leave the table, children,' she says in the middle of the dinner.

They get up quietly. Oluf and Nini, Christella, Herman, William and Ingeborg.

Hanne is standing outside the door carrying Sofie on her arm.

The second course is not brought in.

From the dining room they hear a loud rasping noise. It is father moaning and weeping.

*

The best thing for Thora Bang, the pastor's wife, would be to go to a spa. But that is not possible. She has her little flock to care for, the pastor and the seven children. How would they be able to look after themselves without her, the dancing, singing, wasteful, helpless mother who just leaves everything to the girls while she reads novels and lies in.

The missus has to take long walks to gain strength. The missus has to rest in the sun. The missus has to eat rich food. Meat and freshly churned butter, egg yolks stirred with sugar, simply everything that reminds you of the sun, that's what the missus must put away. The missus is almost nothing but skin and bones.

She sits in the sun, compliantly, with her shawl wrapped around her. She attempts to read and wakes up with a start when the book falls on the floor.

She tries to clean her plate, obediently, and everyone has to stay at the table for a long time because of her coughing. She forces herself to eat the butter and drink the wine which makes her cheeks glow. Father grabs her hand and pours some more. The wine goes down the wrong way and she coughs until tears flow.

One day she loses a button on her coat and announces triumphantly that she has put on weight. And they celebrate with champagne.

Her steps get smaller. She has to lean on Herman when they go window shopping. She feels cold, even in the September sun. He wants to give her furs, black fur coats and white fur coats and long coats trimmed with wolf fur. But all she wants is linen, white linen and elegant nightgowns like a bride.

'Remember me,' she says suddenly at the bookseller's window. 'See to it that they don't forget me.' She is crying and he promises her everything. He will become famous, he assures her. And she will be present in everything he does – for the rest of his life.

But why she had wanted bed sheets, he only understands the day she stays in bed for good. Her hair fans out on the pillow. Black and silvery like cobwebs in the morning sun. Her face is all white, and he squeezes her handkerchief in her hand. Her teeth are much too big for her face.

At times she looks like an old woman and at other times like a very young girl. But she will never become staid, and when she lies in bed eating jam, she hardly seems like a mother. She never reads to them any more, but instead reads poems about unhappy love over and over again to the point where the books fall open to the right pages by themselves.

Herman reads along with her over her shoulder. He imagines her as young and childlike. She goes for a walk in a forest where she meets a man with dancer's legs. He is dressed in sky-blue velvet, and he makes her a present of poems written by himself, and he tells her that he will love her until the end of his days and that she will be his queen.

Perhaps he asks the postmaster for the hand of his daughter in marriage. She is much too young and much too soft-spoken to say no. She is compelled to say 'yes' to whatever she is being asked.

She is invited to Copenhagen as a guest in her future father-in-law's home where she gets dizzy from all the lights that burn day and night and the champagne that makes her skin tickle and tingle. And the Royal Physician, His Excellency Oluf Lundt Bang, takes her hand and kisses it, and he, too, writes poems about her face and her hands and her hair. Her parents are not invited. Only she is there, seated at the table, eating with a silver fork. Afterwards they go to the theatre, and her youthful head fills with poetry and lights. In the late mornings they go visiting, or she will be warming her hands in her muff while watching Frederik Ludvig Bang skate.

One day her father-in-law asks her to accompany him to the small study. He tells her that his favourite son, Frederik Ludvig, has a flaw. It is a weakness in his soul, a particular kind of sensitivity that he cannot help, a type of nervous excitement. That's all. But she is not to mention this to outsiders. If she were to sense something unusual she should always come to him for help. It is nothing to worry about, and perhaps it will disappear completely once Frederik Ludvig takes up his office, has a pretty young wife and hopefully soon some children. The old man gazes at her with a look that confirms his blessing and his happiness as if he were the one getting married.

Thora bites her lip somewhat dispiritedly. She doesn't ask what nervous excitement means. She is a well-mannered young girl.

Frederik Ludvig, whom she now calls Fritz, offers her his arm and takes her out on the ice. She feels awkward next to this man who does figure eights and outside edges while all the ladies gawk at him. It seems to her that he is wearing out the ice to the point of it almost breaking. Now and then he turns towards her and waves and laughs.

At the engagement party that same evening, their eyes meet during the speeches.

Drops of perspiration form on his upper lip, a hectic flush spreads over his cheeks, and it seems to her that his eyes are like water, slightly frozen. He grasps her wrist and squeezes it until she begins to cry. She breaks away and flees up the stairs and into somebody else's apartment where she drops to her knees and sobs with her head in the lap of an old and rather stout man. She just wants to go home, home, that's all she's asking for.

She has told the story often. 'Imagine, the servant found me weeping with my head in Oehlenschläger's lap, Adam Oehlenschläger himself,' she usually recounts. 'For of course, it was none other than the great poet who lived upstairs in the big grey house near the palace.'

'Why were you crying?' the children ask.

'I was overcome with emotion,' she answers, 'or perhaps with joy.'

But Herman finds it difficult to imagine a newly engaged girl fleeing from happiness.

She must have been in love with somebody else, he thinks. But she has never had the heart to make anybody but herself unhappy.

During the night she wakes up the whole house with her coughing, and they have started giving Herman a couple of spoonfuls of sleeping draught. He falls into a deep sleep that sits in his bones the entire next day although he has only rested for a few hours.

One night he thinks he sees his mother standing in his room looking at him like a child with frightened eyes. He tries to rise from his sleep, but it is as if he is held down in deep black water that closes around him regardless of how much he fights to get to the surface and reach her, his lovely mother, who has become as small as a child. Her movements have become light and airy, the nightdress hides her feet and her hair brushes against the hollow of her knees.

Then someone shakes him roughly.

'Herman. Herman!' It is Nini's voice. Nini drags him out of his sleep and says that mother is about to die.

When he bends over his mother's hand, it is still and cold and white. He knows that she can't see him any more. At that very moment everything changes. And she will always be with him.

Once again father's raspy wailing fills the whole church while the curate delivers the funeral oration by Thora Bang's coffin, the pastor's wife who carried her cross with patience and was a good wife and a good mother. Moreover, she had a soft spot for those in need. And he speaks of pastor Frederik Ludvig Bang who delivers soulful sermons and is a conscientious spiritual advisor. God will help pastor Bang and his seven dependent children through these hard times.

'Dependent.' It sounds like an orphanage. Herman will soon be confirmed in the church. And if he hadn't been attending grammar school, he would already have been serving an apprenticeship for quite a while.

He glances at Nini. A young girl who has been touched by frost and now has narrow lips and tightly dressed hair. She passes a handkerchief to Ingeborg who is blowing her nose in her mitten.

You cannot really call Nini a dependent. Not Oluf either. He has signed on on a ship and will be sailing to the East.

All the fine furniture seems suddenly too big and shiny. Time and time again the children are drawn towards their mother's empty room. The green plants are withering and leave shadows on the wallpaper.

One night Herman bumps into Nini who throws her arms around him and hugs him tightly.

'Herman, little brother,' she whispers and won't let go of him.

'Nini. Yes, Nini. What is it?'

'I am so afraid.'

'You, Nini, are you afraid?'

'Yes, yes, my little brother. Yes.'

'Why?'

'Father has gone out. He hasn't returned home.'

'I know. It would have been better if he had died instead of mother.'

'Don't say that kind of thing, Herman. Or I'll never speak to you again.'

'I won't say it again, Nini.'

'Help me. Won't you sit with me. I am too afraid to sleep.'

'I can't sleep either.'

'No, that's why people think we are odd. We never get any proper sleep.'

Nini pulls him into her room. They each sit down in an easy chair, holding hands. They don't light the lamp and they only speak in a whisper.

Finally they hear their father's footsteps. They hear him open a bottle, and they hear him getting bread and cold meat in the kitchen and carrying it back to the dining room.

Suddenly he begins to sing. It sounds as if he is moving in circles around the table. The melody is a waltz, and after a while it changes to a galop.

Herman flinches and strokes his sister's cheek gently.

'Nini,' he whispers in her ear. 'Why are you crying, Nini?'

'I fear the worst – the worst thing of all,' she whispers back.

'What is the worst thing of all?'

'But you know. If father begins to laugh. If father begins to laugh that laughter again. Oh, dear God, let sadness remain with us.'

'Yes, Nini. Yes.'

They hear a chair being knocked over, and they cling to each other.

The next day father suggests that they go to the theatre.

'No,' Herman says. 'The repertoire is not suitable.'

'No,' Nini says. 'We will never go to the theatre again.'

Father lowers his head, mortified. 'But at Tersløse it won't be possible.'

'Tersløse?' Nini asks. 'What is Tersløse?'

'It is a smaller parish by the town of Sorø. As your mother isn't here any more, I cannot stay here either.'

3.

Tersløse parsonage. He remembers very clearly the mornings where the fog was still covering the fields like a mysterious veil. Here no one knew about the pastor's weakness, and because the pastor's wife had passed away, people looked upon the children with pity and mumbled something about time healing all wounds.

'Come, time, swaddle me in cobwebs,' Herman wrote on the window pane covered in mist. And he was nervous and bit his nails down to the quick at the thought of soon having to begin school at Sorø Academy where everything would be very different from Horsens. He missed Julius and his girl friends. Moreover, his heart was racing and he had a stitch in his side. And could you die from that?

Naturally he would die young. But not until he had become famous one way or another. He couldn't be a doctor like grandfather. For he fainted when he saw blood just like his father. That is why he kneeled down in Sorø Church to pray to his ancestors for a sign. That his prayers were pagan didn't occur to him. But it surprised him that the Hvide clan showed itself in the form of coldness in his hands and knees.

He didn't ask his father to tell him about his forefathers. For just think if he began to tell the story about his mother again, about the barber's daughter, grandfather's poor, young beloved who gave birth to three children and died in childbirth without having as much as touched a silver spoon. The poverty and the young woman's tragic death didn't fit into the image of grandfather as a Royal Physician.

But the pastor prepared his son for confirmation. He spoke to Herman about God and the Trinity and about all the trials that humans have to suffer with patience and preferably with gratitude. An unfamiliar softness had come over father, and nothing or no one was to throw him off balance.

'You don't think it will happen again, do you?' Nini whispered.

'Never.' Herman was shaking his head energetically while praying: 'Dear God, don't let father become mad. Don't let me become mad. Let me die instead. Let Ingeborg's oddness be hidden by her hair.'

He learned scriptural passages and hymns by heart. Not for all the world did he want to be a disgrace to the family, especially not to father, the pastor, who had more than enough to wrestle with.

None of the girls from Als came with the family to Tersløse. After all, it was the missus that they had been attached to. It would be awkward having to instruct a new girl in the ritual with the water bucket. As it was, the pastor only trusted the daughters' governess. But she had thin arms and was past fifty. Herman ought to be the nearest. But clumsy as he was, he would most likely fall over backwards with bucket, chair and everything.

Yet, father and son grew closer. The future confirmand read through all his father's sermons, corrected awkward sentences, crossed out repetitions and on the really bad days where the pastor sat with his feet in ice-cold water and had rags tied around his head, he rewrote the whole sermon. For on those days the pastor spelled the words as if the letters had come tumbling out of a bucket.

'It is an excellent exercise,' his father used to say. 'If only you could write larger and more clearly.'

The confirmation itself was a real feast.

Without being the least bit nervous he, the pastor's son, answers all the questions correctly. And they are all proud of him. Nini who smiles with her little restrained grown-up smile, Christella who looks at him adoringly, Ingeborg and Sofie who would rather be jumping up on the bench to see better, and William who sulks because it isn't his turn yet.

The pastor brings his newly confirmed son with him to a

wedding in the country. They eat roast chicken and drink weak beer, and when the fiddlers stomp their feet to the rhythm of a galop, it is Herman's turn to dance with the bride. Her ample bosom is level with his ears, and it seems to him that it softens the sound of the violins. He looks up into her pretty glowing face, and she smells nice and warm – and of a whiff of beer. And he discovers that he has dancer's legs. He forgets about his racing heart and the stitch in his side. Afterwards the bride needs to sit down and pause for breath. And the bridegroom wipes her forehead fondly with a white handkerchief.

It is nearly dawn when they return home. Nini is waiting in Herman's room wearing a woollen shawl over her nightgown. 'How did it go?'

He tells her about the galop and the bride beaming with joy.

'It is father I am thinking of.'

'He didn't dance at all.'

'Thank God. And Herman, you shouldn't have danced either.'

'Why not, Nini? Why?'

'I don't think we are allowed to be happy.'

As usual Nini is right.

The following day the letter from the shipping company arrives, informing them that Oluf has died from typhus.

'Why?' Herman cries, 'why couldn't I be the one who followed mother?'

Christella looks at him, her eyes bright with tears, and at that very moment he knows that he doesn't really mean it.

For several days father talks about sharks. The water is full of sharks. The ship has paused for a moment. The captain has spoken, probably very briefly. The crew members have been on deck, their heads uncovered in the presence of God and of the sun, and then Oluf has been lowered into the sea. But has the sea been blessed? Are sharks among God's animals?

'We haven't been mournful enough,' Nini says. 'Now we're being punished.'

'We should write to grandfather,' Herman suggests.

'Not until father begins laughing. And only if he does it in public.'

'Yes, Nini.'

'Yes, you and William are lucky. You attend Sorø Academy. You only need to come home during the vacations and occasionally on Sundays. This girl has to stay put and look after things.'

'Nini, I am telling you, that academy is worse than a military camp. – The food alone – '

'What about it?'

'The famous Madame Mangor would have crossed herself. You could write a whole book about it: four hundred fish dishes and six hundred recipes for porridge and gruel.'[4]

'You are just picky.'

'What's more, they poke fun at me. But that's only what you would expect.'

'Yes, you probably have yourself to blame. William doesn't have any problems.'

'Nini, if you knew how much I long for home.'

And the first few months he really does wish he were back in Horsens. He misses his girl friends and Julius Schiøtt and the streets and small canapés with salmon and asparagus and the rusks with blackberry jam.

Instead, here you are met with the smell of dust and varnish in the long hallways. The smell of sweaty bodies in the changing room. The chill of the gymnasium, the windows high up on the walls as if to prevent escape by that route. And there is the smell of fish, of boiled milk, cabbage, liver pâté and cinnamon.

But there is also the Academy garden with its secret hideaways, tall shady trees and wide lawns where you can stretch out on the grass and study your Latin or read sinful French novels. And his cozy room with the family photographs and the secret drawer.

And there is the kindhearted headmaster who treats the students almost as if they were his own grown children. And then there is the French teacher who gives him praise and lends him Musset from his own library. And the Danish teacher who reads his compositions aloud because of the unusual language and who, incidentally, turns him away from a lesson because he has shown up in his new shirt with the open Byron collar. And when he is being teased, he knows that he is also being admired or at least noticed.

'Are you going to church again?' his schoolmates ask when he walks out of the Academy's gate and turns towards town. His lips are sealed with seven seals. He doesn't talk about his forefathers and definitely not about his home. But in his brain the words form like a litany of afflictions: 'Mother is dead. Father is mad. My younger brother is dead. My older brother is dead. We are all odd. Here they believe in Darwin. Suppose Mr Darwin is right! Dear God, don't ever let Mr Darwin be right.'

They can tease him as much as they want, all those healthy and plucky boys who can swing from the ropes and who enjoy fencing and playing ball and jumping over the vaulting horse as if it were nothing. They don't bite their nails, and they are not apt to shed tears, to have heart palpitations, to faint or to have a stitch in their side. But they don't have his sense of irony either. If someone mocks him ever so slightly, he is able to counter with an answer that draws the laughter over on his side. Besides, he does well in nearly all subjects. He comes second almost without any effort just like at home in Horsens. In Latin and French he comes first, unquestionably. He does independent studies in French in Sorø's lending library where an absent-minded old gentleman keeps the shelves full of all the new French titles.

'A notebook,' he says as an alibi.

The old man shakes his head gently and points at the worn books that contain perfumed boudoirs where beautiful, fallen women with hearts of gold or stone abandon themselves to pleasure on red velvet sofas. He swallows the books where silk rustles and satin sparkles and white hands are heavy with rings. He writes his first play in an exercise book, and he writes poems about his cousin's beauty. Margrethe Black who is as blonde as wheat and so very calm and pure and inscrutable. If Margrethe should ever become a fallen woman and drag her lace through the gutter, he would come and rescue her. He would help her into his carriage and dry her eyes with a Swiss handkerchief and forgive her everything in advance.

When he is writing, he can see himself from the outside as a figure in a novel. Sometimes he is so touching that he makes himself cry. But he can also make fun of himself as if he were to prick himself with pins, and then the little jabs would make him laugh like a child who is being tickled. It is a kind of magic, and he locks his drawer with great care.

In the Academy's literary club he shines in the company of the other members, especially as a critic. He takes Holger's fairy tales apart and puts them together again, he criticizes Cantor's and Graa's short stories, smiles overbearingly at Rosenberg's three poems and praises the fourth one to the skies.

'We will print it in our journal,' he says.

'Which journal?' Rosenberg asks puzzled.

'The one we are going to set up,' Herman says and knows that now he will have to ask grandfather for an extra allowance for 'writing supplies'.

Rosenberg who up to now has been one of his opponents becomes one of his faithful supporters. At least after he sees his poem in print and spends the honorarium at the bakery.

They never become friends, though. Neither Herman nor William has yet had the courage to invite schoolmates home.

But the first Christmas in Tersløse is a feast. The church is full, and the pastor's voice is carried through the pews by the warmth and expectations of the parishioners. Afterwards comes the relief followed by the red wine, the goose and all the presents from Copenhagen.

'Did I do well?' father, the pastor, asks, his eyes fixed on Nini who is lighting the candles on the tree while carefully estimating the distance between branches and candles.

'Yes, father. Yes,' say the children.

The day after Christmas Day they have invited friends, family and neighbours. Cousin Margrethe arrives from Copenhagen, and from Rodvigsballe come the old playmates Rikke and Peter Holst. Suddenly young voices can be heard chirping away in the living room, and Rikke almost makes her sentences sing because she has fallen in love with a Norwegian. 'Henrik,' she says over and over again: 'Henrik Ibsen.' – 'But,' she suddenly adds, 'it is probably not going to be him, anyway. After all, he appears somewhat self-important – you know, a bit odd.'

'How?' says Nini without looking at Rikke and without waiting for an answer. For Nini and Peter Holst only have eyes for each other.

Herman smuggles a poem into his cousin's hand, and she makes it disappear up her sleeve.

They sing, dance, dress up, play charades and guessing games. And Miss Benedicte Arnesen Kall, the distinguished old translator of Molière, lies down flat on the floor in her black silk and asks for a large map of Denmark. The servant girl brings it and wraps it around the old maid's flat chest, her belly and her knees that are undoubtedly bony and sharp.

'What am I supposed to be?' says the old maid. 'Guess – you will never guess it.'

They guess and guess in vain until she triumphantly reveals the mysterious answer: she is supposed to be 'Made/Maid in Denmark.'[5]

Nini laughs with her elbows jammed in the white keys of the piano. The pastor laughs and helps Miss Benedicte up.

It is over and done with, Herman thinks. The laughter is no longer dangerous. And when he returns to the Academy, the days become light and indistinguishable like fine snowflakes that fall around him and drift into weeks and months.

At Easter he and William are back in Tersløse again. The 20th of April is confirmation Sunday, and that day Herman is both a birthday boy and a Sunday's child. But he fears the worst. The pastor's head is wrapped in rags and he is talking about Job. Herman has gone through the whole sermon and edited it the best he can.

And even so it happens. Up by the altar, surrounded by the confirmands' young faces full of excitement, the pastor forgets everything. 'Sharing with your neighbour,' he says. 'What is yours is also mine.' But suddenly he looks up at the ceiling or heaven like a dog seeking something.

Heaven's dog, Herman thinks while whispering and miming and trying to catch his father's eyes. But the pastor sees neither Easter nor confirmands and the birthday child. Gone are all the scriptural passages and devotional words, and a couple of the girls begin to cry when they hear their sensitive pastor chanting:

The cat and Miss Cruel
fought over some gruel.
'Ouch!' cries Miss Cruel.
'I got burnt on the gruel!'

'Your fault,' says the cat.
'You could've giv'n me that.'

At the festive tables the soufflés begin to slump and the roasts get cold while someone sends for the curate.

Nini and Herman hold their father, the pastor, between them in a firm grip, and all the while his beautiful voice rises towards the spring sky. At home the servant girls hide in their rooms. The governess weeps out loud. And Herman telegraphs grandfather in Copenhagen.

Already the next morning the Royal Physician's carriage pulls into the courtyard. Grandfather speaks with the bishop. And grandfather helps his favourite son into the carriage and kisses the children on their foreheads and tells them to stay calm. If anyone should ask for their father, he has gone to a health spa.

Nini cries quietly. Ingeborg slaps herself on both cheeks, and it is not until Christella takes her hands in hers that she begins to cry. Thankfully Sofie is still too small to understand. She sets a white feather afloat in a puddle. Herman puts his arm around William's shoulder and senses that from now on the two of them must stick together. When his brother frees himself from the affectionate touch, Herman discovers that William is a whole head taller than himself.

The following day they travel back to the Academy. It is a relief just to see the gate and to stroll in the park and hear the blackbird and the great tits and watch the spring flowers unfolding. The days are once again safe and a matter of routine, and the only thing Herman truly fears is the examination in mathematics.

'Pray for me,' he writes to Julius in Horsens. 'Pray for me to all the saints that I will receive pass marks in mathematics. I have few claims to lay in that regard – and even less proficiency in the subject matter. In Latin last month I received the following top marks: sixteen A's for oral work, seven A's for the written, and no other marks. But Latin is my best subject anyway.'

And he ends with:

'You are probably aware that father is ill but now doing much better. Ah, dear friend! We have reached a dark point in our lives, we are devastated that things have come to this. In three weeks time he will go to a spa and stay for a month – times have been very very hard … it broke out on my birthday with more intensity than ever before – believe me, to watch your father go mad is painful, so very painful! Be well!

Best regards from William!

Give my regards to every person, anywhere, who would care to receive a greeting from

Your faithful friend Herman'

He seals the envelope and picks up a letter that has been lying about for a couple of days, practically screaming for an answer. Holger, the frequent contributor to the literary journal, wants to know how and why one becomes a poet and if it is at all a good thing.

Yes, if he only knew the answer himself. The word 'good' seems in any case to be completely wrong. Only one thing is for sure: one must be unhappy. But if only that was sufficient, he would have been a famous poet long ago. He is just a schoolboy who bites the pen holder when writing poems to his own cousin although he knows that she shows them to Nini.

The family line, he thinks. Perhaps it is all because of the family line. And the pen is flying and splatters ink while he thinks about mother who had a debauched opera singer in her family, and about father and grandfather who could compose a rhyming poem faster than an ordinary letter. And he thinks about the Hvide family and about art and about Holger's wide, innocent face.

*

'If I am a poet, it is because I have wept the tears of the family line and wallowed in their wretchedness and dreamt the same dreams – and one of the thousand tears we shed becomes our poetry's baptismal water, and one of the million sighs they heave becomes a curse on the world.

So, is it a good thing to be a poet, and if it isn't, why not flee from it?

It is impossible. Once you have felt the fire in the sea of torment and been immersed in the burning waves, the soul will always yearn for the flaming bath of the process, and from under the infinite torment it will seek to rise up above the unending suffering.'

*

He knows he was born to sorrow and fame. Just the thought makes him euphoric. And outside the weather is so bright and beautiful that he wants to treat himself to a stroll along the lake. Afterwards he will visit the church and pick up his pictures at the photographer's.

The sun is still high in the sky, and right by the rushes a mother duck is swimming with her flock of newly hatched ducklings. Suddenly he senses a flicker of movement in the air. And the cat seems like nothing more than a black shadow when it jumps into the shallow water and snatches a duckling. The duck spreads out her wings and turns towards the cat in a rage while the rest of the brood bobs up and down in the water like downy balls. In a split second Herman meets the tomcat's yellow, defiant gaze, and he watches the duckling's small feet swim in the air. He turns quickly the other way and heads for the church.

When he opens the door his first thought is to turn around. For the roar of the organ fills the church with music that only exists for its own sake. The family's ancestral space saturates the sound with sorrow and joy.

He has no idea what is being played. If truth be told, he is not particularly musical. To him, music has always been associated with words, with hymns, plays or songs. But the organ seems to be self-conscious and passionate at the same time, and it is as if the sound stirs a whole new feeling in him, untouched and fresh.

It is not the Hvides' music nor his mother's – when during the long winter afternoons she let her fingers run over the keys. And yet it is maybe like her after all – when with the table cloth draped around her head she recited a tale of love that was both innocent and forbidden.

It is like a column of water that suddenly shoots up. A happy, bright declaration. A passion that wants to break all the rules.

Suddenly the church feels bare without a sound. He hears footsteps. Actually, he didn't even think about the music as something being played by a person.

He lowers his head the moment the man passes by him. Then he straightens up and follows him. He sees a figure in black, slim and straight. He sees that the man stops for a moment and rubs his hands together, then interlaces his long fingers as if he wants to keep the cold at a distance by embracing himself. And Herman notices the nape of his neck and his black shiny hair just before the figure practically disappears in a coat that has been lying in one of the pews. The moment the gentleman turns up his collar and faces him, Herman feels like a small child who has been caught doing something wrong.

The man smiles. His teeth are small and very white. The smile is neither affectionate nor compassionate; it is more curious and at the same time knowing and perhaps slightly ironic.

The man has stepped out and entered his carriage when Herman discovers that he himself has been wringing his hands and biting his lip to the point of almost drawing blood. But then he suddenly remembers his pictures and hurries off to the photographer.

In front of the shop he looks at himself in the display window and smoothes the fringe of his hair. But it is not a true reflection that he sees. It is life-size and in black and white. It is his face and his skin and hair behind the glass. And it is his mother's exotic beauty in a boy's body. His features are soft like a child's with a thick, unruly fringe above a domed forehead and with eyes that are large, dark and inscrutable. His nose is delicately shaped and his lips full and sensual. That's what the man has seen: an Oriental prince.

'Thank you,' Herman says and smiles at the photographer.

'I have done some retouching, sir. I was wondering if I should cut some of the ears off?'

He shakes his head. He hasn't even noticed the ears.

'No, you don't notice them too much at this angle. But the gentleman does have somewhat large and protruding ears. So, we let them be?'

'Twenty, please. I want to order twenty photographs.'

'Certainly, sir.'

And he flew back to the Academy and his room where he dedicated the first picture to Margrethe.

He writes 'An exceptionally handsome young person' across the surface. He simply cannot help himself. And the accompanying letter is written on the finest of paper:

'I hope, my dearest, that you notice that I write to you on grey paper and that I have made more than the usual effort with the writing which, incidentally, makes it even more illegible; but, as I mentioned, the will is there, and one cannot ask for much more. You have, when you read this nonsense, already understood the reason for the grey and its content – the fact that I send you this picture will have to justify my audacity in writing a poem to you which I myself find flattering, notwithstanding a typical and impressive silence on your part. It would hardly be appropriate for you to descend from your height to those who lay down the song of their lyre in front of your ambrosial throne with its musk-fragrant cushions. So, may my picture move you and may you look at the beautiful, noble and yet so cold features until you yourself warm up, as though you had eaten buttermilk soup. Tune your harp and let Nini ready her lyre and then write a song that can preserve this ephemeral beauty for immortality. Observe in this gaze everything that love's eye can see, longing, emptiness and melancholy. Read in this picture a man's suffering – and write a powerful poem, preferably on an empty stomach or you will be too highfalutin, and Nini is already high above me, yes, she has literally reached sufficient height. Farewell, my picture will say the rest, it will speak for me with the irresistible power of irresistible beauty.

Your Chatterbox'

But Margrethe doesn't answer, neither in prose nor in poetry, neither with passion nor with nonsense. And he regrets that he has written her at all. Imagine if her letter had been intercepted or worse yet, his letter. In both cases he would be the one to be ridiculed. He will write a letter that cancels out the previous one. But it is no longer the pretty blonde Margrethe he imagines when he puts pen to paper.

It is a dark-haired gentleman in a black coat. It is a man who caresses his own hands and suddenly turns his gaze towards him, the boy, and smiles a smile that is knowingly arrogant and perhaps a bit mocking. And that man will understand everything.

To him he would be able to speak of his mother, the family and the dream of finally being noticed one day. And he imagines places where the two of them can meet, rooms filled with the sweet fragrance of flowers and a soft dimmed light that barely makes it possible to discern the letters on the page. For he wants to read it out loud. He reads better than anyone, they say. And the man will be moved by his voice and the expression on his face. And perhaps there will be a caress. A hand that will touch his hair lightly. And perhaps he will take that hand and press his lips against the spot where the veins flow like rivers under the skin.

It is the language of love from all the French novels that comes flying like a flock of doves, finally returning home. He hides the notebook in the drawer. In the mist on the window pane he corresponds with the night until he sees the first light of dawn and the mist above the landscape.

The entire next day he is teased for his yawns and the dark rings under his eyes.

'You are in love,' says Cantor.

He doesn't even have the energy for a retort.

One Sunday Margrethe visits Tersløse. He sees her the minute he turns into the garden. A young girl in pink. A small arched foot that pushes the swing back and forth with a lazy nudge. An abundance of blond ringlets that cover the nape of her neck and fall on her shoulders.

He could sneak over behind her and give the swing a push that would make her laugh and scream at the same time. Or he could cover her eyes with his hands and make her guess.

'Margrethe,' he places himself right in front of the swing. 'Did you get my picture?'

'Yes – '

'But you didn't answer.'

'Women don't write poems to men.'

'But why! I have written at least ten to you.'

'Would you perhaps ever consider writing a poem to a man?'

'Yes – absolutely.'

'Herman. – It is only the words that you are in love with.' She bends her head forward and her face disappears behind the curls. Her voice sounds small and disjointed. 'Women can't do that sort of thing – it would be – '

'Be what?'

'It would be too forward.'

'Men, then, have greater opportunities than women.'

'No. No, not at all.'

'So, what can women do that men cannot.'

'We can wear pink, for instance.'

He bends down to kiss one of the long shiny ringlets but discovers that a wasp has gotten the same idea. He blows it away.

'It is the cognac,' she says matter-of-factly.

'But Margrethe, are you drinking?'

'No. Of course not. But I always rinse my hair in cognac to avoid singeing it with the curling iron.'

'A brilliant idea,' he says and kisses the tip of a curl. 'The next time we meet, we will wear pink.'

'Herman, you will disgrace us. You will disgrace both of us if you wear pink.'

The empty swing moves back and forth, and Margrethe disappears in a cloud of pink.

He will not write to her again for the time being.

For there is a man who is more beautiful than any woman. As beautiful as Shakespeare's boy heroines. And that man has brushed his shoulder, touched him with the tip of his fingers and smiled at him with an ironic, mocking and tender expression. He didn't say: 'My friend.' He didn't say: 'My love.' But he, Herman, knew that he meant: 'My own, beloved friend.'

And there was no letter. For letters of fire must be turned to ashes. That kind of love must never speak its name. But Herman wants to imitate all his movements, and Herman suddenly hears his tone of voice in his own voice and becomes paralyzed with fear that somebody should hear precisely that tone.

And he meets him in a garden, in a greenhouse, in a sitting

room. And they both act as if it were by chance. As if it were not fate that the man would pass his hand over Herman's eyes and close them. As if it were not fate that he would slide and sink toward perdition. That he would open his mouth. That the man's hands are like protective wings – although not totally. That he, the boy, would open his mouth which suddenly is a landscape. Teeth for cliffs, a domed palate, a silent tongue, soft against the thrust of a member. Against a liquid flower that is warm and salty.

And if someone came now. And if someone saw him now, there would only be one way out. In the lake. And there he would sink to the bottom and let the water seep into his eyes, ears and mouth. Not to cleanse himself. But to die. For that's what he deserves.

And most of all he wanted to run away. And most of all he wanted to wipe his mouth. Or spit. But the man holds him back. And he knows that he is damned. And he wishes that the two of them could go for a walk around the lake arm in arm. That there would be restaurants where the tablecloths would cover their hands and feet and their caresses. That there would be rooms where the two of them could be together forever. And that their hands would never fly apart like frightened birds.

And he dreams about amethyst grottos where a mild salty rain falls on naked bodies, and where snakes with beautiful heart-shaped heads rest in their coils. And their brains are much too small to comprehend any feeling of hatred.

He writes about the man again and again. 'Fragment' he calls his story. For it is so very little he can disclose about his love:

He, himself, is sitting by a table reading out loud. He is still only a child with soft features and downy cheeks. But he is as beautiful as in the photograph, and his voice is soft and melodious.

On the settee a woman sits and listens. She is much older than him, a Juno with an ample bosom and large hips and a gaze that soaks up his youthfulness.

The two of them are in the same room. But their longing is caged in the wrong bodies. There are only words and a casual touch, a kiss and then his tears streaming down his face onto the woman's hands.

There is no ending at all. There is no way out of this room where love is an acute pain or an illness that must be kept hidden.

'Read something to us yourself,' says Rosenberg, and Cantor and Holger and Graa pester him: 'We know very well that you write. Why do you just restrict yourself to critiquing the rest of us. Is it because you don't dare?'

He attempts to appear reluctant when he rummages around in his secret drawer, and he pretends that it is completely by chance that he finds 'Fragment.' And he reads about the boy and the woman with such passion that he needs to blink his tears away and bring out his voice with force.

For a moment he thinks his friends are overwhelmed by emotion. But they are in fact convulsed with laughter, guffawing at him, their faces copper red. And he tears up the notebook and tosses it into the fireplace before hiding his face in his hands, sobbing. He weeps over his entire family line, over mother, father, Aage, Oluf and over Margrethe whose brow he will never get to dab now with a white handkerchief. But he weeps mostly because not a single soul is touched by his art and all his suffering.

The friends are embarrassed. They were not laughing at him at all, they say. It was something entirely different that they suddenly happened to think about. But he can only weep and weep. And it is only after they have left that he notices that they have salvaged the notebook from the fireplace. He glues his 'Fragment' together again and decides to rewrite the story.

But soon there are other things to think about. For the following day the headmaster announces that the royal actor, professor Phister, is coming to Sorø to act in Holberg's *Jeppe of the Hill* along with the senior students at the Academy.

*

The welcoming committee from the Academy is at the station well in advance. The boys expect to see Phister alight from a first-class compartment, wearing a cloak and accompanied by a manservant. But it is just a little old man who steps out of the train, carefully as if he is afraid of falling and breaking something.

When the students introduce themselves, he nods absent-mindedly. He has definitely not come for their sake. An elderly couple who have also been waiting for him take his arm, and the gentleman carries Phister's suitcase to the carriage.

The bouquet of flowers is not delivered, and Herman Bang's welcome speech is not given. The students at the Academy are stunned.

But the next day the whole Academy is acting under the sign of Holberg, and it is boring. The professor measures the floor and draws lines and squares with a piece of chalk so that he can place his fellow actors at the right distance from himself. He orders them about for six hours. He measures out pauses to allow for laughter from the audience. There is neither drama nor passion. It is really only when Nille is on stage, shouting in her rough, breaking voice that it becomes lively. Herman usually plays women's roles. But those women were melancholy, graceful and coquettish. His physique and temperament don't match those of Nille. Now he is a barrister and has plenty of time to observe how the professor strips down the art and only leaves the scaffolding behind.

Finally, once they perform for the audience, the real drama begins. Professor Phister has stage fright. When he is off stage, he is nervous about his lines, about his costume, about every single step. As soon as he is acting, he is wonderful. The audience laughs appropriately, all according to the plan. He is blind to his fellow actors. They are merely serviceable parts of a clockwork.

But during the courtroom scene the professor's mind goes blank. He gets stuck and then jumps back half a scene. What Herman sees is an old puffy face and eyes that look up towards the ceiling or heaven. And he hammers his fist on the table and shouts into the royal actor's face: 'This you have already said, you scoundrel!'

And for just a moment Jeppe really does notice his young barrister, and after that he plays the scene to the end without any trouble.

At the curtain calls Jeppe drags the barrister onto the stage. The two of them stand in the light while the audience is applauding, and in one dizzying glance Herman sees Nini and Margrethe, Christella, William and the headmaster and the unfortunate friends who don't have any roles to play. When the curtain comes down for the last time, the professor looks at him approvingly and says: 'You are obviously going to be an actor.'

Afterwards he dances with Margrethe and with the headmaster's daughter and with the matron's daughter. The girls hover around him in spite of the fact that he lickety-split has tied pink laces in his shoes, knotted a pink necktie and donned pink gloves.

His sisters and Margrethe leave early. But he doesn't pay them any attention for the professor has promised that he himself will coach him.

And not even the examinations can distract him.

For everything he longed for as a child will happen now. The light will shine on his person. Everyone will see him and love him, and he will pass into the chrysalis stage, change his shape, turn into other creatures altogether, and in this way finally become himself. Everything that he has experienced has led him to this one goal.

Aladdin, Hamlet, Tartuffe – he will disappear behind these characters. All the Nordic heroes will speak with his voice. He is still a bit too short and inhibited. But the family line will help him. 'By the holy blood of God, how proud and fair she is,' he recites until the window panes rattle and Rosenberg, whose room is next door, knocks on the wall and asks him to be quiet and think about his examinations. But he doesn't need to do that. He needs neither Greek nor Latin to become an actor.

Still, he passes his final examinations with top grades.

'How about that!' says his father and squeezes his hand almost shyly.

Nini and William hug him, and Christella and the little ones shower him with good wishes and endearments. And there are parties upon parties and still more parties. Spirited speeches, night outings on the lake, the small shadows of the bats, the freshness of the wild roses, and the sunrise that they absolutely have to wait for. The birds etch the air in blue, and the young girls in their light dresses dance and tread ever so carefully in the grass wet with dew. He offers them his protective arm and brushes their exquisite, round cheeks with his lips, and everything is otherworldly and splendid.

The summer in Tersløse is gentle and endless, and when he has had enough of it, he moves to Copenhagen to live with his grandfather and becomes a pampered young man with polished fingernails, embroidered gloves, silk socks, patent-leather shoes, monogrammed handkerchiefs and from London: rose-coloured stationery with gilded edges.

He patronizes Tivoli Gardens, the theatre and À Porta restaurant. And he can afford to treat his friends. Every morning his grandfather slips him a couple of bills and in the evening he asks if Herman doesn't have 'something on his mind' for, after all, a young man needs quite a bit to provide for clothing, books and a tutor. They both avoid the word 'money.' Money is something you have. And grandfather has a heart of gold.

Following the wish of the Royal Physician, he studies economics, and grandfather dreams him into a diplomatic career. And it occasionally happens that he too imagines a life of diplomacy, especially a travelling life with large leather suitcases and a manservant with the Hvide family's coat of arms on all his sparkly silver buttons.

But he especially dreams about the big roles. The applause that surges towards him and bouquets that beautiful, spirited women throw to him. Perhaps they will fall in love with his Hamlet. In any case, they will finally see a Tartuffe who is young and handsome and seductive.

Unfortunately it is not that kind of role that Phister gives him.

'Wait,' he says. 'That kind demands maturity.' The professor loves his Holberg and wants to make him into a perfect Leander.

But Leander is just a dry, elegant young man who falls in love with a perfectly ordinary girl in a perfectly ordinary manner. And to cap it all, the two dull creatures get each other by means of a bit of cunning. No passionate monologues, no death scenes. He gets Leander's lines all mixed up. And one day he suddenly plays Molière instead of Holberg.

Professor Phister looks at him, just looks and looks. Then he closes the book.

'I don't listen to lines that haven't been learned,' he says. 'I always knew my roles.'

His weary face seems simultaneously authoritative and tired. And the student Herman Bang will have to get up and leave.

He is embarrassed but not despairing. Outside the door, the city is waiting for him with its colours and gas lamps. It is as if the light envelopes him in a protective membrane. And the day the telegram arrives and grandfather opens it and says that father has died, he doesn't begin to cry.

He takes it with the same stoic calmness as the Royal Physician who says that it was the best thing that could happen. 'Now the impasse has finally been broken. Now your father doesn't have to fight any longer.'

It is only in the train on his way to Horsens that he gives way to his grief and sees everything in a fog. But it is just as much due to the thought of his mother's grave and Aage and Oluf and grandfather's poem that he has to deliver to the newspaper.

Then suddenly he hears Nini's voice. 'But Herman – surely you are going to change.'

'Change – '

'Yes, I assume you have bought a black coat to wear at your father's funeral.'

Only then does he notice that everyone is wearing black. Sofie's delicate flower face disappears behind a black bonnet. Even Ingeborg's hair is hidden under a black hat with a black elastic band that is cutting into her chin.

He hadn't thought about it, not at all. His coat is light beige, the fashion colour of the year.

He is the last person in the funeral procession, all by himself, staggering and stumbling.

No, suddenly Margrethe's cool fingers grasp his hand. Her voice is clear like a bell: 'Herman. If only you didn't want to become an actor.'

'Why?'

'It would never be the right – the right kind of family life.'

4.

No, Margrethe with the cognac-scented ringlets never did get the right kind of family life either. She became a spinster and learned English.

She spent her vacations with him and Nini those summers when he could afford to rent a house near Hotel Marienlyst in Elsinore. He helped her financially, quietly giving her money behind his sister's back. And got her a job at long last as a translator at the newspaper *København*.

And she was very able. Mr Witzansky himself said: 'That woman you found me is an excellent translator. She selects her material with good judgment. I am exceedingly glad to have her here at the paper.'

That was indeed a very different tone from the usual one. Witzansky made a practice of ordering his journalists around as if he were still a non-commissioned officer.

Margrethe got a permanent post as a translator of serial novels. She would be sitting in the dining room on Gammel Kongevej in those days when he and Nini shared a household. From noon to three o'clock she would cover the entire table with her English novels full of secrets, last wills and murders.

And her horn-rimmed glasses would slide down on her long nose that never seemed to quit growing. And her backside got wider and flatter as unfortunately often happens to women. And her hair darkened and was gathered in a bun. And then a tinge of white that with time turned to streaks. A thin salt-and-pepper braid coiled up like a snake.

But it wasn't just the dreams of the theatre that separated him from Margrethe.

There was a man who was more beautiful than any woman. And he would have to surrender himself to his destiny. He was lost.

But he would always be fond of her and help her. 'You must send Witzansky a couple of stories so you can earn some money. He has only received this "Tiger Hunt," and, after all, you are no longer so pretty.'

No, she had long since fallen from her ambrosial throne onto a mere dining-room chair. But how he misses her now. If only she could have travelled with him around the world. If she were sitting across from him right now, people would think they were a married couple – the kind of couple where the wife is older than the husband.

Margrethe would have understood what people were saying, and she would have been able to subdue each and every electrical installation in New York.

He wouldn't have been alone, enduring the train's rhythmic pulse throbbing through him: 'Life, death. Life, death.' And then this dizziness that makes it impossible for him to concentrate on his travel articles. And he absolutely must write them. And the papers will have to accept them. It is a matter of life and death and a bill from the tailor. For he has still not paid for his wardrobe in Copenhagen.

Otherwise he wrote to friends and acquaintances: 'Help me if you can. If you could lend me a hundred kroner or just thirty. I am travelling around the world, and I have no clothing to my name. Tropical clothing is probably called for in Japan. And I gave my spring coat away to a poor man.'

The train stops with a jerk that hurls him forward. His nose is running. And what will happen to his voice if he should get a cold? How will he cope with all the big halls that swallow up the sound?

It is blood. A tiny blood stain on his handkerchief. Haemorrhages, seizures and fainting spells – all that he is familiar with. Fortunately they don't affect his voice.

A smell of wet fur is in the air. A gentleman clad in beaver furs walks by so closely that he can feel the fur touching his cheek.

Once he had a fur coat himself. Black and luxurious.

When he looks up, his eyes meet the gaze of the waiter. Of course, in a dining car you are supposed to eat something.

He opens the menu with an arrogant gesture and points at the cheapest item.

The waiter smiles, as if it were anything to smile at, and shortly after places a tray with tea, toast and a soft-boiled egg in front of him.

He warms his hands on the teapot while the waiter walks over to the stove, shakes the ashes down and adds two scoops of coal. He feels the heat stroking his back. The same kind of heat as the time he woke up with a fever in Valkendorf's Student Residence.

*

She nursed him, the porter's wife. And she took care of his housework. She dusted all the silver frames with the photographs of family members and actors. The rag passed across the forehead of the Niobe figurine and right into the corner of the eyes of the Antinous bust. She fluffed the cushions on the chaise longue and casually folded the Royal Physician's old afghan so that the monogram was visible.

Finally she would pick up the animal skin from the floor and shake it out the window. She thought it was from a panther although it was just a black pony. She had a mixed look of fascination and disgust on her face when she rolled it up, getting ready to wash the floors.

He dozed off. Maybe it was rheumatic fever he suffered from. Maybe he would soon die like his gentle sister Christella. Or like grandfather who took his own pulse and was lucid right to the end.

When he knew where things were heading, he called for Herman and gave him a wallet with 1500 kroner. 'Just so the transition won't be too difficult,' he said.

But it was not a transition. It was a fall. The day the Royal Physician was buried, Herman was without protection and without a home. He only had his books and the afghan and then the 1500 kroner that he changed to smaller bills and hid in his desk drawer so he only had to stick his hand in and grab a few without counting them.

The woman pushes her two small sons from corner to corner. They are not allowed to make noise and be in the way. And he opens his eyes and says in a weak voice that the children may sit on the settee and eat from the big box of chocolates. She shakes her head disapprovingly but humours him, bends down and wrings the cold, dirty water out of the rag. Her wedding ring is very thin and cuts into her finger a bit.

'You shouldn't work so hard, madam,' he says. 'Perhaps I am going to die soon.'

'It has to be kept clean all the same. – But couldn't you wait until you are called just like the rest of us,' she adds bashfully.

The two boys look at each other. The younger one jumps across the newly washed floor in his stocking feet, pulls three flattened daisies out of his pocket and places them on the eiderdown. And soon both children are sitting on the edge of the bed while he tells them about the white house and about Tine and about his mother who lets the cows and horses loose just to see them run. And in the winter she jumps on ice floes like a circus acrobat and on legs as thin as a goat's legs. But when he wants to try it himself, he falls into the water and pokes his head up like a seal.

The woman kneels and unrolls the black animal skin on the floor. She can't help stroking the fur carefully. Then she hustles the boys out. And before she leaves, she puts a small tray with tea, toast and a soft-boiled egg beside the bed.

'Madam,' he says and hands her a piece of paper. 'Would you or your husband kindly send for these people.'

'But Mr Bang, surely you are not going to give a party now?'

'No, I want to write my last will. And your sons are going to be my heirs.'

She seems more alarmed than happy. She holds the scrubbing brush and the pail in one hand, the paper in the other hand away from her as though she is afraid to stain it should it touch the wet spot on her apron. Even so she attempts to make a curtsey.

And he must have been out cold in his feverish state back at the Student Residence. For when he opens his eyes, he thinks he is at home in Horsens. Perhaps it is because of Julius' voice. For Julius Schiøtt, Cantor and Graa are looking down at him, lying in the bed.

He asks them to help themselves to the carafes if they wish. They find some glasses. And finally he can begin the dictation, that he, who is so young and has suffered so much in order to write just a little, now wishes to will the rights to his works to the porter's young sons. The money shall be used for the children's education.

Cantor raises his eyebrows slightly but writes it down.

The children are probably too young to appreciate the furniture and the paintings. They will remain in the family.

'In addition,' he says, 'I wish to bestow a watch studded with diamonds upon Nini, my dear older sister. And a necklace with blue sapphires to my younger sister, Sofie. They will go well with the colour of her eyes.'

'Tell me, Herman, are you in actual fact in possession of this jewelry?' Cantor pauses with the pen in the air.

'I have to say, I have never seen your mother wearing anything like that,' Julius protests.

'No,' he sighs. 'You know very well that I don't have the jewelry. But my uncle is very rich and can easily buy them.'

'Herman,' Cantor was already a know-it-all then. 'That's not how you write a will.'

The young Herman Bang leans back and sinks into the cushions resigned: 'Then I don't know what it means to respect the last wishes of the deceased.'

Shortly after he asks for a cigarette.

'You should give up smoking,' says Julius. 'Smoke and bronchitis don't go together.'

'Over my dead body. Cigarettes are chic and French. I would rather do without food and drink.'

He gets his cigarette. And the long draw goes straight to his lungs and his brain.

*

Exactly like now.

And in reality they haven't changed much, his friends. Cantor, the decent, sensitive lawyer, has helped him time and again without charging a fee. A book with a friendly note inside, that was enough.

Incidentally, Cantor had reminded him of the will just before his departure. He had suggested that they should draw up a new one. But he had shrugged it off.

And Graa – Graa can spellbind Herman Bang completely and never tires of telling how Herman Bang borrowed his first shirt with collar stiffeners from him and forgot to return it. And without make-up and without his waistcoat, Herman Bang looks no more than a little Italian shoeshine boy. That's the kind of rumour that Graa spreads. And of course the rumours get back to him. Sooner or later.

And Julius Schiøtt. In everything that others attempt to do, he succeeds. His marriage is harmonious and stimulating for both parties. He was an accomplished translator of French and a splendid editor. And now the director of the zoological garden. His last success was having the garden's Brahma bulls slaughtered and then treating the journalists in Copenhagen to Brahma-bull steaks and peacock eggs. And that generated publicity.

Yes, of course Julius would be the first to warn him against cigarettes. But not the last.

Just prior to his departure, it was his physician, Doctor Wasbutzki, who, by the way, isn't at all stingy with the morphine.

And one day when the doctor was out, Mrs Bertha Wasbutzki took his right hand and looked at it with sadness for a long time. She called him God's finest work of filigree and said that his yellow fingers spoiled his hand gestures and the hand itself, so small and shapely.

He smiled a melancholy smile. For his teeth behind his sensual lips are and always will be yellow. And it doesn't matter how much toothpaste he puts on the brush.

'A kiss calls for white teeth,' says the advertisement. And well, yes, that sounds very fine and true.

It wasn't a kiss she wanted, the doctor's wife. But she shared her problems and worries with him. If she tried to confide in her husband, the physician, he would immediately become professional.

Now she is probably still in Berlin, missing her Herman Bang. And when he returns, she will be at the train station with an armful of white roses and lilies.

If he returns, that is. For only one thing is for certain: he will go to his grave with yellow fingers. And perhaps they will fold his hands and hide them under a wreath adorned with long white ribbons.

He had never thought about that kind of thing when he was young. And in truth, a great deal ought to be changed in that will from long ago.

His body must neither be photographed nor sketched. And no death mask. For maybe his facial expression will look foolish. He even thinks about his appearance when he has fainting spells and seizures. And he has the photographs retouched a little. Unfortunately he has never been as handsome as on the pictures. But death does not retouch the image. And suppose his corpse looks comical.

Otherwise he is not afraid of dying. Time and again he has imagined death sitting by his side like a faithful friend or liberator. Total obliteration, finally, or one long continuous sleep. But he doesn't want to be a hideous corpse with tousled hair and a gaping mouth letting in the darkness.

Also, he doesn't want a headstone. People who don't know him are certainly not going to write things on a stone and place it on top of him. He can only imagine what Nini would think of putting on a headstone like that, a stone that would survive much longer than his books. For to be sure, he doesn't believe that they will last.

No, he is just a diligent talent. And he has utilized each and every millimetre of that talent, stretched himself and laboured until his brain nearly burst. But only geniuses will endure, Shakespeare, Michelangelo and the Bible.

Of course it happens that he runs into admirers who call him a genius. It happened as recently as the day before yesterday. 'No,' he said. 'No, I am merely a talent. I reach up to here.' And he stretched out his fingers until they reached quite high up on the doorpost. 'But the geniuses,' he continued and pointed up where he couldn't possibly reach. 'They are way up there.'

But there is a difference after all in knowing your limitations and then letting Nini and the horrible Pastor Fenger give him a posthumous reputation.

Actually, he would prefer being buried without ceremony or

mourners. All right, maybe just Fritz. That is, if Fritz would come at all, if he wasn't touring or in the process of cavorting with some questionable woman and if, needless to say, he had money to buy a train ticket. And then he could come and sing with his young, fresh voice: 'How Sweetly Beckons the Path Ahead.'[6] Without pomp. His voice would still sound young. No longer innocent, but clear. And it would accompany him to the grave, which would merely be a hole in the ground. A wound in the green lawn that would soon heal. And the linden trees would smell sweet, and lovers would tread noisily above his face.

All that he hadn't managed to put in writing. Back then at Valkendorf's Student Residence he had been thinking of the two children first and foremost. He had wanted the boys to remember him as a young man who had let them eat all the sweets they fancied and who had left them the last bit of grandfather's money: about three hundred kroner.

Perhaps it wouldn't even be that much today. The statements from his publishers are and will remain in the red. He is almost afraid to open the ones from Gyldendal. And from Germany the shortfalls are even worse. But then Sammy Fischer writes very politely that he should only take the figures as advisory.

At least back then he had three hundred kroner and his expectations.

The family expectations would have shrunk to nearly nothing by now. He remembers very clearly Nini drawing herself up, a head taller than him. 'But Herman, how could you think of becoming an actor? A man who makes a display of himself. And you with your first-class diploma?'

And aunt Fanny, sweet aunt Fanny, marches up the stairs of his residence and spends an entire evening explaining to him that he is a layabout and a daydreamer. And he will go directly to the dogs if he doesn't immediately pull himself together and do something about his studies in economics. As if you could become an envoy with suitcases and a fur coat simply by pulling yourself together.

'Yes, but I do in fact do something.'

'What?' She slams her ringed hand on the table. 'Would you please tell me what that might be?'

But he was still waiting for replies to his letters.

'Valkendorf's Student Residence / St. Peder's Street Copenhagen
15.8.78

When I plead with you, Sir, to please read the enclosed short article, I am following the advice of one of my literary friends. For I have been told that I should send you a sample of my style and approach without delay, and when you have read it, you would agree that I could be of use to you.'

But there was no reply from Vilhelm Topsøe, the editor of *Dagbladet*.
And he has written polite applications to the theatres in Copenhagen and enclosed photographs. 'With the enclosed pictures you will be able to familiarize yourself with my appearance – slightly "idealized", naturally.'
Oddly enough with no results.
In his desperation he has written to Odense Theatre.

'*Sir*,

I am writing to you to inquire whether there is any possibility of my being associated with your company. I am twenty-one years old, a student, and I belong to one of the most respected families in the country. Since my earliest years I have had an overwhelming desire to be part of the theatre. I was fortunate to attract the attention of one of our greatest dramatic artists – and he approached my grandfather, Privy Councillor Bang, to obtain his permission for me to become an actor.
I had then a great sonorous voice of rare beauty and power. Due to over-exertion, it lost some of its strength but not its singular softness.'

*

Odense doesn't respond either. But aunt Fanny's ringed hand has left a pale star-shaped mark on the table's surface, and she has called him a dreamer and a layabout. Time will show her. She will be eating her words one day. Time will show all of them. Nini and William and Margrethe.

He puts pen to paper and writes far into the night while all decent folk are asleep. For a brief moment his head drops to the table and he tries to go to sleep. But sleep brushes him off. He is wide awake again and he continues writing. He speaks out loud but not to himself. Those are lines he shouts and sighs out into the room. And by the following morning he has written a short one-act play.

He sends his play to *Folketeatret*, and since he has to wait for a reply anyway, he writes a couple of articles that he sends off to the newspaper *Jyllands-Posten*.

'Write more,' says Vilhelm Møller at *Jyllands-Posten*.

'Yes, it is not any worse than any other twenty-year old's debut,' says Fritz Holst at *Folketeatret*.

Twenty years old and making his debut. '*You and I*. Herman Bang,' says the playbill. And he follows the billposter all the way to Østerbro to observe how his name is displayed all over the capital of Copenhagen. His feet barely touch the ground and not only because he is wearing patent-leather shoes and silk socks in the slush.

'Now, what do you say, Margrethe? And you, Nini? And you, aunt Fanny?'

'But it is nothing solid, Herman.'

'Better keep your shirt on.'

'It will hopefully soon be forgotten.'

But he was happy right up to the rehearsal when he sat in the box listening to his own lines spoken by the actors. He followed Betty Borchsenius in particular. She who as an eighteen-year old had captured Horsens with her smile and her youth, fresh and delicate as a windflower. She had matured, twenty-seven years old and not only pretty but outright beautiful. She elevated his lines until there weren't any more to elevate, and the actors looked at each other. There was no ending. It just ended.

'I must say the last line so the audience is entranced,' Betty Borchsenius said. But he, the poet, didn't have the faintest idea of what she should say. Together they wrote sixteen different endings. But nobody could find the right line. And at the opening night the audience applauded politely and infrequently. *You and I* was definitely not a success.

But Herman Bang had become a name. *Jyllands-Posten* printed him. From *Jyllands-Posten* he moved to *Morgentelegrafen* where the rooms were small and the air hot and sweetish because the journalists used to fortify themselves with alcohol diluted with warm water. Especially in the evening when they realized that nothing was working out. On the other hand, the column inches were plentiful. He took up so much space as a theatre and book reviewer that he sometimes had to call himself *Mr?*

One day *Mr?* received a book for reviewing. And that book seized his heart, occupied his brain and made his pulse race while he filled up the waste basket with drafts before he was able to complete his column.

And *Mr?* received a thank-you note from Topsøe, the editor of *Dagbladet*. He was the anonymous author of *Pictures of Our Time*. *Mr?* was very welcome to pay him a visit and, if possible, to write for *Dagbladet*.

There he sat, Vilhelm Topsøe his literary hero, playing with an ivory paper knife, and seemed surprised that *Mr?* who possessed a fine sense of nuance and language could be so young. Only one word in the review had bothered him a little: 'sentimental'.

'I thought about that, but to me it is not a negative thing to be sentimental,' he answered.

Topsøe dropped the paper knife on the desk: 'Would you entertain the idea of writing for *Dagbladet* – only as a freelancer for the time being – you will deliver twelve articles per year. Can you do that?'

As if he couldn't. Granted, he couldn't make a living out of it. But writing for *Dagbladet* brought prestige. And from *Dagbladet* he jumped to *Nationaltidende*.

Permanently employed with 150 kroner monthly. That was twice the amount a police officer earned and more than a royal actor.

The family was dumbfounded.

'You must invest it, Herman, so it yields interest.'

'Be careful you don't fritter it away.'

'You should buy bonds.'

On the first of every month, Emil Bjerring, the secretary, paid out his wages in gold, and the money burnt a hole in his pocket. He used neither a wallet nor a pocketbook, and he wouldn't dream of putting it in the bank.

He remembers clearly how he steps into his modest lodgings, and without turning on the light he throws all the coins up towards the ceiling. In the dark, he can hear them roll around in all directions. Only then does he light the lamp and kneels, some of the gold coins he picks up and others he shoves under the bed, behind the wardrobe, under the carpet and the washstand. A few he buries in the flowerpots. That's how he takes care of his money. He never counts it. But at the end of the month he goes down on his knees and crawls under the bed, fumbles with a coat hanger under the wardrobe. And it is just as exciting as when he was looking for Easter eggs as a child, and when he finds a coin it is as if he has earned it twice.

He is well aware that these kinds of things cause rumours to spread in the city. Especially after a couple of his friends have seen him dig with a small stick in his flowerpot and, in reply to their question of what was going on, received the answer that he was digging for gold.

The money simply disappears, and one day he visits the loan shark Andreasen. He has been warned. But it is as if the warning itself drives him to go there. Perhaps it is just that he wants to write about a loan shark.

He faces the door with the big brass sign. If he rings the doorbell and no one is at home, he will just run out into the street and never come back.

He puts his finger on the doorbell and hears how it rings through all the rooms and pulls a person out into the hall. A woman with short, hard steps. He imagines dark hair and silk stockings with crooked seams.

The woman is blonde and about fifty, and she gives him a friendly smile when he hands her his visiting card and says that he would like to speak with Mr Andreasen.

And does he happen to have an appointment?

No. He looks down at her feet in elegant, pointed shoes. And she practically dances in front of him to the door and right into the library where Mr Andreasen sits behind his desk without looking the least depraved or mysterious.

No greasy vests or frayed cuffs. Mr Andreasen is a tall, well-groomed man who smiles and asks what he has on his mind.

And it is suddenly so easy. So easy to tell about his inheritance that won't be paid out until he turns twenty-five. So easy to say that he must establish himself, live decently after all. And his salary will of course increase.

'But why don't you go to your uncle, Mr Bang?'

For a moment he doesn't know at all what to say. Then he mumbles that he doesn't want to trouble his uncle with so little.

'And how much is a little?'

'A thousand – perhaps a thousand.'

Mr Andreasen begins to write in a large, flowing hand.

'If you would please sign here, Mr Bang, and if you wouldn't mind asking your uncle to sign here, then it shouldn't be a problem.'

He is both disappointed and relieved when he later walks along the Lakes on his way to his uncle. For what will he say? And aunt Fanny and Margrethe?

What if he just pretends he was passing by and decided to make a visit.

Aunt Fanny would ask if he had time to wander around in the middle of the day.

He will say that he is searching for material.

And aunt Fanny: 'There is no material to be found here.'

Margrethe will probably say that she has read his article about spring fashions, about the hats and the dresses that long to emerge into the world.

Aunt Fanny will say: 'Nonsense.'

He will then mention his articles about pig breeding, the dairy industry, foreign politics, theatre and books and the miserable working conditions of home seamstresses. And he will tell them about the firetraps in the neglected tenement houses in the neighbourhood of Nørrebro and about the tenants who simply threw him out because they didn't want their misery to be put on show in the paper.

Most likely, he won't be saying that much.

Uncle is probably not at home. Like a child he starts counting the cracks between the flagstones. 'At home, not at home.' He counts buttons. A black cat crosses his path from the right. It starts raining. He seeks shelter under a chestnut tree. A branch breaks off and hits his shoulder. He counts rowing boats on the lake. There are eight. He hurries home.

He unfolds the documents and writes his name. And it is just child's play to write in uncle's large, left-sloping hand. But he doesn't want to go back to Andreasen. As soon as he has read all of it carefully, he will tear it to pieces and burn it.

Someone is knocking on the door, and he gives a start and pushes the IOU under his books. Maybe it is uncle or aunt Fanny or Nini.

Outside is a small boy carrying a laundry basket. The boy's cheeks are red from exertion, and his hair is spiky from the sweat.

The laundry and the bill. He had forgotten. He takes the basket from the boy and nearly drops it.

'It is much too heavy for you,' he says.

The child smiles. He has lively greyish-blue eyes and a small snub nose. He has taken his cap off.

'The bill, sir.'

'Just a moment, boy.' And there is no money is his pocket. He has to get a teaspoon and dig in the English geranium. He is probably damaging the roots, and he is thinking about asking the kid to come back later. But then, he will most likely take the clean shirts back with him.

Herman Bang polishes a coin with his handkerchief.

'Here you are.'

'I don't have enough change, unfortunately.'

'Just keep the change.'

'But it is way too much, sir.'

'Then buy something for yourself and your siblings.'

'Thank you, sir.' The boy makes a low bow, politely and clumsily. His sweaty hair is still standing on end like spikes on a hedgehog.

'Now, don't run around town and say that I am bizarre.'

'I don't know what bizarre is, sir.' The boy is already on his way down the stairs with the basket in one hand and his clogs and cap in the other.

He looks out the window to see if the child remembers to put on his clogs before jumping out in the rain. He does.

Herman Bang himself carefully picks out the shirt that he will wear tomorrow when he goes to see Andreasen.

Andreasen has been expecting him and offers him a glass of port. The money is ready to go. After he has looked at the paper, he pushes the money across the table with a nonchalant gesture. It is only a formality.

On his way down the stairs, he stops to do something so unusual as to count the money. There should be one thousand. But there are only nine hundred. He must have dropped one hundred. He slips off his shoes and sneaks all the way up the stairs. Not a single krone. So, he sits down on the bench on the mezzanine. Counts, closes his eyes and counts again.

He remembers suddenly the words 'instalments and interest'. On the first of each month Mr Andreasen demands an instalment and interest.

But there is no danger. As long as he is working, there will be no real danger. He sticks the money in his pocket, puts on his shoes and visits the amusement park Tivoli. And even there he is working. Sounds, colours, profiles, the light, everything turns into words, and he writes notes on a serviette and runs to the editorial office.

He is the *enfant terrible* at *Nationaltidende*. He is so quick. He fills one column after another. He can simply go on and on. It is annoying how easy it seems to be for him. Some times he is superficial, but he can always mask it with his style. And the ladies actually write to the paper and praise his serials. It turns his head and he becomes even more mischievous and flippant.

'Your social behavior,' says Emil Bjerring. 'And your attire. But of course, it is no good giving you advice.'

'I always listen to your advice.'

'Yes, you do that. You listen patiently. But you only follow your own wishes. Even though we here at the paper know what is best for you.'

'Three young ladies have written that they have profited from my article about wedding gowns.'

'Yes, and the servant girls snigger at your socks and gloves.'

'They admire me. And the laundry wants to put my linen on display.'

They hear clinking sounds and someone swearing. And everyone who has been watching Bjerring and Bang up to this point now looks at the oldest correspondent at *Nationaltidende* who has just knocked over his inkwell.

'It is impossible to concentrate here in this building,' he snaps. 'Now look what happened.'

The young journalist laughs and skips down the stairs, all cockiness. 'What do you need an inkwell for, anyway?'

*

On the first floor in newspaper owner Ferslew's rooms, Herman Bang is like a son of the house.

'Mr Bang,' whispers the maid. 'Today is not a good day for staying for supper. We are having porridge. But tomorrow is veal.'

He just manages to pour himself a glass of red wine from the carafe before Ferslew's little boy pulls him over to the toys. No one can build castles like Christian and him. As big and beautiful as those in the fairytale books. They hold their breath when they add the last towers.

For a moment they sit very quietly and admire their work. Then Christian thumps the table or Herman blows down the blocks. The castle collapses with a loud bang, and they start all over.

He has become Christian's playmate, and Mrs Ferslew is his motherly friend. They borrow books from each other. He reads his articles and short stories to her, and she shakes her head when she thinks he is too sentimental. She weeps for hours at his description of paupers' funerals, and she laughs out loud when he requests in writing to borrow her husband's fur coat for just two hours.

'What in the world do you need it for, Bang?'

'I only want to look presentable when I attend premieres and appear in public right before my book comes out.'

'Have you written a book?'

'It is nothing. Not even a real book. Just articles that I have compiled. *Realism and Realists* is its title. It is only newspaper articles and aphorisms. What I wrote about the theatre for *Dagbladet* and then what little I have written about French literature. And then a bit about the Nordic authors that I am fond of, J. P. Jacobsen and Topsøe and Skram.'

'Tell me, how old are you really, Bang?'

'Twenty-one years old. – I am already twenty-one.'

'And you are publishing a book?'

'I have barely dipped my pen yet. My head is full of novels and stories – '

'I am not lending out my husband's fur coat. It will look ridiculous on you, anyway. It is much too large. But couldn't you do a reading of one of your stories? – It is for charity. An old seamstress needs a new sewing machine.'

'Yes,' he says. 'Yes, thank you.'

He practises. He reads the short story about the old pastor with the hymnbook from Greenland to the point where he knows it by heart. But when he finally stands in the big hall, he reads poorly. The walls absorb his voice. There is a clinking of champagne glasses. The women's fans cut his sentences to pieces. He himself feels that his voice doesn't reach out to the audience. They are bored, and he and the sewing machine are only an excuse to socialize and show off pretty dresses.

Patronizingly, theatre director Holst puts his arm round his shoulder and says: 'Dear friend, it is for a charitable end, as we know. But don't repeat it.'

'He can work like a horse,' he hears Ferslew say. 'A horse with wings.'

'You wouldn't know from looking at him,' says a gentleman and gives him a rather condescending look.

But Ferslew sells *Nationaltidende* like never before. Herman Bang writes under ten pseudonyms. He is Copenhagen's leading journalist, and he knows it.

'The two of us,' says Ferslew, 'we can build the best newspaper in Denmark.'

'In Scandinavia!' says Bang. 'We will attach the best Nordic writers to the paper. Lie, Levertin, Tavastjerna, Strindberg.'

'Strindberg – is that necessary?'

'Absolutely, yes. He will create a storm. He is necessary. – And by the way, could you also give Emil Bjerring a promotion?'

'Bjerring? – Why in the world should I do that? He has a good position.'

'It would please his old mother immensely if he were to become editor. If she could witness that before she dies.'

Ferslew looks at him tenderly, shakes his head and pours a glass of cognac.

Some times it is night time when he walks home. He looks in through the few lighted windows. Lovers who are putting out the lights, their faces turned towards each other. A mother who covers up her sleeping child. And suddenly he stops and hides in a gateway and watches an older woman doing ballet exercises by her bedpost. Her leg stretched far out to the side and up towards the ceiling. Finally she takes hold of her white skirt with both hands and does a low curtsey.

'Irene,' he thinks at the sight of the lonely figure. 'Her name must be Irene Holm.'

The next day he reads on her nameplate: Alvida Back Nielsen. Dance teacher.

He couldn't write the story yet. So many things stood in the way. The journalism, the novel, Anna. Miss Anna Ferslew.

In a way he knew her before they met. He had seen pictures of a little girl with chubby cheeks wearing a white dress with a cherry-red ribbon around her waist. She had returned from a children's ball carrying an armful of bouquets, her cotillion presents. She rushed to her father, triumphant and beaming with joy.

'Remember,' he said, 'when somebody shows you that much attention, it is only because you are my daughter.'

No, she was not to be spoiled by riches and flattery. She had to learn about duty and propriety like everybody else. Incidentally, she was much too independent for a girl. She had barely turned seventeen when she fell in love with a lieutenant, and they had to send her to a convent school to make her forget.

All that he knew from Mrs Ferslew, and he looked up at the portrait of the seventeen-year old Miss Ferslew and imagined that her waist had been laced up and her profile retouched.

Their first meeting wasn't promising at all.

He had come to return a book to Mrs Ferslew. Piano music came from the sitting room. He didn't think at all about the fact that Mrs Ferslew seldom played.

Miss Anna had not been retouched. A slender back, shiny black hair and a pretty profile.

'Please, continue, miss. You play beautifully.'

But she practically jumped off the piano bench. The look on her face was disdainful and vulnerable at the same time.

'Forgive me,' he said.

She didn't even ask him to sit. She just introduced herself and said that she had returned from Montmiraille.

She put the book on her mother's sewing table.

Perhaps she thought he was praising the newspaper proprietor's daughter. But there was something lovely and sentimental about her touch on the keys.

All of Copenhagen notices Miss Ferslew when she strolls down the fashionable shopping street Strøget wearing her new handkerchief dress that consists of little squares joined together with lace. She wears long gloves like Sarah Bernhardt and carries a parasol.

And he hears her young, fresh voice in Ferslew's rooms, and he knows that she reads French novels and weeps over *Madame Bovary* and loves premieres.

The Ferslew family have their regular seats at the end of the row in the theatres of Copenhagen, and they arrive exactly just as the lights go dim. In that way you make the point that you are not there to be seen. But no one can avoid noticing Miss Ferslew who rushes in at the last minute with her cape fluttering behind her and her silver bangles jingling. At least a dozen on each arm over the long gloves. Gifts from girl friends. All young girls collect them. She wears a sheer sky-blue shawl around her hair and loosens it while holding the fan in her mouth.

During the intermission all opera glasses are turned towards Miss Ferslew and Herman Bang. It is as if the two of them are out together. They discuss the play eagerly. They look at each other and know they are being watched. They play their own game and know that during the intermission all opera glasses will turn to them and the audience members will study each and every one of their movements.

She leans over and inhales the fragrance of the lilies of the valley he carries in his buttonhole. She snorts with indignation at the sight of his embroidered gloves.

Or she pulls suddenly away from him: 'Mr Bang, if you only knew how boring it was at the convent school in Montmiraille. But mother sent me your serials.'

Is it because of him that Miss Ferslew all of a sudden is being sent to learn the finer points of housekeeping in the kitchen in the crown prince's quarters at Christiansborg Castle, no less?

No, there was nothing between them. After all, they were never left alone. There was perhaps some gossip. And then the older colleagues at *Nationaltidende* who were afraid that he, the youngster, would gain too much power.

Every morning the young lady walks or is driven to Christiansborg Castle where she smiles to the guards before putting on a large white apron adorned with an embroidered crown and spending four to five hours producing cakes and pâtés, arranging them very elegantly, some times even on silver platters and marble columns. She is the only one of the young girls who is not going to use that education for anything. The most important thing is that she doesn't get ideas in her head and that she keeps up her French and attends to her riding and piano lessons. She is on her way to becoming a lady. But she still collects friendship bracelets and portraits of actors and poetic quotes for her album.

'Would you write something, Mr Bang?'

Surprised, he takes the small book with gilt edges and pale blue leather cover. And he does his best to write in a nice clear hand.

'Contentment is not happiness, but at least it is a respectable surrogate for happiness in humble households – and that is the best I can wish you in this our humble life.

Yours sincerely, Herman Bang.'

She reads it quickly. Then she turns on her heel and slams the door to her room behind her.

Maybe she had expected a poem. But he was in an entirely different space. He was thinking of his novel 'The Generations' that would reveal everything. His entire life, his entire generation, his hopelessness and all his hopes were going into that book. It was alive in his head. But he hadn't had time to put even one chapter on paper yet.[7]

The newspaper took up all his time. If only he could put some money aside. If he could just ask for a few months off. But his money seemed to vanish into thin air. And one of the entries in his accounts is Mr Andreasen.

On the first of every month Mr Andreasen arrives. It is of no use pretending that you are not at home. For he will wait. He has time to wait, he says. It is of no use hiding out at Restaurant À Porta. Because suddenly, there he is, standing in front of his table, smiling. And that smile of Andreasen's chases him all through the city and right home under the blankets. And that's where he remains, feverish and convulsing.

And he thinks he can hear footsteps. And he thinks he can sense Andreasen's shadow behind the door. Carefully he touches it with his forefinger, and it is certain, a person is standing outside. And he might as well open the door.

The shadow turns out to be newspaper owner Ferslew paying him a sick call. 'We miss you at the paper, what is the matter with you?'

And it is impossible not to tell him what weighs on his mind.

'You are one of my best paid journalists, Bang. None of my other employees have these problems as far as I know.'

'But all the problems will disappear the day I have written my book. "The Generations" – that book is going to capture the spirit of our time and my entire soul life.'

'Your soul – shouldn't that belong to my paper with the salary you are getting? – Well, try now to get better.'

The newspaper owner sees himself out. But the patient can hear him stop and put something on the console table. As soon as he hears the door shut, he jumps out of bed and tiptoes out to the table.

He heaves a sigh of relief that turns into shouts of joy. For right there is the very amount that he needs. And a little extra. Now he can pay Mr Andreasen and all the other bills. And in the summer he will rent a room at Hotel Marienlyst and write. Just write.

He tosses the money up towards the ceiling from sheer happiness. Only then does he hear Ferslew go down the stairs with a confident and springy step.

The following day he shows up at the paper and is invited for dinner. And that evening he finds it necessary to revise his opinion of Miss Ferslew.

Suddenly she gets up from the table, and perhaps it is the red wine and the liqueur that cause her face to blush and her eyes to shine irresistibly. She bangs her ivory fan on the table. A white, flapping wing. He has hurt her feelings, she says. Hurt and offended her by comparing her to a humble household.

Ferslew's cigar goes out. His wife's lace bobbins come to a halt. Miss Ferslew runs into her room and gets her little book with the pale blue cover. 'Please, write something else.'

This time his hand is shaking as if the pen were a bird. No, he didn't know her. He had no inkling that she was so sensitive and proud.

'Without knowing you I recommended you contentment as a good surrogate for happiness in humble households; now, where I have perhaps assumed more than I am entitled to, I will still advise you to seek contentment, fearing that you will play the dangerous game of seeking happiness, – a game where the questers often lose and where the heart that desires too much will often give us pain.

Herman Bang'

'It is because of the sewing machine,' says Mr Ferslew. 'In our youth, the young girls had enough to think about. They sat in their rooms and hemmed sheets.'

'It is because of spring,' says Mrs Ferslew.

However, it is not Miss Ferslew's anger that occupies Herman Bang, but the actor Martinius Nielsen's debut. The young man is gifted in every way. A fine posture, a voice that can reach all the way to the back rows, and good looks that make the women notice him. And only him.

Herman Bang reaches to his shoulder and looks up to him and helps him. And it is only reasonable, for 'Martinius Nielsen is a natural talent,' he says to anyone who wants to listen.

'If you heard Martinius read.' 'If you saw Martinius.' And: 'Dear Mrs Ferslew, would it be possible to arrange an evening of readings?'

'What would you read, Bang?'

'That all depends on Martinius Nielsen.'

And he helps his younger friend to choose roles. He helps him to select photographs that can be included in his applications. And he helps him formulate the letters.

'Thank you,' says Martinius. 'You are really doing too much for me. You are truly a friend.'

'I will do anything for you – I will walk through fire and water for you.'

'But why?'

'I just want you to be happy more than anything.'

'Yes, but I am in fact happy. You know, I am going to work with Mrs Oda Petersen. She is very helpful to me.'

'Oh. Mrs Petersen. The widow. The one who came back from Paris.'

'Mrs Oda, yes.'

'She is eight years older than you, as is well known.'

'She is the prima donna. – And she plays the role you played when we rehearsed Gérard. But you will of course come and see us.'

'I will come and see you.'

He sees the beautiful Martinius with the beautiful Mrs Petersen, and there is something other and more than art between them, and he wishes he had a fan that would hide his face.

That same evening he tries to write a letter to Martinius. But it is impossible, and he gives up and writes to Mrs Petersen.

'*Monday*.

It is only my simple duty, Madam, to tell you how deeply the scenes with Gérard affected me yesterday evening. There is only one thing to be said about it, which is that a man who has not heard a woman speak to him in this manner, he has never been loved and has never known happiness.

If you would kindly bestow on me the privileges of a friend for an hour, after which I will never take advantage of these again, I believe, Madam, that I would be able to say a thing or two that would make you even 'greater' than presently is the case. If you would give me permission to speak to you about your art for about an hour in private, and without speaking to anybody else about it, I will enquire tomorrow at one o'clock as to when it would suit you. Please, defer any impression you might have of my being bizarre until then.

Respectfully yours
Herman Bang.'

The lady didn't answer. Neither did she when he wrote that she with her virtuosity gave Heiberg's musical comedy *No* such rough treatment that she killed the profusion of flowers. The flowers of spring.[8]

But later, when she played in Erik Bøgh's musical comedy *All Sorts of Roles*, she mimicked him, Herman Bang. And she made him very, very bizarre.[9]

She became Mrs Oda Nielsen all the same. Eight years older than Martinius. No budding flower. No spring chicken. But a prima donna.

Herman Bang had to capitulate.

But he had 'The Generations' on his mind. He would write the book of his life in a matter of a few weeks at Hotel Marienlyst, and then Ferslew would send him to Brussels. And writing travel articles for *Nationaltidende* would be pure recreation.

*

At Marienlyst he is happy with his twenty-one years and with his whole life and the family line as his material. He writes about the Hvide family resting at Sorø Church, about his beautiful mother who dies sedated with champagne. And about Nini and William Høg – the hawk – who become their father's keepers. For he allows himself to give his protagonist his younger brother's first name. William was, after all, the one most loved.

He writes about the chilling moment when he realized that everybody thinks his manic, lively father is the healthy one while his son seems abnormally weak, sickly and nervous.

He writes about his ambitions, about his dreams and about a man who is more beautiful than any woman, a man who understands him better than anyone. And the man is transformed into Kamilla Falk – the falcon – with the deep contralto voice, the knowing look and the organ that fills up the ancestral church. And the falcon and the hawk fly together, they soar towards the sun. Their wings slice the air. The two of them glide majestically and untouchably, different from all the others right up to the day when he, William, must break away. And only loneliness and longing remain.

And he writes about Bernhard Hoff who hides his sensitivity and diligence behind a superior bohemian attitude.

He writes until the early hours. When the sun strikes the paper, he wraps a blanket around his shoulders and steps out on the balcony and gazes at the sea and the green lawns.

The chambermaid knocks carefully on his door and leaves. The shoeblack puts the guest's polished shoes in front of his door. Bang sleeps for a couple of hours, orders coffee, wine and a light meal and continues writing.

Or friends, men and women, come to visit. He acts like a magnet for the curious. It is written all over his face that he is writing his life's work, maybe the book of his generation. Everything will suddenly be as clear as if it were on a stage. William Høg's life stands as a warning. But Herman Bang himself will finally be able to make good use of all his troubles and all his flaws. Nothing has been in vain.

All of a sudden the hotel bill is on his table. He hasn't given it a single thought. He has been thinking all the time that he would finish the book, or that a miracle would happen. But he is not even half finished, and in two days he is travelling to Brussels. And before that he must pay the four hundred kroner.

If he could only run away. If he could only tuck the manuscript under his arm and run across the lawn and jump on a train. But that is impossible.

He tries to squeeze a couple of sentences onto the page. But he is dizzy and throws up in the washstand and has to lie down.

Darkness seeps in although the morning light is very bright. And a kind of sleep that isn't real sleep overtakes him. He hovers above the bed, but feels a heaviness and an ache in every joint. He is trapped, and a buzzing moan rises from his chest. And the more he moans and tries to break free, the more he gets entangled in the thin, strong threads of this spider web. He, a poor buzzing summer fly, is caught in an evil swing of dizziness and death.

He opens his eyes. The pillow is soaked in sweat. Outside the large seagulls are flying high in the sky, summer clouds float by, and the sun is shining above the lawn. He danced here one night. He had a ball all by himself and thought that nobody saw it. But in the morning he gathered from a woman's smile that she must have been awake.

His seizure eases off. It is doubtless the book that paralyzes him. It grows and grows, sucks all life out of him. He promised to have it completed a long time ago. He has had the deadline postponed time and again. And has received an advance and then another advance and then one more. And his doctor has warned him that he is putting his health on the line. There is nothing to be done but to write to his publisher one more time.

*

'You know that I took care of my business matters in the early part of the summer, but this arrangement doesn't allow me to travel without making a certain deposit, which I am unable to do. However, it is Mr Ferslew who is paying for the travel expenses, and he will most certainly be terribly angry when I have to announce on Monday that I cannot travel, and I cannot travel because I am completely in my creditors' power ... I implore you, dear Langhoff, not to speak about this to anyone, but the past two months I have suffered from temporary paralysis on one side. If no help is forthcoming, *Hopeless Generations* will be my last book. I have consulted a known French doctor in writing. Only by undergoing a treatment can I be saved. Otherwise I will be crippled in half a year. Were I to undergo the treatment here, I would end up being a poor copy of Heine. A different solution would be preferable; but I could undergo the treatment during my sojourn in Brussels. It is a question of life and death. – I write this with all the calmness that my desperate uncertainty can afford, but what I have suffered under these circumstances during my struggle to raise money, I leave for you to guess. Paralysis when you are only twenty-two years old! You have written, and rightly so, that I have received so much in advance that it is impossible for you to give me any more. But I implore you to consider that it is literally a matter of a death sentence, for today it is Saturday, and by tomorrow I must make a decision. *Hopeless Generations* has to be done. You know that I am ambitious, and I want to have it out by Christmas. Should I die before, my guardian will probably pay for everything. Should I become crippled as the physician bluntly wrote, I would live maybe another two to three years, and the money would be lost. A treatment would in all likelihood prolong my life by six to eight years, and the four hundred kroner will be paid in ample time ... At this very moment I am fighting for my life. Tomorrow I must leave, and I have given my word not to depart from Marienlyst before I have paid the four hundred kroner. You will receive this letter by five o'clock. Think about it until seven and then send off a telegram. But please bear in mind that I have been driven to despair, and what I have written here is only known to the doctor and to you and me, whose sentence it is. "A Fragment" was thus the fruit of an entire life.'

He cries and has to rinse his eyes and face in a trickle of water from the pitcher by the washstand. The whole room has a bitter smell, and that letter has drained all his strength. He only manages to get it to a waiter by late afternoon and asks to have it delivered by messenger.

And then the wait and the rejection that makes him cry even more. For how can it be that his book and his health are of no importance to Paul Langhoff who has always acted as if he was fond of him? Doesn't he even wish to see him turn thirty?

But off he went just the same.

He succeeded in borrowing from a friend at the eleventh hour. He lied and said that his money was stolen. When the friend began to talk about the police, he was so shocked that he burst into tears again.

But the minute he boarded the train to Brussels, he was completely and utterly happy.

He travelled abroad to experience the world with youthful, wide-awake awareness. Everything he saw and heard became writing material. The articles practically flew from his pen and directly home to *Nationaltidende*.

*

And now. He puts on his glasses. He labours to find words to describe the landscapes and towns the train passes through. He acquired the glasses in order to see the new world in clear, fresh colours. But the old pictures intrude. It is as though everything returns to him.

Even the crumbs on the tablecloth, the sparkling grains of salt and the egg only remind him of meals of the past.

Once he ordered half a dozen eggs and a carafe of port after a successful reading tour. That was his breakfast.

And once when he held a literary salon, the guests complained that the eggs smelled bad. Quickly he grabbed his eau de cologne. Poured half a bottle of Es-Bouquet over the eggs. It was reckless and extravagant. And the taste of perfume and rot was unequalled.

A young woman accidentally bumps into his table and apologizes with a smile. She is wearing small beige travel boots and a beige suit. When he answers her in Danish, she peers at him with curiosity through the hat veil as if he were an animal in the zoo. Then she hurries over to the fur-clad gentleman's table, and shortly after a woman of approximately forty-five arrives – a nice little family – mother, father and daughter. A cheeky daughter with dark shiny hair and small nimble feet and a slender back. Simultaneously ladylike and brazen with the self-assured air that comes from fine boarding schools and money.

Her mother pats her on the hand and tries to get her attention. But she is looking intently at him, this elderly gentleman who is writing. The smell of his perfume still lingers on in her nostrils.

'Anna,' says her mother. 'Anna, you stare and you stare. But you ought to know that it is rude.'

'Maybe he is an actor.' She is playing with a little ivory fan.

Her mother shakes her head indulgently. 'I think he is a deviant. And then in first class to boot!'

'Mother, can nothing be done about it?'

Perhaps that's what they are saying. In any case, they are talking about him quite openly in their completely incomprehensible language.

5.

'We are very satisfied with you, Bang. Your articles from Brussels, Hamburg and Düsseldorf are excellent. You really know how to observe.' Ferslew was impressed, and his wife praised especially the descriptions of Geel – the city of the nuns and the insane.

If only he were there now. For he had wandered completely relaxed and freely among the mad. There were no locked doors or straitjackets. And he had announced that if he should become incurably insane, his wish would be to go to Geel. There his father, the pastor, with his magnificent voice and the rags tied around his head could have had a suitable congregation, and his younger sister Ingeborg could have found happiness there. He realized that she was mad already that time when the spider danced on her eiderdown and when she tore off the rose petals in order to understand their inner being.

She paraded around in her nightgown, her hands full of millipedes, speaking to them in a reverential voice. And she frightened off three young men although they were enthralled by her abundant hair and the intensity of her eyes. In Geel she would have been a princess surrounded by worthy admirers. Instead Ingeborg died a grey death at Middelfart Psychiatric Hospital while working on a plaited floor mat.

Betty Borchsenius could perhaps have benefitted from staying there a couple of months. This actress who suddenly refused to play her youthful roles as a blonde angel and now claimed the right to be natural, clumsy and plain. To cap it all, she allowed herself to become older. She who could conquer a whole performance with her smile and a song wore out her beauty. In the corridor she played the roles she had long wished for, and she began to put words on paper, and he, the twenty-two-year-old journalist and poet, became her confidant. 'Will you give me some advice since death evidently won't have me?'

He put everything else aside and let the errand boy wait while he read her letters and hastily scribbled notes. Sometimes several in one day. He answered right away and blew on the ink to dry it, and sometimes he would forget, and the writing would smear when he tried to help with good advice, with money, with getting her stories placed in journals and by saying that he believed in her talent. Her natural talent.

'Is it possible to stifle the scream in one's throat in order to breathe and gain a new life?' she asked.

He thought it was.

He talked about the fecundity of the summer and the splendour of the autumn when she wept tears over her plumpness. He encouraged her when she went on a water diet and renounced everything to be thin and dainty again. Not for the sake of the theatre but for the sake of her young son. He told her that she was a good mother even if she was divorced. And she bought the tallest and greenest Christmas tree in the city to please little Kaare and him. And she wrote a perfectly naïve and light and joyful little song when Kaare turned ten.

But nothing could stifle the scream in her throat. Not even the collection of stories that she eventually had published. That same year she was declared insane.

He knew about the scream from his own experience.

One day he had screamed in the middle of the Ferslew family's large sitting room where all the furniture was lined up in straight rows.

'I cannot bear it!' He banged his fist on the piano keys.

And he hadn't seen her at all. Not noticed Miss Anna Ferslew at all.

'I have faith in you, Bang,' she said with a voice as clear as a jet of water that suddenly springs up.

And he bowed and took hold of her hand where the veins were still buried deep under the skin, and he kissed it reverently.

There was something tender and at the same time defiant in her eyes, and a blush spread across her cheeks. And it was during those few minutes when no one was keeping an eye on them through opera glasses and pince-nez that he possibly should have fallen to his knees and said: 'Miss, Miss Anna Ferslew – Will you do me a great favour?'

Without doubt she would answer: 'Yes, with pleasure.' Her voice would still be polite and distinct but would perhaps sound a bit concerned due to his position on the floor. The situation would continue:

He: 'Will you marry me?'

She: 'Marry – I know people are talking about us – but I have not at all imagined ... that I should marry.'

He: 'Perhaps it is as well that you haven't thought too deeply about marriage if you are going to marry me.'

She: 'Why?'

He: 'There is so much you need to know first.'

She looks at him with anticipation and almost whispers: ' – Yes – '

He: 'My mother died very young from consumption.'

She looks surprised and sad. She holds out her hands as if to stroke his hair. But instead she fiddles with her fan. Her bangles jingle, and her hands drop to her side: ' – Poor thing – '

He: 'She died like a flower snapped in two.'

She: 'Poor you – '

He says it quickly and resolutely: 'And my father died mad.'

Horrified, she now backs all the way to the window.

He continues almost as if he wants to comfort her: 'I will die young. You know that I am writing a novel, and I also dream about becoming an actor.'

Fortunately she doesn't throw herself out of the window. She is smiling. There is something childishly curious in that smile. 'But how do you imagine our marriage, Mr Bang.'

He: 'To be together the two of us and be happy. And then I want to write about you, Miss Ferslew.'

She: 'In truth, I have also written about you but not publicly. – Only in my diary.'

He: 'What do you write?'

She: 'I write: "Some times I find him unequalled. – But then he immediately says something that destroys all that brilliance." – But promise me at least one thing.'

He: 'Yes – everything – '

She: 'Promise me that you will never become an actor.'

He jumps up like a coiled spring and practically shouts: 'But I know you love the theatre. You are there almost every night. It is like your own sitting room.'

She: 'I don't want to marry a man who puts himself on display – and who wears make-up. – And you must completely stop using perfume. By the way, I hate your embroidered gloves. A man should only smell of clean linen and maybe a bit of tobacco!'

*

And then she will probably shout that he is mad and run in to her mother and sob loudly and defiantly like a little girl, hiding her pretty, confused face in her mother's lap.

But it didn't happen. There was just this moment of tenderness and intimacy. It was like a summer morning where everything awakened. And his crimson lips against her small hand. For in those days when Miss Ferslew believed in him and his book, his lips were crimson and sensual.

At Mrs Nimb's boarding house they also believed – in him and the book. He had moved to a room facing the inner courtyard where his furniture took up much of the space. And he wrote. He wrote as soon as he came home from the editorial office until his head dropped on the manuscript. Sometimes he would wake up the next morning still in the same position.

And every morning she, the maid, stood outside his door. She could never finish her chores because of him. She knocks so quietly that it merely sounds like a faint scratching. He knows that she is standing out there with her mop and her pail and that she is humble and lovely and intensely irritated that he, this sleepyhead, this bohemian, won't even bother to get up and leave his room when all the other guests have long since gathered around the tea urn.

But Mrs Nimb forgives him – most of the time. One day she pulls him aside right after dinner and asks him to join her in the kitchen.

'Mr Bang, I want to have a serious word with you. You are a quiet lodger. But I am getting tired of having your creditors coming and going here. Your tailor and especially that fellow Andreasen.'

And his only defence is the fact that he is working. That he is writing most of what is in the newspaper *Nationaltidende* and that in six weeks he has written three hundred pages of his book. '*Hopeless Generations*. What do you think of the title?'

'I don't know. I know that you burn candles and that you soon will be nothing but skin and bones. And besides, I suspect my cook has been stealing cigars from you. Every evening she sits in her room puffing away.'

'Yes.'

'What do you mean, "yes"?'

'She is welcome to them. I can't very well offer a woman cigars, don't you agree? She has first-rate taste. She prefers the Brazilian.'

'Mr Bang, how much are these cigars?'

'I don't remember.'

'How much money do you in fact owe people? It must be possible to make some arrangement.'

He dashes into his room, pulls out the desk drawer, returns and pours its contents onto the well-scrubbed kitchen table.

'My God!' she says and throws up her hands in alarm. 'There is no end to it.' She begins writing down the numbers on a piece of brown wrapping paper. Every now and then she licks the little indelible pencil.

'What is Es-Bouquet?'

'Eau de cologne.'

'But you are buying quantities of it as if it were milk. And shirts and gloves. That's how much I spend at the butcher's for an entire year. And still we live well. And paper – do you really need this expensive paper? You can use my paper.' She nods toward the shelves where the thin tissue paper from the baker and the heavy brown and white wrapping paper from the grocer and the butcher are stacked neatly next to the yellow coffee paper.

'How much do you actually earn from a book like that?'

'I don't know. – Perhaps five hundred – but I think I have already received that.'

'Can you write one every month?'

'It is written in my heart's blood. And the day I finish it, I will do something out of the ordinary.'

'Well,' she says, glancing at the pile. 'I had no idea that it was this bad.' And she shakes her head in resignation.

The day he finishes his manuscript, he is in the dining room early before dinner. He, who usually comes last, arrives before the students, the secretary, the widow and the shopkeeper's apprentice. Mrs Nimb serves the soup, and he takes off his shoes and climbs up on the table and walks around between the plates as graciously as a cat.

'He has finished,' cries Mrs Nimb. 'He has finished the generations!'

And every one at the boarding house has champagne with the soup, the roast and the dessert. They all want to drink a toast to him. Anticipation and joy envelop him, and never, never before has he felt this happy.

Later he drives to the Ferslews'. They must be told. At least he wants to share his happiness with her, the one who believes in him. Miss Anna with her clear, lively eyes and hands whose veins are still buried deep under the skin.

He runs up the stairs and rings the doorbell. Only the maid and little Christian, who is asleep, are at home. But the master and the mistress are sure to arrive soon, and he sits down waiting with champagne and happiness racing through his veins. And the day the book comes out, he will want a lot more than kissing her hand. He will drive with her through the city in an open carriage. The two of them will run across a green lawn, and the air will be saturated with the fragrance of roses, jasmine and camomile. And they will pick dandelion globes and blow at them. And her hair will come undone, a wonder, so long and lavish, dark and shiny.

And he remembers how his mother and the children in the white house moved the furniture around when his father wasn't at home. The chairs turned into houses and ships, and the whole drawing room became a landscape.

He moves the little table that Miss Anna hit with her ivory fan and turns it at a new dramatic angle. Chairs and lamps follow. He pulls the large upholstered sofa out from the wall with great effort, moves columns, pedestals and palms, and voilà – a fashionable salon. Cushions, carpets, table cloths and foot stools, he frees everything from their usual locations. He unfolds the entire space into light fan-shaped arrangements. Plants, candlesticks and screens form intimate nooks. He moves the paintings around so the light will fall on them in new and different ways. A handkerchief is draped over a lamp to dim the light. All the candles are lit. He has given the whole room new life.

When the family arrives, only the missus' sewing table and the piano haven't been moved. Mrs Ferslew has to sit down to recover herself. Ferslew practically runs off to his study. Miss Anna just stands there, staring open-mouthed like a little girl. Then she runs through the room and throws herself on all the chairs and sofas as if she wanted to try them out.

'A party. Our drawing room is fit for a party!' She lifts her arms and twirls around until her yellow silk skirt fans out like a sun around her.

And she is so close, and he puts his arm around her waist, and the two of them waltz round and round, and he can feel the stays of her corset against his hand, fine and hard like the bones of a bird skeleton.

'Children,' says Mrs Ferslew. 'Children, really!' Her voice is subdued and mild, and she shakes her head at her daughter and at him. He who is like a son of the house.

'We are going to have a party. A ball,' says Miss Anna.

To celebrate his book, he thinks.

'And you, Bang, are going to take care of all the flower arrangements,' she says.

Still he could think of nothing but the book.

And then it came out.

He stayed up and waited until the first newspapers were out. Then he walked towards the City Hall Square. He bought copies from all the paper boys he met. He carried a whole armful of papers as if he were going to sell them himself. He pressed his face against the bundle and inhaled deeply to take in the bitter smell from the fresh ink. And he wished that he could buy her blue, sweet-smelling hyacinths. And he wished that he could just stand under a lamp post and read or spread all the newspapers out on the cobblestones and crawl around in this landscape that was now his.

He hired a cab after all. He paid the driver almost without looking and didn't wait for his change. The warm breath from the horse brushed his cheek, and it felt like a caress, a good omen. Then he ran upstairs to his room.

There was not a single positive word written about his book. He began to read and let the first couple of papers drop to the floor. But he had bought so many that he could now read the same words over and over again. They cut right through him. They slashed him from neck to toe. And he covered the whole floor in newspapers like someone who is about to travel far away and is worried about moths.

Edvard Brandes thought the book was three times as long as necessary. *Aftenbladet* thought the book was 'so immoral that no woman should be reading it.' Dear Nini studied this particular review closely and returned the 'Generations' to him immediately, unread.

In *Dagens Nyheder* Erik Bøgh referred to *Hopeless Generations* as 'one of the most unhealthy and in many ways one of the most irresponsible books sold on our book market in a long time.'

And did it help that he wrote to Nini:

'One may hear many falsehoods, dear Nini, and to know my book only from hearsay is not enough for the love of a sister who surely wouldn't refuse to do the one thing I beg her to do: to read before making judgements. Don't you agree? – It would only be doing me justice.'

No, it didn't help that the stationery was adorned with lily of the valley. She didn't read the passage that 'Nina had grown strong in this life. The grief, the task she had been given and that had become too great for her physical strength, had not crushed her spirit. But the premature pain had traversed her soul like a frosty night, and the night's hoarfrost had lingered there for a long time.

With all her warm-heartedness she embraced "her own": William and Sofie –she shied away from strangers.'

This portrait she didn't see. She only knew that her younger brother had tittle-tattled about the family's secrets, and also that he was immoral.

Then the satirical magazines came out. Everybody could read in *Punch*:

'... Loathing for everything except the sordid underside of backstage life and the seamy side of life in general. Kisses, long "generous" vampire-like kisses, ever so desired. Extensive embraces every two hours. Fear of the light of day. Craving for the semi-darkness of dawn and dim lighting effects. Obscure reasoning. Clear, coherent, logically organized speech is not possible for any of the characters. Fertile dreams are frequent. Strong desire for champagne with or without mustard, for women with or without costumes, for chaise longues with or without women. Blood deficiency, iron cravings, preferably for iron cuffs. – Strong penchant for kicks and restraints and a passionate need for a straightjacket. The creator of these "hopeless generations" seems to be in a totally hopeless situation himself (pornographic mania), the reason why I most definitely must recommend that he be put under close observation and supervision to the extent that it will be impossible for him to form, deform and reform the generations.'

*

No one replied, not a soul defended him.

Ferslew said that he should have stuck with what he is best at and also think a little more about the newspaper.

Bjerring proclaimed to the whole editorial office: 'Yes, one thing is for certain. If Bang has sinned, he has sinned out of ignorance.'

Topsøe invited him for dinner and praised his book. But Topsøe could not prevent Herman Bang, the grandson of His Excellency the Royal Physician, from being accused of writing pornography, nor that *Hopeless Generations* was banned.

The day it was printed in large type in the daily paper *Berlingske Tidende*, he left the editorial office early. It was as if the earth had vanished under his feet, as if all of Copenhagen had disappeared into a deep, dizzying hole and he would sink into it from shame.

Apparently the book was dreadful. It was going to be removed from the book sellers' display windows and forgotten. But the accusation would stick forever to his name, for ever and ever. It would hurt Nini, Sofie and William and come between him and his loved ones.

He dragged himself up the stairs. Mrs Nimb was standing in the hallway, she must have been waiting for him.

'You shouldn't give in, Bang. Keep your chin up.'

But he could see that she had been crying. And he could hear the sound of sobbing from the kitchen. The girls were crying over him.

He retired to his room and lay down. If he could only hide there like a dying animal. If he could only fall asleep. Three gulps of sleeping draught. To be dormant, motionless, without the images, without time.

But sounds penetrated his shell. Two voices arguing about what was best for Herman Bang. For a moment he thinks they are the voices of higher powers. But one of them is Mrs Nimb and the other one is Bjerring who suddenly appears in the middle of the room and lights a lamp. The light hurts his eyes and the pain shoots through his head.

'You have to get up, Bang. We are going to The Royal Theatre. You have to show your face in the stalls, act completely unconcerned and wear your usual outrageous attire.'

He begins to cry like a little boy who doesn't want to go to school. He has a fever, he says. And a headache. His whole body is aching.

But Bjerring doesn't take hold of his wrist with his soft, well-groomed fingers. Bjerring tears the door of the wardrobe open, pulls out his dress suit and puts a shirt on the bed along with a sprig of lily of the valley.

'I cannot. There is nothing I want to see.'

'You have to go to be seen yourself.'

'I cannot. Not even for the sake of my book.'

'You must. For your own sake. For the sake of the book. And not the least for the sake of *Nationaltidende*. Do think of the Ferslews.'

'I will never go out in public again.'

'Show yourself like a man.'

'I cannot.'

'You must. You could have learned that at the battle of Dannevirke.'

'I was only a small boy, then. – And besides, I have a squint. I could never be a soldier.'

'That's a pity. In 1864 I stood by my captain's side when a shell blew the cigar out of his mouth. And I pulled out my cigar case, offered him a fresh cigar and lit it.'

'But we lost nevertheless. Both the war and the island of Als.'

'We lost with honour. Now, hurry up. The carriage is waiting.'

And he could just as well have been driving to the scaffold wearing his elegant gloves and the lily of the valley in his buttonhole.

But the minute he enters the theatre it is as if he sees himself from the outside, and he walks as tall as he possibly can. His heart is pounding. A red bird flapping in a cage of bones. But no one knows. All the opera glasses are trained on his back. Even in the dark he feels their presence.

During the intermission Peter Nansen introduces himself and shakes his hand. 'A writer whom nobody attacks is an insignificant writer.'

'Thank you. Do you really mean that.'

The handsome Peter Nansen smiled his most captivating smile: 'I am only quoting your own words.'

But the next day he took to his bed, and he really was ill.

How could he defend himself against the criticism that his protagonist is sensual and his book obscene?

The satirical magazines had already portrayed him as a little boy put in the corner, weeping and sucking his fingers. And he knew very well that at least some of his colleagues wished the 'Monkey' and the 'Theatre Flea' all kinds of bad luck.

He couldn't make sense of it. That the Brandes brothers should despise him in such an undisguised manner. He had always admired them. They were fit, intelligent and handsome. Some women would die for them. And not only that, but their mother was still alive.

But when he meets them at a party held for the author Jens Peter Jacobsen, he overhears Edvard Brandes hissing: 'Bang and his "realists". It is disgusting. He drools over Balzac and Flaubert and Zola and Dumas. I could have done it a hundred times better. But now he has done it. He has simply snatched the intellectual bread from my mouth.'

And there is only one thing to do. To pretend that you haven't heard it. He takes his glass and asks the guests to rise to their feet and drink a toast to Jens Peter Jacobsen who is quiet and looks pale as if he doesn't realize that he is the guest of honour.

But Edvard Brandes practically jumps up and declares that unfortunately his friend Jens Peter Jacobsen is unable to speak in this polluted room, but that he personally wants to say that Herman Bang is not worthy of proposing a toast to Jacobsen. He is not even worthy of shining Jacobsen's shoes.

And everyone looks admiringly at Edvard Brandes.

Only Holger Drachmann reaches across the table to shake Bang's hand: 'I am with you, Herman.'

He has put his glass down and with his hand wipes his forehead nervously, pushing back his fringe.

'Yes,' Edvard Brandes looks him up and down. 'Even if I were to let my hair grow long enough to reach my stomach, nobody would give two hoots.'

He leaves the party.

Later on, he ventures into a polemical debate with the elder brother Georg Brandes who brushes him off with the words: 'He has a blind spot in his head, for he simply cannot think. I mean scientifically. He has no understanding of philosophy, no sense of conceptual thinking ... His intellect is that of a middling female. There is no manly stride in his thoughts; they have clearly never been subjected to that rigour which governs and protects against perpetual stumbling.'

He withdraws from the debate. He has no training in petty spitefulness, he says. And Georg Brandes responds with indignation that he has only been fencing with a blunted foil.

No, only the women love Herman Bang. Mrs Nimb who toasts his bread the way he likes it. Mrs Ferslew who has sent him a jar of grape jelly and wishes for a speedy recovery. And then – Miss Anna.

Otherwise his only enjoyment is reading Ibsen's *Ghosts*. Osvald – that's him. Finally his role has been written. Osvald who completely innocently carries the seed of insanity. Osvald who asks for the sun.

One day he will play Osvald. It is this thought that makes him get up and go to the editorial office.

There on his desk is the satirical magazine *The Raven* that practically falls open on its own on a page with the headline 'Idolatry.'

And it is he who is kneeling in front of a woman's laced-up corset placed on a pedestal:

> 'Herman Bang adores Ferslew's girl,
> will bite the dust for that lovely pearl.
> The "deep thinker" with joy must extol
> this shell, besides her body and soul.'

He has damaged her. Miss Anna.

It is very quiet around him. He can hear his own breathing. The blood pounding in his temples. And the dust particles that dance like gold in the sun. In front of him he sees two broad backs shaking from suppressed laughter. Now he knows that he must pay Ferslew a visit.

The stairs down to the first floor have never felt so steep. It is as if his legs are going to give way any minute. Then he will lie in the dust, empty of thoughts.

But the maid is smiling as usual and shows him into the parlour where the furniture is still arranged the way he left it. Christian puts his little warm hand in his, and Ferslew and his wife inquire about his health. He still looks very pale, Mrs Ferslew says, and does he get enough 'real' sleep? He knows that 'real' sleep is the kind before midnight, and he knows that she prefers reading novels and that the newspaper owner thinks the satirical magazines are nothing but a waste of time. But Miss Anna's lips betray a small knowing smile, and her handshake is warm and firm as if she is confirming an oath. She is his ally. They are a couple.

His pen is virtually dancing across the paper:

Dear Miss Anna Ferslew

Our names are linked together. But when we meet we are bound by the thousands of considerations and conventions that exist between man and woman; and we remain locked up in our respective cages.

Since the day when I understood that you also seek perilous happiness, and from the moment you let me take your hand, I have sensed that a meeting of our souls is a possibility.

Dear Miss Anna, I don't believe in God. But I believe in the soul. Perhaps you still cherish the beautiful faith of your childhood, which is all for the best. As for me, no longer do I see a ladder ascending to heaven.

As you know, I have had many disappointments and suffered much grief, and now I am alone as much in life as in the literary world. Only you and your family have shown me the kind of affection and friendship that no human being can live without.

One day I hope to make up for it. In the future I will do all that is in my power to make *Nationaltidende* the country's leading newspaper, a newspaper that not only has wide distribution but also political influence.

I have still two plans that you will be the first to know. One of them is a novel – a modern Phaedra which I hope will be moving and impressive. The main character is a woman whom I saw striding into the hotel's dining room wearing a red silk dress. She walked between her husband, who was stroking his large beard, and her stepson who was looking at her with a sad, lovelorn expression. She was sipping red wine or she would cool her pretty face in a bouquet of roses. No one knew if the bouquet was from her husband or her stepson. But everyone was guessing. All attention was directed at her.

Your image, Miss Anna, blends in with hers. Your face at the moment when you promised to have faith in me. But also the stroll with your parents where you suddenly screamed at the sight of a grass snake. And the many times when I saw you run into the theatre, excited and stylish in your evening cape, your small fur-trimmed galoshes, your light dress, holding the fan with your teeth at the moment you loosened the sky-blue veil around your hair.

You will find your voice and gestures in the book, and also the many silent moments at dinner parties where we exchange glances over a glass or an open fan.

So far I haven't progressed far with my novel, and with respect to my other project, I am afraid it will cause you grief. At least your father will be awfully angry. I still don't know how to carry out my plan. But I must and I will act Osvald in Ibsen's *Ghosts*. Osvald, that's me. Finally my role has been written, and one day I must succeed in the greatest of all the art forms, the dramatic art where one stands face to face with the audience.

Only one thought frightens me. The possibility that your parents with the best of intentions will send you away after having seen the picture in *The Raven*. I am terribly sorry, and I wouldn't be able to bear seeing you go abroad in order to be cured of the confidence and affection you have shown me. Maybe the love between souls belongs to the guilt-free landscapes of dreams. Maybe the era of souls is yet to come. And we will become fools for love. But I know that you will never marry mere contentment, and that you will always be in my life's most honourable dream. Travelling with you to a faraway land would be utter happiness.

Yours sincerely
Herman Bang

He puts the letter in one of the blue envelopes that he has used so often when getting her one of the actor portraits she collects.

He asks the messenger boy to deliver the letter to the palace kitchen. But no sooner has he seen the boy run off than he runs after him to be assured that the envelope is delivered to the right door.

He leans up against the door and discovers that he has forgotten both his hat and his coat. The spring sun almost blinds him. But he does see the boy come out and shortly after he sees her, a young woman walking tall, wearing a lavender-blue spring coat and a lavender-blue veiled hat, beautiful and framed by the sun with the palace in the background.

He sees how she stands still for a moment and sniffs the air. How she wipes her brow as if to remove something painful. She has probably excused herself with a headache, then, in order to get away.

His heart is beating. Beats as if it wants to fly out of its bony cage.

She walks so beautifully on her feet, lightly like a dancer. She stops and touches her cheek with the letter, part fan and part caress.

She tries to open the envelope. But her glove prevents her from using her nails.

She pulls a hairpin out of her hair. She smiles. A lock of hair flutters like a dark wing across her cheek. And never before has she been so beautiful. The pin rips the envelope open. Excitedly she pulls the veil up over the brim of her hat before looking at the loose sheets. She reads the pages in his special order: one, three, two, four.

She leans forward, bites her lip. The wind takes hold of the sheets, but she doesn't let go of her letter. She hangs on to it for dear life and reads while walking, taking tiny little steps on the round cobblestones.

If he could only run over to her right now.

One of the guardsmen watches her closely and winks and smiles as if they know each other.

But she doesn't respond to the smile.

She sticks the letter inside her muff and starts running.

'Miss! Miss Anna!' He hears his own voice shouting for a young woman who is running on a windy spring day. And the following day he is called to a meeting with Mr Ferslew.

The letter is lying on the desk. He sees it right away when he enters, sky-blue among all the white, brown and yellow.

Ferslew asks him to sit down. He clears his throat and begins without further formalities: 'Dear Bang, you are young and have no one to guide you. That explains a lot. Our Anna is still very upset. Naturally, she hasn't read your letter; no young girl can take a stand on that sort of thing. She gave the letter to her mother who of course gave it to me. So now, we won't talk about this matter again, but if you wish to keep your position here at *Nationaltidende*, you are never again to influence my daughter in writing or in person.'

'But I am very fond of the young lady.'

'Yes, Bang. So are we. Incidentally, you have a peculiar way of showing it. As far as I understand, you are practically asking for her hand in marriage while you at the same time wish to travel the world playing a syphilitic.'

'But Osvald is innocent.'

'That doesn't change anything. You are a good journalist, Bang. Stick with what you are best at. My wife greatly appreciates you, and my daughter possibly likewise. But you are clearly not the kind of son-in-law we wish for. Surely you can see the other side of the picture. – – And Anna, our Anna is a ray of sunshine.'

The newspaper owner walks over to the window and looks out, and the large man's voice turns soft and tender: 'Naturally, we want the best for our daughter. We have decided that she should train to be a kindergarten teacher. But first she will be travelling to Germany with my wife and our old friend Miss Berthelsen. It will be a kind of educational journey, and afterwards she will have enough to think about. – That will be all, Bang.'

He practically falls over the doorstep on his way out, and on the stairway he runs into her: 'Miss Anna Ferslew.'

The two young people stop abruptly like birds flying into a window. Then they flutter away, confused, in opposite directions.

Shortly after he is on the street, stunned as if he had been punched.

6.

– It was not the day
neither was it life.
Only a morn it was,
a summer morn
when our garden awakes –

No, it wasn't life. The newspaper proprietor's daughter had to study psychology and pedagogy and learn that a young woman must never turn her gaze so openly towards a man, and not let passionate promises fly out of her mouth. Her desire is bound by her father's will, and her dreams belong in a diary that can be locked away in a secret drawer.

In the theatre they still sit in their usual seats. But during the intermission he keeps company with Peter Nansen and Gustav Esmann. They are three puppies, three fops smelling of patchouli, pomade and Es-Bouquet. They lean against the pillars and turn their backs on the conventional bourgeoisie. They have the sharpest pens, the most provocative opinions and decadent habits and elegant shoes with thin soles. Other young men join them. They comb their hair over their forehead and wear showy rings and silk handkerchiefs. They act as if they have nothing else to do but attend the theatre, frequenting cafés and barber shops only to hang about pillars like odd, limp plants. From time to time one of them bursts out laughing for no apparent reason, especially the one in the middle, the most outré: Herman Bang who seemingly gathers them around him, all the young men who read and write and most likely never do a day's work.

Mrs Ferslew in her grey silk and discreet pearls, well-preserved and amiable, sweeps past him, leaving behind a pleasant fragrance: 'We never see you on the first floor. Come for tea tomorrow afternoon. I will be at home alone.'

Tea and fine English biscuits. But he seems to be distant, and she is maintaining a certain reserve. She won't even borrow the books that he has brought.

'No, Bang. I don't read Zola. I am afraid that our daughter does it to keep up with her French. She is so inexperienced and young. It is not easy raising children nowadays. At least not daughters.'

Christian pulls at his sleeve: 'Do you want to play, Mr Bang?'

'Yes, the two of us will build the tallest castle in the world. And you will blow it down.'

'I don't blow castles down any more. I build solid houses.'

'That is probably the most sensible thing to do, Christian. Where did you learn that?'

'In kindergarten. We are not allowed to run wild. To play is a kind of work. Do you want to see my kindergarten bag and my milk bottle?'

'Yes, Christian. It is a very nice bag.'

'That's because my father made it.'

'Designed it,' Mrs Ferslew laughs. 'My husband really did design the bag himself, allowing space for a song book, a milk bottle and a lunch pack. And now he is designing a factory at Kattinge. He has bought half a forest.'

'Then it might be the last time you spend your holidays on Strandvejen.'

'Yes.' But she doesn't invite him. 'Christian,' she says suddenly. 'Don't bother Mr Bang any more. And you are probably busy.'

'Yes, I have rented accommodation at Middelfart Seaside Hotel in order to finish my book undisturbed.'

He needs a long stretch of time, and only in a hotel can he be completely independent. Besides, he needs to get away from Copenhagen not only because of the correspondance that keeps piling up but especially because the satirical press has announced that he is working on a new novel with the portrait of the chief of police hanging over his desk. And regardless of what he hangs on the wall, it is as if those eyes look straight through him just like when he was a little boy and God looked right through him as if looking through a transparent hard candy.

Unfortunately the eyes follow him to Middelfart. Even though he labours to the point of there not being room for any kind of vice.

He gets up at eight o'clock, has tea and writes letters until nine o'clock. Exactly at nine he starts writing his novel and continues until four in the afternoon – only occasionally does he interrupt his work to go for a thirty-minute walk along the wharf. At four his first copyist arrives, and he dictates until six. After that he eats dinner and goes for a stroll. At half-past seven copyist number two arrives and writes after his dictation until ten o'clock. And then – finally he recognizes that the novel is progressing much too slowly. And he is thinking that he would have enjoyed spending just a couple of hours on Strandvejen before leaving. But perhaps he doesn't deserve it.

And: Poor, poor Miss Anna, he sometimes thinks when standing on the wharf looking out over the sea. But she will recognize herself in *Phaedra*. She will be able to see how fond he is of her. And then – maybe.

*

But the novel was not finished. He had to return to Copenhagen. He wrote his serials, tried to find new ideas, suggested new writers who could fill the paper's columns. A certain fatigue or rather edginess like a trembling nerve had set in. And he got himself a family.

Herman Bang, Peter Nansen, the midwife Mrs Astrup and her two small daughters Ida and Louise rented a large, posh apartment and divided the rooms so the midwife and the children had their own, he and Nansen each had a study and a bedroom and shared a parlour.

The parlour was particularly wonderful. Rumours about it are circulating all over Copenhagen. The extravagant dinners, the wine, the flowers and the greenhouse heat and this abundance of columns and silk cushions. Everyone who is someone or who hopes to become someone frequents it: poets, actors and critics. And it is Herman Bang who does the talking, who entertains with anecdotes from the theatre and the editorial office, and who has plans for the future.

When the guests have left, he and Nansen sit on the green pouffe and talk about all the things they are going to do. They are going to work together, and travel together to distant cities where rivers flow by outside their window and where the potted plants are like trees in bloom and the rooms are like dance halls. And they want to get rich and buy diamond rings and cufflinks with golden chains.

And he calls Peter Nansen Don because he is so handsome. And Don is fond of him, and Mrs Astrup admires him, and the two small girls wait for him in the hall when they hear his footsteps. And it is not only because he has given them new shoes and boots and wide silk ribbons for their little braids.

'I wonder if you are not doing too much for the people you live with, Bang,' Ferslew says with concern. 'What is really in it for you?'

Under Ferslew's fatherly gaze he becomes tongue-tied, and so he answers him in writing:

'Perhaps – especially as I have no right to do it as yet, because it is not really me. But you don't know the real reason. I act out of selfishness. The two young children are provided for, and my life is so very empty. One person knows so little about another, and that must be so. But the past year has been the richest in my life: now it feels like the calm after the storm, but even the calm sea can fill us with bitterness. My only hope is that everything I have experienced one day will become genuine, serious art. Then all these years of suffering won't be wasted, and my loneliness now is just a gathering of strength.

The reason I remained silent yesterday was because of your mentioning that what I am doing is too much; for I felt that you had the right to ask. I can only say that now everything is progressing quietly and with restraint. – – – Promise me now not to be angry, and promise me that all this remains between you, your wife and me. – – – I put my trust in you and yours entirely. – – – There is one thing I really and truly wish for Christmas – an artificial plant. I wouldn't be upset if somebody gave it to me anonymously.

Yours,
H. B.'

He didn't receive an artificial plant anonymously. But Ferslew was not angry. He laughed and dropped a picture of a young woman on the desk just as Herman Bang was proofreading a theatre review.

'Look, Bang. What do you think of her?'

'Arma Senkrah. Violinist. Is she a gypsy?'

'Attend the concert and give her any nationality you fancy.'

And in the evening he sat in the first row and watched a young Austrian woman, eighteen years old with a mass of blond hair and large bright eyes. With her childish demeanour and her violin she had control of the whole orchestra, forty-two men, trumpets, strings, percussion. Everyone followed her.

'A wee maiden in her first silk gown, so slim and fine and delicate with the youthfulness of an eighteen-year old that one can only try to imagine. This is how only a young girl can whisper about her longing, her untainted dreams that are like a veil of mist covering the meadow on early summer mornings when the earth wakes like a virgin after a night's slumber.' This is what he wrote in his review.

The next evening he sat in front of the podium again, and he sent her flowers and showed her and her mother all they had time to see of Copenhagen before she had to rehearse and change her clothes and once again stand in front of the orchestra.

Mrs Harkness would oversee things from the back of the carriage, keeping an eye on her famous daughter, Miss Arma Senkrah, whose name was spelled backwards due to an impresario who thought that female violinists had to appear exotic.

From time to time Mrs Harkness would grumble and demand that the driver turn around, for her daughter had to rest and drink tea with milk and eat two biscuits before the concert. But Arma laughed and whispered in French that little Maman worried too much and was overly cautious. For little Maman was unusually knowledgeable about all the things that could happen in this terrible world full of dangers, especially to young girls who play the violin.

She called Herman Bang her 'cher ami' and 'liebes Kind' and assured him that he was her only true and best friend. She held his hands between her own, and her grip was firm and energetic. And after the concert, the two of them fled. She carried an armful of flowers, and in his pocket he had an advance payment that was soon converted into champagne. And they both leaned over the table so that he could admire the medal for 'Kunst und Wissenschaft' which the Duke of Sachsen-Altenburg himself had fastened to her decolletage.[10]

'Do you think I have deserved it?' she asked, blushing from pride and champagne.

She confided to him that she was afraid of her next concert. It was going to be in Stockholm, and the Swedes were so difficult to engage. He immediately sent a telegram to his Swedish friends. 'Arma Senkrah is coming now – the most delightful creature that has ever played the violin. She is beautiful, eighteen years old and unassuming – and a great artist.'

He read it out loud to her. They laughed and in their high-spiritedness smashed their glasses, and the small fragments gathered around their heels like diamond dust. All of a sudden they began speaking at the same time, 'La vie est bien triste, laissons rire,' and just then tears began to run down her cheeks at the thought of little Maman who was waiting at the hotel – very angry and, especially, very worried.

But Mrs Harkness forgave both her daughter and him, for the reception in Stockholm turned into one long party with spectacular reviews, bouquets, endless applause and invitations.

Arma Senkrah glued glossy scraps into her letters. 'Liebes Kind. Cher ami,' she wrote. 'Mother was perhaps a tiny bit unfair. But now she has infinite faith in you. Don't ever leave me. You will never do that, will you my dear child. How we laughed. It was a happy evening that I will never ever forget. How it saddens me to hear that you are ill. Why is it always the best of us who must suffer the most? We have once again received some very bizarre and wicked letters about you. Tell me what I should do. I will fight for you. Little Maman is still very shocked. Parents are not always one's best friends. But you I will never lose.'

Her French mixed with German and her small, concentrated handwriting. When he was abroad, a card would suddenly arrive at his hotel:

'Nous serons vraiment fachés si vous ne venez pas.
Mille amitiés
Senkrah'

He came and he gazed into her large eyes whose pupils swallowed him up. And she folded her hands around his.

Then she got married and had children, and she no longer gave concerts. One day he read in the paper that she had shot herself.

*

He stood up with such force that the table fell over and the teacup broke. 'She loved me!' he cried.

He understood her.

And suddenly he also understands her mother.

*

Everything goes black as if they are driving through a tunnel. A scream is trapped inside his head, and a dry faint smell of coal dust settles in his nostrils.

The light returns. He is standing up, and perhaps he has been crying out or actually screamed, for all the passengers are looking at him.

The waiter bends down to pick up a teacup or more precisely the shards of a teacup. The waiter looks at him, concerned. The waiter taps his shoulder and pushes the chair back in place so that he is gently forced to sit down again. The waiter removes some crumbs, checks the teapot for warmth, leaves and returns with a new cup. All this the waiter does for him, the passenger.

The middle-aged gentleman in beaver furs looks at him, shaking his head. And the daughter. Now he remembers her. The young American girl who reminds him of Anna, of Arma, of all the young girls he has known. She is standing by the window. She must have turned around suddenly to face him; she looks startled like a child, her lips slightly open. She presses a half-eaten apple that she holds in her hand against her blouse, leaving a stain. She is breathing quickly as if she has been running or is feeling ill from the stuffy, confined space. Then she turns around again and leans her forehead against the glass. He looks out the window to see what she sees. A small, delicate furred animal that he has never seen before is running outside. A grey squirrel. Maybe it is a young one, maybe it is very old. There is no one to ask. Peter would have known. The handsome Peter Nansen whose brilliance became more and more apparent with age and who is now the head of a publishing house. Perhaps he is at this moment thinking about what to do with the letter that Herman Bang, his old friend, wrote from Hotel Astor in New York while gazing at the city that refused to turn dark. Cars roamed the streets, and the sky was pink, turquoise and green.

'*My friend.*

It was not in order to press the publishers for money. But because it became clear in Hamburg that it would be completely impossible to go through with the journey, I wrote telegrams and letters. On the transatlantic crossing I saved money by only getting injections every other day, even though for many years I have had them done daily (Doctor – 5 marks per injection).

I only go to the barber every other day.

I have saved on shirts (eighty pfennigs per shirt), and one must wear a dinner jacket!

Now I only possess 2300 marks.

But what I didn't learn until I was in Hamburg – a scheme created by the ocean liner – was this: the "World Tour" will not start before San Francisco, and therefore I have to pay for everything during the seventeen days here in America – in the most expensive country in the world. When I reach San Francisco, I will only have one thousand marks – to last me four months. And that is impossible. The journey will be hellish. I also have to buy a tropical suit. I am simply losing my mind.

And where have the thousand marks (there were originally 3300) gone? To pay for rent in Copenhagen, for Miss Thune's wages, for the stay in Berlin and Hamburg, for purchases (cabin bag, shirts).

Due to the stupidity of the Danish-Americans, I will not be able to do any readings in Chicago and San Francisco. Here I will receive one hundred dollars.

All along it has been my intention to write two books:

1. Bergen – New York (about my lecture tours) – I will send the first draft for this book from Japan.

2. Vacation (about my world tour).

But San Francisco is the last station, the last one on the entire journey, where a telegraphic authorization can reach me. 250 dollars must be authorized. For I cannot face these four months in this way. I will lose – without exaggeration – my mind.

Address (4th - 5th February): *Cleveland*. San Francisco.[11]

Herman.'

It couldn't be expressed more clearly. Surely, Peter Nansen must understand. After all, an attachment still exists between them due to their early friendship and working relationship. In those days when they sat on the green pouffe talking the nights away, holding a glass of red wine in one hand and a candle in the other.

'Don,' he said. 'Remember this during your sleepless nights: it is not where we have arrived that we have to reckon with, but what we have done.'

And Don looked at him with such a surprised expression that he realized that he still didn't know about the prickly, uncontrollable thoughts that haunt people during sleepless nights.

But he didn't realize that he himself in time would stop saying Don and instead call him: Peter Nansen, Peter the Married Man, Per Parterre, Nansen the editor or simply Nansen, and that he would sometimes use formal address and call him a scoundrel at least twice.

Back then they would laugh loudly and wholeheartedly when reading in the provincial paper *Fyens Stiftstidende* that the fashion in Copenhagen was now so outlandish that 'The well-known writer of serials had appeared wearing a blue tailcoat and a white waistcoat, light-grey trousers, gold-plated buttons, a golden hair ornament, and a spray of roses instead of a tie while his companion wore a tailcoat with shortened sleeves and long twelve-button gloves that only ladies usually wear.'

But they had to swallow their laughter when they saw their portraits in *Punch*: Peter Nansen standing, his attractive, steady gaze fixed on the reader. Herman Bang sitting slumped in a soft chair, his gaze fixed on Nansen. Two creatures with pointy high-heeled shoes, frills, narrow trousers and legs ready to dance the pas de deux, with roses around their necks and glittery tiaras in their pretty pageboy hair.

And at that time he himself usually dressed in browns and check patterns to give his frame more fullness, with the addition of a discreet blue tie, blue socks and a white handkerchief with a blue border. How was he going to manage his planned reading tour?

'You could cancel it,' Peter said. 'For once you could cancel it.'

'Cancelling – that would be the same as giving up. That time Bjerring advised me against giving a lecture in Stockholm and Lund, I took the Swedes by storm – simply by stepping down from the podium. And when Nini had Ferslew forbid me to do a reading in Horsens because she feared a scandal, I went to Horsens – and did a reading.'

'And how did that go?'

'When I finally arrived, Nini welcomed me with roulades, stewed fruit and mild resignation. And the attendance was much too low for a scandal to unfold.'

'I will accompany you.'

'Promise? Then it will be a success.'

Don shook his handsome head indulgently at Bang and pushed *Punch* away.

But the drawing of the two serial writers turned out to be a perfect advertisement. There were full houses everywhere. In Randers a theatre troupe had to cancel, for everyone wanted to see Herman Bang.

Especially the women flock to see them.

And he does his best, not only to triumph but also to give them an experience. He is simply grateful and touched that they have come.

The tailcoat, the boutonnière, the golden buttons, even the half bottle of red wine, all that is for their sake. And as soon as he begins reading, he is neither affected nor bizarre.

It happens that somebody laughs in the wrong place. To all appearances he doesn't notice it. Not until he says that now he would like to read something funny so that those who were amused by the tragic parts would get an opportunity to laugh with all their heart.

When the young farm boys show up with their hair combed down over their forehead, he looks at the audience and declares that it pleases him to have come to a town where the youth is so fashion-conscious. And when a couple of demure matrons walk out in the middle of an erotic passage, he looks up and says: 'Why! It is a pity the ladies are leaving just as we got over the worst part.'

But he doesn't win over the audience through laughter alone. Every single night he lets them into his world, he captures and moves them, and they reward him with applause that is warm and spontaneous like a caress.

He is still in a state of intoxication when he walks back to the hotel.

'I managed it once again, Don. They come out of curiosity, and then they become enchanted.'

'Why do you think so?'

'They can feel that I love them just for them coming. Perhaps it is only that.'

'I wonder if it is that simple?'

'No, I think that it is purely because I am an actor.'

'You believe that one swallow makes a summer.'

'Yes, right now I believe it. And when *Phaedra* comes out, I will demand my artistic freedom. You have read it, and Bjerring has read it. I have worked hard, very hard, and I know I am master of my material. I am no longer twenty. I cannot spend the rest of my life working for a newspaper.'

'You try to convince your editorial director of that.'

'I will do that, yes. My position at *Nationaltidende* must be reassessed in the New Year. The serials I will pass on to others. I have now spent my entire early youth on those kinds of things.'

'But the money – '

'Yes, the money. – – But I am so very tired of Ferslew running his paper like a business. Everything must pay. At Salomon and Riemenschneider the tone is completely different. They don't think of money at all. Only of quality. They are young like us. My next books are going to be published there.'

'Do you think that enterprise is solid?'

'The families have more money than they know what to do with – – By the way, I am going to edit their journal. – – I will speak with Ferslew as soon as I get home.'

And it was easy. Surprisingly easy.

Ferslew asked him to take a seat and offered him a cigar.

The smoke formed patterns between the two men, and he felt like poking the smoke rings with his finger and playing with them like a child. But he was no longer the 'enfant terrible' of the editorial office, he was the poet Herman Bang, demanding his artistic freedom.

The newspaper owner nodded. Both he and his senior correspondents had also been thinking along those lines. A less permanent association with *Nationaltidende* would be an advantage for both parties.

'Yes, dear Bang, you have yourself brought so many fresh young journalists to *Nationaltidende*. – Nansen, Esmann, Carl Ewald. We understand completely that you would rather write your novels. But the acting – that you must give up. Nothing but misery will come of that.'

Ferslew smiled, a fatherly and indulgent smile, and invited him to Kattinge in the days around New Year. Bang's future was near to his heart. He was once again invited to the Ferslews'. He would bring orchids for the lady of the house; they would be available at florists around that time.

The shops sparkled in red and green and gold and silver. In December the city was more beautiful than usual. Ida and Louise made woven paper baskets for the tree with small, stiff fingers, their tongues sticking out at the side of their mouth. Ida burst into tears because she had made a mistake in the middle of a heart-shaped basket.

He tried to console her: 'We will turn it around so the nice side is facing out.'

'But I still know that it isn't nice.' She started blubbering uncontrollably. Her nose was running, and her small, bony shoulders were trembling.

'Ida, when something doesn't work out, you must try to make another one that is better and more beautiful. And then you will forget it happened. Come here.' He cut the green and the red paper straight and carefully. He helped her weave the pieces together while thinking about his novel and the Christmas publication and the days around New Year.

Then *Phaedra* came out, and it was like *Hopeless Generations* all over again. Only Erik Skram thought that the love scenes were moving. Otherwise all the reviews were negative.

There are many ways to shed tears. Over a glass of champagne. Where glass and teeth collide, and the drink whose fizz speaks of elegance and expectations turns lukewarm, stale and flat.

Or the heavy kind of weeping that pursues you in your sleep. Tears mixed with a tot of rum and a spot of sedative. Tears that roll down your cheeks, smearing your eye makeup. Black on white. In the future his bed linen is going to be black and practical.

Or when he paces his room, crying. Black tear streaks covering his olive complexion, almost like the beautiful animal called a cheetah.

But no one sees him cry in public. He only confides in Don: 'I saw Henriques. And then he says: "It is bad, that book of yours. You are not a human being. You will never be able to write a good book." I lost patience for the first time ever. My response was somewhat bitter. It was foolish.'

But he tries to act unaffected. For instance, he doesn't cancel his lecture on the art of acting held in *Casino*'s small hall. But he wished that he had. For in the morning he is called to the office of Salomon and Riemenschneider.

He runs to their office filled with apprehension, and the minute he enters he knows that the worst must have happened. The police are sealing off cabinets and drawers. Employees and nosy parkers from the street are wandering about aimlessly. No one is working.

All they know is that the two managers have taken flight.

He remains standing against a wall that feels damp because nobody has thought of lighting the fire in the stove.

It must have to do with the money. All the unrealistic large sums that drifted by like stars in the sky out of everyone's reach. All these promises, then, have only been a dream or an illusion. He knows that in Riemenschneider's drawer is one of his own visiting cards with the words 'When does the money arrive?' written on it. The big investment that was supposed to come from the family in America and made from the kind of material that money is usually made from: paper with ragged edges, a watermark and numbers printed on it.

He is waiting because of the visiting card. Imagine if the police believe that he has anything to do with what they have found. The printing press for counterfeit money in the cellar. The many thick bundles of banknotes that have been wiped in a hurry with a dirty sponge before being brought to the bank to meet the deadline for repayments.

This much he learns before rushing home to change his clothes and drive off to *Casino*.

That evening he can hear his own voice giving the lecture. And he hears the audience applauding. He takes one bow after another, with a smile even. But a visiting card with his name and writing on it is buzzing in his brain. And that card conncects him to August Riemenschneider and to a dream of something great that is now disappearing.

The following day he reads in the paper that the two young men have been arrested and have confessed to everything. They had hoped that the counterfeiting would help the publishing house get through the crisis. Riemenschneider, who had a flair for graphic design, had produced the bills himself the night before the deadline. The bank had noticed that the bills appeared a little odd and wet, but had accepted them nevertheless. But when one of the creditors held a bill up against the light, the two managing publishers fled on foot out of town. At Damhus Inn they paused for a cup of coffee before boarding a train. In Roskilde they were recognized. December the 18th: Scandal, bankruptcy. From now on he will take a sedative and stay in bed on the 18th of December.

The visiting card is returned to him by a young constable who shakes his head with a smile and says 'Humbug' when he inquires about the two publishers. Peter Nansen has gone home for the Christmas holidays. Mrs Astrup and the two little girls walk on tiptoes. Four times a day the postman runs up and down the stairs with Christmas cards and letters. The last letter he receives is from prison.

'*24.12.83*

Dear Bang

You being the only person among our literary acquaintances with whom we have shared more than business interests and the only one among our "friends" for whom I have felt affection, I feel the need to write to you regarding the case of the publishing house. – It would break my heart if all our beautiful plans now come to an end because nobody understands them and nobody has the ability to carry them out. Do you think somebody, for instance Ferslew? would wish to take up our cause? It seems to me that for a man of his genius, it would be an enticing thought to add this venture to his other activities. He would undoubtedly become the most powerful man in the literary world. Think about it and suggest it to him. For a modest amount he would be able to obtain a good publisher, an excellent idea and a secure position, and my honour as a businessman will be saved. Should the business be closed down and the publisher and the weekly *Vor Tid* be dispersed, what would you, the writers, do then? There is not one person among the younger booksellers who is capable of understanding *Vor Tid*, and as far as the older publishers are concerned, your relationship with them will not be pleasant.

Think it over, dear Bang, if anybody can bring the idea to fruition, it will be you, and for that I would be most grateful. The thought that people will say "It was all humbug" is too dreadful, and that is precisely what people will say if the publishing house is not rebuilt and relaunched towards our goal. –

Adieu, dear Bang, we will most likely not meet again in this life, but do think of your unhappy friend every now and again.

Aug. R.'

This letter is in his pocket when he arrives at Kattinge carrying an armful of green orchids and is greeted as a dear and sorely missed guest.

Mrs Ferslew shows him the house from cellar to attic. Ferslew guides him around the factory. They shout to each other through the noise. The machines are at once so threatening and enchanting that he wants to make use of them in a novel. He will describe them as large independent creatures that steal employment while the sound of them cuts through the industrial kingpin's brain night and day.

There are dinners and coffee parties. Champagne, red wine and cognac. He doesn't see Miss Anna. The parlourmaid tells him that she is visiting friends in Copenhagen. The parents avoid talking about her. He in turn avoids talking about August Riemenschneider, and to all appearances Mr Ferslew doesn't think about his newspaper at all.

But then it happens. During the after-dinner coffee, precisely at the moment when he takes a spoonful of the thick cream that forms pearls on the coffee's surface like tiny floating nests with even tinier white cream pearls inside. White round eggs that the spoon crushes and causes to converge.

'We ought to talk business as well,' says Ferslew.

The instant he mentions the name of his friend August Riemenschneider, he knows that it isn't wise. But he must do it. He jumps from ice floe to ice floe over a deep black sea. The publisher is so young, so daring and idealistic. And what's more, Riemenschneider is newly married. One must pity the young wife. 'And,' he concludes, 'the publisher and the journal could possibly be taken over – '

'Yes,' says Ferslew. 'I can take a hint. But I cannot take on a business that doesn't pay. I myself started from scratch, and I was in a much less fortunate position than your friend. Oddly enough, one of his banknotes is in my possession. You have to hold it up against a bright light to see that it is counterfeit. Your friend has a remarkable talent for graphic design.'

He sees Mrs Ferslew blink back tears and withdraw from the glow of the lamp so her kind, lovely face seems only a pale oval in the dark. And he hears his employer say: 'We would rather not see you disappear from the pages of *Nationaltidende*, dear Bang. You will receive a payment above and beyond the usual for every piece we accept. You can submit new ideas, articles, stories. – From now on you may consider yourself released from all editorial duties.'

He stares at his coffee cup. It is white with a pattern of pale-green leaves, a very lifelike representation of the maidenhair fern. For a moment the graceful plant fogs over before his eyes and almost appears like a dark grating.

'The salary?'

'You will receive a salary for the next four months. Four months would seem to be a reasonable transition. Of course with the provision that you don't write for other papers. The articles that you write will belong to *Nationaltidende*.'

'But without my salary I have no authority.'

'No, dear Bang. And I will make no secret of the fact that some of our old, loyal colleagues are very annoyed with your reckless behaviour. Incidentally, you express opinions that are completely contrary to the official views at *Nationaltidende*. And lately we have had plenty of opportunity to notice that our paper runs very well without you.'

'Bang,' says Mrs Ferslew in her soft voice. 'We will always be friends. You can always come to us.'

And he feels that he is losing control over his voice: 'But you are reducing me to the level of a stage manager's errand boy. You are dismissing four and a half years of work as if it were nothing.'

'I wonder. Now, go home and sleep on it.'

Sleep. As if he could sleep.

Peter, dear Don, is probably sound asleep in his father's parsonage.

'Dear, I am so devastated by all this that I don't know where to turn to get away from myself. Not being able to move past it and leave. Wish you were here just to issue a few grunts and a "calming" comment.

But everything here that reminds me of the days ahead of me, is so repugnant to me that it makes me ill ... . Sold his freedom and his conscience by tender! Do you think I can accomplish enough in order to endure the misery that is coming to me? ... .'

He complains to Bjerring. Four and a half years of employment and a salary that has gradually increased to three hundred kroner a month. How is he going to manage without it? Peter is dependent on him as well as the midwife and the children.

But it is Ferslew who decides: 'After all, it is your own wish, Bang. Freedom, your artistic freedom.'

But he loses his financial security as swiftly as you can knock over a child's castle of blocks.

'Don, my friend. It is over. I cannot stay at the paper on Ferslew's conditions. But for my sake, Bjerring will give you enough work to live by.'

'And you? – '

'Something will have to happen now. I feel the excitement. Admittedly excitement combined with anxiety. But it grows and grows and forces every thought in my brain towards this one thing: The Theatre.'

Peter Nansen shakes his head and looks at his friend who begins to walk up and down the floor while reciting lines from a play that Edvard Brandes has written. Despite that, Herman thinks that the play is accomplished and that the role of the young man who abandons his fiancée because her father went bankrupt is a suitable one for his acting debut.

'Herman, it will not work. It is wishful thinking and always will be.'

But he is still absorbed in his role and speaks to an artificial palm while gently shaking it. Not until the scene is finished does he turn around to face Peter and explain to him that the tour has been carefully planned. In addition to Brandes' *An Engagement* the Jutlanders are going to see Peter Nansen's *Friends* and Herman Bang's *Within Four Walls*.[12]

The premiere will be in Aalborg, and two royal actresses and Johannes Marer have promised to take part. 'Now, what do you say, Don?'

'I am hopeful. Mostly for you, naturally. But also for my *Friends*. By the way, why Marer?'

'He has such force of stage presence. And then he is also a graphologist. He can tell from my handwriting that I am an actor and always will be.'

*

'The Herman Bang Tour.' Never before has he seen his name in such large print. The ladies cling to him when they board the steamer to Aalborg. Camilla Lerche and Julie Secher in their light summer dresses and with their shawls flapping about. Pale pink, golden and white, colours like summer clouds. Admiring glances and fragile expectations.

In Aalborg they play to a nearly full house. It is a promising start even if it is mostly the ladies who receive applause. But then the reviews come out. *Aalborg Stiftstidende* writes that his acting is an immature attempt, and in *Nordjyllands Folkeblad* he is told that his voice is lifeless, his mannerisms odd, and that 'his posture and gait, his facial distortions – that serve as mime – his bodily contortions and noticeably affected gestures – that serve as action – have a nearly parodic effect.' Why have such fine actors allied themselves with him?

The ladies smile cheerfully, Marer pushes the newspaper far away, and they take a drive through the town in their beautiful, light clothes. The veils on the ladies' hats blow against their faces. Bright eyes and smiles are caught in a net. Only their laughter escapes.

Afterwards he sends a telegram home to Nansen:

'4/6 1884

I was rejected. Success for *An Engagement*. Ill-behaved house. *Friends* saved the evening. Greetings to all …

Your Herman.'

In Randers he is heckled and told that even his gestures are womanly. He goes for a drive with the ladies and buys gloves. Dusty rose, blue and white gloves. The two actresses wear black. Black shawls against pale cheeks and two small noses dripping from disappointment or from a cold. He himself is wearing beige. But in his letters to Peter, he is weeping:

'What I have to do now is to leave *Nationaltidende*. I don't want to stay and expose myself to all this agony. What saddens me the most, my dear friend, is the fact that we must separate. I have been looking forward very much to working with you, being with you until the day you get married. Now I have to go abroad. My financial affairs force me to live on nothing. Whatever will happen to the children, I don't know.'

'I am so foolish that I am beginning to cry again, but I cannot bear to think that we shall separate and that I shall be separated from so much that is dear to me.

But continue as a writer the old way – that I cannot do.'

In Ribe only a few tickets are sold, so the ladies decide to return home and there isn't much else to do than to follow suit.

At home he practically topples over as he enters the parlour and slumps into the nearest chair. He has just enough time to notice the artificial palm's long, dry leaves and Peter who rushes towards him with a glass of water. Then he gives up and faints.

'But I told you so.' His friend's lovely, soft voice pulls him out of the darkness and makes him open his eyes and look up at the stuccoed ceiling that soon will cease to be his. Never before has he studied the plaster rosettes, ribbons and fruits so carefully. It must be the first time he fainted here.

'Tomorrow,' he says, 'I'll have to prepare Mrs Astrup for the move. Then I'll travel to Sweden, and when I return to Copenhagen, I'll have to move into a garret.'

'Are you going to Sweden to have a rest?'

'No, to work. The fiasco must be transformed into a success. Bjerring says that there is a drama hidden in *Phaedra*. And if I strip it, cut it to the bone, it might perhaps succeed. *Dramaten* in Stockholm has shown interest in me – also as an actor. And Theodor Andersen at *Dagmarteatret* has to all intents and purposes commissioned me to submit a play. I just have to get used to the reactions coming from the audience. And you know that I have a will made of steel.'

*

Sure enough, three days later he has found a fencing instructor in Helsingborg and lodging in Ramlösa.

He turns to face the bright sky, puffing his chest out and sucking the metallic Swedish air deeply into his lungs. He wants to fold the cold and the brightness inside himself like a folded knife blade, all sharpness and shivers.

But he finds time to write to Peter:

'I have had two fencing lessons. I am completely exhausted.

I do physical exercises every day and make progress. If it were possible – but unfortunately it is not – I would stay here all summer to make a full recovery, reconciling myself to the future and much more.

I drink four litres of milk and four bottles of porter every day. This representative of all hideousness at the theatre must first and foremost attempt to appear less pinched and less sickly. I speak in front of the mirror for an hour every day.

And during it all I feel a longing, and I don't know for what – a longing that is tearing my soul to pieces.'

'True, I say that I have courage, but I wept bitter tears last night for a couple of hours because I am so stupid as to be who I am – and not like others who live contentedly by loving a little, pursuing their goals a little, being married a little and having children.

I, who am otherwise never envious, envy people this contentment that doesn't exist for me.

Farewell.
Your Herman'

7.

But he didn't regret it. Well, there is one thing he does regret – still: that he wrote Mrs Ferslew and asked her to arrange for him to get his job back. He promised to mend his ways, and if anyone could help him, she would be the one. He admitted that he deserved to be dismissed considering how he had behaved. But just the same – the way it had happened was hurtful.

He wished that he had never written that letter. But he wished even more that she was still alive.

If only he could have written to her from the dining car with its stained table cloth, and where a bit of egg shell and a few grains of salt are sticking to his hand. If he could have told her that he was on his way to Utah, to San Francisco, to Japan. That the mountain air is like knives in his lungs, that his heart is pounding from fear. That America's sunsets are terrifying. That the sun practically draws sparks out of the grass and the trees, and it is like driving through fire.

Dear Mrs Ferslew would have understood. She was his friend, motherly and wise – and besides, both generous and wealthy.

He needs something stronger than tea. He orders port, and the waiter nods.

It is still as if the train is driving through the sun. The other passengers are standing by the windows, pressing their foreheads against the glass and evidently enjoying the view. But he wished that it was cooler and milder, and that the smell of wild roses, lilacs and camomile would fill the air.

There is something dangerous about the red colour. He won't be able to sleep until this sun has set. The fear overpowered him already at Hotel Astor. It was after he had finally managed to tear the telephone plug out from the wall and made his way to the bed that an evil red eye on the wall started flashing at him. Letters emerged from the eye. He wrote them down. It said: 'Message for you.' He didn't mention to anybody what he had seen. For if you have seen words written in flames on the wall, you have met God, or else you are going mad.

*

The fleeting sweetness of the port. And the sky as he has experienced it only once before: 'a fire all yellow and a flaming sky all red, and the air like one large phosphorous cloud – .' He still remembers the date written on that sky: 3.10.1884. Christiansborg Palace was burning, and he happened to be on the palace square.

In the archways he had seen two lovers. He saw their bodies lean against each other in the secretive shadows. Her slender back with its fine curvature, dressed in a lavender-blue coat. A white veil billowed out at the nape of her neck as if she were a bride-to-be, and under her arm she carried two thick books.

But suddenly they were caught in a flood of people, and he himself was caught in a crowd. There was much shouting. 'The palace! The palace is burning!' Everyone wanted to watch and flee at the same time. There was panic and screaming, a rain of broken fragments and ashes when the flames burst through the roof. And he saw: 'the blazing pages of hundreds of books that were suddenly lifted by the storm above the palace like a swarm of frightened birds taking flight.'

He watches. And his body is pressed against other bodies, so closely that he feels somebody's breath brushing his cheek, and he turns around and sees her, her hair covered by the white veil, her eyes large and terrified like those of a child.

'Miss Anna – Miss Ferslew. I hardly recognize you.'

'I have changed. I have come to my senses. I am engaged now, but secretly.' She flashes a smile at him, a smile that is at once girlish, cheeky and sultry.

Her hot breath and her lips against his cheek. But just then she turns on her heel and shouts: 'Let me pass. I live at the palace!' And she cuts a path through the crowd with her textbooks in pedagogy and psychology.

He surges forward with the crowd closer to the burning building. He sees how the soldiers form a chain, how the firemen battle the fire and how the sparks are being carried by the wind across the city. The smoke is making him cough, and his eyes and nose are watering. But he doesn't feel it. All he knows is that the fire is a catastrophe and that he is the one to report it.

He breaks loose from the crowd without knowing how. But he has probably woven his way through the mass of people and used his elbows to get to *Nationaltidende*'s editorial office where the windows are blown out by the intense heat and sparks are flying above Mrs Ferslew and Bjerring who are moving the last boxes of archival material to safety.

'I need a place to write. A peaceful place.'

Mrs Ferslew takes him downstairs and into a small room in the family's private apartment. He sits down by a dainty writing desk.

'Fire in the middle of the fire. The consuming clouds of smoke and stairs that collapsed – and chasms that opened up, and halls that were buried.'

A window bursts. Shards scatter over his papers. But he is unharmed. And in any case, he can shake them off. The only thing that really bothers him is the soot, for every time he runs his hand through his hair or just scratches his nose, his hand leaves black marks on the paper.

It is not until he has finished writing that he discovers that he is sitting in Miss Anna's room where everything is dainty and pink and sky-blue.

On the desk is one of his own envelopes. One of the actor portraits that she probably still collects was once inside. He has written a greeting on the envelope. But the corner, where he had written his name, has been torn off. Censored away. Swiftly, brutally and demurely. The envelope is blue and as thin as a butterfly's wing.

His eyes are stinging. He gets up.

In the parlour the crystal chandelier has fallen down, and family and friends have gathered to witness the drama.

'How inappropriate,' an old uncle huffs, 'letting him have access to Anna's room.'

Mrs Ferslew pretends not to hear it. She just looks at her daughter Anna who is standing right there with flushed cheeks and letting the young student Levin embrace her as though he had rescued her directly from the flames.

Ferslew himself didn't witness the catastrophe. He had been in Kattinge at his factory, but the next day he could read the reportage in his paper.

'This is the best you have written to date, Bang. Please, come for dinner tomorrow.'

He didn't have high hopes. He only came to experience one more dinner with the Ferslew family. The candles, the laden table, the champagne, the wine and the speeches. And Bjerring, the best friend of the family that one could imagine. Bjerring who so obviously enjoyed being pampered by the ladies who in turn assumed that this charming, cultured gentleman must have suffered an unhappy love affair.

Miss Ferslew swept past him with her student: 'Yes, Bang, I will marry Reason after all,' she laughed. At least she didn't say 'Contentment'.

She had become more plump. Perhaps it was happiness that had made her rounder.

He went home early. And the image of Mrs Ferslew's mild face stayed with him. She had seen right through him, and she was fond of him.

At his lodgings he had gotten a new motherly friend. Mrs Ottosen with her rough, manly voice. Mrs Ottosen who can slam a door so the whole stairwell shakes. She is of the age where her femininity has begun to fade away. The first down has appeared on her upper lip, and her flesh has become loose and earthbound. She runs her fingers through her thin, greying hair that was once a fiery red mane. Furious and desperate, she lifts her hands and turns her eyes towards the ceiling when forced to take his coat and boots as security until he has paid the rent.

But in this Fury with her thick fingernails and worn-out body, he sees a young woman with full lips and lively eyes and high breasts, dressed in a white, pleated negligee. She flings herself down gracefully on a sofa, and her hands are small and delicate. And her index finger is neither dirty nor rough from counting money.

'Lovely,' he says to Peter, 'she must have been lovely in her day.'

When he leaves, Peter Nansen will take over his rooms. And the thought of him being in his rooms and touching his things will keep the bond between them alive.

But a certain distance has entered their friendship. They no longer talk the nights away. They never read to each other any more. They work separately. They don't any longer have common interests. And Peter doesn't tell him about whom he has met, whom he has visited. Why he never drops in on him. Or why he so seldom is at home himself.

Peter makes excuses, says that he has to take care of his brother Emmanuel. The lazy pup will be sitting his examinations soon.

'Bring the pup. We can eat together. It won't be late.'

But Peter remains silent. Peter tells him one white lie after another without wanting to do so. And it is humiliating for both of them.

For he knows very well what it means. Peter's silence, Peter's beating about the bush and all the little untruths.

'Just say it as it is. You have begun associating with the Brandes brothers. You are leaving *Nationaltidende* to join *Politiken* – aren't you?'

'You could join as well.'

'Never. – I am not judging them. Not at all. There are probably other people to whom they show generosity and devotion. But they are different from me in temperament and spirit. And they have humiliated me – both as an artist and as a human being. – – Perhaps it is better that the two of us no longer see each other. That we just remember how it once was. Back when we were close – when we really did understand each other.'

'You are too sentimental, Herman. And too fanatical about your friendships.'

'Farewell, dear Peter. I will never be a newspaper man in Denmark again. – With you I will never compete. And working with Edvard Brandes – that is impossible. It will never happen.'

He went away. He had bought a black fur coat that clung to his body like a precious caress, and he saw that the coat made an impression on Nini and Sofie.

Neither one of the sisters wept at his departure. When the train began moving, the elegant Mrs Nini Holst and the pretty young Mrs Sofie Göttsche drew close to their husbands and waved mechanically with their handkerchiefs. It was not at all like the time when their younger brother William suddenly left for America, and they all stood on the quay, sobbing.

'Gothenburg, Stockholm, Helsinki, Bergen,' Nini laughed. 'Before we know it, you will be back home again.'

But then, she didn't know about his other plans or his meeting with the great impresario Mr Theodor, formerly a specialist in corns and bunions and now an artist in his field.

Mr Theodor, who receives visitors every morning dressed in long brownish undergarments, a dressing gown and a morning wig and with a voice like a foghorn, tells of all the stars he has created. The rising and the falling stars in his personal sky. Mostly the falling ones lately.

'Sir,' says Mr Theodor, 'the agents are destroying the market. We are flooded by celebrities – in ten years time I won't give a hundred marks for a world-famous personality.'

And he got lost in memories about the curlyhead Dengremont with his child-size violin who had played to the tune of two million. 'But incidentally, I do appreciate children. They don't cause trouble, you can get them where you want them: they will play without complaining … .'

To be sure, the young Herman Bang didn't complain in the least when the former specialist in corns and bunions held the lamp up against his face, turned him this way and that as if he were an object, inspected his ears, his nose and his eyes and inquired about any diseases he might suffer from.

'Only a bit of haemorrhaging, seizures and fainting spells,' he said very nonchalantly, relieved that Mr Theodor in the end found his appearance suitable for electric lighting and wanted him to sign the contract right away.

Finally Mr Theodor advised him to travel by night in order to save on hotels. And naturally he would have to travel third class. But when approaching his destination, he should most certainly purchase a supplementary ticket for first class and move in there with his suitcases. For people of talent must arrive in style.

He nodded excitedly and in agreement with Mr Theodor's whole approach. Humbug, charm, experience and illusion were going to help Herman Bang conquer the North. He was going to lecture on the art of acting, on Henrik Ibsen and Turgenev, and he would finally, finally have an opportunity to perform in the role of Osvald.

The tour begins in Gothenburg. The friends receive him, and the hotel room fills up with flowers even before his performance. A young man throws himself at his feet and covers his hands with kisses. He himself doesn't move, is surprised, feels a bit awkward and ultimately pities the man. For the young man is neither handsome nor particularly interesting, and the passionate kisses merely feel like lukewarm rain on his hands.

After the lecture on Turgenev, an older Swedish lady approaches him. She gives him a small lock of grey hair tied with a blue silk ribbon.

'I closed Turgenev's eyes,' she says. 'And you understand him as if you had lived with him. I cut this lock off Turgenev's hair when he died. It now belongs to you.'

He sends the dead poet's hair and three laurel leaves to Peter. And in the newspapers they compare Herman Bang to Georg Brandes and believe that he actually surpasses the doctor.

Unfortunately he must continue on to Stockholm. And he leaves a room filled with bouquets and laurel wreaths, already a professional tormentor of flowers.

In Stockholm he has hired a servant to receive him at the station and carry his suitcases to the hotel. And how he wished that he hadn't permitted himself this luxury or insisted on taking a detour.

No one notices him or the servant who is tramping along like a horse. The waves of the Riddar Fjord are ominously dark, and he is frozen to the bone from the cold wind in Västerlanggaten.

The night before the lecture on the art of acting he lies awake.

And he bites on the pillow to keep his teeth from chattering.

Afterwards the critics tear his lecture apart. All that is left is a shell of a man.

In *Smålandsposten* he is described as a humbug equipped with a camelia and a chapeau claque and later as a monkey in a cage. – And what good, then, does a lock of hair from a dead poet do you? And what good are flowers? Or champagne? One day the reception is bubbly and effervescent. The next day you only have an empty glass.

He has to move on. In Uppsala he finds it necessary to rent a hotel room and spend a day in bed. He has seizures, and every time he lifts his head the dizziness pushes him back into deep nauseating darkness. Finally the dizziness turns white and painful and is full of pictures: a humbug with a camelia and chapeau claque and the monkey in a cage. Those pictures have long since flown to Copenhagen. In black and white.

He tries to concentrate on a fixed point in the ceiling. But there is no pretty mitigating rosette. The ceiling is bare and white with an ochre-coloured stain that most likely stems from a knocked-over chamber pot.

A stain of urine. A blinding light. And gulls outside with evil stares and red feet and beaks.

But he has to get up and move on. Herman Bang is on the bill in Helsinki. He has to speak, perform, stand in the white, blinding light. He is not to appear weak or dull. The audience mustn't be disappointed.

Helsinki is his town. All tickets are sold days in advance. After his lecture the applause is endless. And a delegation of young Finnish ladies give '*Phaedra's* Poet' a laurel wreath and an impressive lyre of red and white roses. And finally he is going to play the role of Osvald for the first time.

He is nervous, exhausted and nearly in a trance. But as soon as he has spoken his first line, he is inside his character. He really does become Osvald. He utters cries that even frighten himself. Osvald acquires expressions and movements he has never previously imagined or rehearsed in front of the mirror.

Uneven and completely out of control, he thinks. He bites the nail on his index finger until it bleeds while standing in the silence between the two actresses, waiting for the audience's reaction.

Then the applause breaks loose. It is thunderous, a roar, a stomping of feet and clapping of hands, expressions of surprise, enthusiasm and emotion flooding towards him. More intensely and passionately than he has ever dreamt of.

He is called before the curtain again and again. The audience will not let him go. And afterwards he is drowning in compliments, kisses, gifts and invitations.

For a moment he tears himself away from the party to telegraph Peter:

'Merci Osvald succès complet.
Herman'

The following day he is declared a genius by a unanimous press. He has nerve, soul and temperament. He has moved and shaken the spectators. A young critic is of the opinion that he has violated the most basic of the laws of acting and gotten away with it. A physician advises him to avoid subjecting himself too often to this kind of agitation. But it doesn't spoil his pleasure. He has been Osvald, ill, provocative and loved.

He will need his newly acquired visiting cards. He gets invitations from actors, directors, poets and counts. And at a soirée the famous pianist Sofie Menter approaches him. She has fallen in love with his voice, precisely this voice that he has worked on so much. The voice has tones she hasn't encountered before – it is at once soft and slightly husky – a sophisticated, odd and raw beauty that she would like to accompany.

He cannot fathom how he has the nerve. But they put together a programme and perform in Åbo. She plays Mendelssohn, Schubert, Chopin and Liszt. And he recites two short stories and Osvald's monologue.

Once again a cheering reception. She squeezes his hand, and he can feel the strength in her long sinewy piano fingers. And afterwards a supper with oysters and champagne.

Her cat is brought in and sneezes into the ice-cold shellfish while she mixes beer with the champagne to sweeten it.

'The two of us, Bang. We will perform together. We will conquer the whole world.'

'Do you think so, Mistress Menter?'

'Mistress –,' she smiles, and there is both coldness and sadness in that smile. 'I am thirty-nine and soon to be divorced. My husband is a violinist and very famous. He and I are competitors.'

'Do you think I will be famous?' His voice quivers with longing.

'Bang, you are better off seeking happiness.'

But right now happiness doesn't interest him. Because a woman interrupts their conversation. She introduces herself as Princess Demidoff and wants to meet the Royal Physician's grandson. And before he knows it, his travel plans have changed. There is absolutely no reason to rest up before invading Norway. From Helsinki he can sail to Saint Petersburg – the gateway to all of Europe.

The Princess will recommend him to the court. Empress Maria Feodorovna is of course a Danish princess and probably remembers her old doctor. Perhaps she has heard of the grandson's success. In any case she will be pleased to receive news from home. 'And Bang, you conduct yourself like a young diplomat.'

He bows deeply to the Princess and shouts with joy on his way to the hotel. Now all doors are open to him. Bang: an actor, a writer, a diplomat.

The next morning he is on his way.

The ship creaks from the ice pushing against its sides, and he imagines his audience with the Empress. She will be wearing sable and velvet. And diamonds will twinkle in her hair and weigh heavily on her hands. And he must remember to walk backwards when leaving the room and to lift his feet high over the threshold.

Finally he sees the city's golden onion domes and the entirely unexpected shapes and colours – Saint Petersburg – a dazzling, lavish fairy tale that takes him by surprise. The lights along the Nevsky River. The elegant French-speaking ladies and gentlemen that never get up before midday and don't see the sun all winter. They live only at night. They go to the opera or to parties and balls. During the day they doze off and dream, listless and pale and disturbed by the city noises. But he:

'13.5.1885

Heaven and earth – that's what the Empress was. Getting up at seven o'clock to see the damned court tailor who had inspected my attire and found my trousers to be too narrow (!) for the court and therefore had to sew me a couple of new pairs in a matter of ten hours. They cost a mere trifle of thirty rubles (sixty kroner) and fit horribly. After this I made two modest attempts at getting a shave, the time was now half past eight, but I didn't succeed – so I waltzed off unshaven to meet the Empress. Nevertheless, I looked very distinguished – all in black – the yellow buttons and satin cuffs had been sacrificed – I haven't been dressed this modestly since my confirmation. The ride to Gatchina is bleak through a flat, bare and unattractive landscape. All along the tracks are sod houses where unhappy soldiers are permitted to crawl in at night after having stood on their feet all day by the railway. Every two hundred yards you find one of these souls standing at attention. I rode in the same car as the minister of war, an old doglike gentleman – all Russian generals look like bulldogs – who in the course of one hour on the trip made short work of thirty cigarettes. Mr Mynter, a friend of father and very much a protégé of the Empress, accompanied me. Gatchina station is well guarded and, as expected, a dozen sly police eyes followed my humble self but gave way timidly to the royal carriage that the servant opened after which we quickly drove off. A young grand duke flew past us in a small, light, luxurious trap. Everything that has been said about the cordons of soldiers and such is nonsense. At Gatchina the guards are no more numerous than at any other palace. Only a single Cossack was posted at the entrance to the enormous park. The palace is as enormous as the park – a huge half circle and two wings. We were allocated a couple of rooms and had tea, after which Her Majesty was gracious enough to let us wait for an hour and a half. She had been on a hunt with the Emperor the night before until six o'clock in the morning and was now resting, which I didn't begrudge her. Finally the door swung open, and a remarkable-looking lackey appeared, sparkling like a rainbow in yellow, red and green. Through a vast number of corridors we reached an infinite number of chambers. Servants were loafing around everywhere. Describing all this splendour for you is impossible because my words cannot convey the picture adequately. Everything that marble and gold and paintings, everything that heavy velvet and the plastic arts can accomplish – imagine that, and still you will not be able to visualize the Roman gallery where the busts of Roman emperors radiate in all their barbaric whiteness along the curved wall; meanwhile the entire opposite wall, all of glass, opens up to a view of the marble park where all the pagan gods shine standing on their plinths. We passed through another gallery that was hung with Persian carpets. A jumble of silk and colours. But this one thing you can surely imagine: the entire colossal space, the galleries and the chambers are saturated with an intoxicating fragrance that penetrates everything. From all corners, from all staircases and every landing, heliotrope, reseda, yellow roses and lily of the valley emit a blend of strong scents. The golden flower bowls are overflowing.

The number of servants increased. Finally we reached the Empress' chambers. She lives on the mezzanine floor where the ceilings are not as high as in your apartment. A group of servants lined up in two rows, and we were ushered in to the imperial children's playroom where some very ordinary toys for the miniature-highnesses were displayed. Then Mr Mynter was shown in to Maria Feodorovna, and I was moved to another room. It was the Empress' antechamber, very plain, only some French paintings of the modern school adorned the room. From the neighbouring room I could hear the Empress talking and laughing very loudly. Then it was my turn. In the middle of a small boudoir stood a very youthful person in a green dress. She wore a single pearl as a brooch. Her beautiful eyes and her lovely figure are captivating. I think she was abashed for a moment at seeing my youth (I suppose I looked twenty-two), but a second later she offered me her hand, and we spoke for about twenty minutes. Everything in the room reminded one of Denmark. During the conversation the Empress pointed and said: Have you seen my Melbye! – a wonderful painting of a blue sea. The room was small, very small and low-ceilinged. In the corners were large rose trees in bloom … . Yes, said the Empress, there isn't much room here, but there is still space for a piano … . We spoke about grandfather, about

Turgenev and Dostoevsky – how she laughed when she corrected my pronunciation and said: Yes – oh – Russian – God, how difficult it is. I think that Maria Feodorovna can very easily turn into a giggling girl – to be sure, though, she is most unassuming and adorable. One of her ladies-in-waiting told me that during the days when they feared a war was impending, the Empress was the only one who was happy and cheerful. Oh – nonsense – she said – there won't be a war … And she was right, but most likely she had also worked very hard on the quiet to that end.

Finally she offered me her hand again – I had addressed her as "You" and not as "Your Majesty" throughout the meeting and felt obliged to apologize. She responded with her silvery laugh – and requested that I send her a copy of my next book. She had read many of my serials in *Nationaltidende*. I bowed, and the audience ended.'

At the end of his letter, he forbids Peter from making any of the content public. He has his reasons. It is imperative that he be allowed to return to Saint Petersburg. Never before has grandfather's dream about a diplomatic career been so nearly within reach. He knows that he has made a good impression. He didn't trip over the threshold when walking backwards, and had he tripped, he would have done it gracefully right at the feet of the charming Empress.

But in the meantime there are performances and contracts, travelling and lectures. He is not longing for home, only longing for news from Peter, and in Gefle he eagerly reaches for the stack of *Politiken* that is waiting for him at the station.[13]

Well, he must admit that Peter is truly passionate about his paper. There, printed on the front page, he sees his own letter from Saint Petersburg.

'*Gefle 21.5.85*

My dear Peter

You are completely mad. I arrive at the station and see in *Politiken* – in large print and on the front page – my letter from Petersburg.

It was easy to recognize, and if I am now unable to cash in my pay for the last two months from *Nationaltidende*, then I will seek compensation from you – which would probably be of great use to me.[14]

I am now on my way to Norway.'

He is travelling towards the very idea of spring. And Bergen opens up to him already on his first leisurely walk. The pretty, cheeky servant girls are like a chorus of Holberg's Pernille characters. The Bergensians' temperament has a southern touch, and his impresario has assured him that he, Herman Bang, is indeed the man for Bergen. Bergen will receive him with open arms.

But at the theatre it feels almost as if he is an inconvenience.

They are polite, gracious and worried. Just now *Ghosts* doesn't interest them much, in fact the tragedy is at odds with the theatre's plans. All the actors are occupied with rehearsing for comedies by Holberg and Hostrup on account of a distinguished Danish guest performer. Olaf Poulsen is coming to Bergen to play his famous roles. And Herman Bang as Osvald cannot possibly compete with the royal actor playing Lieutenant von Buddinge in Hostrup's *The Neighbours*.[15]

But he is still drunk with the feeling of victory and doesn't understand their worry. And the manager Gunnar Heiberg does in fact find a spot for just one Herman Bang evening. He will recite two of his stories, 'Love' and 'The Pastor,' and act the role of Osvald. The eight hundred tickets are snapped up. He sees no reason to be worried.[16]

The unease doesn't become apparent until the dress rehearsal.

Gunnar Heiberg is gracious, Mrs Sperati, who plays Mrs Alving, is gracious, and Didi Heiberg, who is Regine, is very, very gracious and as pale as a corpse underneath her make-up.

'If you will just remain calm,' says Gunnar Heiberg and looks as if he would prefer to cancel the event.

'But Osvald is not at all calm. Osvald is nervous and tense.'

'It is too much for Bergen.'

Gunnar Heiberg, of all people, who himself is a dramatist and is considered self-confident and provocative, that he should have doubts. That is incomprehensible. All this distrust intensifies his nervousness. It is like a tic that makes his whole body shake.

Mrs Sperati takes his hands and holds them. 'If you will just remain calm. If you play like you do now at the rehearsal, everything will be fine.'

At the actual performance he senses very clearly that the audience is not moved by his stories. The applause is polite, cool and utterly mechanical. And how depressing is that, this gutless sloppy sound.

He changes his clothes, powders his face pale and sits down on the stage. Osvald must and shall stir them. Osvald will make them clap until their hands hurt.

Mrs Sperati brings a glass of water.

'What is this? Osvald doesn't drink water.'

'I thought you were ill, Mr Bang.'

'No, I have begun acting the role.'

And then he becomes Osvald, and he is ill and desperate, and she, the mother, Mrs Sperati, will not give him the morphine capsules that he has secured in order to commit suicide. She wants to keep him as a poor helpless child whom she can feed and nurse and be kind to, someone she can bring water to.

She holds the morphine capsules tightly in her clenched fist, high in the air. She will never help her Osvald to end his life. She doesn't want to understand that death is his only liberator, his only friend. She won't let him join the dead. As a good mother, a good nurse and a self-sacrificing woman, she wants to keep her innocent syphilitic child alive.

How he hates her that very moment when he hits her in her chest with his fist. He sees the fear in her eyes, and her scream is loud and piercing. But she doesn't lower her hand, she tries to flee. And he chases after her, quick as a cat. Chairs, tables and stools fall over. The entire stage is vibrating, and she is helpless, frightened out of her wits because of this mad person who is yelling and screaming and wants to beat up his mother.

But she won't let go of the capsules. She is supposed to hang on to them; Ibsen has said so himself. But this Osvald refuses to understand that he is the weaker of the two, and that, regardless, it will not do to kill her.

Mrs Sperati turns towards the audience with a helpless imploring look, and they understand her. All eight hundred of them rise to their feet and begin hissing steadily, loudly and dramatically, and the curtain goes down and Osvald collapses on the floor.

'Are they hissing?' he asks, confused.

'I'll say they are.'

'But they loved me in Helsinki.'

'Helsinki is far away from here, Mr Bang.'

They hiss and hiss. A sound like thin, thin flutes. A sound of metal. A shrill penetrating sound. Tall, tall wheels of metal that move through your heart, through your body. A sound of scandal, a sound of shame, a sound of mocking laughter that cuts right through your bones and shatters your dreams.

The next day he was ill. He took to his bed, they said.

Mrs Sperati paid him a visit and seemed relieved that he wasn't truly insane. He appeared to be completely calm and composed and sighed at the sight of her hefty Junoesque body while trying to imagine where she might be black and blue.

He gave her his portrait as a present with the dedication: 'Oktavia Sperati. With thanks to my mama – from Osvald.'

*

Peter sent him a rather non-committal letter, and it was definitely not a consolation to him that all of Copenhagen knew that he had caused a scandal as Osvald in Bergen.

His lecture was received with enthusiasm. The applause lasted longer than the heckling. In fact, the audience clapped for more than fifteen minutes.

He listened to this wonderful sound. But no one could make him go in and take a bow. His ears took in the applause. But the Bergensians' heckling still had a hold on his soul.

He went to the theatre. Not to see Olaf Poulsen act, but to throw him a bouquet of flowers as a fellow countryman. The bouquet was big and beautiful and hit the stage with a thud.

'No,' a young woman said. 'Now you must hear it after all. Before your arrival Olaf Poulsen talked and talked about you so that we came to expect you to be quite ludicrous. And then you give him flowers.'

'Too bad for Poulsen,' he answered, 'that the audience didn't laugh me off the stage. That would have pleased him more.'

The rest of his stay in Bergen he avoided Olaf Poulsen and never talked about him.

'The only revenge I have grown accustomed to taking against these people is to remain the gentleman. People like them don't have a place in my soul or among my kindred spirits. They can hurt me; they cannot force me to engage in any sort of fellowship.' This is what he wrote to Peter whom he called Per Parterre, for Peter was after all a kind of spectator.

*

He straightens up at the thought of it and knocks his hand against the table in the dining car. He tries to ignore the noises from the train that sound like obnoxious jeering and hissing. Sharp metallic sounds, shrill pistons and whistles and the enthusiastic voices of the passengers admiring the sunset, their foreheads pressed against the windows.

'The sun – Give me the sun.'[17]

Did he manage to say the words before this hissing broke out, the whistling that brought down the curtain on his dreams?

He feels a twinge of pain. A red twinge. It comes from his chest – maybe the heart. It grows narrower by his throat, is concentrated, throbbing and cruel. It is a pain that summons up images.

8.

On the visiting card was printed Herman de Bang. His pseudonyms were: Bernhard Hoff, Lecteur, Felix, Alceste, Liseur, Vidi and finally the reclining crescent moon on grandfather's coat of arms. He had three suitcases, two with his clothes and one with books, manuscripts, photographs of family and friends, a couple of silk cushions and a rather threadbare afghan. He was twenty-eight years old when he travelled to Berlin – not to seek happiness but to become famous.

He carefully hung up his fur coat on the coat hook so as not to wear it out too soon. 'Mr Wretchedness in furs' would have to pretend that money was of no concern to him. How else would he be able to conduct himself in the metropolis of Berlin?

He leafed through his manuscripts and books. He tormented himself by looking for errors, and once more he unfolded Bjerring's letter and read:

'*25.11.85.*

Dear Bang

I know very well that I am unable to make you budge even an inch from your chosen path, for no one, and especially those among us who want the best for you, has ever been able to do so, and yet the path has almost always led to your – unhappiness. Whether it concerns your health or your financial circumstances or your "artistic" work, or your social conduct, attire etc., you have always listened politely to well-intentioned advice, but have never followed it and in the end always cried over humanity's wickedness and abuse. If you publish the controversial story, you will in my opinion be "a man overboard", and your only rescue will be a ship that happens to pass by. But that is evidently what you want.

Better just to publish the two other stories by themselves. Better to spend the next twenty-four hours writing a new "harmless" story of the same length. Anything else would be better.

For the sake of your health, going into exile in order to avoid the anxiety in the wake of the verdict may be a practical and sound precaution. But that's all. The other day I painted you an ugly picture; here is another one. A naughty boy leaves a mess behind him in the classroom and runs out before the teacher can scold him. He knows that he is being naughty, his friends beg him to stop, and only one person supports him and says that it is well done. His friends are ashamed of him, and he is chased out of the school.

It is perhaps too harsh to speak in this manner. In any case it is useless, for you will go your own way, you will not listen to any warnings. Very well, now the only hope left is the passing ship. On occasion shipwrecked persons have been known to be rescued from the sea.

All the same, I want to thank you because your last letter attests to the same deep devotion you have shown me in your previous letters.

Yours Sincerely
E. Bjerring.'

He reads again the story about Frantz Pander, the impoverished lad with an exceptional sense of beauty, the waiter who desires all the luxury he serves to the rich. The young man who shows himself off to wealthy women in the hope of being desired in turn and in this way getting closer to them. He knows that he is nothing but an object and that his well-groomed hands and perfect body are part of the hotel service.

'A mess that a naughty boy has left behind in the classroom.' He puts his eccentric story away. They will probably once again call him unhealthy and perverted and overly excited. But he feels compelled to write about these caged creatures. The waiter, the child prodigy and the circus performer. The harassed and the exploited. This is the only way he can protest against the barriers that laws, conventions, economy and gender have created to keep people apart.

He could write another story. Or he could rewrite the story without much trouble. Had Frantz Pander been a woman, a pretty chambermaid, everybody would forgive her for desiring luxury, silk and perfume. But no, the beautiful, penniless Frantz will have to be a man.

If Frantz had been a woman, the story would have been less brutal. The sensual maid wouldn't have hanged herself, the gentlemen would have understood the gaze that spoke of her dreams. Or she would have hoped, patiently and at great length, and perhaps eventually given up.

He himself had all sorts of reasons for accepting his fate with resignation. The road to Berlin was paved with failed projects. After Osvald in Bergen the theatre directors responded to his letters with lofty silence. It didn't help that he promised to be diligent and humble and swore not to write a word about the theatre, at least for the time being.

And the dramatization of *Phaedra* that he had rewritten over and over again and that he had assumed that August Rasmussen would have been grateful to put on at the *Casino* theatre with the author himself as director. That play had simply been rejected. Very amiably and with deep regret to the point where he could barely allow himself to feel hurt. But of course he was hurt – financially as well.

But worst of all was the Sofie Menter Tour that should have earned him 1500 kroner. It was a complete fiasco.

And they had worked together, he and Mrs Sofie Menter. They had truly prepared themselves. She had invited him to her castle in Tyrol, and there, in her Turkish drawing room, they had planned their trip through the northern countries. And there, at the piano, she had accompanied his voice and praised his musicality. Words and notes had flowed together, it was a whole new form, and the audience would be enchanted just like the time in Åbo when she in her magnificent concert dress had held his hand in a firm grip.

He wrote poems to her:

'How beautiful she was,
her silk dress a river of diamonds.
No queen adored by the crowd
was more beautiful than she.
Flying across the piano,
her lovely arms
tempted the multitudes.'

The two of them would laugh together and be sarcastic. He had outgrown the role of the page. He was the the star's confidant.

He got to know her really well on that tour. The hard work behind the facade didn't surprise him. Neither did her temperament: her generosity when encountering a talent, or her meanness when she cheated the waiters out of a tip with the excuse that she didn't travel for pleasure.

He saw the frankness and the self-assurance in her personality and the vulnerability that made him wish that he could protect her to help her concentrate on performing elegantly like a queen, wearing her expensive concert gowns. He loved her touch on the instrument, and he admired her business sense. But it surprised him that this girlish woman with her beautiful arms and her sensitive features was able to cut and slash in a sharp and steely manner. To cut to the bone. And that right after their first performance together – which didn't go as planned.

It was solely Sofie Menter people had come to hear. She was received by a cheering crowd. But Herman Bang's voice didn't move a soul. At best the audience seemed bewildered.

The following day he read in the Stockholm paper a notice posted by Mrs Menter. She announced that her concerts in Sweden would be without Herman Bang's participation, purely and simply. And once again the satirical press arrived on the dot. The pianist's notice was compared to advertisements by certain small hotels that claim to be free of bedbugs.

That finished off their partnership but not his admiration. In fact he almost convinced himself that the great artist had every right to do what she did. But in any case, after her announcement and especially after the comparison with the bedbugs, the northern countries were now closed to him.

The lady travels through the north with her silks and furs trailing behind her. And he – 'Mr Wretchedness in furs' – travels to Berlin in third class and takes lodgings at Hotel Askanicher Hof, 21 Königsgrätzer-Strasse. He arranges his cushions in the chairs, places the afghan at the foot of the bed, puts books, manuscripts and pictures on the table. Then he presses his forehead against the window and watches the lights of Berlin, the metropolis that he intends and needs to conquer.

The noise from the carriages reaches his ears through the glass, and as soon as tomorrow he wants to go for a walk in Tiergarten, and he will pay his translator, Councillor Emil Jonas, a visit and tell him that he will accept sharing all the honoraria equally. But the Councillor must act quickly, and the Councillor must recommend him a language teacher. Emil Jonas must use all his connections to promote Herman Bang's name. And he himself will pester the editorial offices with visits, just like when he was very young.

The city tires him out and makes him dizzy. The city makes him wander around in circles. He passes by the large show windows. Jewelry, boots, shoes, spats, hats, silver-mounted walking sticks. It is solitary window shopping. A craving without the liberating laughter of his childhood. For had he the means to do so he would immediately have donned the somewhat stiff but elegant Berlin fashion that hugs the contours of the body.

And in Councillor Emil Jonas' parlour he sits drinking weak tea and eating fine, thin biscuits. He reaches carefully for his cup, for all the chairs are equipped with white, crocheted pieces of cloth, underneath which the upholstery is worn down to the padding. The wife moves around soundlessly in her soft slippers, and the Councillor's movements are refined and subtle, and it is as if the light emanates from his beautiful, white hair. For the lamp is not lit until late, and the wife pulls down the curtains as soon as the sun comes out so as to protect the furniture from fading. He realizes that the older gentleman needs his fifty per cent as much as he does himself.

It seems to him that Berlin is devoid of any gracefulness. But he courts the editorial offices of the newspapers and journals, the weekly magazines and the theatres. Take me on, use me, make me famous. The German teacher drills him until the language flows from his mouth and his pen and onto his manuscripts. When *Schorers Familienblatt* commissions him to write a short story, he produces eight drafts in five days and has them translated.

He works until he is feverish and must take to his bed. He lies sleepless and knows that he has neither the time nor the means to be sick. And he sends articles and short stories to Scandinavian newspapers and journals. Maybe they will print them in Copenhagen, Stockholm, Kristiania and Bergen. But payments are not coming his way. He will have to write to Peter Nansen:

'And when all these shiny carriages rolled past, I swore that I wanted to conquer this city.

I will leave no stone unturned. Will not spare myself in any way. The world never does. He who wants to tether it and who wants the one thing will have to use every rope available. I am no longer sentimental; I will step aside from passion; trivialities that occupy so much space in our lives bore me; I don't feel tempted like so many others to imitate the small dogs that run around and sniff every tree; it is, after all, the same stench that fills your nose.

I read my book on the train to make a note of any errors. Nothing is more painful – when something is still so imperfect – but it is necessary. A talent can only approach genius by dealing with its shortcomings.

I will commit myself mercilessly to work, which will have to earn me money, and to success, which does not depend on work alone. I only wish that people would refrain from interpreting my resolve from the way I appear – and this they do with pleasure. Just a year ago I still looked rather helpless. Now I look too self-confident. That is frightening. I would give several years of my life to have my soft mouth back, the mouth that tempted kisses from so many women and – men. But I don't have it any more. Age will knock the weapons out of our hands just when experience has sharpened them.

Do you find much "cruelty" in this? It is only plain speaking. If you remember me from long ago, you will perhaps agree that my vital functions have had their share of troubles with many consuming acids and such – oh yes – certain chemicals can practically eat the heart right out of your chest.

I have been thinking on this journey about something I would like to ask you. I need your help and advice in this matter. I don't know what is the wisest thing to do, and I only wish to do what is wise – not what is conceited. One must swallow the indignities. They are like castor oil – and in this case they are served without the jam we were given as children.

It is the business with *Politiken* and the money.

I have said "no" to receiving money from Dr Edvard Brandes. You know my reasons. These two men hate me after all. It happens that we experience a certain attraction for each other – this goes for me too – but deep down we harbour a strong aversion, a sense of alienation. We pursue too many of the same objectives as well. To submit to those people and take their money – to me that is like swallowing castor oil. But is it the right thing to say no. I need all I can scrape together to give people the impression that my position is financially sound. And it is imperative that they believe so.

You are sensible and know how to weigh the arguments against one another.'

Oh yes, Peter Nansen knows how to weigh the arguments against one another. In the future Bang will receive an honorarium for all his published articles. 'Write,' Peter urges. 'Preferably something amusing, something political or provocative.'

'Write. Just write,' says the young arrogant editor at *Berliner Tageblatt*, examining through his gold-rimmed glasses this Dane who is applying to be a theatre reviewer.

And he writes and writes after he has seen Josef Kainz in the role as Don Carlos in Schiller's play and knows that he has seen a genius. 'Slight, delicate with the face of a gypsy, the voice of a consumptive, odd in appearance,' he noted.

And he sees him as Romeo, as Mortimer, as Hamlet and as Prince Friedrich of Homburg, and it is as if he encounters his own thoughts, his own soul and impatience.

He sees Josef Kainz as the actor of his generation.

But there is another Don Carlos, another Romeo, another prince. Max Appel with the stage name Eisfeld is a blond northern German, a quiet personality whose voice sounds very soft. He is sitting by himself, silently, dressed according to the Berlin fashion, subdued and styled like a uniform. Mr Eisfeld is in the limelight at night, but during the day he is completely anonymous.

Herman Bang cannot mention Max Eisfeld by name in his writing. For Max is more beautiful than any other creature who has set foot on Berlin's cobblestones. Max has an inquiring gaze, a straight back, and when he lights a cigarette it is as if he is picking a flower. And the two of them have dined together at a table with a white tablecloth while the waiter kept a close watch on their movements. Their hands would touch lightly as if it were just by chance that they had put down their wine glasses simultaneously and stretched their arms and fingers to shorten the distance between them. Both of them looked down and immediately after turned their eyes towards each other. Max dropped his napkin just so he could move a bit closer. He himself pretended to have forgotten both his cigarettes and matches so he could feel Max's hands near his face.

Afterwards they walked for hours. They talked about performances, books and opening nights that they absolutely didn't want to miss. Almost without noticing it, they took turns accompanying each other to the hotel. They lived only a few streets apart. Had they stayed at the same hotel, then. Maybe. He looked up into Max's face and imagined his body. And one day he will lean his head on Max's shoulder. And they will seek each other under a moon of liquid silver. Afterwards they will rest, damp and smooth, as if they had been washed up on the beach, carried away from a distant shore. Intertwined like a cipher they will promise each other everything in the early hours of dawn.

Max touched the tips of his fingers lightly to signal his departure, turned around and walked back to his hotel alone. For if the two of them had climbed the stairs together. And if somebody had heard the creaking of those stairs. And if somebody had suspected anything and gone to the police with their suspicions. If and if and if.

There would be a knocking on a door. He and Max would fly away from each other like birds.

There would be a key turned in a lock. And perhaps a scream. And shame.

He and Max would probably be securely locked up in their respective houses of correction. And it would be all over with their dreams and plans to make their careers in Berlin.

But in his dreams he saw Max. Max walked through a long hallway further and further away from him. A pink light enveloped his body as if he were wearing tights of very fine silk. You could see each and every one of his muscles, and he floated across the floor as if walking a tightrope.

He woke up and thought that if he and Max could become circus acrobats, they could travel together. They could pose as brothers. He would perform as a clown. He would step into the ring and begin to laugh, just laugh, until every one in the tent was laughing. And just then he would burst into tears until streaks formed on his cheeks. And Max. Max is so beautiful that it doesn't matter what he does. He would simply sit and gaze at him, proudly and triumphantly, like when you gaze at your beloved.

For a moment he was so happy that the only thing he wished for was money. He wanted to give Max a present for Christmas.

On that Christmas Eve he was all by himself in the hotel. And he began writing a letter home to Peter.

'*Christmas Eve 85.*

Thank you, dear Don, for your letter and for taking care of the money. No – my friend – I will not go to bed but will write to you and then go out to look at this city's windows behind which so many strangers are celebrating Christmas. Everyone here at the hotel has a Christmas tree, the waiters, the maids, the hotel keeper and the grooms. In my thoughts I can see your tree at your manager's and next to it your tree from last year. How sober-minded you have become – that comes with age. This thing we call love is difficult to deal with – like the hammock at Hotel Marienlyst – but once you are there, you feel good and comfortable.

I will not trouble you. But let's say that a bee could possibly settle on your nose, and the pain that this bee causes you (perhaps it is only a quick afterthought on the part of the bee) would at once remind you that our habit is to make life narrower, to reduce sensitivity – in short, make yourself less young.

But let us not talk about that. I always avoid talking about these things as far as the lives of my closest friends are concerned since I cannot know them fully. Falling in love is one of these things. Until I have seen one of my acquaintances drunk, I don't know how he behaves when drunk – how love shapes you, my friends – what you seek in it, what you seek to complete through love in yourselves – that I don't know.

Cannot judge either how this or that woman can effect the growth of bad or better qualities in you.

In that regard you leave me unworried. You love too little to let yourself be changed fundamentally. If that were not the case, perhaps some of the women with whom you have lived would have caused me to be anxious for your sake. But the thing is that you in reality, like so many souls who are basically extremely pessimistic (due to an unconscious feeling of weakness, I wonder?), give up love from the outset, that is, you don't make great demands apart from pleasure or a certain interest – and reserve the noblest and deepest sides of your nature for the devotion that you give certain individuals who are less demanding, that is, who ask less of you, are less central.

And still I wish, in spite of all I know, that I will receive your quiet but deep devotion – that one fine day a great desire will seize you and take you away from everything but this one thing: your passion.'

Now Don will shrug his shoulders and think that he is much too sentimental. And why does he talk about passion, anyway?

He reaches for Max's parcel. He opens the gift and expects to find a book. But inside are letters. A woman's right-slanted handwriting on pink stationery. Julie's letters. Words of love came rushing towards him. And perfume, silk ribbons, pressed flowers. And a dried red rose stuck in a letter whose corners have been singed, most likely with a curling iron.

This is how he would have written to Max had he dared. This is how he would have wished that Max had written to him: 'I am waiting for you, my love. Yesterday I waited in vain.' Or: 'You came towards me. Your blond hair, your eyes framed by black lashes as shiny and curved as the bright feathers on the drake. You brushed against my shoulder. A branch of glowing flowers ruptured under my skin.'

Is it a gift? Revenge? Or simply a way of recommending yourself?

On Christmas night he will read the pink letters. And he will finish the letter to Don. And then he will write yet another letter. He will write to Mrs Ferslew and tell her how hard he has worked and how little he has earned. She will understand that he has to get out of the hotel where the bill is ballooning. That he needs a home, just two rooms where he can work undisturbed and receive guests once in a while. She would understand that. And at Christmas you are allowed to make wishes.

*

'Now, be reasonable, dear Bang,' Mrs Ferslew reprimanded him in her New Year's letter. But she understands that he is longing for a home and sends him money. Much more than he had dared to hope for. He can pay his hotel bill, he can rent two rooms, he can eat. That is, if he could eat at all. The bread sticks in his throat, and he coughs, and he must force himself to drink a little wine or water to keep it down. His clothes hang like a sack on his frame.

But on the table in his new lodgings are irises and lillies. And he has bought a palm that wasn't terribly expensive. And the afghan is draped over the easy chair. Candles are lit. And Max Eisfeld is impressed.

Max with his blue eyes and blue tie drinks in a gentlemanly way only very little, while he himself is so nervous and so happy that he could empty the glass of white wine in one single draught. He offers him fruit, sweets and cigarettes, and for the first time it bothers him that the fingers on his right hand are yellow although he has washed himself thoroughly in ice-cold water and eau de cologne and polished all of his twenty nails and pomaded his hair.

Max is relaxed, almost arrogant. And yet. There is a little tic by his left eye. It encourages him.

'Thank you for the letters, who is Julie?'

'A colleague. We are good friends – she and I.'

He is both relieved and upset about the word 'friends'. But at the same time he knows that he would stomp on the faces of his friends with his heel to get just one smile from Max.

Max Eisfeld loves him. Like a bird against the window. He drops his glass on the floor, that's how suddenly the truth hits him. And shards bring luck. And they are both young and beautiful and free. And the landlady is visiting her sister as luck would have it.

And they move as gracefully as swifts mating in flight, rising towards the light. Max is as beautiful as an angel. Even his sweat smells sweet. For a moment he leans his head against Max's shoulder and dreams of being lifted towards the light, carried like a child.

There are small, fine wrinkles at the corners of Max's eyes. In a few years time, there will be crow's feet. He was moved knowing this, and knowing that the skin of his hips is sensitive and very white, and that his lips in his sleep take on a satisfied and childish expression.

'Darling. My own darling.'

Max gets up and stops for a moment under the lamp's globe, wearing only the light.

'One day I will write about you – '

'Will you write me letters?'

'If I were to write you a letter, you must burn it immediately. – But I will write about you.'

'About me? – You mean in your reviews?'

'Yes. In *Berliner Tageblatt*. That's where I will write.'

They drink the last sips of wine from the same glass. And Max Eisfeld is gone long before the landlady's steps are heard on the stairs.

Love, he thinks, is to be two together and to be happy.

Finally he is able to write about Berlin. Only now does he notice that the city has not received him as a stranger but as a guest. 'Write,' the editors have said. And they have received his articles with enthusiasm. As if they were in need of exactly his talent.

Berlin is the city that 'opens up its doors to a stranger. Privately, too, the "metropolitan", the Berliner, has learned the kind of hospitality, the gesture of giving the stranger a helping hand, which stems from his eagerness to gather everything and everybody in his city.'

Finally, here he can work.

Of course, it is disruptive when a nice young man wants to pay him a visit just now. He doesn't know him, and it is not even twelve o'clock yet. But since he has already been interrupted, he might as well hear what the man wants. Just to get it over with.

Whether Herman Bang likes Berlin? What does he do in Berlin? What does he live on? Is he married? Where was he born? Where might he be travelling to? How long will he stay?

Always. Maybe always. But why must he answer all these questions?

The gentleman replies that it is only reasonable that visitors attract attention, and he hands him a visiting card that turns out to be a police identification card.

'Where do you publish, Mr Bang? We would like to have a complete list.'

'But why?'

'It is just a formality.'

German, Danish, Swedish and Norwegian newspapers, journals and publishers. He writes while the gentleman watches his hand that begins to tremble as if it is about to cramp up.

'Isn't one missing?'

He adds *Bergens Tidende* to the bottom of the list.

The gentleman says goodbye and leaves.

From the window he sees him turn the corner. He then lies down on the bed, and every time he tries to get up, he sinks back in yet another swoon.

Bergens Tidende. He pushed the thought aside, far away. As long as the police don't take an interest in Max and him.

Time crawls along on its small black insect legs. Finally he falls asleep and dreams an endless dream about sleeplessness.

But the next morning he puts on his fur coat to deliver a couple of articles to *Berliner Tageblatt*, and on the way he goes by the university to see Doctor Hoffory. Not because he knows him personally or has any wish to meet him. But solely because this doctor in his youth was expelled from the University of Copenhagen.

Hoffory receives him with a smile, he is very young for a doctor.

And they lunch together while talking about the metropolis of Berlin and the backwater of Copenhagen.

'Berlin is a city for a man like you,' says the doctor. 'In no other place in the world is there as much freedom as here in Berlin.'

'The police paid me a visit yesterday.'

'It was just a formality. You will be happy here – You will be received with open arms. People like you are needed.'

'Do you think so?'

'Now listen. I was expelled from the University of Copenhagen because I attended a party where a gentleman was wearing a pink tailcoat. I myself was very drunk and recited the Lord's Prayer. – Here in Berlin I am a doctor.'

'One can only hope – '

'Let us make a bet. You will be successful. And I will be a professor. That's how Berlin is.'

That night he slept soundly, and he was still in his deepest sleep when his landlady knocked. She stuck her head round the door which gave him the opportunity to notice that she wore a hairnet to bed and that her nightdress wasn't entirely clean.

'There is a gentleman here to see you.'

He looked at the clock. It was half past seven.

'Would you please tell the gentleman to come back later.'

'That won't do. He is from the police.'

His hands are shaking when he gets dressed. It must be a misunderstanding. At any rate, it is not just a formality being apprehended before eight o'clock.

'What do you want from me?'

The constable only asks if he prefers to take a cab, and if he usually takes first-class or second-class cabs.

First-class. Naturally first-class.

And he leans back in the carriage and tries to look relaxed. He is thinking about Nini and about Sofie. If they knew that he had been apprehended by the police. He sees servant girls running with baskets full of fresh bread. A woman emptying a bucket on the sidewalk, a cat running off on her wet paws. And the postman. Perhaps the very postman who will bring him money.

Finally the carriage comes to a halt, and he, the impeccably dressed Herman de Bang, is placed in a room with vagrants, minor offenders and drunks.

He waits for a long time. At ten o'clock he ventures to ask how long you usually have to wait. No one knows. It varies.

At long last he is called in to a desk where he is lectured about expulsion. He has to be out of Prussia in twenty-four hours, otherwise he will be transported to the border after having served a sentence.

'But the reason?' he asks. 'What is the reason?'

'Will you please sign? – No reasons are given here.'

'But I am not some carpenter's apprentice who can pack his knapsack just like that. An expulsion will attract attention.'

'Surely it is not as bad as all that.'

The man points at the spot on the paper where he has to sign.

'But forty-eight hours – could you just give me forty-eight hours to pack up and leave.'

The man nods and waves him away like a fly.

He goes to *Berliner Tageblatt* to say goodbye to Arthur Levysohn. Levysohn looks suddenly affectionate and eager behind his gold-rimmed glasses. 'That expulsion. It is the chance of a lifetime. Hurry off to the photographer. We need new pictures, and we will take anything that comes from your pen. Of course, it is a misunderstanding. But in twenty-four hours everyone in Germany will know your name. Write. Hurry home and write.'

Arthur Levysohn offers him strong coffee and shakes his hand before he practically commands him to go home and write. It is simply the most brilliant prospect for success that Bang has ever been offered. All the liberals are excited. At all the liberal papers the best journalists are dipping their pens to weave a martyr's crown of words for him to wear.

He drives out to the envoy himself to present his case. The envoy is speechless and promises to contact Prince Herbert von Bismarck the same day.

And then it happens, unfortunately, that Prince Bismarck puts a newspaper down in front of the envoy. *Bergens Tidende* has been forwarded to Berlin by the Norwegian consul. Inside is an article. A short, second-rate piece that Herman Bang wrote in October. He wrote it one evening in Hamburg after having seen the faces of the Hohenzollerns at a photographic exhibition. The article was easily written. And he needed the money. He doesn't remember if he was ever paid. But the words are there:

'The kaiser – the kaiser – he has become a trembling old man: William the Conqueror … The military mask has dropped off. Everyone knows this face of a non-commissioned officer whose entire substance speaks of callousness … How little soul there is in those Hohenzollern faces.

Look at the crown prince. He looks like a cavalry officer who knows how to swing his saber without pretension, as it happens, for he knows very well that this is all he is capable of. It seems that fate intended him to be a commander of a parlour.

His son is Prince Wilhelm. You can tell he is of the third generation. All too clearly. He does not understand how to project the traditional broadness of the Hohenzollern males. He takes up combative poses with a blasé smile, and his face, which is more refined than those of his grandfather and father, does not express anything but cold and detached indifference …

His little son – has a mouth that reaches up to his ears.

People say about thrones: "They are sometimes so shaky these days that they collapse on top of those who are waiting to ascend them.'"

*

And he ought to have known. He knew of course that you can say anything about the state and about the city of Berlin. But the kaiser is ninety and more of a god than a person. The kaiser is a symbol, and he and his family cannot be critized.

And all that is left to do is to pack one's suitcases and move on. And to send a telegram to *Bergens Tidende*: 'Stop the article. Don't pass it on. For my sake. It is a life-and-death situation.' And it is even worse having to go to *Berliner Tageblatt* and ask for their silence.

The photographs. He still has them as postcards. He bought a whole stack of them that time at the exhibition in Hamburg. He looked at them while writing his article. Sucked all life and facial expressions out of them while writing. He laughed at the kaiser who rode in an enormous automobile, gruff and heavy under a bizarre antique headdress. 'Good morning, Sofie,' he wrote and sent it off to his younger sister. Nini got the prince in his hunting costume.

That evening the photographs were a joke. And became so again, later on. He sent them to his nephews and nieces, and it was like confidental, self-deprecating laughter: 'I, too, was young once. And committed blunders – '

9.

On the main street of the principality of Meiningen, where all the merchants were purveyors to the court, a fur-clad gentleman who looked like a young count was strolling along. He installed himself at Hotel Erbprinz. It was noted that the establishment housed the banished poet and journalist Herman Bang. But everyone was polite and pretended that they didn't have any inkling of what had happened to him.

He spends most of the day in his room. He says he is working and that he doesn't want to be disturbed. In reality he is lying on his bed with a cold, damp handkerchief on his forehead, trying to muster enough strength to write letters. He needs to send word to his closest relatives, and he needs money. The banishment itself came like a bolt out of the blue. But he is actually very calm, not paralysed. Just quiet. Only one thing is certain, he wants to return to Berlin.

'I must go back. The strange place where I find myself now is part of this plan. Here you are close to a duke. And this duke, who is married to an actress and who is a theatre director himself, is intimately connected to the court in Berlin. I will make a plea to disregard said article. It is the only thing to be done,' he writes to Peter.

And Peter Nansen suggests he should write a humorous article about his banishment.

'No, my friend – humorous! Thank you. One must sacrifice the smaller things for the greater. And I wish to succeed in Germany.

And Germany is Berlin.'

Emil Jonas is both angry and disappointed. How will he now be able to sell anything by Herman Bang in Berlin? Perhaps the only possibility is to obtain a pardon from the kaiser. That's what Councillor Emil Jonas will personally advise him to do.

He imagines how he will prostrate himself on the floor in front of the throne, penitently and dressed in black. And the gruff ninety-year old gentleman will just shake his head. No:

'Such an action would be futile. If I were the kaiser, I would not forgive the boy who had so recklessly written those foolish things in the Norwegian paper – until the same boy through his labour had shown that he deserves forgiveness.'

Taking back your words is not enough. Even if he had literally swallowed the entire Norwegian article right in front of the kaiser's throne, it wouldn't have been enough. He will simply have to prove that he has become an entirely different person. Wise, noble and distinguished, altogether different from the young journalist. And until then, he will have to write under a pseudonym if that is possible.

'If you, dear Councillor, believe that a pseudonym is possible – if I don't live in Berlin it will be easier to keep it a secret – then I will stay in Germany, and after having struggled for years to secure just one name, I will struggle for the next seven years to get an additional one.

I think, dear Councillor, that though you might still be angry at me for my recklessness, you do harbour a bit of affection for me in your old heart. I now beg you to look into the matter and seriously consider the options.

Your letter to me will be crucial for my future.

Do you think I could live in Leipzig? Please, consider this as well. Staying here will be mentally stultifying in the long run. Leipzig has many advantages. The envoy told me that the government will not take any steps to prevent me from living somewhere else in Germany.

If your answer is: "Using a pseudonym is difficult if not impossible. In my opinion your position in Germany is impossible" – then I will leave.

The Moor has failed. – The Moor may leave.'

Those are the kind of letters he writes in Meiningen. But every single evening he is transformed into the city's most elegant gentleman, and he sits in one of the most expensive seats in the duke's theatre even though the progress of the play is wooden and the actors' recitations are boring. And when the soldiers who have been called out to serve as extras, shoot and let out a roar in the wings, he jumps in his seat.

But he craves being in the same space as the duke and the duchess. He watches the duke enter his box with the duchess, the actress Ellen Franz. Then the lights are dimmed. But even in the darkness he watches them through his opera glasses. He can see the pearls around the duchess' neck. The padding in her high-piled hair, the pores in her skin, the duke's beard that perhaps is dyed. But they don't see him, the recently arrived poet, the city's most elegant gentleman.

And it wouldn't have helped, if they had seen him. For on the third of February the receptionist looks the other way rather demonstratively when he, the guest, reaches for the *Hamburger Nachrichten* that he wants to read with his morning coffee.

In the paper is a serial story about journalist and infamous author Herman Bang. H. V. Boldt, Master of Law, has written a 'Copenhagen Letter' on the occasion of Herman Bang's banishment. It emerges that he is the son of an eccentric pastor and morphinist. He has several years of imprisonment due to him in Denmark, and as he was born on Als and is therefore a Schleswiger by birth, the correction might as well take place in Germany.

He puts the newspaper down. He drinks his coffee. Does he smile at the receptionist? Yes, he actually manages to smile and ask for his mail.

There are two letters from Copenhagen. One is from the loan shark Andreasen and the other from Ottosen. Just think that she, the sometime lovely lady, has taken the trouble to write to him. She probably misses him. She would scold him. But he was the only one of her renters that she didn't quarrel with.

The letter turns out to be from her husband who informs him

rather laconically that he has read Boldt's article in *Politiken* and now wants his two hundred kroner back immediately. And he makes terrible threats should the payment not be made.

And he had happily forgotten about that money. But now he recalls the wife's arms around his neck – and those arms could lift him up and crush him as though he were nothing. But all she said was: 'Let's forget about the last two hundred for the time being.'

Well, that was her way of putting it.

But then the banishment is a known fact in Denmark as well. And people have been able to read Boldt's article in Peter Nansen's newspaper – and especially in Edvard Brandes' paper.

And Peter with his handsome appearance couldn't do anything about it at the editorial office. And Mrs Ottosen with her bony arms and flat backside couldn't do anything about it against her husband's will.

Ottosen and Andreasen, both of them.

Julius – the only hope left is Julius Schiøtt. He will have to go to the creditors and ask them to take human suffering into account.

He will have to write to Nini and Sofie himself and try to make them understand that he is innocent. Nini will shake her head and say that where there is smoke there is fire. But she absolutely must help him with money. Holst is a wealthy man.

And Boldt's article. – If someone could stop it. Or if somebody could respond to it on his behalf. And state that it wasn't true.

Suddenly he realizes that Berlin now is further away than ever before and that he might not even be able to stay in the dull little principality of Meiningen.

He opens Andreasen's letter just to make sure. It's what you would expect. And he sinks into a state of blissful unconsciousness, where he wishes to remain.

But the sound of footsteps forces its way into the soft, nauseating darkness. The kind of grand, disciplined, almost dancing steps that you can only learn at the theatre. They come closer, very close. And only those steps can make him open his eyes.

Through a fog he sees Max.

Max, standing just inside the door.

Max, looking at him, horrified, fondly.

Max who makes him jump up. And the first thought that comes into his head is whether he looks decent. But the image reflected in the mirror is hazy.

And if Max Eisfeld would put his arms around him.

If only he himself could sink into Max's arms.

For a moment they both stand still. One of them dizzy. The other one ramrod straight. Then Max takes the first step and the next three steps. 'I was just passing – on my way to Vienna. I heard that you were here.'

And the people in the city notice two handsome young men strolling along the streets together. They radiate a kind of happiness that seems provocative. Especially considering Herman Bang's situation.

They even have the audacity to go to the theatre together. To look at each other and smile. And sometimes there is something ironic in those smiles.

But the letter to Julius was sent off.

'In all probablity you have read the lampoon in *Politiken*. That a fellow countryman can stoop so low as to write the like is inconceivable to me. Just think, what an ocean of meanness – and how defenceless I am in this foreign country.'

Just then he realizes that what he had hoped for was that Peter or Julius or Cantor had reacted to the article. That they would have said that they knew him personally. That his father, the pastor, had been insane. That it was a misfortune, a sad situation that ought to have stirred compassion, and that the son Herman Bang was their friend and not at all a criminal.

But that much he cannot ask for. He has no hope of receiving moral support – just a bit of practical, financial help:

'I beg you, dear friend, to talk to Ottosen. The man is going to place an advertisement in the Scandinavian papers that will complete my ruin. He is the most stony-hearted person on earth, but the limited standing that I still have he probably won't destroy for the sake of his two hundred filthy kroner.'

Julius must be able to explain to him that under no circumstance will it pay to make the debt public.

Still worse is the situation with Andreasen who doesn't want to understand that until the writer Herman Bang has submitted a manuscript, no money can be collected from the publisher. But now Mr Andreasen has learned that Mr Bang evidently has other sources of income.

'Enclosed is the letter received from Andreasen today. You can see his threats for yourself. He wants a bank transfer from *Politiken*. But both a share of the wages from Schou and the entire catch from *Politiken* – a scanty catch at that – would be impossible to grant him, however. Do go and see him, dear Julius, and show him the book imprint so he will believe us.'

Julius will have to do it. He is, after all, both his childhood friend and his editor.

But Max came because he loves him.

Max Eisfeld offered to respond to the lampoon in *Hamburger Nachrichten*. But he shook his head and sealed his lips with a kiss. Writing a public response would be to give himself away.

He walked back to his own room from Max Eisfeld's.

The police knocked on Herman Bang's door at five o'clock in the morning.

He had expected it and had thought about whom to notify.

'*Meiningen 19-2-86*

This is just a brief letter, dear Mrs Ferslew, as I am so exhausted that I can hardly hold a pen. This morning at five o'clock I was awoken by the police. I went to the city hall and learned that I have been banished from Meiningen. That is, from Germany – for the foreign ministry in Berlin has informed the governments of all the duchies and principalities that my presence in the empire is no longer tolerated. This new blow has almost knocked me to the ground. I have fought so desperately here and suffered so much.

Counting from this evening, I have twenty-four hours before having to leave. This month I have sent out twenty-one articles, and I have only received 120 marks from the entire world. I am now facing banishment without any means. I will not send telegrams home. That will only get the drums beating again. I have only written about the banishment to you, no one else in Scandinavia, and to two business people in Germany. Otherwise, I have just made it known that I have left for Vienna.

It is no use going to Denmark. What can they offer me there: a newspaper that I have no sympathy with – friends who are now enemies, and enemies who are apparently now friends.

I must go to Vienna with the little that I have. I will arrive without a penny. I have only you to rely on. I just need two weeks of rest – for these battles and the emotional turmoil have nearly destroyed me. Naturally, in Vienna I will be at risk from starvation, literally – but I will be stronger than my troubles. I will get my position in Berlin back when the emperor pardons me, and as far as my new book goes, I am writing day and night. – – – Reason for banishment: (I was informed by the minister here) only the Bergen article (and Boldt, I believe).

Herman Bang,
poste restante
Vienna.'

'Events are moving in my favour,' he says and smiles to Max who sits across from him in the third-class compartment.

Max shakes his head, and Max is always right. Poverty is eating them up. And he wishes that he, like his mother, had strength enough to bend down and rinse his hands in the glassy pond.

Perhaps it is love itself that makes him see her person in front of him, so young and always ready to laugh.

But there is another face that merges with hers. A woman he saw years ago. A young woman he saw through a window at a small Danish country station. Sitting between palms and blooming cacti, staring out at the train with the large, shiny eyes of an unwell person. She didn't move at all. She just sat there resting her head in her hands.[18]

He starts writing notes on a napkin, and when Max asks him what he is doing, he starts telling him about the stationmaster's wife Katinka.

'But in the end – what happens in the end?'

'He leaves, and she dies.'

Max shakes his head. 'Is that what you have to offer your lovers?'

'No, – in Vienna we will rent a small apartment. In Vienna we will disappear into the crowd. But meanwhile a hotel will do.'

And will the fur, the duke's visiting card and the three suitcases be sufficiently impressive to obtain room and board on credit?

They impress sufficiently at Hotel Hammerand. But his hand is shaking when he signs in, and as soon as he is in his room he gathers everything that can be pawned: the silver writing tools, two golden rings, a silk vest, the not-too-threadbare tailcoat that he wore so often to the theatre. The fur he is still wearing. But the air is warming up a bit. Perhaps he can do without the fur. He tiptoes past Max's door, nods to the receptionist and looks without doubt like a tourist who wants to take a bit of fresh air before dinner.

He drifts down the main street and then on a sudden impulse turns on to one of the side streets. And the only annoying thing about that pawnshop is the way the man shakes the fur before throwing it into the heap of other furs where it most definitely will be infested with fleas.

He looks at himself in the shop window and thinks he resembles a skinned cat, but the money is whispering in his pocket.

He knocks on Max's door: 'Come, let's go out on the town. We are going to see Vienna.'

'Yes, but aren't you going to wear your fur coat?'

'We will eat it. And afterwards I will appeal to my creditors.'

Late at night he borrows a pen in reception and writes to Councillor Emil Jonas on his last sheet of rose-coloured paper with gilded edges. He has kept it for eight years and has really wanted to write Max a poem on it. Now it will be used to plead for an advance: 'Dear Sir, I am writing on this fine paper because I don't have anything else.'

And if Emil Jonas could just send him a small amount, he will settle for a third of the honorarium for translated texts in the future.

And he writes to Nini. And he moans to Peter Nansen: 'Good God – such a misery. What would my entire life be worth, if so many tragedies, a certain amount of talent and a good deal of resignation would not one day give rise to a *great* work?'

But he doesn't miss the fur coat. When he and Max stroll along the streets of Vienna, the city becomes an erotic landscape. And it is a mild spring, the sun shines through the leafless trees on the avenues, and there is a throng of people and carriages. 'Every street urchin knows that he is "Viennese", every woman knows that it is her duty to look as beautiful as possible or in any case as un-hideous as possible. And this dying city has yet another charm for the sophisticated: decadence. All women are yearning, and every man looks as if he wants to possess them all – and does what he can to achieve it … little by little.'

He jots down notes and wishes that he could afford just to enjoy the city when Max asks if he wants to join him at the theatre.

'My tailcoat has been pawned – and my gloves.'

'The *Sulkowsky Theater* is a theatre school. I act there gratis. The others are students and have to pay to act. The theatre is located out in Wieden in a dilapidated palace. And I have looked at a couple of rooms in the vicinity.'

'After I have paid the bill, we have no money for a deposit.'

'I spoke with the landlady. – The first month is free of charge.'

They go by tram through areas that are so dreary that even the slums of Copenhagen with their firetraps seem less grey and hopeless. They walk the last stretch, and there at the outskirts of the city is the palace in a garden where the weeds have long since choked the roses and peonies.

Once seated in the theatre, he felt no hunger, fatigue or pain. Max Eisfeld introduced him to the professor and the students. They decided that he should observe some of the rehearsals and perhaps write about the theatre. They had to run through the park to catch the last tram. That night he slept without a sedative, and the next morning he collected his mail.

There were two letters. One from Nini, he kissed the envelope as soon as he was in his room, one from Emil Jonas, hopefully money. And then a journal, *Freiheit* – the international anarchists' magazine.

He opened the magazine without any misgivings. Rather, he took his time in order to delay the moment when he would have to read his actual letters. And then – right there was the dreadful article about the emperor and his family. The story was splashed across the page with a picture of the banished writer and journalist. It didn't help that they called him 'the learned Dane Herman Bang'. Apparently now he was an anarchist as well. It would be of no use to object, neither would a fainting spell do any good. He let the magazine drop on the floor before opening the letter from his beloved sister.

Nini's words appeared in a fog, and regardless of how much he blinked, the words reached him slowly as if through water. She couldn't ask her husband for money, she informed him.

So, she simply believed he was lying.

If she knew the state he was in, she would have sold all her jewelry and the two silver candelabra and the silver spoons. She would have implored her husband or else forged his signature. No, not the latter part. Nini was honest and proud.

He tore the letter into many bits.

That's how far they had grown apart.

Emil Jonas wrote very kindly that presently it was difficult for him to sell anything by Herman Bang. The eight hundred marks that Schorer had paid in advance were not even close to matching the repayment. Unfortunately he was not able to help him financially himself. He couldn't even afford a short vacation. He and his wife were condemned to spend the entire summer in Berlin. And it would no doubt be stifling hot.

Once again he looked at his name under the article and knew that now it would be even more difficult for Emil Jonas to sell his short stories. Schorer's homely family magazine would most likely have none of it. He felt himself far, far removed from the enchanted city of Berlin. Then Max came and asked if anything had changed. He handed him *Freiheit* and shook his head. Keeping his chin up he paid the hotel bill, but he had to ask Max to pay for the tram.

Their new home turned out to be a room with two iron beds, two chairs and a table, and with access to a shabby parlour where a rather motley crew of characters were playing cards.

'Max, are you saying that we can work in this place?'

Max nodded and began rehearsing Don Carlos rather demonstratively. His voice rose from a soft longing to a pitch of anger and despair that could make a stone weep. Even the ugly stones behind the yellow wallpaper where the bedbugs were hiding.

He himself sat down to rework 'Son altesse' and decided to send the princess to a convent.[19] He revised a few things in an article about snow. And he felt elated that the weekly magazines were anticipating Christmas. And now Councillor Emil Jonas had to understand that it was serious:

'If you haven't sent any money – then send it right away. I found yesterday – in an outlying district, in a slum – a room full of bedbugs, and cannot afford it.

My last pennies went on buying stamps and paper. Even thirty marks would be of help for the moment. I will stay here for the summer to save money.'

Afterwards they moved the beds out from the walls, and he sprayed them with eau de cologne to safeguard against the bugs.

On the stairs he had stepped in some filth from a rat or a cat. He would never have debased himself to wear the shoes again had he had another pair. Now he could only hope to be able to scrape off the muck on his way to the theatre.

Max was once again immersed in his role. He addressed a crack in the wallpaper as if it were his beloved. He, for his part, returned to his manuscript, to the childhood of his unhappy princess, and he let her have dance lessons with a chair as partner.

They walked to and from the theatre. And they collapsed on beds that looked like the lairs of wild animals. Luckily for them they didn't sleep in each other's arms, for at five in the morning two policemen knocked on their door.

It was fortunate that Max Eisfeld could confirm that he had come to Vienna to perform at the *Sulkowsky Theater*, hoping that he could later get engagements at one of the big Viennese theatres. It was only due to poverty that they were forced to share a room, he remarked so innocently that the men immediately turned to the anarchist Herman Bang.

But that morning at five o'clock he was self-assured, genteel and arrogant. The article was a mistake, but he denied having any connection with the anarchists. He pointed out that he had had an audience with the Russian Empress. He mentioned his grandfather without it making any impression on the men, and he handed them his visiting card.

They detected poverty and eau de cologne. They hinted that he likely was funded by a secret anarchist organization, that he was exploiting Mr Eisfeld and performed acts that were against the natural order of things.

Finally they left.

He clutched Max's hand. His own hand was shaking. They listened for footsteps. Maybe one of the men had remained standing outside, maybe they had gone down only one flight of stairs in order to return quickly. No, they retreated swiftly and without stepping in anything whatsoever.

They heard the front door slam shut. And they made love desperately without noticing the skin of the beloved, prepared to flee from one another. He knew that Max was and always would be a prince with smooth eyelids and lashes that were very long and dark in comparison with his hair. He would rather die than lose him.

They both knew that they had to separate. From now on two policemen would be keeping watch night and day on their hands, feet and lips.

'I will return to Berlin as soon as I have finished acting here. – Will you write about me?'

'Yes, I promise.'

Every day he accompanied Max Eisfeld to the theatre. He watched the rehearsals and got to know the professor. He admired the professor's technique that encouraged the students to draw on themselves instead of imitating celebrities.

Proud and deeply moved he watched his beloved on the stage. He watched the prince fight defiantly and fiercely for his love. And this surge of emotion was not due to the dark-haired girl in her silk skirt. She was no more important to Max Eisfeld than a crack in the wallpaper. Max loved him.

That same evening he wrote his review and sent it to Emil Jonas along with the article on the theatre.

'You shouldn't advertise so strongly for your personal acquaintances,' replied the Councillor.

'Dear me. Two lines about Mr Eisfeld. – Does that amount to a lot of advertising?'

But this means that they must know about it in Berlin.

Finally a money order arrived from *Politiken*. – Very disappointing. Only a fraction of his travel pieces and articles had been accepted. But at least he could pay the landlady a small instalment and have dinner with Max for the last time.

At the café he only wanted to touch Max's hands with their fine, manicured nails. It occurred to him that his beloved was able to groom himself as perfectly and cheaply as a cat.

But just then they caught a glimpse in the wall mirror of two persons they knew. Two young gentlemen in police uniform were enjoying a meal very close to their table.

Max Eisfeld stood up. With the suitcase in his hand he turned around one last time and smiled with lips that would tempt any man or woman to kiss him. And then he was gone.

Bang returned to his room alone where there was only work, fainting spells, seizures, bugs dropping tirelessly from the ceiling and finding their way under his clothes. And the landlady who reminded him every day of the rent.

For four days he lived on two eggs and a chunk of bread. And the same dream appeared again and again.

He knows he is dreaming. And in the dream a body lies close to his own. He stretches out his arm, maybe because he wants to wake up. But in the dream the body is firm and warm. He and his lover huddle like two birds in a nest.

Just then a sense of dizziness occurs. A trembling and a creaking. Somebody is shaking the tree with such force that all the branches quiver.

He wakes up and knows that he has had a seizure.

*

One night he woke up. The landlady and two large lodgers were looking down at him in his bed and talking about cholera.

Early the next morning he jumped on a tram and rode to Hotel Hammerand where they showed him to a room right away, for he had no debt there, after all.

10.

He telegraphed Max Eisfeld:

'Thank you, my friend, for everything. For every kind and encouraging word – for all your help.

Herman'

If only Max could be with him at Hotel Hammerand. Max who thought that his friend didn't give love enough room. The hero leaves, the heroine dies. Sad. But not sentimental, no, not at all sentimental. For he wants to weave some gallows humour into the story about Katinka – the stationmaster's lovely wife. He can still see her face, a soft, resigned face as if her longing had tired after having fluttered against the window. She has kinship with his mother; she who broke like a delicate flower.

And there are other pictures that reveal themselves. Other books that he must write. The book about Copenhagen. When he strolls around Vienna, he compares it with Copenhagen. Or rather: Copenhagen lies like a shadow behind the houses – or under the cobblestones, like a happy sunken city right there where he is walking. Copenhagen – the city that made him dream. The city that gave her children everything and then devoured them. A city with its theatres and facades that instilled in its youth the hope of obtaining easy money and fame.

And then the collapse.[20] For a young man it was unforseeable. Only exhausted women, housewives who were accustomed to reckoning, would have suspected it. The dreamers were innocent. Adolf Riemenschneider was innocent. Bang will defend him in his book. The book about his generation. And about the city. And he won't return to Copenhagen before that book has been written. First *By the Road* about Katinka and the confinement of love in the seemingly idyllic provincial town.[21] And then the great work – about the city. And he is consumed by longing, desperate longing.

But if he really wanted to, he could stroll along the fashionable shopping street Strøget in the city of his youth. *Dagbladet* has offered him a permanent position as chief editor.

It was a flattering offer. Nothing else. He didn't consider it seriously.

Councillor Emil Jonas' paternalistic concern was depressing. Not to speak of Mr Schorer's remark that Mr Bang has apparently lost his talent. Once upon a time he could write eight short-story drafts in five days. But now – where are the manuscripts? The editor of *Schorers Familienblatt* is not amused.

If they would only believe him when he says that he is working on something bigger. *By the Road* could be an excellent serial. The ladies would recognize Louise the Eldest and Ida the Youngest and their mother hen. They would shake their heads and feel sorrow for the teacher Miss Jensen with her pug and her variegated artificial hair. Agnes, the intelligent, awkward daughter of the pastor with her big troubled heart, they would hold her dear. And the little woman who becomes pregnant again and again and weeps at the thought of it not stopping until she is old. And the happy girl who gets her lieutenant and is later tyrannized by a captain. And Katinka – especially Katinka whose girlish dreams don't measure up to the realities of marriage. What do they say to each other, Katinka and Huus? Bang doesn't know. Love makes them as mute as fish. And suddenly he thinks that Huus, the foreman, is a terribly thin fellow.

He takes a walk at dusk. It is several days since he has been out for a walk. He follows the strolling couples. He notices how their hands and eyes meet. How their bodies lean towards each other almost imperceptibly. And then they disappear into cafés and tearooms.

Perhaps it would help if he himself could go in and drink a cup of hot coffee and eat a piece of cake covered in dark, shiny chocolate that would snap under the fork. No, that is not Katinka's cake. Katinka bakes pound cakes. Butter, sugar, flour, nine or perhaps ten eggs and a touch of lemon. Katinka's cakes are basic – nice, honest and light.

When he returns to the hotel, a telegram from *Politiken* is waiting for him. He opens it with trepidation. Telegrams never arrive with money, but rather with bad news or words of congratulation. And he certainly doesn't expect any of the latter kind.

And yet: Hørup is offering him Edvard Brandes' position at *Politiken*. Brandes has left the paper, and Peter Nansen has followed him. If Herman Bang accepts, the position is his. He must respond immediately.

It feels like a conspiracy, as if everyone wants him to return exactly now when he has decided to stay. He could send a telegram right away with a 'yes'. He could ask for money. He could pay his bills, purchase a first-class train ticket and leave for Copenhagen. And there he could settle behind a desk, call himself chief editor and draw a proper salary, preside over the entire newspaper, compete with Ferslew and take his revenge on him – and finally, finally take his revenge on the Brandes brothers. He will show them what he can accomplish with his 'petticoat-brains'.

But Peter. – Peter Nansen has left with Edvard Brandes without uttering a single word about it to him. That settles it:

'*Vienna. Hotel Hammerand. 8th District. Sunday.*

My dear Peter.

Nothing can describe my surprise at receiving the enclosed letter.

As I already telegraphed you, I replied with a *no*. First I will tell you my reasons for doing so – for saying no – which it is impossible for me to change to a yes. I find *your* decision regrettable. Of course, I don't know if you have something better, but I find it unfortunate that you should leave a paper whose great success is linked to you and your name. Perhaps I also feel personally that you ought to have written to me a week ago before taking this step, dear Peter, in which case I would have been less worried for you and your affairs. In short, your decision seems "reckless" to me, but nothing will convince me to enter the place that you have left. There must be reasons for Brandes leaving, I suppose, and for your following him. But what connected me with *Politiken* was you, and when you are no longer there, I cannot imagine working every day with people to whom I otherwise feel quite distant.'

Councillor, translator, literary agent Emil Jonas is appalled. Interest in the works of Herman Bang might exist in some small place or other, but it is not in Berlin. There are no sales of his translated texts, no commissions. Jonas advises him to accept the offer from *Politiken*.

But no, no and again no.

'And I will tell you why. If I accept either of these offers, I cannot stay in Germany any longer. Both positions are in administration, as chief editor, and I know from my three years as leader of the literary division at *Nationaltidende* that it will absorb all of my time. Because of that, my production suffered a gap of three years between *The Generations* and *Phaedra*.

So, a choice must be made, and I have chosen.

But for that reason your long letter was the more painful to me: I had sacrificed two positions – you know how significant that is in Denmark – I turned down two offers which would have kept me free and unrestrained and would have given me a high standing at home. I did it in order to remain in Germany and with Schorer. And then I can see that because I received eight hundred marks (which the gentlemen call an advance although they have surely collected enough manuscripts for the marks), I am almost considered a "blackmailer" there. It would have been nobler had they shown more consideration for the unfortunate things that have happened to me.

Now that I have realized how weak my position is at Schorer's, I see even more clearly how terrible my situation is. I know that they are furious in Denmark, and that they are literally starving me in order to force me to return. And here – what support do I get? Yes – you, dear Sir, and I know that you would do everything that is in your power – but you, yourself, don't have any.'

For a moment he doubts whether he has made the right choice.

His short stories cannot be marketed.

He has offered to write texts to accompany illustrations. He could do it very easily and under various pseudonyms so no one would guess who the author was. But, no.

Everything he owns of any value has been pawned. By Sunday the landlord will have taken possession of his linen and thrown him on the street. And everyone will say that it serves him right. But if he waits just one more day, perhaps then something wonderful will happen.

His hope is so strong that he for a minute thinks that the letter from *Politiken*, which the landlord is waving around, is a money order. But it is just a laconic message announcing that both Edvard Brandes and Peter Nansen have returned to the paper.

All doors have been shut. But somebody ought to have helped him. At least his closest relatives. Nini and Peter Holst:

'*4 Vienna Universitätsstrasse. 9th District*

It is possible that a regular letter hasn't reached you. Therefore I will write again. The day that I, in spite of all my efforts, will have to give up the struggle and literally be out on the street – a place where you don't want to be in a civilized country – that day will not go by without leaving its mark. The day when Herman Bang succumbs to these last unhappy events, people will ask – and ask in public: but had this man no family at all?

As expected, I am no longer at the hotel. You can still reach me at the above address where I have found a room for a week. I might be able to get some work and a position here, but until then, how can I stay alive?

I will not burden you with any more letters.

Herman.'

It is his birthday – he is turning twenty-nine and there are no congratulatory cards, no money. He is in his thirtieth year and no longer feels young. There are only two days until Easter. Two days of sadness, on Saturday the landlord will probably throw him out. And he will not find a red egg decorated with a golden star on the pavement. Not even a hardboiled egg that he could roll in salt. If only steaks grew on trees, or if only he could kill a rich Jew and steal his purse. But of course, it is not likely that anyone would let himself get killed.

He is standing by the window, looking down on the street. This is the only entertainment he can afford.

Suddenly a man comes around the corner. He scans the house numbers as if he doesn't know the area well. A wealthy traveller who has strayed into the district that has the cheapest hotels. He looks like Bjerring. He looks exactly like Bjerring. His erect bearing and the cane that swings lightly along the cobblestones. It has to be him, no one else has that particular gait. But lately it has happened that he has seen a familiar face in a stranger's features. And he has been close to addressing the person – and then backed away. Perhaps it is his poor vision. Perhaps his nerves. Or simply hunger.

The elegant gentleman stops in front of the hotel. And he can hear Bjerring's voice from the lobby. Bjerring's footsteps on the stairs. And then Bjerring is in his room dressed in his beautiful, tailored spring coat, and the two of them shake hands. And finally, finally he hears his mother tongue again. Danish in Bjerring's slightly nasal voice. And Bjerring waves his manicured hands in the air, those hands that once paid out his wages in gold: 'This place of yours, Bang, is nice. Modest but nice.'

Bjerring orders wine and canapés and cakes. And there are no contemptuous looks coming from the staff, no dragging of feet. And he recalls how he himself had power once as an editor. In those days Bjerring had teased him and said that he, Mr High and Mighty, was less useful than an old mother knitting socks for her son. Bjerring believed in him, expected so much of him, and precisely for that reason he mocked him.

All that is in the past now. Bjerring looks at him with a mild, worried, almost affectionate expression. And only now does he realize how much he has missed his language – missed speaking Danish with somebody. He tells Bjerring. And Bjerring smiles. Actually, he has come to give Bang an invitation. Newspaper owner Ferslew and his wife are in Vienna, and they would be delighted to see Herman Bang at dinner and afterwards the theatre.

Everything is as before. And yet it wasn't. He hardly had anything chic to wear. He ought to be wearing a spray of lily of the valley in his buttonhole, and he ought to bring roses for the lady. And gloves – all his gloves are pawned.

Mr Ferslew has grown heavier as has his disposition. His wife has become more staid. Her features are still pleasing and soft, but somewhat looser, and there is a little hesitation in her movements as if her weight bothers her.

And he himself. It is not only because he has lost his looks that he cannot be lively and entertaining at the dinner table the way he could as a young man. There is a hint of reservation, a feeling of doubt inside him. What is on Ferslew's mind when he cuts into the beautifully prepared meat? And Mrs Ferslew when she takes her seat next to his in the stalls in the *Burgteater* and looks over her fan, smiling? Perhaps they are thinking: 'Now we see the other side of the coin.'

Afterwards they invite him to Café Bauer. They converse over the fine dry wine, and he asks them to give his regards to Christian and let him know that he will always remain his good friend. And Anna – no, not a word about Miss Anna.

The next day Bjerring paid him a short visit to give him a 'belated birthday gift'. A thick brown envelope graced with a blue silk ribbon, tied by a woman. Once again Ferslew – and especially Mrs Ferslew, most likely – came to his aid with: money.

There was no need to think it over. It was just a matter of getting out of the hotel and moving into a room that he had already looked at, let by a widow with six children. Everything was so worn down and untidy and inadequate that he at first couldn't fathom how she could manage a lodger. But she explained that she and the children would move into the kitchen and the adjoining pantry, and then he could have the living room. When he said that he would think about it, she sniveled with an expression of patience and sadness.

And of course she hadn't been able to rent that cubbyhole out to anybody else. And he moved in, sat down at a blue-painted kitchen table and worked on the story *By the Road* while the children's thin voices and the mother's shushing could be heard through the wall.

Katinka never became a mother. There were no children to soak up her affection or to interrupt her when she prepared for birthdays, Christmas or picnics. The pound cake. He had to have a whiff of it before he could continue. He rushed out to buy butter, sugar, flour, eggs, and asked the widow to bake Katinka's cake.

The widow stirred the sugar and butter until it turned white and fluffy, her face turning red from her labours. With the flour, he had to slow her down, but with the eggs she put up resistance. She covered her face when he broke the tenth egg in the bowl and the children stuck their fingers in the dough.

But with the door ajar and the pleasant smell from the kitchen drifting past his papers, he could write effortlessly and quickly. In six weeks he completed *By the Road*. The characters had lived inside him for a long time. Now he set them free.

It wasn't until after he had sent his manuscript to Emil Jonas and to Copenhagen that he noticed men's voices coming from the pantry.

These men made the children as quiet as mice. And the mother answered with a voice that was a little hoarse and jumpy from nervousness. There was something special about that voice. And perhaps it was this something in the voice, this raw, hoarse and subdued quality that attracted men. For more and more of them showed up. And when he questioned her, she said they were suitors. She had advertised for a new husband.

He hoped that she would make a decision soon so he could get used to hearing just one voice. It occurred to him, however, that the gentlemen didn't speak the language of love. And how could she afford all this advertising when she could barely bring herself to use an egg. Besides, the gentlemen often came in pairs. When he met them on the stairs, they would look at him with deep suspicion, and somebody had rummaged through his papers.

'Is it the children?' he asked.

Finally she confessed. The young men were not suitors at all but detectives. They showed up every single day asking whether the gentleman had had any visitors, whether the gentleman had been out during the night, and whether any Russians frequented the place. As soon as he was out of the apartment, they would read his manuscripts. They didn't understand them, but they looked for certain words: anarchist, nihilist, those were the kind of words they were looking for.

He immediately went to see the Danish envoy who confirmed that he, Bang, was indeed under suspicion in Vienna. And he packed his manuscripts and his light suitcase, his only suitcase, which the landlady clung on to while moaning about being a poor woman – and about him owing her at least thirty guilders.

He tore the suitcase away from her and gave her twenty. Then he ran with her cursing trailing behind him into the mild spring air and on to the train station where he bought a ticket to Prague.

*

How swiftly he could run in those days. He and events loved each other. And Prague, the golden city with its sweet smell of acacias, became his favourite town.

The traveller passes his hand across his forehead. He had drifted off, far away. Far into his story of the time he was on the run from enraged landladies and all sorts of detectives.

In Prague he hailed a cab and asked to be driven to a hotel. And with great confidence he climbed the stairs in Hotel Blauen Stern where the rooms were the size of ballrooms and where Count Bismarck himself usually spent the night. No one could see that he was as poor as a church mouse, and no one was waiting for him.

These days, when he gets off the train, a welcoming committee will be waiting for him. They will give him flowers, and they will carry his suitcases to the carriage. And beautiful women will turn their faces toward him because he is so famous now.

They expect that he will entertain them before the reading and after the reading and of course during the dinner. They know he will be charming, animated and elegant. He can recount things in a lively and light manner, his language and self-deprecating irony will sparkle. They say that he is a treasure trove full of stories, that – frankly – he is bewitching. And he performs as expected until he senses the first signs of weariness, the kind of exhaustion that makes the air around him seem to vibrate and the smiling faces to cloud over as if he were seeing them through water. At that point he excuses himself and retreats.

It is like a lid that snaps shut when he leaves the room. But he wants them to remember him as witty and irresistible, not fragile and worn-out. For everyone has expectations of him. Even his close friends will complain about receiving letters that don't live up to his previous letters. And then he will have to pick up his pen again and write more thoroughly and more stylistically polished and apologize that the last letter was not meant as a real letter but just as a reply.

Everybody is tearing into him. And he needs to rest. He wants to look at his watch, but it slides out of his hand. It doesn't matter, time is not important here, it is a foreign time. He passes his hand over his face. His skin feels creased and dry. He must look like a scarecrow.

Glasses, papers, pen. He practically sweeps it all towards him with a movement he knows must look clumsy and ugly. But the passengers in the dining car don't notice him. They just sit there, lethargic, with their books, newspapers and drinks.

He steps into the corridor. He wants to find a porter and ask him to make up his berth if it hasn't already been taken care of. He wants to lie down and find the sleeping draught in the pretty lacquer box filled with make-up, eau de cologne and miracle medicine.

The train, this piercing, nerve-racking metallic sound that grinds its way into his brain. He wants it at a distance – with the help of morphine if necessary.

In front of him he sees a young negro with a wagon. On the top shelf are clean, very white, starched linens, and on the lower are crumpled, dirty sheets. The young porter is whistling, moving along the corridor almost like a dancer. It is not a waltz or a galop but a warm, swinging melody that makes the traveller feel like dancing himself with steps he doesn't know.

The young man turns around suddenly as if he feels that he is being watched. Then he continues down the corridor quietly and stiffly with his wagon.

The traveller wants to ask if his berth has been made up, just to say something. But the train moves so fitfully and roughly as if it has run out of energy. And he, the well-known Danish writer, falls against the wall, and two diamond rings slip off his fingers and roll down the corridor.

The porter catches them and approaches him. The fine, pink open palm that for a moment closes around his own hand, and the rings that are being pushed back onto his thin fingers, give him a jolt. Two golden circles on his hand. Yet another figure eight. He lets the porter help him into the compartment.

Everything is clinically clean, and a glass and a carafe with water are placed next to the berth. The mirror shows much too clearly the lines around his eyes and mouth. He takes one of Doctor Wasbutzki's morphine capsules – and thank God for the doctor and his wife who worships and loves the artistic Herman Bang, at least platonically.

The globe lamp above him sways back and forth. And here is the morphine with its touch of bitterness, and the water which tastes differently from that at home. And if only sleep would settle in. He closes his eyes and tries to force them open again. For behind his eyelids is a swinging, dizzying white globe. And in the middle of the light is Max, wearing pale pink tights, so pale they are almost white.

Max lifts his arms, takes hold of the globe and begins to play ball with it, gently and gracefully.

It's a waltz, thin and jittery with a metallic sound.

And he tries to get up and face Max who doesn't see him at first for he is only a shadow of himself.

Suddenly Max throws the globe towards him. But he is too slow to catch it, his arms are heavy. He screeches like a bird. The globe shatters and transforms into a cloud of shards.

Max stands in the light, beautiful as an angel or a beast.

Max came to him in Prague.

At Hotel Blauen Stern they would laugh in front of the mirrors and imagine that Count Bismarck had stood exactly there brushing his moustache.

And he wrote to Peter and asked him to send two neckties,

twelve handkerchiefs and a pair of cufflinks. For he was completely cleaned out. Everything that he had owned of any worth was now to be found in various pawnshops. Only the fake and tinny were left.

And Peter Nansen charmed his tailor into increasing his personal credit. And the lavish cufflinks especially bolstered Herman Bang's creditworthiness at the hotel.

On the other hand, Peter was much too slow writing him to tell what he thought of *By the Road*. Maybe the story was a flop. Maybe it wasn't a story at all.

When the letter finally arrived, he nearly burst into tears of joy. Yet Peter had reservations, especially concerning the style. Which Bang knew:

'Yes. – The style, my dear! Now, that's scandalous. I'm damned if I will ever learn to write. I still write in exercise books like eight-year old kids. "Impressionist" is precisely the word. I am making a supreme effort capturing the impressions, each and every impression clearly and carefully and in keeping with the characters, and I never think about the totality of the story – and the style explodes into a thousand fragments that are as discrete and hard as cobblestones. Shocking to even imagine it.'

But his publisher Andreas Schou sent him a letter of congratulation after having read the manuscript. And that had never happened before. And Julius Schiøtt talked about passages that one couldn't imagine being better.

As for himself, he thought of his new book that was going to be a real opus. And he hoped that *By the Road* could finance it. Only one thing worried him. *By the Road* was going to be published together with 'Son altesse' which now seemed to him to be lifeless and much too long.

And the book was not a success, neither in terms of reviews nor sales. Schou was disappointed and wrote that his next book really had to work out or else the game would be over.

Emil Jonas had translated *By the Road* with great enthusiasm, but he was not able to sell it.

The very day he waved goodbye to Max, the cufflinks went to the pawnshop and he himself had to abandon the hotel's big comfortable bed.

The ant Mr Bang had to find new accommodation – a new anthill. He worked feverishly, but it wasn't easy when he had to share the bedroom with another person and the living room with a whole gang while trying to visualize Tivoli and describe the fireworks and all the people in evening dress.

Everyone else grew in stature after a book publication. Only Herman Bang didn't.

Granted, Sophus Schandorph who was an author himself wrote to him: '*By the Road* is beyond doubt superb. Unless an old rat like me is no longer able to sniff out some good cheese, this story will become a classic in our literary corpus of novellas.'

Henrik Ibsen thanked him a couple of years later: 'As far as my correspondance is concerned, I am unfortunately guilty of negligence.' 'But,' he wrote, 'your fine melancholic work *By the Road* has remained very clear in our memory. It is as if we ourselves have lived through it all.'

Also Bjørnstjerne Bjørnson thanked him warmly for the book – and a bit belatedly because 'the ladies had taken it.'

All this was not known to him back then in Prague where he had to go hungry and was afraid he would collapse and faint on the street.

Only one thing was certain: Max Eisfeld loved Herman Bang.

That certainty was more potent than morphine.

11.

He stayed in Prague. At Veith's pension in Balbingasse he got a room and ate soup from an earthenware bowl and added water to the cheap wine all the while dreaming of dining in Tivoli, enjoying an abundance of shrimp piled on bread followed by a cool slice of melon.

New clothes – he had given up on that. And one day he actually began to do his accounts.

It was due to a letter sent from Mr Andreasen, addressed to Andreas Schou's publishing firm and forwarded by Julius Schiøtt.

There were endless lists of numbers. Old debts, interest and compound interest and a new loan that was going to pay for a smaller part of the debt and then one more loan that he had forgotten about.

It emerged that for several years at the beginning of each month he had paid 100-150 kroner to Andreasen. The hundred kroner were instalments plus interest.

And yet the result was that five hundred kroner were to be paid immediately.

He remembered the words debit and credit from his mathematics book. But his answers had always been wrong.

Only one thing he knows for sure: debitors forget, and creditors remember. This debt will follow him wherever he goes:

'*Monday*

Dear Jules

I would have written to you already yesterday – but I didn't have any money to pay for the stamps.

To Andreasen's letter I have the following to say:

I believe that the 425 kroner that he received from you in the fall must be written off against the debt which then amounts to 2615. We acknowledge this debt, and because I truly want to accommodate the man, if he is reasonable – I will pay him 5% of the sum (2615 kroner) in interest.'

He added and subtracted. He promised that Andreasen would receive three hundred kroner the first of February. The debt would then be reduced to two thousand.

He got a headache and felt nauseous just from trying to figure it out. Or perhaps it was cholera. There was cholera in Graz. And if he fell ill, who would take care of it then?

Old Mrs Veith smiles when he rushes down the stairs and nearly knocks over the postman. She thinks that he is expecting money to pay for the two months' rent that he owes. She has no idea that he is hoping to collect a sum that will take him far, far away from there.

A thick envelope with Danish stamps and Andreasen's handwriting. The worst of all: a threatening letter.

Mr Bang has sent an extremely rude person named Schiøtt to Andreasen's address. But Mr Andreasen is not so easily intimidated, for he has a clear conscience which is more than can be said for Bang. If the outstanding five hundred kroner are not paid out immediately, it will give him, Andreasen, much pleasure to expose Bang, the swindler.

All his accounts will be disclosed. Other creditors' accounts likewise. Everywhere where Mr Bang has lived, unpaid bills and people in distress are left behind, while Mr Bang himself is travelling far and wide and living it up. The satirical magazines have already shown interest.

The letter knocks him off his feet. It falls out of his hand and lands by his feet and apparently pulls his entire body down to the floor, for suddenly he is gazing at Mr and Mrs Veith from below, their faces floating like two gentle moons. Next to him are a glass of water, a chunk of bread and a small piece of meat. A damp, ice-cold cloth, ribbed and possibly one of the wife's undershirts, is placed on his forehead. He takes pleasure in this luxury and in her voice that asks if any of his close relatives has died.

'Most of them – ' he sighs.

And the compassion that he sees in the eyes of the two old people will probably translate into another month's grace. That same evening he borrows money for stamps and sends Andreasen's letter off to Julius Schiøtt.

And that same night he realizes that it was the worst possible thing he could have done.

He can hear Julius' voice: 'Why don't you go to the police?' And Peter's voice: 'But this is pure and simple extortion. What are you waiting for, go to the police.'

And he can picture very clearly how Julius Schiøtt, Peter Nansen and two constables go to confront Mr Andreasen who is seated at his big desk. He pictures those heavy hands that can write so easily. And the surprised housekeeper who smiles at the constables.

Mr Andreasen is calm and appears altogether trustworthy. There must be some sort of mistake, he says. A malicious attack by a person who owes him money. A writer who has been expelled from two countries and convicted of pornography.

He shows the policemen his accounts and Boldt's article and of course that terrible piece in the anarchist paper about the emperor. For Andreasen has a handle on his affairs, and Peter and Julius are merely two young men. In addition, Peter is handsome and is probably still combing his hair over his forehead.

The worst – the police were the worst thing he could think of.

'*Tuesday*

My friend

You will laugh, and it is not at all laughable – when I ask you to write me immediately to promise that you will not go to the police about Andreasen. On my honour – you are acquainted with the whole case. But my head is feeling weak, and I cannot bear any more nights like the last few where I couldn't sleep at the thought of a never-ending police investigation that will tarnish my name. – Write to me at once, old friend, two lines, that you will not do anything but convince the man that I won't withdraw everything from Schou. My head is too tired. I cannot bear it.

Your Herman.'

Julius' reply was reassuring. They hadn't dragged Andreasen to the police station. But they were getting good and tired of his turning up at the office insisting on gaining access to Herman Bang's accounts.

But what is happening with the manuscripts? Andreas Schou would like to see at least a portion of the novel.

He has to pull himself together. He will have to revise the first long, shimmering chapter of 'Bernhard Hoff' thoroughly, correct, cross out, cut and paste.[22] He has to show Schou something. The envelope will be thick and the postage costly. And if the manuscript should go astray, how is he going to reconstruct all that bustling and pulsating life, the feeling of anticipation in the theatre, the fireworks in Tivoli and all the characters?

Letting go of a beginning is dreadful and physically painful. If he could just get a book to translate. Any cheap novel that could finance his own slow work practice. As things stand now, his journalistic work is wearing him out while he waits for a financial miracle.

At last Schou replies.

He hurries upstairs with the letter. And it is as if he sees himself, the writer Herman Bang, far off in the distance, reading his publisher's polite, almost fatherly letter:

'As far as Bernhard Hoff is concerned, I regret to have to tell you that what I have seen so far of this book does not satisfy me. I have now read all of the first chapter (the introduction) and at any rate, I find it much too scattered; my impression has been that it is a roman à clef, and if that is so, I must warn you to be careful. I think that you should put this work aside for the time being and write a story, not too long, along the lines of *By the Road*, in which case I could publish it in the spring. If you agree to this and the work succeeds, I believe that it will strengthen your position here, and you could definitely do with that.'

He laughs out loud as if someone is tickling him, and he runs quickly through the rest of the letter. Schou doesn't have any translations to give him. The financial affairs at the publishing house are suffering badly. And moreover, the dear old gentleman is afflicted with a leg sore.

But there is one more letter. Schou must have regretted it. It says 'Another suggestion.' Schou is not heartless but just couldn't make himself tear up the letter about the finances and the leg sore. Schou wants the best for Herman Bang. He is a publisher who is committed to his authors.

'After having written the enclosed letter, another idea occurred to me: give up Bernhard Hoff. I think it will be a book that will not benefit you at all, and it seems highly unlikely to me that the remaining chapters will be of a kind that I would want to publish. I am fully aware that this suggestion will upset you and hit you hard, but I beg you to steady yourself and listen to what I have to say further. Today and the following Mondays in December, that is, the 6th, the 13th, the 20th and the 27th, I will send you, in addition to the eighty marks that you already received in advance, fifty-five marks each time. I hope that in the meantime you will have some peace of mind and make plans for some new work of the sort I hinted at in my first letter. Think it over and let me know as soon as possible whether you will accept my offer, in which case the money will be sent off straightaway.

One thing I must finally ask you, in addition to what I have urged you in previous letters to consider regarding language and style: write your manuscript in larger and clearer handwriting. You can of course use the thin stationery paper that I get from Russia as the postage might otherwise be too dear. It is hard for me to read your writing, and also for the typesetter.

I remain yours sincerely
A. Schou.'

He lies down on the bed and visualizes his novel as if through thin
Russian paper. And he can almost hear the voices of Andreas Schou
and Julius Schiøtt: 'Write something light, my friend, something
humorous. After all, you can be really funny. Or write something
touching. Write about this dance teacher Alvilda Back-Nielsen. You
observed her from your hidden spot in the doorway on the street
when she was doing her exercises by the bedpost. Later on you met
her in a provincial town. You saw her giving dance lessons to seven
clumsy toddlers at the inn. And she invited you to the end-of-season
performance. While she was dancing solo, you took note of her bad
teeth and flat bosom. Write a short story about her and about all
the other poor creatures that you have encountered in the shadowy
corners of the cheap boarding houses. Pull yourself together now
and write.'

He weeps so much that he has to dry the pillow on the windowsill.
Afterwards he spreads out his papers on the floor and crawls around
among notes and drafts: Mr Adolf, Asta, Mathilde, Mr Theodor,
cabinetmaker Martens, the large French chef who drops the good
meat into the ashes.

The theatre with its chubby cherubs of cardboard and gold dust.
The Victoria Theatre.

Stucco and Facades. Stucco and Facades.[23]

He must write that novel. And he will have to accept Andreas
Schou's offer. No one will understand it. Not even Peter.

Being subjected to censorship and having his style dictated. That
amounts to a new 'expulsion' and of the worst kind.

He sends Schou's letter to Peter and attempts a show of
resignation:

'"Bernhard Hoff" was deep into the second out of the ten chapters.
It was developing nicely, and I felt in full control like I did when
working on *By the Road*. It should have been published on my
birthday – dedicated to you – a settling of accounts with our youth,
a summary of our generation's errors. I have so few people to talk to,

and I sleep so poorly that I have a lot of time to dream: I have dreamt so many things for this book. The construction of the "Victoria Theatre" in five chapters, and then the descent in five chapters: first a subtle creaking and rumbling and then the collapse – the ruin. There were some "sublime" passages, at least a couple. And the interiors! And then a young man who dies – a kind of symbol of our errors that were beautifully thought up and yet so common. And his parents had been struck severely enough.

Perhaps you will say that I should demand a definite answer from Schou, an unconditional "yes" or a "no", in which case I would look for another publisher. But I do have a contract, and I think I am obliged to let Schou read all the manuscripts before I can pass them on to another. And even if he waived this demand – after all, I don't owe more than eighty marks – where to find another publisher? Every other person will ask like Schou: "Yes – but I need to *read* this manuscript" – and I for one *must* be paid per sheet.

I have therefore accepted his suggestion. Even more so since I have had to do without money for a whole month, and now it is winter. You might argue that it is very unlike me. Perhaps it is. But remember that this is written during the last month of the last year before I enter my thirties. At that point you are inclined to keep your contracts and resign yourself to the circumstances.'

He posts his letter and thinks that now Peter Nansen and Gustav Esmann can discuss his case at home in Copenhagen and, if nothing else, feel fortunate that they don't have his problems. Their pens fly across the paper, and their light, elegant books have readers.

Then his first chapter is returned, carefully corrected by Schou. And suddenly he himself thinks that it is thin and shows no talent.

But he is on his way to something. He can visualize his characters, hear their voices. They are with him day and night. But not with the reader – not yet. And yet he cannot let go of them and write the kind of short story that Schou can sell.

He needs time. More time.

Perhaps he should have stayed with Paul Langhoff – Paul would have been able to see the plan of his novel. But Paul doesn't pay per sheet.

A book translation would be of great help. Paul will understand:

'But where can you root out material for a short story? For God's sake, it is not the same thing as driving out partridge from a field …

That king who shouted: "A kingdom for a horse" was not as badly off as I am. A novel that you feel you cannot write, and a short story that you could write if only you knew one small thing: what it should be about!

Dear Langhoff – I beg you in all my agony: find me a "book of sermons" to translate, or whatever you wish – I am prepared to do anything, damn it.'

No novel for translation was forwarded. But one day Max Eisfeldt showed up in Veith's pension with a suitcase full of tights, boots and cloaks fit for a knight. An additional bed was prepared, and two bowls of soup were served. Thank God that the first instalment of money from Schou had arrived.

The two of them stroll through Prague's golden arcades. They look at coats, boots and rings. Finally they enter a pet shop. There are whining puppies, ruffled kittens and newly castrated dogs and cats, moaning, imprisoned in a painful dream and with dark blankets thrown over the cages.

The smell alone is enough to make them turn around and run out. But then they notice an aviary with budgerigars. The birds are nestling against each other, rubbing their beaks together and feeding their downy chicks.

They leave the shop with a golden cage, each holding a paper cone. Through the rolled-up paper they can feel a bird's beating heart and its small claws scratching inside. Back home they place the cage on the table and carefully let the birds in. After a bit of fluttering, the love birds find each other.

Dusk turns to darkness, and the lamp is lit. There is a sense of calm that will never be habitual, a safe haven, a state of happiness. He watches his friend reading, and he loves that face that unconsciously expresses love, bitterness and anxiety as if the soul lies right under the skin. To his own surprise he is writing poems:

NIGHT

It was night already
and quiet was the room
where they both sat – reading
by the glow of the lamp.

Only faintly could be heard
the crackling fire
and the rocking sound
of the chair – his chair
against the floor.

They read like this, in peace
till all at once, both looked up
and eye met eye
in a lingering smile.

How much we l o v e, he whispered
– and their reading resumed.

It had come to him so easily, and yet he made a fair copy and tore up the first draft into small pieces. – Exclusively for the purpose of changing 'his' to 'her'.

It was lucky that he had done it. For the next morning two constables knocked on the door with a warrant. Both entered the room and looked around. The shorter one poked a finger at the birds. The taller one went into the bedroom and inspected the beds and the clothes that were folded neatly and placed on separate chairs.

Then they went through his papers. Evidently they were interested in everything. Manuscripts, love and economy. They took a fair amount of his correspondence with them.

He proof-read a couple of pages of his manuscript so he could send it off in time. And he asked Julius to send him a hymnal so he could sing a couple of his childhood hymns by the Christmas tree.

That night he barely slept. There was only a brief moment where he practically plunged into deep sleep. He looked down into a river.

The water was deep and it flowed calmly and gently. But suddenly it rose, and the river divided. He woke up and couldn't understand why it felt like a physical pain. In the dream he had wept over the river's two lonely streams that had rushed towards the sea.

Max slept peacefully and soundly. And as soon as they had consumed their morning coffee, they strolled down to the police station as if it were another outing.

Max Eisfeldt, the actor, flashed his dazzling smile when Mr Bang was called in, and that smile – at least at the start of the interrogation – contributed to a posture of arrogance that was only matched by the officers' boorish behaviour.

'Why are you staying here in Prague?'

'I am fond of the city. I am working here.'

'What kind of work?'

'I write.'

'For socialist journals.'

'No, never. – My grandfather – '

'Your grandfather is of no concern to us. – But we believe that you are receiving support from a secret socialist organization.'

'You are mistaken – '

'Where do you make your money?'

'My publisher in Copenhagen pays me by the sheet.'

'When exactly?'

'Approximately every week.'

'No "approximately" here. – We want a precise date and time.'

'It all depends on the post.'

'We understand that you write for newspapers.'

'Yes.'

'About politics – presumably.'

'No, never about politics.'

'What do you write about?'

'Theatre – literature.'

'Can you make a living doing that?'

'A modest living.'

'Why do you share accommodation with a gentleman?'

'We are both strangers to the city – and we don't have much money.'

One officer was writing and another was questioning him, and his head was spinning with new inquiries and variations of earlier ones. It was as though they were just hoping that he would get entangled in a web of lies and contradictions.

Finally he himself asked why he had to be dragged through this painful interrogation. 'Do you in fact have any evidence against me?' he shouted in desperation.

'You owe ten guilders to a landlady in Vienna.'

'If you intend to expel me, let me know immediately.'

The answer was not particularly friendly. But if Mr Bang was not guilty of any offence, he could most likely stay. For the time being they would keep him under observation.

When they finally let the alleged socialist go, Bang realized that the interrogation had lasted an hour and a half.

The interview with Max Eisfeld lasted half an hour. And during those thirty minutes Bang chewed his nails so hard that blood showed. For what if Max ended up hating him. And what if Max couldn't lie when he was questioned about the shared rooms.

When they were on the street again, their first inclination was to embrace each other. But they had to make do with a light handshake, their finger tips barely touching.

Max wanted to eat out to celebrate the occasion. But Bang insisted on going home. He had to write letters.

'Letters? – Do you want to write about this?'

He nodded. It was important that Peter Nansen should know about it and make sure that all his articles about politics were published under a pseudonym. Even though he would surely shake his head at this, believing that Herman Bang clearly suffered from paranoia. And Emil Jonas – if the police should approach him, he would have to know what had happened, in which case he would have to have a letter from Herman Bang to show. He already had his closing words formed in his head:

'I beg you to inform me, dear Councillor, whether one is forced to accept such treatment, and if I cannot demand to know what they want from me.

It is hard to believe that we live in a civilized century. I haven't written or done anything untoward.

Yours,
Herman B.'

It would sound appropriately innocent and appropriately indignant. In addition, he would ask for an advance of thirty marks.

Back home Mrs Veith went about her business with red eyes. Her husband had been called in for questioning along with the boy who polished their boots. Both of them would tell the truth: that they had never known any lodgers more quiet and peaceful than these gentlemen.

The post arrived with a little blue letter to Max Eisfeld while Herman Bang received: *Hamburger Nachrichten, Berlingske Tidende* wrapped in paper, and letters from Julius Schiøtt and Mr Andreasen.

In the Hamburg newspaper, Boldt writes that Herman Bang will most likely be expelled from Prague too. The review of *By the Road* in *Berlingske* is scathing, at least at first glance. Andreasen intends to see Mrs Ferslew, who apparently has a soft spot for Herman Bang, and collect the amount due to him. Julius is of the opinion that the author is wasting his time with journalism. Now he really must concentrate on the book. No more articles for *Politiken* – not for now, and preferably never.

If Max had been able to read these letters, he would have understood his hysterical laughter that turned into tears. A fainting spell and absolutely no wish to return to consciousness.

And Max would not have shaken his head and said that he is only hurting himself when he gulps down the wine too quickly and grabs the pen again.

'Jules,' he sighs. 'Please help me. I know that I have to get away from *Politiken*, but I cannot do without the money. I want to come home but not to Andreasen and not without my book, Jules!'

The thought of Andreasen at Mrs Ferslew's makes him shiver. With his amiable smile, he will hand Mrs Ferslew a copy of 'The Bang File'. The lady will glance at the long columns and notice that the irregularities had already begun during the time when she had patronized Herman Bang as a young journalist. Andreasen will explain to her that she had opened her home not to an innocent child but to a professional swindler.

Jules will have to make sure that it doesn't happen:

'The past never dies, and I don't know if it can be atoned for. Do me the favour of telling Andreasen or letting it be told – preferably the former, which will give us some peace for a time – that he will receive five hundred kroner within the next year. We will have to manage without it. But then he must leave me in peace. He won't dare – to be sure the only hope for the future lies in the hands of Mrs Ferslew if I ever wish to return home – he won't dare to approach the Ferslews. But don't linger. Also, tell him (the word cannot be spelled out) what I have written to you here.

Herman.'

He posted his letters and splashed cold water on his face. He and Max walked past two officers of the law who were standing outside Veith's boarding house, keeping an eye on the two criminals.

They went out to eat at a cheap restaurant. They caught snowflakes that melted on their hands. He had written Christmas stories for family magazines both in Germany and in Scandinavia. For if he wasn't going to be expelled, Christmas was going to be rich and Danish, with a goose and gifts and a tree.

He wished for a white Christmas and imagined the two officers standing in snow up to their knees, with heavy snow collars resting on their shoulders. He regretted his thought immediately, for if it snowed too heavily, the postman would perhaps not make it there.

'Max,' he said. 'If it snows – if the post doesn't arrive in time before Christmas – '

Max smiled completely unconcerned as if tree, goose, hymns and gifts were of no importance to him.

The snow was falling and falling. It swept into deep drifts. And not only in Prague but all over Central Europe.

Every morning he leaned out the window. He noticed that the officers had given up. But the postman hadn't given up yet. He caught sight of him and ran downstairs. And there were no money orders for him. And then it was the 19th and then the 20th, and still no money. The postman shook his head and smiled apologetically.

'*Prague. Wednesday.*

Dear Councillor

Now winter and snow are coming my way but no mail whatsoever. If you can – kindly put ten or twenty marks in a letter so that I don't have to freeze on Christmas Eve. Oh – May God help us!

Herman B.
Merry Christmas!!!'

'*Prague. Thursday.*

Dear Jules

I don't hear anything from anyone. It is very likely that the police are intercepting my letters. I am under strict surveillance here and am taken for a socialist agitator supported by a secret foundation!

Enclosed is one sheet of the manuscript. That makes two sheets including the last one – but send the money right away. I don't have any more, you understand. And ask Schou to write on the back in German: In payment of sheet number this or that of the short stories – seventy-five kroner.

You will receive this by Saturday. Please, send the money without delay since it is held back here for a long time. It must be mailed out on Saturday.

I am writing and writing so I will be able to send sheets every other day.

I haven't received anything.

No proofs.

No hymnal.

No letters.

Nothing.'

Nothing came. Nothing at all.

There was nothing else one could do other than accept old Veith's invitation to a Bohemian Christmas with carp in a sweet-sour sauce and carp with prunes. Later on he would make people laugh at this Christmas Eve where the wine was served in kerosene cans, and the goose had shrunk and transformed itself into a carp in prune sauce. But on the actual evening there was no self-deprecating laughter. Only disappointment and sadness. Here he was – in Prague – and had so obviously been forgotten.

After Christmas the money orders arrived. He fanned them out like a deck of cards and invited Max to a restaurant. He enjoyed watching Max picking up the glass by its stem as if vintage wine was something completely ordinary and fitting.

His own hands shook whenever a shadow darkened their table. He had begun seeing policemen everywhere. When he was working, their voices would suddenly pop up in his head. They shattered the rhythm of his phrasing. And back home in Copenhagen, old Andreas Schou was anxiously reading page after page, correcting and polishing, all with the best of intentions so that Herman Bang's nervous style would be grammatically correct and suitable for publication in any ordinary family magazine.

Perhaps he simply wasn't capable of writing any longer. Many a time he would stall at a sentence or a word, and when he looked in the mirror, he saw his father's face with a wet, white compress around his head. Oh, Jules, if you could just see me now.

'To you I will write the truth so you can understand that this uncertainty must come to an end. My dear friend, I am in despair and fight day and night against this derangement of my mind. This year has been truly awful. Since New Year's I have – like father in his day – been misspelling words, and I have to fight like someone possessed just to remember the right word order. What I am suffering in this struggle – which a perpetual persecution mania will only intensify – let the saga be silent thereof.'

Tears mixed with water dripping from the cold compress bleed onto the letter. But it is still legible.

'When one day I enter the eternal night, this letter will bear witness to how early I knew of my fate.'

Accidentally he rips off a corner of the wet paper.

'And to cap it all, now the doctor wants me to move because of a mould infestation in the house.'

'Mould!' He shouts it out loud, and Max looks up from his script and asks if he isn't going to take a rest – just for an hour.

But he cannot relax, not even at night time. The characters in his novel *Stucco* about the Victoria Theatre won't leave him alone. He is back again in Copenhagen, facing Adolf Riemenschneider and Miss Anna and Mrs Ferslew and all the journalists at *Nationaltidende*.

The plot of the book is going to be the actual architecture of the theatre. The stucco represents not only superficiality and mannerisms, it penetrates the very soul of the structure. The young dependable Herluf Berg is now the protagonist, and the elegant cynic Bernhard Hoff has been banished from the novel. That much he has agreed to alter. But his publisher, old Andreas Schou, nevertheless intervenes and corrects, deletes, revises. But:

'Nothing can alter my view that censorship and excessive stylistic editing are more than I can and will tolerate. My work is my sole possession. In this respect the right to make my own decisions is my essential right. Without it I will lose any hope of victory in the future – the only thing I live for now.'

He looks up from his papers, distracted by Max's voice. Max is rehearsing Romeo with the birds as an audience, lying prostrate on the floor in front of their cage.

A pulsating distance has arisen between Max and himself. One requires silence, the other needs movement and words. Their quarters are too cramped. Poverty has imprisoned them. And the fear of suddenly being apprehended, being caught making the wrong gesture, is wearing them out.

Shortly after he notices Max applying white stage makeup to his face.

Which means that he has also thought about it.

Exactly as he had once mused. Circus performers can travel

together from town to town. Two lovers can call themselves brothers, and people will believe them.

He gets up and reaches out his hand. But just then the mask cracks.

'This is all I can hope to be offered here. A mute role, a Pierrot-role.'

Max removes his makeup quickly, almost brutally. Tiny white pearls are still stuck to his eyelashes when he puts on his coat.

'Wait. Wait a minute. I am coming with you.'

'But you are working. I will go by myself.'

'Where are you going?'

'Nowhere – just want some freedom – '

'Freedom– from me – '

'I am going to a rehearsal – if you must know.'

'But that is not until this evening.'

'We are rehearsing privately. – You just stay here with your characters. Now you will get some quiet.'

And if only he had remained there with his book. But he only waited until Max was down on the street, then he followed him with light steps. Like a shadow.

Max stops. Max enters a door and climbs the stairs. And he – he crosses the street and slips in to a doorway.

There she is, on the third floor on the left: The Woman. Her face appears white against the window. Her hair is dark and let down. Her eyes are large and her lashes long. Very likely her eyelashes are very long. A face that is all eyes and soul.

And she tears herself away from the window, runs to the door and opens it. Maybe Max lifts her up for a moment in his arms, maybe he shouts with joy, dances, swings her around.

They stand by the window a little while. They turn their faces towards each other. They don't say anything. The lovers are silent.

The light goes out. Nothing else.

Oh. Yes. He is there, climbing the stairs in the dark. He, the lover, puts his ear against the door and hears a waltz, a thin nervous waltz. And he had no idea that Max could whistle. But of course he can. For it cannot possibly be her, a woman lover doesn't whistle like some street urchin.

He can hear their voices but not the words. He can hear Max burst out in a young reckless laugh. He imagines that the woman wraps him in her long, dark hair, that she hypnotizes him with her silk, her bracelets, her small delicate hands, her tapered nails and her golden shoes.

Max is lying in her arms. For he, Bang, recognizes this voice that rises and then dissolves in a melodic whimper.

The woman's sounds are short and sharp. Like a swallow that soars towards the sky to catch its own cries.

He tiptoes down in the dark. And if anyone saw him now, they would think he was a thief.

He walks home through the empty streets and wishes he could die. He lies down on the bed. And if he just stayed there, his heart would slow down, and he would turn cold. His love is dead. But he is a corpse that keeps vigil.

The love birds are on the swing. Even after he has covered the cage with a black cloth, the sound is in his head like a small metallic cry.

Someone is whistling a waltz on the stairs. Max lets himself in and lies down to sleep, calmly and peacefully.

And he wishes that words and thoughts didn't exist, and that he never had to try to be understanding. He wishes that he could simply kill Max like another Othello.

And then Max gets up early in a cheerful mood, asking if he would like some coffee, if he has a headache or if he needs a powder, a cognac, a glass of water.

He stays in bed, silent as a stone, and the silence causes Max Eisfeld to betray himself.

'There is no need to take it so seriously,' he says. 'Julie and I are friends. We act together and see each other for the sake of friendship.'

And why did he have to hear his own lifeless voice uttering: 'But I thought that we were of one flesh.'

And Max who shouted: 'You and yours! I am Max Eisfeld! And I will never ever be yours!'

Just then he realizes that Max is a completely different person from the man he loved. The fact that Max can abandon himself to someone without real abandon. That he perhaps just acts like a lover with all the gestures of love out of friendliness, pure and simple. That he always wants to remain his own self.

'To me,' he says, 'you meant everything.'

Max stares at him with an expression of childish surprise. He seems almost sad that he hadn't noticed it before.

'Do you mean more than all your writing?'

'Yes.'

'More than your entire family – '

'I loved you more than any other living creature.'

'More than your mother – '

'She is dead. Why don't you just leave. Go back to Berlin.'

Max wants to touch him, but the warmth emanating from his skin is like salt in an open wound. He screams and knocks over the coffee cup and the glass and watches Max jumping out of the way.

'Stop it now – somebody might call the police.'

'It doesn't matter now.'

And then Max Eisfeld went off to his morning rehearsal.

And he, Herman Bang, didn't die. He got up, and worse than that: he also had something to eat.

And he sat down to work on his book. In order to reflect his own times, he had to add a prostitute to the plot. Sexual instinct had taken the place of love, and the tears of love were being shed for a whore.

Max Eisfeld's soul he could only love now on the stage. But his body he continued to love.

Sometimes it was almost like before. But it was only a faint reflection of a distant sense of happiness. Light and shadow fell on them – separately.

'I am finished here,' Max announced. 'I am going to Berlin.'

He had pictured it. And sometimes wished for it. It was if it had already happened.

The parting was easy. Max left the door open. But he didn't follow him.

He could hear how Max kissed old Mrs Veith on both cheeks and on her hand. After that he probably embraced Veith.

Max Eisfeld was a ray of sunshine.

'It is summer here now,' he wrote to Peter. 'At the foot of the

"Vineyard Mountains" the whole city lies bathed in sunlight and blue skies. I nurse my plants and my two birds, and I never see a soul. The only human being I knew, saw and lived with – Eisfeld – has left to take up some work in Berlin where he belongs. And I don't know anybody else.'

Otherwise the correspondance with friends has almost ceased. The book is draining him of all his strength. And as soon as he stops writing, he feels pain. His head aches, and a winter has settled in his bones and muscles which he tries to soothe with wine. Once in a while he laughs. He roars with laughter while writing about the ball at Graversens. And afterwards he is amazed at having heard his own laughter in the midst of all the despair.

He has allowed the whore Paula to step into the novel. And he insists on keeping her there. Even when Andreas Schou very kindly lets him know that for that reason he can no longer act as publisher for the novel *Stucco*.

Then the nerve-racking days follow where Paul Langhoff reads the written chapters and wants to see more and promises to publish the book. When that is done, the notes become paragraphs and the paragraphs form chapters. And Paul Langhoff is a quick reader who is able to enter into the spirit of the novel and give good advice. But he feels it is an insult that the man allows himself to go on vacation in the middle of the work process. At the very least it is insensitive:

'*Prague 22.6.87*

I cannot claim, dear Paul, that your journey to Jutland has stirred up much enthusiasm in me. I had hoped with certainty to hear from you every week – to have your assessment passed on to me as it flows from your pen; your observations, and *enfin* I had hoped for cooperation. And you, *cher*, travel to Jutland.

Enfin.

When you return home, I will have completed the first chapter of part two. It deals primarily with a conversation between Berg and Councillor Hein and then the scenes between little Gerster and Mrs Stern. The latter scenes have caused me much trouble.

So, you will be reading IV and V (of part one) and I (of part two) together. You will be able to see my method clearly: that individual lives are revealed through and in the big scenes. My friend – it is an enormous undertaking. And I am only at the beginning of this new direction in the art of narration. Will I be thanked for having paved the way? Will I be understood at all?

Dear Paul – come home soon from Jutland. Support me with your advice, urge me on with your praise and criticism. It is an immense amount of work, and I often feel anxious in my loneliness.

Is the ending of V too "intense"? Do you want it changed? First and foremost, dear Paul, come home from Jutland.

Your friend
H.B.'

Towards the end of the summer he was finally finished and could have gone home. But 'Irene Holm' practically danced from his pen, and he sent the short story to Julius Schiøtt's magazine. And then, finally, he could allow himself to be genuinely sick. Fainting spells and seizures kept him in bed while the days drifted past like clouds, and he managed to avoid three weddings.

Because his friends were getting married at home. Esmann had brought his bride home from Norway. At their first meeting she became so enamoured of him that she broke an earlier engagement by telegram. And this in spite of her former fiancé being a handsome and rich aristocrat.

Peter simply announced in an official manner that now he was getting married. And the society wedding of the year was a stab in his heart: Miss Anna had married Reason.

' – – – Yes – I don't begrudge Levin his happiness. He loves her. In order to win her, he has employed means … that I probably would have shunned. I wonder if she will be able to love him in the long run as well. She and I will not see each other any more in this life, that is, we won't be talking to each other … But she will, as long as she lives, be thinking of me often – just as I will be thinking of her.

Funny that all this is happening at the same time as the autumn publication of my "book", this odd book about Copenhagen – well, "odd" is not the right word, for the book is *tout au contraire* very even – and it will move you deeply in places.'

Finally Herman Bang went home. The changes were not surprising.

The lucky Levin became an official censor. A well-groomed industrious man who on the orders the minister of justice, Alberti, weeded through everything from cabaret singers' lyrics to The Royal Theatre's repertoire.

When Herman Bang chanced upon Mrs Levin, he would usually cross to the other side of the street.

He and Max Eisfeld met as friends at Hotel Marienlyst. Max was fond of the sea.

Actually, he also killed Max. He let him die in the character of the young lieutenant Appel in *Tine*. It was out of discretion that he used Max's family name and not his stage name.

He already knew he was going to do it when he was in Prague.

Perhaps you could read it in his face. His boyish looks were gone. By way of experiment he had begun to grow a moustache.

That moustache created a sensation in Copenhagen. Strictly speaking it was the only new thing about him, seeing that he moved into his old rooms at Ottosens and began working as a journalist again.

'My entire time is spent on writing. I have in these two months been in the theatre only twice – which is otherwise my main diversion! I have acquired a large beard – well, a moustache, really. When a portrait equipped with this adornment was on display in Nygade, a crowd of ladies gathered. I wish to God that I could have charged admission,' he wrote to Emil Jonas.

'That moustache,' Mrs Ottosen said, 'that's just what was missing. A man without a beard is like a bed without pillows.'

But it didn't prevent her from locking his boots and coat away until he had written the lines that would pay the rent and a part payment of the two hundred kroner.

'My coat is at the tailor's,' he wrote to his friends when they had waited for him in vain at dinner.

12.

He wakes up and it is as if he could fly out of the berth and get dressed. And it is hard to believe that he is on board a train on his way to San Francisco. For someone is speaking French.

The voices were a dark woman's voice and maybe that of an adolescent boy.

The woman said: 'I can read the future in your palm.'

And the boy: 'I can light a cigarette with my toes. I can twist myself like a snake. But I am missing a silver tail.'

No, he must have dreamt it. That kind of conversation belongs to tents and caravans and not to first-class compartments on American trains.

He opens the curtain and looks out the window. The speed and the window form a thin protective membrane against the night that is probably full of wild dogs, wolves and maybe hyenas with their witches' laughter and glowing eyes.

Maybe there is also a lonely rider out there who is riding with passion and rage like the horsemen he loves to watch in the circus. He admires circus riders, acrobats and animal handlers who risk their lives every single night. An actor risks only his reputation, after all.

He passes his hands over his face. His moustache is black and shiny. He has brought his personal dyes and makeup along for the whole trip. He touches the box nervously. If that box disappears, he will lose face, literally. Golden brown, black and a little crimson.

They go well with his wardrobe and his eyes.

How beautiful they once were, those eyes. A warm brown with jet-black pupils, and his slight squint was only an extra refinement. His gaze still has a pronounced demonic appeal. To some people it seems dreamlike, to others snooty.

*

It was his eyes and his moustache that made the ladies flock to the photographer's display. And then the novel *Stucco*, of course, that was much commended and much maligned.

But he had grown. Also in a literary manner, they said. He had matured. To be sure, some readers had been bored, but perhaps it was because of the many impressions and characters that had simply exhausted them. They confused fatigue with boredom. And talent – that was beyond dispute.

Maybe his sisters would finally take some pride in him. The thought alone was intoxicating.

There was a tiny glimmer of appreciation in Nini's eyes when they met on the lawn of the Lyngballegaard estate. The sisters approached him slowly. Sofie carried her little son in her arms. But Nini held a little girl's hand, the prettiest girl he had ever seen. Her large dark eyes were bright and self-conscious. It was like looking into the eyes of a grown woman. The child's hair was braided tightly, and the parting was glaringly white.

'Nini, my dear Nini, why haven't you written? Why haven't you told me anything? She is her mother's spitting image.'

'We have adopted Bertha from the orphanage, Herman. Don't be so overwrought.'

At first sight he felt a kinship with the slight little girl. He bent down, and she touched his cheek lightly. He and the child had formed a secret alliance.

He wanted to invite his sisters to join him on an outing and later for dinner.

Sofie laughed, shaking her head.

Nini reproached him: 'But you cannot afford that kind of thing.'

But it so happened that he had a hundred-krone bill that day which he took the liberty of waving in front of them.

'But Herman, be careful! Wrap it up in your handkerchief.'

He obeyed his older sister and regretted it. For after the dinner he accompanied her and Bertha to the station. The train started moving. He pulled the handkerchief out to wave and saw his bill fly out onto the tracks. He screamed and ran and saw Nini covering her face with her hands and the little girl looking confused with her nose pressed against the window.

He looked for torn bits and pieces along the tracks and was elated to find a whole corner – which the bank, however, refused to accept.

The dream of an overcoat and his plan to settle in the provinces, to isolate himself completely and get away from his friends, away from Copenhagen, had vanished into thin air along with the banknote.

He wants to write Tine's story. First an idyll. He will marry his beautiful mother off to a forest manager. And the two of them will stay together and be happy. Their love will be devotional and uncomplicated. His mother's only problem will be her habit of having a lie-in. And he himself – the only child – will jump in her bed like a squirrel.

But the protagonist is Tine. Tine with her puppy fat and her lovely voice that soars to the sky. Tine who can look quite pretty in the morning. His childhood playmate who grows into a tragic heroine. She is the green tree, the girl who runs to meet her lover wearing a little childish bow in her hair. The child who in her sorrow gives herself to the man, without being noticed.

No one judges Tine. But the deacon's daughter judges herself. She leaves her shoes at the edge of the pond and walks into the water. Not to clean herself but to die.

He feels he must write that novel, and the urgency pushes him to leave the city where friends distract and beleaguer him.

Peter Nansen and his wife invite him to dinner in their elegant home where they resemble two handsome children playing grown-ups. The young and rich Johan Knudsen invites him to caviar and champagne and oysters and absinthe. Johan with his blond curls and knife-edge creases and sharp opinions looks at him with admiration which makes him think that Johan really wants to be a poet or perhaps an actor. But Johan is simply too neat. He is so clearheaded and wholesome that his only worry is the thought that he lacks artistic temperament and flaws. Maybe he is inviting the writer in order to become acquainted with anxiety. And Marer invites him so they can talk about the olden days. And the Skrams invite him because the eccentric Herman Bang has such a wonderful calming effect on the desperate Mrs Skram, and moreover, they have a mutual admiration for each other's books. And professor Feilberg – and especially his kind wife – invites Bang together with the Skrams. Mrs Amalie Skram and Herman Bang are both patients of the professor – and a little famous as well.

So, there he is, sitting across from Mrs Amalie Skram who sits next to her husband. Mrs Feilberg sits next to him. He sparkles and charms his dinner partner, and the wine makes him excited right until he turns his eyes towards Mrs Skram.

Black shadows around nervous, probing eyes; and she is thin, my goodness, how thin she is! He knows how miserable she feels. She has written to him about it. A long, rambling letter that has taken her more than a month to write. Her young daughter, an afterthought who arrived after her sons were grown, keeps her on the go night and day. When she finally finds a moment's peace, she falls asleep sitting bolt upright in her chair. And what about all those ideas she has? All those sentences that are never written down.

The pen feels suddenly so heavy in her hand. And nobody understands her when she cries and says that she loves the little one but just wants to be alone, to have some time to herself.

They speak to her as if she were an unreasonable child. Surely, she will have time to write later – and who knows, now she has different things to think about. And a child is, after all, more important than a book.

He glances at her. A thistle of a woman, straight and unbending.

He completely forgets to drink a toast with Mrs Feilberg. He only notices Mrs Amalie Skram, and he wishes her all possible success with her next novel. And when it comes out, he will give a lecture about her and her writing and watch her blush with happiness.

'The two of us,' says Erik Skram and gives his wife an encouraging smile. 'We have just written a play together.'

'The two of us!' A violent, sneering outburst is heard from his wife. 'The two of us!'

Erik Skram quickly puts his hand on her arm and pats it reassuringly. But she shakes off the touch as if his hand were an insect.

Mrs Feilberg looks at them both with pity.

The professor shakes his head. 'No, this cannot go on any longer.'

And Mrs Amalie Skram empties her glass and puts it down so forcefully that the stem breaks and a shard cuts her hand, only superficially, but enough to draw blood.

Erik Skram puts his arm around her shoulder, caringly but firmly, and the two of them leave without as much as thanking the hosts for the dinner.

The waiter removes the broken glass and their plates. Professor Feilberg's guests bend their heads once again over the shellfish. With small silver forks they loosen the pink lobster meat from the shell and smother it in mayonnaise.

'But Mr Bang, you eat like a bird. Listen, come and lunch with us on Sunday; my husband and I will be by ourselves. The three of us can have a good talk, then.'

'On Sunday I will be in Nakskov.'

'You could travel from Nakskov to Copenhagen, or we could visit you in all your loneliness. In any case, you must promise to write to us. We will want to know how you are.'

'Yes, dear Mrs Feilberg. If I have enough money for stamps.'

She laughs. How odd it is that she, the professor's wife, is laughing. That she is apparently enjoying herself immensely.

But, of course, he still writes to her from Nakskov:

'It seems to me that Mrs Skram is seriously ill. I think it is their marriage that is ailing, and that the play they have worked on is an attempt to keep together all that which is falling apart. But maybe I am mistaken.

I wake up during the night soaked in sweat because I can see the landlord with a bill I cannot pay.

And during those first days when I was still well, I enjoyed complete happiness in the solitude which has become the last and most delightful passion in my life. To be alone means to be able to think again – and through the act of reflecting to be able to share humanity's joys and sorrows and to love the mother country from the depth of one's soul. Only in solitude can you be a whole person. Only then can you truly be near your friends. Only then do you find goodness and the meaning of renunciation.

My existence is this one thing: writing a book. Which means that I suffer through all the nervous afflictions that could possibly exist. I am digging my way through this monstrous mountain of material under unspeakable pressure – and whether any of it will succeed, I dare not say. To produce is like an illness. All these strange pictures and ideas can only be put down on paper through a warped process in one's brain. And for me this "sickness" is so agonizing that it sometimes feels as if I should die from it, that my brain will burst. It feels as if my back is on fire. When I wrote *By the Road*, I think I felt less sick – and perhaps it will be my one and only true book. Unfortunately.'

He doesn't mention that he is romping about with the landlord's children, up and down the stairs and through all the empty rooms at Hotel Skandinavien during the quiet winter months.[24] That he considers himself an 'adopted son of the house.' And that those pictures that almost cause his brain to burst are not only those of war and death and injuries but also those from the country of his own childhood.

He remembers every single path and every single bush in the garden around the white house. He remembers the terrible night when he and Christella were hiding under the table. And he makes use of everything that Bjerring has told him about honour and loss.

But he is unable to pay off his debts to his friends. Peter Nansen has to wait for the thirty kroner. Two lawyers and the retreat at Dannevirke intervened.[25] But Peter is soon to see his dear ten-krone notes again:

'Yesterday I finished the Dannevirke-night. At least something in that passage has turned out well – something. But ought it not to be something great? – I would give my life, really, my life for the sake of this book if it could only be a lesson for our wretched country.

For I have nothing to love other than my fatherland. I think of it constantly, and one fine day the stupidity that prevails will cause its destruction – an injustice that torments me as if it were aimed at myself. This country is fundamentally so good, so patient, so honest – why then have there always been so few who loved it, people who didn't just love their party, their own interests and themselves? Why have those who labour always been taken advantage of by those who only talk?'

Twice a day he went for a walk. He was deeply affected by this quiet anonymous life, the semi-dark shops and the streets where seemingly nothing was happening. He stayed in Nakskov until the novel was finished and until he could finally write 'In memory of my mother' on the book's first page.

In everything he had written, he suddenly heard the sound, the tempo, the fear in the alarm signals that had ordered the troops to flee.

And then spring came to Nakskov and Lolland in the course of one single night. The hotel woke up from its winter sleep:

'When I stepped out of my room, the chamber maid was leaning out the hallway window, singing into the bright day, and down in the yard the waiters – the fine, honest and happy waiters of the provinces who are as helpful as friends – were wrestling.

The soil was steaming under the full sun, and the earth looked as if it was eager to conceive.

And Lolland's ugly willow trees gleamed like silver in the fields.'

He quickly wrote down a sketch that he could send away when he came to Copenhagen. And the summer was all expectations and journalism.

In October 1889 *Tine* came out, and the novel moved its readers and was much admired.

But a bad review walked up his stairs. A tall, stately woman knocked on his door without prior warning.

The woman steps into his room, and he asks her to sit. But she prefers to stand. The desk hasn't been dusted in a long time, and the ashtray needs to be emptied. But it is especially his papers that she stares at with disapproval.

'I don't believe that you remember me, Mr Bang.'

Oh, yes, now he remembers. And he wants to embrace her, but she pulls away. Catharina Marie Petersen, born Kjærbølling, now the wife of a landlord, is definitely pulling away from him. In fact, she has come all the way from Skåne in Southern Sweden to express her righteous indignation.

She neither wants to sit nor partake of anything offered to her; she has simply come to tell the author Herman Bang that she has recognized herself and her family in *Tine*. But she has never in her life had a relationship with a forest manager. During the war she was bedridden, sick from typhus. And he knows that.

'Tine, – Tine – '

But there was no 'dear Tine' coming to his aid. The dust from the buttercups had blown off her chin. No white stockings. No dizzying summer.

'Promise me that you will never write about me again.'

'But Tine, I am so very fond of you.'

'A pretty way to show it, putting me into a novel. And you cannot even stick to the truth. Remember, from now on we are no longer on first-name basis.'

And then the lady's quick and hard footsteps echoed down the stairs. Mrs Ottosen opens the door a little to see who has paid him a visit.

'A landlord's wife from Skåne. My old nurse, in fact.'

But he doesn't cry. He just slumps a bit in his chair. Then he gets up and pulls out the top drawer of his chest. In the back are fifty kroner. He puts them in an envelope and mails them to Alvilda Back-Nielsen, the dance teacher. Julius Schiøtt has told him that she recognized herself as Irene Holm and that she actually enjoyed the story. But the ill-fitting dentures – he shouldn't have mentioned those.[26]

For fifty kroner she will surely be able to buy a natural smile made of white porcelain.

It was not his intention to hurt anyone.

He was so vulnerable himself. He read the love poems from Prague again. The jealousy poems.

It was sheer pain. A memory like a scalpel cutting from head to heel. Deep into his heart and brain. Love had perished, and the body had to carry on.

He showed the poems to Peter who said that he couldn't rhyme at all.

'But aren't they still as gracious as dancing mammoths?'

'I only know that if you publish them, you will destroy everything you have gained with *Tine*.'

'These poems are part of me. I want to bring them out.'

Peter talked again about aesthetic flaws and asked if he perhaps regarded his opinions as nothing but rubbish.

And of course he should have listened to Peter.

No sooner had the poems been accepted and printed in a small edition than he imagined how Esmann, half stifled with laughter, would recite: 'That morning a corpse woke up.'[27] He would find it ever so comical that Herman Bang could be so unlucky in love – and then write about it to boot.

But the first review he read was favourable. Erik Skram saw in the poems a strong man's lament about the ephemerality of love. And Amalie Skram thought she had prevented all attacks. Because she had run into Mrs Henriques on the street. And this woman had told her that her husband had read the poems to find material for his satirical revues. But he had closed the book reverentially and said that he would never have suspected Herman Bang of being capable of writing anything that good.

Then the New Year's issue of *Punch* came out. And the writer could see a caricature of himself as the cadaver-poet Herr Manbang, riding a three-legged, headless ghost horse. The resurrected corpse, addicted to painkillers, quinine and morphine.

'*Odense, Thursday*

Dear Nansen.

It is a very big problem that I am asking you to sort out for me – if you can, please. It cannot go on any longer; I have literally gathered all my remaining strength to write this letter. Since my *Poems* came out, I have been more than ill. I suffer from paranoia and cannnot relax, neither day nor night. The last three days I have been falling and having fainting spells one after another. The best thing would probably be to get myself admitted to a mental hospital; but it would hurt my career as a writer too much.

But carrying on as things are now is out of the question. Untold amounts of cognac and port only give me a couple of hours of sleep, and it is destroying me.

There is only one possibility left – that I leave. I always feel better when I am abroad. In Norway I could get myself admitted to a sanatorium without it being noticed if a temporary stay in a small remote town wouldn't work out. As soon as I felt reasonably better, I could then embark on the longer journey – either to Japan or South America.'

The world tour. He was talking about it, planning it even at that stage. It had been a possibility for more than twenty years. His young Norwegian friends were rich. In Norway he could travel from family to family and stay in country houses with views over the fjords. And he would dine and ride in sleighs, and the ladies' furs were elegant and better tailored than their dresses that sometimes had creases in the back.

The young ship owners would offer him luxurious cabins if he wished to be alone. Or they could easily secure him a passage on a ship to the Far East.

'Japan,' they said, 'is the country for you. That's exactly where you would feel at home.'

They had noticed the blood-red fan that he usually waved in the theatre. That kind of thing had not been seen in Norway yet. They marveled at his chain bracelet and gave him two diamond rings as presents. But they laughed at his gloves, for in Norway even millionaires wore knitted mittens.

He wrote about Norway's landscapes and towns, about the youth that was ever so fit and free. About Norwegian literature that he admired. He befriended Henrik Ibsen, Bjørnstjerne Bjørnson, the very young Arne Dybfest and Jonas Lie whose young daughters were always sitting at the piano. Two fine, blond necks, their heads slightly inclined. Two vegetative creatures in another world, enchanted by their own music.

'What happens when Ida and Erika get up from the piano bench?' their escorts would ask teasingly.

The day they finally got up, they had become two fully formed concert pianists.

Norway was full of surprises, was so big. He met the young wives of sea captains who had travelled with their husbands for years and had now returned home, their persons radiating a different aura.

He wrote about them. And he also wrote about the gull hunt on a mountain lake. They would row past the tall rushes and the pristine white flowers. Then they would sit silently until the gulls came.

'The white birds came sailing past the rock face, first a solitary one, then a flock. You couldn't hear their wings beating. Fish were jumping seductively out of the glassy water, while Magdalon was waiting with his gun.

The birds circled closer to the water.

Then the first shot was heard; a word was spoken, a quick pause. A bird is hit. It tumbles, sparkles and – falls through the bright air.

How quietly it floats on the water, its wings spread out, its head bent while the entire flock of gulls circle above the dead, emitting their drawn-out screams of terror.'

He will never forget that sight. And one day he went into the tunnels of a mine and was pulled on a wagon towards the mountain's dark, chilly heart. He lay very still and securely with a fur hat pulled tight over his ears. And above him glowed the bright veins in the ore.

Otherwise there was only darkness, the sound of the wheels and the bitter coldness of the rock.

But there was no pain. The frost had not yet penetrated into his heart and lungs.

*

He will take just another sip of morphine.

But first he wants to turn on the light. And his hands shake at the thought of pushing the wrong button by mistake. Perhaps the window will open automatically and let in the cold night. Perhaps a propeller will start spinning here too. Or a waiter will fling open the door and ask something he doesn't understand.

But his fingers push the right button. The light practically blinds him. But he finds the powder and mixes the morphine carefully with water.

He was met by a strong odour of urine coming from the washbasin. It must have been from passengers who had occupied the white berth before him and who didn't have the energy to get dressed and walk down the long passage to the WC where, incidentally, you could watch the earth fly by through a hole.

It is understandable that they wanted to spare themselves that experience.

He measures the distance from the floor to the washbasin. He steps tentatively up in the berth. Of course, just then the train sways abruptly to one side. They are tall those Americans. Perhaps they eat something special. In any case, their height is impressive.

He sacrifices a little of his eau de cologne to the washbasin, pours a few drops into his palms and swallows down his morphine. Then he lies down with his hands pressed against his face. Like a small child who is hiding, or an older child who is counting, playing hide-and-seek.

Until the effect of the morphine sets in, he will think about the time after the publication of *Poems*.

He travels to Norway, not to visit his rich friends but to sit in the living room of his Norwegian physician Dr Nissen, telling him and Erika Lie Nissen, the pianist, about all the fiascos of his youth. About how he acted the role of Osvald in Bergen, and how the audience hissed at him. About his recitations and theatre tours in the provinces. About the indomitable impresario Mr Theodor, his humbug and his long brownish undergarments. And about how Herman Bang was expelled from Germany, and how he celebrated Christmas Eve in Prague.

Doctor Nissen laughs, and Erika Nissen laughs, and the children turn red from laughing, and they pull on his sleeve and shout: 'Tell us – tell us about this fellow Herman Bang!' And he continues, becoming increasingly more self-deprecating. Suddenly he sees himself as a moving, tragicomic figure that he too can laugh at. And that laughter, and especially the bright bubbly laugh coming from the missus and the children, is better than any medicine.

'Write it down, dear Bang,' says Mrs Erika. 'You must write this down. You have so many talents. When you tell stories, you are an actor. I think you could be a theatre director. If you made use of all your talents, I think you would be less unhappy.'

He wrote about his 'Ten Years' the way he had recounted them in her living room, and he dedicated the book to her. And she, who had had great success in Copenhagen, thanked him, excited from happiness and giddy as a schoolgirl.

Here in America he thought for a moment that he saw her again. She came towards him completely unchanged and smiling. And her gaze was modest and yet very open at the same time.

– Erika – his lips formed her name although he knew that both she and her husband were dead.

The young woman was their daughter Jette. She looked like her mother in the same way a butterfly that emerges from its chrysalis resembles its progenitor. Same features, same sing-song language and same lovely laughter. While reading and while partaking of supper, he only had eyes for her.

She accompanied him to the train. And he flung open the window, leaned far forward, reached down and put his arms around her neck.

'Dear child – I wish that I could have been your father.'

The train's whistle and speed tore them apart. She ran along the train, and her handkerchief unfolded like a white, fluttering flower.

Back then when she laughed her childlike laugh, he himself broke away. One day he felt well enough to travel to a health spa in Laurvig.[28]

Here he surrenders himself to the doctor, the nurse and the masseur and to spring water and heat and cold baths. His body no longer belongs to himself. It is only a material substance that needs to be improved. It is nothing but bones and tendons and blood and muscles that cause pain, fainting spells and seizures.

They were talking about tension in his muscles while digging deeply into his neck with their fingers. They shake him like a cat. And they send him off to the baths and wrap him in soft towels and blankets and praise him for his bravery. And sit him in a deckchair in the park.

The swallows are flying high. The birds gather and scatter. The last roses smell cold and metallic and are probably full of bugs. And far out on the green lawn three dogs are approaching. They are not particularly large and far from being beautiful. The one in the front is short-haired and black. She is moving slowly and patiently. Once in a while she stands still, for the next one, a small yellow dog, is lying across her back. Locked into the movements of the mating effort, the yellow dog walks on its hind legs, completely exhausted, caught by its own sexual instinct. The third dog is a poodle that follows the other two at a short distance, looking exceedingly sad.

At last the dogs disappear. They seek shade away from the sun. Towards the east.

When he returns to his room, he wants to read today's letters again. One of them is from Peter. Peter the Married Man – the Don of his youth who doesn't love his wife any longer. And it appears that she has stopped loving him as well. They are parting ways – these two perfectly charming children.

The other letter is from the new daily paper *København*. Johan Knudsen has bought himself a paper like you would buy a fine hunting dog or a thoroughbred. Now the paper is commissioning a serialized novel by Herman Bang. 'If you would be so kind.' As if it were a steak with Béarnaise sauce.[29]

When the nurse comes to help him back to his room, he sees the three dogs returning in exactly the same positions as before. Which means that the poor creatures have passed at least one hour in this manner. For that is as long as he usually rests after his bath.

As soon as he is alone, he collapses at the desk. A novel – as if it were just a matter of shaking one out of your sleeve.

Outside he hears the swallows' light and bright twitter, as if they want to cheer each other up. It is a sound of metal. Two love birds on a swing in their cage, squeezed close together. A sleepless night, freezing cold. A night of glass and metal.

He has to drown out that sound. He hums a waltz. A love waltz. Enchanting and sentimental.

Amour, amour
oh, bel oiseau,
chante, chante
chante toujours.

He heard that waltz at the circus. The trapeze artists were flying
under the dome to that tune. Maybe they were called Fritz and
Aimée and Adolfe and Louise. Once upon a time they were four
betrayed and troubled children. But now they were stars in the
circus sky. The women in black tights were flying with their hair
flowing. The men were wearing pink 'so pale that it seemed white.
Every muscle was visible – their bodies looked naked.'[30]

Sing. Sing. Go on. It must never cease. This moment where
they float in the erotic space under an illuminated sky must go
on. Catching each other's bodies, flying back and forth, innocent
like angels or birds that are oblivious to their own being, emitting
rousing cries as if this toying with death is an act of love.

There, under the sky of the tent canvas, the acrobats are angels
and devils, sensuous but sexless. Their costumes are almost akin to
nakedness. The light is aimed at them and forms patterns that look
like coats on exotic animals. Their souls are reflected in their eyes.

They catch, they fly, happy and invincible until the woman in the
audience pulls Fritz, the acrobat, down to earthly love. She corrupts
him, robs him of his strength and calmness.

Her dresses are like clouds. Her body is not disfigured from her
work. Her hands are soft and her nails are delicate and pink. Even
her smile and her language are of another world. 'A flower,' she says
about Fritz' mouth, and 'her ruin' about his arms. Mutual desires
catch them and hold them in a tight embrace.

And then there is one night when the trapeze artist Aimée
follows her lover and sees the shadows of him and the woman in a
window. The image of two bodies.

'Her entire life, piece by piece, memory by memory, thought by
thought, shattered, swallowed up, devastated, sunk into this one
thing: desire, the miserable desire of the forsaken.'

She, the unsullied and devoted, becomes a vengeful woman with
lifeless eyes and a body that works mechanically until the moment

when she unhooks Fritz' swing and watches him plummet.

'She didn't know that death could be pleasure until now … . when she let go, screamed and fell.'

Herman Bang puts down his pen. Screeches from the birds. Roses full of creepy-crawlies. And desire that is stronger than love.

He looks at the two letters but doesn't read them. He looks at his notes.

If he had only died that time in Prague. Because he had in fact attempted to just lie down and wait to die. But all that happened was that his beard grew. If he died now, his beard, nails and hair would grow a little, and for a short time these faithful cells would call his name. Otherwise nothing.

He closes his eyes and searches the drawer with his fingertips all the way to the back. Neither bills nor coins, but eleven opium capsules. Eleven small moons. – Swallow them. And it will all be over.

He puts them down in a pattern on the table and pours a glass of the fresh Norwegian spring water. It is not at all difficult swallowing them. It almost feels as if it is something he is doing for the sake of his constitution.

Then he lies down on the bed and waits for the eleven pupae to burst. And death will unfold in his body, quiet and white.

But he has to get up. He must write a farewell letter. He wants to write that it is not due to wrongful treatment or to the nurses' sloppy handling of medicine. He has seized death himself, actually stolen it. It is his and his alone.

Everything is swimming in front of him. It feels as if he has to pluck the characters from outer space. The down strokes look terrifying, thick as matches and completely black.

But he makes it to the bed again. Dying is just like fainting. Or, no, when he faints the world disappears for a moment. Now he himself will disappear from the world.

Like a sandbag. That's how he falls through the dark.

And then a light. Blinding, white, hovering above his face. A globe that bursts, and shards that rain down on him.

Shards. No, ice-cold water and hands that slap his face roughly.

A doctor is shaking him.

And the young nurse's shrill, high-pitched voice: 'You, you who are such a nice person.'

And they walk and walk with him. He sways limply between them, so weak that his feet don't reach the floor. Helpless like a newborn, slapped back to life. And after a few days well enough to do an exclusive reading so he can pay his bill and get out of there.

'*24 – 6 – 1890*

Frederiksstad – passing through.

Dear Nansen,

I won't deny that your hasty words felt like a hard blow. Even what is expected can feel that way. I have, perhaps, sensed what hardship you have suffered – but wasn't able to speak when you yourself kept silent. My friend, I will admit that I feel very sorry, so hopelessly sorry for her. For I fear the future, the many years ahead.

This wretched life.

Here things have also deteriorated to the point where the two of us no longer would be able to see each other again. I am so tired, so very tired. The other day I collected eleven opium capsules – five can kill you – and I took them. It is not difficult to die – I know that now. By a miracle, however, they managed to wake me, and the doctor spread the rumour that I had suffered a concussion. Still, I will never die from "old age" – I don't have enough patience for that.

Otherwise there is nothing new. Perhaps I will travel to the North Cape. The doctors have advised me to do so.

All day I have only been able to think about this situation between you and your wife. And I deeply wish – although for the last few months I have scarcely wished for anything – that I could spend a day with you. Perhaps then we could chat for an hour or so.

Adieu, dear Nansen.
Ever yours
Herman Bang.'

The midnight sun was not to shine on him after all. In fact he had to write to Julius Schiøtt and ask for money to pay for his ticket home.

He avoided Copenhagen and went to Hotel Marienlyst for a few days. From there he went to Fredensborg. He couldn't shake the image of the four devils, and he fainted and fell, like Aimée, from the light into the dark.

Every morning he thought about going to Copenhagen to see Peter. But he kept on putting it off until a visit was no longer possible.

A slight, young girl, with the married name Nansen, knocks on his door. Her whole body is shaking while he wipes her eyes and forehead until her nose starts running too. She buries her face in the large soft chair and surrenders herself to childish blubbering.

At last he gets the idea of giving her a handkerchief dipped in cold water and ordering a bottle of champagne.

'I want to return to the theatre. I thought that you could help me,' she says in a small, timid voice.

He promises to do everything he can while thinking that unhappy souls have a tendency to seek out *him* in particular. Maybe he also reminds her of the time when the three of them were sitting in the doll house, Peter and her as newlyweds, and him calling them instinctively 'dear children'.

He rehearses some light roles with her, suitable for her youthful age, and hopes to make her laugh. But she cries her way through the entire jolly repertoire. And they go for a walk in the woods, picking flowers for Ophelia's madness scene.

But they don't make it that far, although he has been looking forward to acting Hamlet.

He looks deeply into Ophelia's distant gaze. 'I did love you once – I loved you not,' he says.

There is a moment of surprise and then sudden awareness in her expression. Then followed by a flood of tears, her mouth slightly opens like a child being wronged.

'Good, dear. Good. – – Get thee to a nunnery,' he adds fondly.

'Yes,' she says. 'Maybe that's a possibility.'

'But, my dear child. You want to get to the theatre.'

'I just want to get away. Far, far away.'

But she stays in the room next to his. During the night he can hear her walking around in there.

In the morning he knocks on her door. A telegram has arrived for her from Peter Nansen. He knocks and he knocks and finally opens the door. She isn't there. Only an awful mess and a bouquet of wild flowers on the dressing table.

'*Friday*

Dear Nansen

Your wife is not here. However, she left the bill and a few of her belongings behind. She has written and telegraphed several times that she will send the money now. I believe that she will be able to get her things back – after all, the landlord has no use for them. But where should they be sent? And what about the rehearsal when I don't know where she is?

Yes – Heaven only knows.
Give my greetings to Immanuel
Your Herman B.'

Being as nervous as he is and lacking focus, he might as well go to Copenhagen and speak with Peter Nansen if Nansen wants to speak with him. And write for the papers, or go to the circus. But he must stay. Maybe she will suddenly show up again with her tears. And incidentally, he cannot leave two bills unpaid.

'*Fredensborg*

Dear Nansen

In the past three days, I have received two letters from your wife in which she asks me for one hundred kroner. Unfortunately I have nothing at all and I haven't received any reply yet from *København* to my enquiry. If I get anything, I will send whatever I can. She wants to – and has to – leave. God knows where. Unhappy soul.

Surely, it must be bad. Otherwise she wouldn't have come to me, knowing that I have nothing.'

Money arrived from *København*. Johan Knudsen was generous, and no sooner had he bought his paper than his stepfather forced him to buy a farm in Vendsyssel in Northern Jutland to get him away from his friends.

'Bangsbo' was the name of the farm. And everything was precisely the way he, Herman Bang, would have furnished it. And he and all the friends came along. Gustav Wied and Ove Rode and Carl Ewald. They strolled along the country roads surrounded by the local pack of dogs. From a landau they basked in the northern landscape, and Johan had the most handsome horses in the whole region. Or they would sit in the humid and hot parlour among the green plants, drinking absinthe before dinner. The servant girls would make their beds with sheets that smelled of sun and wind as the men did in their childhood. Innocence, absinthe, cigarettes and the wide, green lawns at 'Bangsbo' where he would be laid to rest one day.

They laughed at him when he spoke of his burial under the linden tree.

'Too soon,' Johan said. 'But there will always be a room for you here.'

And it was a joy waking up there and being able to write 'Bangsbo' in your correspondence. 'My ancestral farm' he allowed himself to write to his friends abroad.[31]

In return he became part of the editorial staff at *København*. His co-editor spent most of his time lying on the sofa. But the young writers brought him their manuscripts. Among them the young wife of a teacher, dressed in a modest suit, an astonishing hat and with a floating gait enhanced by her small pretty feet.

Mrs Agnes Henningsen wrote rather unabashedly about sex to the point where he had to blue-pencil parts of the text and invent a pseudonym for her. To make her understand that it was necessary, he mentioned his own pornography conviction as a word of warning. Undaunted, the woman laughed – and she was a mother of several children at that. But the pseudonym Helga Maynert she accepted. And he was invited for dinner at her home and was served roast duck with parsley. He left early, probably to her great disappointment after all her efforts.

But he wanted to drop by the circus. When the performance was finished, he would sit with the artists. Their almost petit-bourgeois family life, where skills were passed on from parents to children, seemed both very exotic, simple and ideal to him. He drank Turkish coffee and listened to problems that involved nothing more than muscles becoming too stiff or costumes being too expensive to acquire.

He felt pity for a human serpent – a young boy who wished for a silver costume that would emphasize his suppleness and surely transform him into a world sensation.

The child pleaded, beside himself, sobbing, but the family didn't have the means.

He didn't have any money either and went home in tears. An acquaintance that he met in the City Hall Square asked, clearly concerned, what had happened.

The man's surprised expression didn't go unnoticed when he, who was after all a well-known writer, shouted across the square: 'The boy shall have a tail!'

He wept all the way up the stairs, and Mrs Ottosen followed him and sat down on the sofa without being asked: 'What's wrong with you now, Bang?'

He mentioned the problem.

'Are you saying that you, a grown man, are sitting here bawling because an acrobat brat doesn't have a silver rump?'

He just nodded. And she scratched her head so that hairpins and dandruff flew and landed on his pillows and on the remains of his grandfather's afghan.

'Bang, I have wanted to say this for a long time. I think you are sick.'

'Sick – I have never been well.'

'I mean sick in the head. If I were you I would go to The City Hospital.'[32]

She looks very sad, the woman does. And he has often thought about it himself.

'Do you think, Mrs Ottosen, that they will admit me?'

'Bang, if you behave like this, I am sure they will keep you in over there.'

The only thing left to do is to go there. And when he sits across from the doctor it is like a scene he has practised. Like that time with the famous impresario Mr Theodor.

A sharp light is aimed at his face. It penetrates his eyes, his ears, his nose and mouth. And the light is not in the least flattering. It makes him into a patient.

Doctor: 'Is there any insanity in your family?'

Patient: 'My father was a pastor. He was mad.'

Doctor: 'How did it manifest itself?'

Patient: 'My mother, who was a very beautiful and sensitive woman, was deeply affected – very upset. She died young.'

Doctor: 'It is your father we are talking about. Your father's mental illness. How did it manifest itself?'

Patient: 'By the altar – during the actual confirmation ceremony and also on my birthday, he began to recite an old children's rhyme.'

Doctor: 'Do you remember which one?'

Patient: 'Do you really want to know that?'

Doctor: 'Yes.'

Patient: 'The cat and the hag.'

Doctor: 'Hmm – a very funny man.'

Patient: 'A very unhappy man. And mother and we children – '

Doctor: 'Yes. Were you abnormal as a child?'

Patient: 'Not at all. I was a pretty child, a very charming child. My mother adored me. Mother and I are very alike.'

Doctor: 'Is there an inherited tendency to use stimulants in your family?'

Patient: 'My paternal grandmother was an alcoholic, and so was my uncle. But I am not related to them.'

Doctor: 'I beg your pardon?'

Patient: 'My grandfather, His Excellency, Privy Councillor, Royal Physician.'

Doctor: 'To the point, please. What about him?'

Patient: 'My grandfather was married twice.'

Doctor: 'And you yourself – are you married?'

Patient: 'No.'

Doctor: 'Do you masturbate?'

Patient: 'No.'

Doctor: 'Have you ever been inflicted with venereal diseases?'

Patient: 'Never. I don't consider myself particularly sexual.'

Doctor: 'Are you addicted to stimulants? For example to alcohol?'

Patient: 'In the evening I enjoy a glass of rum mixed with a sedative. But it only gives me a couple of hours of sleep.'

Doctor: 'Do you take any narcotics? Opium? Morphine?'

Patient: 'Only with a doctor's prescription.'

Doctor: 'Any illnesses?'

Patient: 'I have had rheumatic fever. And sometimes I have seizures.'

Doctor: 'When and how do these seizures appear?'

Patient: 'The past ten years I have had them at irregular intervals. First nausea, then feeling faint, and finally I pass out. Sometimes it lasts a long time. It happens especially when I begin working on a book.'

Doctor: 'Couldn't you find something else to do?'

Patient: 'Impossible. It would equate to losing everything. Besides, it would be a loss for literature. – And after the attacks the characters become very clear in my head, almost as if they were displayed on a white sheet.'

Doctor: 'When did you cease being mentally normal?'

Patient: 'Four or five years ago my life took a turn. An event that erased all traces of happiness. The memory of this has festered in my mind, leaving deeper and deeper scars.'

Doctor: 'And this "Weltschmerz" – can you describe it further?'

Patient: 'No.'

Doctor: 'Tell me, have you attempted suicide?'

Patient: 'Only once.'

Doctor: 'Are you thinking of repeating the attempt?'

Patient: 'No.'

Doctor: 'We will try a full diet, eggs, milk, mineral water, massage, sulphur baths and a teaspoon of chloral hydrate.'

Patient: 'A teaspoon – just a teaspoon?'

The physician is writing, and the patient leans forward a little, very discreetly. And his good eye is farsighted.

'His manners and ways of expressing himself are marked by extreme histrionics. Now and then he seems to enjoy his profound "Weltschmerz". Hardly a sentence is expressed in a plain and natural manner but presented in an affected and declamatory style. At the same time a very strong sense of self and an appreciation of his own talent and production are discernible.

There is a strong degenerate air about the patient. The cranium is low with a sloping forehead. The shape of the ears is unattractive. The facial expression is in constant motion. R. eye is blind from birth.

The tongue is coated and darting.

Weight: 55 kg 660 g.'

Herman Joachim Bang's appearance has not been described this unfavourably since his birth.

13.

He survived the opium. Morphine doesn't induce sleep. Your brain keeps on spinning. And your heart pounds. Its soft, dull, dizzying sound fills up the whole train compartment. Fear trapped in a padded box.

The train passes a town. A sky like lapis lazuli. Dark houses and the silvery mirror of a saltwater lake.

The garden at home. The precious exotic plants that grew so well in the summer. Now they are probably covered in snow.

When he returns, they will be able to eat in the garden. He promised his friends dinners under the plane tree when it was only knee-high.

New York, San Francisco, Yokohama, Tokyo, Kyoto. Japanese women, their hair lustrous and shiny like lacquer, and silk kimonos embroidered with lotus flowers and chrysanthemums and herons floating under silvery moons. All that he will write about.

But if he loses his mind, his money, his luggage, or if he gets on a wrong train, he will be doomed.

Someone will wait for him in vain on the platform. Someone will shout his name in the arrival hall or out across the tracks.

But if the light has blinded him. If a doctor who doesn't understand his language has written something in his medical file. If the door in an insane asylum has been slammed shut, nobody will look for him there.

That time when he moved from the Ottosens to the City Hospital in

Copenhagen, he knew that he wasn't forgotten.

The hospital made him as irresponsible as a child. He would sit on the window sill and look at the stars. But he, the poet, knew that he would be discharged. It was just a phase in his life, and when he saw the two rather ordinary nurses, their blond hair brushed tidily off their face, he felt safe. Similarly he enjoyed walking in the hospital's large, quiet garden where the leaves were falling without a sound and the noise from the city was barely audible.

Sometimes he couldn't sleep because of the clatter in the hallway. Sometimes he would sleep ten hours in a row. And room and board were completely gratis.

The first person to intrude was Johan Knudsen. Johan looked around somewhat critically. He praised him for 'Les quatre diables' that had been published as a serial. They chatted about the editorial office, and aside from that Johan, who had just returned from Paris, could inform him that the colour in fashion now was pearl grey in Paris, and that Gabrielle Réjanne was the Parisians' favourite actress.

But they had barely been talking for ten minutes when Johan declared: 'You are exactly the way you usually are. I will get you discharged right away.'

'No. No, Johan. I beg you, don't do it. I intend to stay for as long as the professor will keep me. Here I am finally getting some peace and quiet.'

Just then loud voices, verging on screams, were heard from the corridor. For once Johan seemed hesitant.

'You see, my creditors won't come here to bother me. Not even Mrs Ottosen will be able to slam the door. Here I can really work. Perhaps it is not as good as a hotel – but almost.'

Johan sat on the bed, bobbing his right foot with its well-polished shoe up and down. 'Are you saying that it is just a question of money?'

'Not just money. M-O-N-E-Y.'

Johan laughed: 'We will organize a charity show for you. Everybody will come. At least all the women. And we can easily get somebody to perform.'

'I want a spot on the stage, too. I want to read my farewell.'

And only three weeks later Johan Knudsen, Peter Nansen and

Cantor had arranged it all.

Peter teased him: 'We will get a couple of porters to watch you while you read. Then we can ask twice as much for admission.'

They achieved it without asking and without the porters. Everyone thought he deserved a trip to the Riviera to recuperate.

'And bouquets,' he begged. 'More than anything I must have many bouquets. Even if they are just cabbage leaves, bouquets are good publicity.'

It was of course depressing that it had to be the Swede August Lindberg who acted the role of Osvald in the last act of Ibsen's *Ghosts*. But at least Herman Bang was listed as the director. And when he came on stage to read his 'Twilight Tale' about a young man who leaves his native land, his nervousness and frail voice for once had a positive effect.[33]

The audience at *Dagmarteatret* applauded warmly and vigorously. Women were weeping. A gentleman fainted. And he received eighty-seven bouquets and a very large envelope with the evening's earnings. Cantor, barrister at the High Court, had personally emptied the cash drawer every hour and chased all the creditors away.

And then the newly discharged Herman Bang travelled in high spirits the same evening. Not to the Riviera. But to Norway.

In Kristiania they wanted to see him act in his own tragedy *Brothers*, and he was in great demand in his capacity as director.[34]

In an attractive little dinner theatre he is asked to direct a cabaret with Norway's talented youth. He selects texts. He engages a team of painters for the flats. He listens to poems recited by young strong voices, and he tries to teach a chorus of Norwegian girls to march in step with skis slung over their shoulder.

They are all so keen and fearless. And he himself is practically bubbling over with energy and ideas. And it has to be easy to perform, but definitely not too easy. And the choreography must be perfect, but at the same time flexible so the programme can be changed.

Maybe it is not Norway's best actors that work at the dinner theatres. But all the young performers believe in themselves and in each other and in Herman Bang.

And then – the day before the premiere he reads that Esmann calls the variety theatre pure humbug. It feels like the carpet is pulled from under him. And even worse: everyone gets stage fright and becomes erratic. A voice that had previously been a tad too loud now sounded like a roar in the hall. And the girls who had finally learned to walk in step panic, their hearts pounding and their knees going soft as if made of snow.

He himself remains calm. Even on the opening night when Ibsen and Erika Nissen are seated, the lights are dimmed and three men walk in. They look like lawyers in a comedy with their capes, walking sticks, tailcoats and top hats. They are giddy and drunk. They pop three champagne corks. And everyone's attention turns to them while they fill the glasses of their friends and acquaintances and order more champagne. The pranksters Peter Nansen, Gustav Esmann and a very young actor Jacob Jacobsen drown out the actors and steal their show. Behaving rudely and dressed elegantly, they have travelled all the way to Kristiania to mock him.

'But why? Why did you do it, Peter?'

'Why? There is no explanation. Why didn't you go to the Riviera? Why have you always been so obsessed with everything Norwegian? Why?'

'Who were these three scoundrels?' his Norwegian friends asked.

'I shared everything with two of them in my youth. They dined at my table every day.'

'But the cabaret – you'll have to abandon it. After that premiere and after those reviews nobody will come.'

'The word "abandon" is not in my vocabulary.'

And he managed to turn the fiasco if not into a success then something like it. He cut out the more gloomy acts, rearranged the programme and took an acting part himself.

He fainted on the street from exhaustion. The cold hit him hard, and besides, he had forgotten to eat. Everything went black, and his heart raced at a dizzying rate. But he didn't topple over without warning as he usually did. He flapped his arms like a bird before falling over into a nearby snowdrift.

On that same day he had a visit from Nini's sister-in-law Rikke Tresselt, née Holst. He didn't immediately recognize the playmate from his childhood, the spoiled young girl from the manor house, now a small, slight woman whose face was so gaunt that her chin bore an awful resemblance to the rump of a plucked chicken.

But her eyes were still lively and bright. She had a favour to ask him, she said. When she dies, he must look up Henrik Ibsen on her behalf. Surely, Bang remembers that she had been very much in love with the Norwegian poet and he even more so with her.

He asked why in the world she didn't want to do it herself.

But she had already made an attempt. The press had in fact arranged a meeting.

Ibsen had been seated at his usual table at the Grand Hotel, staring down into his hat which was said to have a mirror at the bottom of the crown.

She had entered and begun to speak right away. 'Well, you seem to have had a more enjoyable time of it than me. You have written your plays. I have just borne children.'

After that there were no more words.

Much to the journalists' annoyance, the poet didn't answer the small woman who had given birth to fourteen children.

The words she had wanted to say, she now passed on to Herman Bang:

'I enjoy Ibsen's triumphs. I understand his celebrations clearly – and I suffer personally – after all – I do know – that in all that greatness – an old youthful dream must be slipping away from him faster and faster – while for me it is my life. Please, do not forget your promise to tell him in your curious, unique manner – when I am gone – and he is still here – how much he has been loved – in spite of my foolishness.'

*

That letter is still in his luggage, locked inside a train that squeals and rattles, moving along at a snail's pace. His heart and lungs take up all the space in the train. A piston-heart and lungs panting for air, pulling the train up the hills, up the mountains, through forests and through deserts. And in the corridors dark-skinned young men dance along with carts full of linen as white as the wings of angels.

And the train conductors are tall and as self-assured as policemen.

Money, passport, ticket. He removes them from his coat pocket and hides them under the pillow. For who knows, there might be thieves on board. And if he loses these things, he is lost.

He is a man without a safety net.

A man who is staying in a hotel without knowing if can pay the bill. For him there will be no excuses.

Fleeing is all that is left.

He knew it already that day in January in 1893 at the Central Railway Station in Copenhagen. The money from the charity concert was gone. The money from Norway had flown out of his pocket. And he had to go to Paris.

There were police at the railway station. And paperboys. The clack of wooden clogs and the fresh smell of printing ink, bitter like the words: Indecent. Perverse. Homosexual. House of correction.

He bought a newspaper to hide behind. The murder he had already read about. An elderly wealthy gentleman had been murdered, and everyone who was thought to belong to certain circles which the victim had frequented was now being questioned. Photographs of young men known from the street and the theatre had been found in the man's drawing room.

If anyone belongs to 'certain circles', then he, Herman Bang, does, and he was in fact rather proud that so many people were collecting his portrait as if he were a famous actor.

Even though he has never visited the murdered man, he knows someone who knows someone who knows someone. And even though he has never disclosed his sexuality in so many words, his back, his socks, his gloves, his handkerchief will give it away. And you would be able to see it in his early portraits – the heavy fringe and a soft and pretty face, the image of an Oriental prince. And the satirical papers placed a tiara on his head and equipped him with a heart-shaped shield.

And even if he burns all the love letters, it wouldn't matter. Including the last one from the young actor Christian Houmark who thinks he is Bang's kindred soul. 'From the moment when my mother read your article about the burning of the castle to me, I began to love and admire you,' the creature wrote.

*

'Yes, dear Houmark, your letter has been burned – it seems the most prudent thing to do. You have a restless heart. I wish you luck.'

But on a later occasion he has called Houmark his 'dear lily' and 'mimosa'. And heaven only knows if Houmark has had the heart to burn it.

He hopes so. Because there will be undercover agents and informers and someone who has heard a rumour. And fear is a room with heavy iron keys. With darkness and blinding lights and voices that question you over and over again behind desks of mahogany and brass. And he, Herman Bang, will be locked up. And the shame will not only be his to carry but also Nini's and Sofie's and little Bertha's.

He has to get away – as far from there as possible. Paris or suicide.

But he needs money.

It's of no use asking the publisher for an advance. Actually, he owes them a novel: 'The Last Dane'. A novel about the political clubs. A brilliant title and an excellent idea. The only problem is that he never got beyond the first very promising chapter.[35]

There is a certain acerbic tone in the letters from the publisher when they send him reminders. And his own letters? Oh well, those are not being answered.

It's of no use asking any of those people he has helped in the past. Either they are just as penniless as he is, or perhaps it was simply criminal helping them out with loans or gifts in the first place. He never asked – or investigated how pressing their need was. He just opened his wallet and gave whatever he had. It was foolish, he realizes it now. Most likely there are one or two blackmailers among them. And those swindlers will soon find him in Copenhagen and ask for more, no, demand more. For once he has paid out, he has made it known that his affairs don't bear close scrutiny.

But it is and will always be nature that has made him this way. Nature has been careless and forgotten something. The same way one can end up with misshapen ears or short legs, or a plant can turn out scraggly. Even a rose can be quite crooked and look intoxicated.

The money. It would be fruitless counting it again. There isn't enough for a trip to Paris. But if he goes to Sæby. At Clasen's Hotel, they will take him in. No one will look for him there. Mrs Clasen is his good friend, and she will not worry about whether he can pay his bill. She will just say that it can wait.

He drags his suitcase up onto the train. His body is his prison. And he will never be free. Fear takes him to Sæby although he knows that he needs to get much further away than to the steep hills of Jutland that remind him of men's necks. And he shouldn't really think this way, but the nape of a man's neck is surely much more attractive and expressive than a woman's, hidden as it is under hair and hair pads and hairpins.

The thought won't go away. Not even when Mrs Clasen squeezes his hands, happily surprised to see him in the middle of winter.

'You are most welcome, Bang. As you know, we have plenty of space.'

Mrs Clasen's face is round and soft. Her neck is wrinkled and her nose slightly red – not from drinking but from the perpetual steam and sizzle rising from her pots and pans. This never-ending rush. The woman is constantly running around and nobody thanks her. No one notices that she makes the beds with nice, starched sheets. But if the water in the pitcher by the washstand should be a touch brownish from the iron in the well … If the towels aren't sufficiently soft or big or white … She bends her head, wears herself down. A little mother for her guests and staff.[36]

She has already lit the fire in his favourite room and brought him some veal roast and red wine when he senses that someone is watching him.

There is another guest with brown eyes, moustache and hair combed down over his forehead. The man is looking at him, not with the sad, pitying look of a dog but with eyes that in spite of the colour are like those of a hunting cat.

Beautiful, shiny teeth. A small ironic smile with a hint of malice.

'We are presumably here for the same reason, Mr Bang. I take it that you are prepared to help a friend in need.'

He doesn't remember having met him before. And he knows it is wrong. He knows that it is cowardly of him to withdraw a small bundle of bills from his pocket and push them over towards the man.

Now, he will have to leave. Now he knows that he has been recognized as a fugitive. And most of all: he will need money. He writes to Doctor Feilberg and reminds him that it is more than two years ago he borrowed money from him last. The professor will surely help him. The same evening, on his way to Bangsbo where lamps are lit in every room, he posts the letter. Johan is entertaining guests and is off to Copenhagen the following morning.

Being with other people is a misery. And in his condition. His clothes: crumpled. His soul: ripped apart. And his suitcase still in Sæby. He practically flees to his bed and lies awake all night until the maid brings him breakfast and a letter from Johan Knudsen. 'Stay as long as you wish.' And money. Two hundred-krone bills. He puts them in his left breast pocket as though they would be able to soothe his heart.

But he couldn't stay. He went to the station and got on a train to Hamburg. At the border he changed to a coach and was let into Germany. He boarded another train, and at the hotel in Hamburg he managed to act like a man of the world. At least, he was shown to a room without having to pay in advance. Apparently, there was no indication of the name Herman Bang being connected with a person banished from the country.

*

He pulled a letter out of his pocket. It was from a real count: Prozor. The count's wife had translated *Tine* and was hoping to find a French publisher.

He wrote to the count that he was on his way to Paris. If *Tine* had been accepted, an honorarium might be waiting for him, something his highness had avoided mentioning. He walked along the wide avenues of Hamburg back towards the train station. He walked close to the buildings, bent over and scared of his own shadow.

The hotel was a trap. Sooner or later they would discover who he was. The train to Paris was not leaving until the next day, so he jumped on the first available train – to Copenhagen.

His nervous fingers drew circles on the window. Eleven little moons and the terrifying number eight. The masculine and the feminine. A snare. A noose around his neck and his foot.

At Copenhagen's Central Station the police constables walked in pairs. The shouting from the paperboys was piercing and nerve-racking. The headlines about murder and indecency had grown in size. He didn't dare to go home.

He drove out to his young colleague, the journalist Kristian Dahl, who had invited him on several occasions and said that he was welcome any time. And he knew that he meant it. For Dahl was ever so good and honest and so inept that his best articles had been dictated by Herman Bang.

He practically fell through the doorway. And Mrs Olga Dahl, who was home alone, greeted him with a sad and sympathetic smile after he had told her that he wished to go underground.

It surprised him that he woke up, for he didn't remember falling asleep. But three ugly dogs had been there and then disappeared in the horizon somewhere to the east beyond the light. And he screamed when he saw his coat hanging from the ceiling. The brown overcoat that had been soaked through had been brushed and hung up to dry on a hook, the very hook, Mrs Olga said, that they had used to anchor the Christmas tree.

For a moment the thought of Christmas made him feel completely calm and safe. And Dahl came home and was truly happy to see him. He had often wished he could return the favour, he said.

No one mentioned anything about the difficult situtation. But Mrs Olga Dahl pressed his trousers with a red-hot iron after having placed them under a white sheet. Steam sputtered and enveloped her sweet childlike face, and those creases lasted all the way to Gare du Nord.

When they accompanied him to the train, she demonstratively pulled off her gloves almost as if she wanted the heat from her skin to stay with him all the way to Paris. And her eyes filled with tears as if it were a coffin they were seeing off.

He tried to smile at her, encouragingly, for Cantor had raised some money, and professor Feilberg had helped out and advised him to take a room at Hotel de Malte where the proprietor spoke Danish.

If he could just work, he would get over it. But he had to write to his brother-in-law, the estate administrator, from Hotel de Malte:

'*Paris. Hotel de Malte. Rue de Richelieu No. 63*

2.3.93

I beg you, if at all possible, not to let Nini know that you have received this letter and in any case don't ever disclose what it contains. It is difficult enough to write this to a man; to a woman or to one's sister – it is impossible.

I came here because I had to get away. Perhaps you have already heard the rumours. This affliction that has been the secret explanation of my entire life, that has chased me from place to place, that has impoverished me increasingly– because everything I had went to people who since my earliest youth have put pressure on me – this affliction that has kept me away from my family and many others has become a terrible threat. If you knew what it feels like to have to drag this curse with you through life. People feel compassion for the blind, the one-eyed, the hunchbacks, the lepers and open the hospitals to them. But for those of us who from birth have been afflicted with this disease – for it is a disease even if you don't think so – for us they open the prisons.

I got away – I arrived here. When I arrived I possessed less than a hundred francs and only the clothes I was wearing. I had left in a hurry and couldn't bring anything with me as everything I own was still in Jutland, and I haven't seen it since. I had to check in to a hotel, I, who haven't set foot in Paris ever. The hotel is small, and I am on the fourth floor, and I eat only once a day. The day after arriving, I began to write. It is four weeks ago this Saturday. Since then I have written forty-eight long and short articles. But today I realized that so far my paper in Copenhagen hasn't had the courage to print anything by me – and in Norway and Sweden it is the same story, for I have received no replies to my letters.

I am now without any means. My friends have deserted me and don't answer me. Today the hotel keeper has demanded his money and given me a grace period until Monday. On Monday he will contact the consul. It will result in a new scandal that will bring all the other things to light.

If I could escape from here without a scandal, I would rent a room in one of the suburbs, and I am positive that I could get enough translation work to survive. Uncle Mikael sent me one hundred francs two weeks ago. But I didn't even have a change of shirts, so I haven't been able to pay any of the bills here.

I pay seven francs per day. Now, when I have to pay them, I realize that everything I have written these past weeks has been a waste and that I have nothing coming to me. Since I am without luggage, they can simply treat me as a fraudster and send me home – which is the same as being implicated in all those cases that are presently being investigated in Copenhagen. Please understand that in moments like these, being deserted by everyone, I neither exaggerate nor misrepresent the situation. It is a matter of extreme urgency, and you must know that I would never have written this letter to you were it not a question of having to save what is left of my name, the same name that was once your wife's.

There is no time to waste. Here in France, they act quickly. When you have received this letter, send a telegram without delay to: "Bang, 63 Rue de Richelieu. L'argent envoyé. Holst" – which I can show the hotel keeper. And send at the same time 250 kroner to the full address listed above. With that money I can leave this place and move out to the suburbs where one can live on less than a hundred francs a month.

I beg you to forgive me the grief I am causing you. Don't let it affect Nini who suffers so terribly at the thought of all this pain we – her family – inflict on you.

Trust me, there is no time to waste, and please act quickly as one would do in desperate circumstances.

Herman

Most importantly: send the telegram to appease the landlord. I give my word that I have written nothing but the truth.'

When it was time for absinthe, he posted his letter and went to the café. He ordered a glass of the strong green drink, a medicine that removed all feelings of hunger and anxiety and settled in his joints like a slight tingling pain. He watched couples moving closer together, buying roses from wretched-looking children. For himself he bought a white rose and tipped the small, thin girl five francs. It was a kind of magic gesture. Now he was certain that his wealthy brother-in-law Holst, the estate administrator, for once would help him. He stuck the rose in his buttonhole and ordered another glass.

*

How he wished he had a glass of absinthe right now. And if he could only speak French or German now. He might as well get up and get dressed and go to the dining car. Just getting dressed helps. It is as if the clothes make him whole. His eyes are clear. His diamonds sparkle. And his watch. He doesn't want to look at it. The beautiful, treacherous watch displays other times than those lodged in his body.

There are only two passengers in the dining car. A woman who has pulled the combs out of her hair so it hangs like two reddish wings around her pale face. A young boy who is lying with his head in her lap in a deep and soundless sleep like a child with a fever.

Maybe the boy is an acrobat or a violin prodigy and the woman, the mother, dependent on his talent and luck. And if her red hair had been done up and her gloves buttoned and her face looked less worn out, she would look like Paris' great actress La Réjane.

The woman is smiling as if she can read his thoughts. But it isn't a real smile, rather a show of the Parisienne's friendly and cheerful ways. In friendships: devoted as a dog. In love: cunning as a cat. That's how they are, the Parisiennes. And in the hour of absinthe, anything could happen. Today's beloved could be tomorrow's friend.

Absinthe – green like the strange underwater light that appeared for an instant in the sky above New York. If the drink and the light could just flood his body, he would be able to overcome his insomnia and forget the European times and quirks that tick away in his nervous and restless heart.

Absinthe – it is not on the menu. But she must have read the word on his lips. Because she shakes her head and points to another drink. A drink made from cactus – strong and mixed with fruit juice.

He orders one for her and one for himself. The drink is red with a touch of orange. A sunrise – she says. And it tastes both strong and innocent like the fruit drinks of his childhood. The two of them drink a sunrise together.

And it is obvious that she wants to hear him tell stories. She, who has to sit bolt upright all night watching over the child, wants to listen to him, the sleepless poet.

'Madame, I came to Paris. And I literally owned only what I was wearing. I was a refugee, a completely unknown man from the North – and I conquered Paris, the world city.

The first few days I walked around in a daze. It was like stepping on to a stage set. But I also had a strange feeling of disappointment. Really, was L'Arc de Triomphe not any taller? Wasn't it supposed to reach to the sky? And the Louvre – wasn't it any bigger than that? And Le Bois de Boulogne – the trees were rather thin at the top.

"I can see you are disappointed," my Norwegian colleague Jonas Lie said. "But you simply have to try living here. Let's talk again in a year's time."

One year. It seemed like an eternity to me. And how could it be done when I couldn't get steady writing assignments with a publisher or have my articles printed?

I wandered around in Paris, and I lay on my bed in Paris with cold compresses on my forehead as if they could heal my wounds and make new thoughts jump out onto the paper.

I wasn't the only one to arrive in Paris with those expectations. There was already a whole Nordic colony. Sophus Claussen who became my friend – he was also the first one I borrowed money from for my laundry, cigarettes and stamps. Jonas Lie who had lived in the city for a couple of years – incidentally, he gave me a rather large advance. And there was Hamsun who also lent me a few francs although he seemed to find my appearance amusing and called me a decent little journalist. And all the painters simply had to come to Paris. They found motifs along the Seine, or they took off suddenly to Normandy: Munch, Willumsen and Fritz Thaulow with his family. His wife, Alexandra, became my wise and helpful friend. Oda

Krohg is her sister, you know, the painter whose husband, Christian Krohg, painted her in the red bodice, her hair let down, her blue eyes animated and her hands on her hips. Oda was the princess of Kristiania's bohemians. But Mrs Alexandra carried herself like a queen in the Parisian salons in her red evening cape shot with gold. She glowed, was so fair that the wives would close the shutters when she walked past lest their men be watching.

One day when we were out strolling, she pointed at a house and said that I should live there because that house looked like me. It was a small, ramshackle, brownish house that seemed lonely and sad, and it was painted in exactly the same colour as the overcoat I had been wearing for two years. I was not offended, and of course I never had the money to rent that house.

But Sophus Claussen got me out of the expensive hotel and into Hôtel des Américains, rue de l'Abbé de L'Epée across from the School for Deaf-Mutes. It was a villa, nice and neat and with a garden where you could eat. I got two bright rooms without bedbugs. Paris in those days was a very inexpensive city. Board and lodging for a day cost you five francs. And the meals consisted of four courses twice a day with wine. You couldn't find anything cheaper in Kristiania, and in Kristiania you wouldn't get four courses with wine. Kristiania is not Paris, after all.

Only Heaven knows how it was possible to serve all that for such a modest price. Perhaps Heaven didn't always know how the food was prepared. The steaks could be rather thin, and the fish not exactly fresh caught the day before. But you got enough to eat, and when we could afford it, Claussen and I, we dined on Saint Michel with the artisans and coachmen who demanded solid meals for their money.

The same Claussen also managed to drag me off to *Le Procope*'s cellar in the Latin Quarter where Verlaine was a regular guest. Forever intoxicated, the poet would drag his cape through the dirt and deliver his poems to the French nation, poems that were like bloody wine in golden bowls. The young adored him and smoked their cigarettes and drank their cheap beer. But I didn't go there often.

I made very different contacts through Count Prozor. Granted, he hadn't been able to sell *Tine*. But he was keen to show me his world, and he filled my pockets with recommendations.

From the first loan advanced to me I bought new clothes so I could conduct myself in style in Paris. A grey smoking jacket with complementary shirts of greyish-yellow linen and a complete ensemble so I could go visiting.

But it isn't that easy calling on a Parisian celebrity. Well, what are you doing there on Champs Elysées, like a bull in a china shop?

The stairs are of marble with beige carpets, and the electrical lamps are supported by caryatides. On each landing is a sofa. I pause for breath on the last one – only one more flight of stairs, and I'll be there.

Dentists and celebrities to whom one must present an introduction ought not to live on the third floor. It prolongs the misery. A valet opens the door. He is dressed in black with black buttons, the celebrity's initials embroidered with black silk on each button. I captured the whole person in a glance … were it not blasphemous, I would say that he looked like an undertaker.

I give him my card and my letter … and the undertaker looks at them as if they were an offering. He has only opened the door a crack – and I am thinking to myself that all that's needed is a safety chain to complete the picture – when he suddenly pushes it wide open: the "lackey" has just noticed the count's crown on the envelope.

"He will ask if the master is in."

Yes, but he is having a bath.

And I wait and wait for this celebrity who finally appears in a night gown of white wool and a fez.

We converse. He knows Count Prozor very well. He met him in Portugal.

And I, I have not been to Portugal.

Oh well, he hadn't really expected as much.

We talk a little about Paris, and with a sudden change of topic, the master of the house says: "Ahem! So, they write novels where you come from … . over there, là bas … ." (là bas means the regions around the North Pole).

And all at once – for I am thinking of all the Nordic novels that

I am fond of – I have the courage to smile, and I answer: "Yes – we try our best."

And so I excused myself and took my leave.

That kind of visit wore my spring ensemble thin.

But at the hotel I felt at home. I knew all the guests: the young couple that always argued about money, the middle-aged woman who reminded me of my cousin Margrethe. I couldn't help taking a special interest in her, even managed to help her obtain an office job. And then there was the concierge with whom I spoke quite a lot when I bought candles. She was a sad, deserted woman. For twenty years she had longed for the same man – not waited for him, just longed for him. She was a lady with an aptitude for resignation. And the servant was so elegant when he left for his breaks that I mistook him for a French nobleman.

On the other hand, people assumed that I was a Polish count and perhaps a diplomat. Those who knew better regarded me as a Danish count – "Illustre comte" was the headline on my first interview in Paris. It was the young Bigeon who wrote about me; he admired me and was in seventh heaven when things turned out well for me.

In the charming rooms in the street of the deaf-mutes my novel began to take shape. In the beginning the sentences had to be gathered from afar. It was as if the escape had caused a membrane to grow between the material and me.

But now all of Ida's childhood came to me in Paris. Life at the estate Ludvigsbakke – that is, Rodvigsballe where I had often been as a child.[37]

And I visualized the nurses at the City Hospital. Their faces under the lamp and Ida Brandt – the self-sacrificing young woman with that lovely gait, a woman who falls in love and is transformed into a seventeen-year old girl. She is no great tragic heroine, perhaps she is a little naive and much too caring. In love she gives all of her self away, and when her lover deserts her, she grows old. She withers away in a single evening.

Oh yes, I was once again back in the Danish provinces and in Copenhagen when I wrote. And outside the acacias smelled sweet. The air was lazy and sticky, and the poor students were studying for their exams.

How were they supposed to concentrate when their female friends and sweethearts were celebrating the summer by putting on the brightest of bright and the thinnest of thin robes?

It was nothing but *joie de vivre* and a desire to dance that led to the students' wailing like a Greek chorus in front of Senator Bérenger's windows. The old reactionary had closed down the ball at the École des Beaux-Arts because some of the models had worn dresses that revealed more than they covered.

They were just hecklers. But the central brigades turned up. Otherwise they are only deployed in cases of rebellion.

Chairs were flying in the air. Six students were wounded. And a policeman accidentally killed a young hawker with a matchbox holder of porcelain.

It was a meaningless tragedy. But not a revolution.[38]

I had been working on my novel and gone to bed when my good friend Sophus Claussen threw a stone at my window and woke me up. There was a big commotion on the boulevards, he said. We had to go and see. I quickly got dressed.

The first stretch of Boulevard Saint-Michel was practically empty. But I noticed that all the metal cages around the trees were broken off. And all the shops and cafés had been shuttered.

We approached the Pont Saint-Michel. There was a horde of people. Especially young men and boys. The students were in the minority.

When we crossed the bridge, Claussen and I, the crowd was relatively calm. The square had just been cleared by the cavalry. And we walked towards the Prefecture of Police.

Suddenly we hear screaming and yelling. The horde is arming itself with stones. Why nobody has thought about removing all those stones is beyond me. There were actually heaps of stones right in front of the prefecture.

I am standing near the large door when it suddenly opens, and a hundred policemen charge out. They scream and behave like madmen. You wouldn't think they were law enforcement officers but a band of robbers waiting in ambush.

In no time the square was almost cleared. But the cavalrymen that were supposed to guard it were bombarded with stones and large rocks. The horde returned. Bigger and increasingly wilder. Kiosks were overturned and set on fire. They burned like midsummer bonfires. It didn't help when the cavalrymen charged the crowd. The horses reared. Only a young lieutenant attempted to hold the fort. He remained on the square all alone mounted on his horse. Pale and facing the flames. Stones showered over him. And finally he too had to give up.

Then everything became almost calm again. But then – suddenly two gates open up. And I think about two hundred men storm across the square, across the bridge and into the narrow side streets. They are armed with swords, and they grab stones and sticks, anything that can be used as a weapon, and they rush at the people who run for their lives. Just a few try to defend themselves by climbing on top of a bus and pelting the police with stones. However, the policemen didn't appear at all calm and collected. It seemed like a massacre. It is moments like these that explain how revolutions get underway.

My friend Claussen and I ran down one of the nearest side streets. But we were not fast enough. Claussen was roughed up so severely by the police truncheons that he could barely use a pencil all the next day. And I ended up with a gash on my head and had to go to the hospital to be bandaged.

But we had material to work with, Claussen and I: "Paris under arms." "The revolution." He wrote for *Politiken* and I for *Aftenbladet*, and there were no problems getting those articles accepted. *Aftenbladet* was selling well back home in Copenhagen.

On Boulevard Saint-Michel there wasn't one undamaged streetlamp left. On Boulevard de Sébastopol the kiosks were burning like big torches in the night. And the horse-drawn cabs bolted through the streets without their coachmen.

Officially there were some twenty fatalities. But I believe the real number was much higher. I am certain that the police seized the corpses.

The revolution lasted a week. But two weeks later, I was still wearing the white bandage around my head while strolling with the beautiful Mrs Thaulow on my arm.

"Take that damned bandage off, why don't you!" Fritz Thaulow shouted one day.

"But Fritz, I want to be a hero for just a bit longer."

Actually, the bandage wasn't exactly white. I took it off. It was out of necessity so I could wear my hat. And when it rained I regrettably had to wear that brown coat that made me look like a ramshackle house.

Count Prozor gave me instructions to follow the rehearsals of Henrik Ibsen's *Rosmersholm* which was going to be performed at *Théâtre de L'Œuvre*. The theatre director, Lugné-Poë, was only twenty-two years old, and his actors were just as young. I don't know anyone who has accomplished as many great things at that age as him. In three months he conjured up a theatre, worked like a dog and laboured for ten. At the same time he was the kindest of all the young people who wanted to bring a new world into being. He dreamt about a theatre that could express the language of the soul – poetic and mystical. *Pelléas et Mélisande* was his favourite play. And it had recently been performed or rather chanted by the actors that wandered about like shadows on the stage, their elbows tucked in and fingers spread like the apostles on ancient canvases, dazed in their exaltation.

Things like that ought not to be done to Ibsen. And with count Prozor's letter in my pocket, I drove out to Rue Turgot and was shown through a courtyard and upstairs to an atelier.

On the walls were canvases with odd symbolic trees. They were the decorations from *Pelléas et Mélisande*. The furniture consisted of a couple of cane chairs, a wooden table and a kind of dais that had served as a throne in Maeterlinck's play. In one of the corners of the hall was a shed constructed from wooden boards. This was the theatre's "siège generale". The French have such charming words for everything.

In the studio was a young, thin, almost lanky man with an angular, oddly fanatical face and a young slim woman with very large eyes, snuggled up in a wicker chair, looking as if she was feeling cold.

The young man was Mr Lugné-Poë. I gave him Prozor's letter and said that it was very important to the count that the former experiments with the Ibsen performances were not repeated. Henrik Ibsen was very much against the practice of creating "philosophy and symbolism" on the stage. The playwright's characters were living people, and the symbol should only shine dimly behind their actions and words.

Mr Lugné declared that it would please him to see me at the rehearsals, and without expecting any confirmation from the freezing woman, I turned towards her and asked if she was going to play Rebecca.

Yes, she was Rebecca.

I confess that "edified" was not exactly the word that expressed my feelings.

As matters stood there was nothing else to do than adapt oneself to the circumstances.

I was convinced that if *Rosmersholm* was to succeed, all the light and the interest had to focus on Rebecca. She had to be the soul of the play – even more so in the French performance than in the original. All in all, Ibsen's plays in France have to capture the audience with the help of their women. In order to reconcile them with the unfamiliar, the slow pace and the longish introduction in the master's work, one must consciously try to centre the interest on his women in this country where women are adored. The title of the French performance of *Rosmersholm* will have to be "Rebecca".

Therefore, when M. Lugné-Poë, who was not only director and actor but also administrator, secretary and ticket seller, stepped into his "siège generale", that is, the shed, for a moment, I pulled Rebecca to one side and said (we were standing on either side of Maeterlinck's throne):

"Yes, Mademoiselle, you of course know that the entire play is you and only you. Rebecca, Mademoiselle – I still didn't know that the shivering woman was Madame Lugné-Poë – is not the protagonist but the play itself. She has to engage each member of the audience mentally, and she has to be felt in every line. She is the play's devil and its angel."

I gave her some practical advice. And while she was acting, I noticed that she had the right look and face.

In the evening I returned to the rehearsal, and for a moment I felt like running away from it all. My courage failed when I saw the actors like strange sleepwalkers mumbling words that were barely comprehensible. And Ibsen more than anyone demands the representation to be the most clearcut and merciless kind of realism.

At all costs. The performance had to be pulled down to earth, so I had to convince each actor that the salary awaiting them was more than they could hope for up in the clouds where they were now floating.

We rehearsed for a week until two o'clock in the morning. There was one evening where Lugné-Poë's young wife, Berthe Bady, threw the manuscript at her husband. It was the final scene that was problematic.

When Rosmer declares that he wants to follow her in death, Rebecca says something like "Are you completely certain now that this is the best decision you can make?"

"Yes, I am certain."

Neither M. Lugné nor his wife were able to articulate those words. They either cried or whimpered when speaking them. Then I said: "Imagine, Madame, that Lugné had committed fraud, that the due date for the IOU had lapsed. He came to you and said: 'Berthe, I have defaulted on the loan. I must die.' And he gave you many a reason, one by one. There was no other way out. And with all the love in your heart (M. and Mme. Lugné had only been married for five months), you would take both his hands in yours and ask very quietly: 'Are you completely certain that there is no other way out?' and he said with his eyes fixed on yours: 'Yes, Berthe, I am certain.'"

After that, the two of them tried again. Now they had found the right tone, and the rest of the evening Madame purred like a little contented kitten. She had good reason to be pleased. On the opening night she was a star. She had a name in Paris – from now on.

I saw it for myself from the wings.

A young actor approached me.

"Why don't you sit in the auditorium?" he asked.

"I am afraid."

"Why?"

"Of Paris."

He smiled for a moment. The he became serious and said: "I understand."

He had come from far away himself, from Romania, seeking his fortune.

But it became a success after all. At first the audience seemed transfixed.

Then, when it was all over, the applause broke out. M. de Mez stepped forward and according to French tradition he said to the spectators who were now standing:

"The play we have had the honour of performing is by Henrik Ibsen." Which gave rise to a new round of applause.

The theatre had had its first success. We had to continue, and the day after the premiere I wrote to Professor William Bloch and asked him to do me and Ibsen a big favour.

Professor Block had directed *An Enemy of the People* at The Royal Theatre – I remembered that performance as a masterpiece. And I simply asked if I could borrow his production of the play.

Bold? – Yes, perhaps. And indeed, it took several days before the professor made a decision. But finally the book arrived in the morning of the 21st of October. And we worked feverishly. I had to take to my bed for three days, in fact. But then I was able to get up at five, write part of my novel and produce some articles for *Berlingske Tidende* – they were of course interested in the Ibsen initiative. At ten I was at the theatre. And we were euphoric, wild and mad.

"I need two hundred extras," I said.

And my dear director and ticket seller smiled. "I will get you 4-500 if you wish."

He was a terrible actor. His body language and diction were miserable. But he was a genius. The following day 267 young poets, painters and student actors had promised to participate. I assume they were his friends and friends of his friends. And he advertised for more.

I screwed up my courage and held the "mise-en-scène" instructions high above my head when I met with close to five hundred extras who had dressed up as Norwegians with caps, knitted scarves, pipes and clappers for mallets. Some of them looked like street ruffians, and their shouting could lift the roof off the house. All those voices, all those bodies had to be tamed. Each one had to stay in his assigned spot and contribute to the shouting at the right time.

The fact that "The Royal Theatre" was written on the book that I was waving around didn't impress them at all. Most of them were anarchists. To tell the truth, they wanted to throw me out. But Lugné-Poë calmed them down. And I gave each and every one of the extras a line or two and assigned him or her a place in the crowd and asked them to remember their lines, places and gestures. With that choreography everything would seem insanely chaotic and terribly spontaneous.

Some of them grumbled of course. Others mocked and laughed at the "little brown fellow". But there was no room for personal touchiness. And I think I also accidentally stepped on the toes of a few ladies. But I managed to keep all these people in check. And when I walked home through the empty streets, I was still full of energy and had no hope of falling asleep.

The première was all sold out, and everything seethed with expectation. And it came as a shock when the extras entered the stage like a wild tempestuous horde.

And afterwards, this thunderous, crackling applause, the hooting and thumping with sticks – it was one of the happiest moments of my life. And the theatre had finally achieved fame.

Unfortunately the play was only performed a few times. In fact it was banned. The whole neighbourhood was alarmed, people believing there was an anarchist uprising afoot.

I was celebrated in the Danish colony. One evening when I returned to the hotel, eighty people were waiting for me with punch. The party lasted until the early hours with speeches, cheers and songs. It was most likely Mrs Alexandra's doing. She had helped me the last couple of weeks when I suffered seizures or had fainted right in front of her eyes. She also wrote some of my letters. Sometimes my hands were shaking so much that I couldn't hold on to my pen. And she had the most exquisite handwriting.

But the future looked promising. *Le Théâtre de L'Œuvre* wanted to put on Bjørnson's *Beyond Human Power* and afterwards Ibsen's *The Master Builder*.[39] Both Bjørnson and Ibsen would pass on their honorarium to me. Unfortunately it turned out later that they were not getting any honorarium at all.

But the plays were performed, and *Politiken* sent their reviewer

Sven Lange to the theatre so he could follow the rehearsals. He wrote about Lugné-Poë's Caesar-like face and about Berthe Bady, a young slim beauty, chaste and with eyes like wild doves.

He wrote about Herman Bang's brilliance and about the impact I had on the actors – simply electrifying.

I was hoping that finally the theatre could move to another venue rather than staying by a railway station where the locomotives sometimes drowned out the speeches. And I was hoping that Poë would be able to earn just a hundred francs a month so the young couple could live more securely. After all, he had done more for Nordic drama than ten of the best writers.

But it wasn't the money that worried him. One day when I visited him and his wife, he looked at us, and his voice was heavy with grief and reproach: "Why didn't I just take a job at a bank. I have founded a theatre, and you people have taken it away from me! I don't want any of your 'movements', your 'transitions', your 'ascents', your built-up sets … . I have dreamt about a theatre where there is no 'acting', where two actors would interpret everything that their souls encompass by simply using their voices … through a song that never ends. I want life. I also want all that which is furthest from life … the unreal and that which is far, far away."

I was shaken. Every time the curtain went up, he had held my hand and smiled, saying: "Don't be afraid."

We had worked together for a whole year. And not for a second had I thought that he had been unfaithful to the best in himself. I had now deprived him of his dreams – his very belief that one day he would be victorious.

As long as you have that belief you can live on next to nothing. I lived on cigarettes, I practically devoured cigarettes. We all did during the rehearsals in Paris. And another two pieces of advice that cost nothing: pull on your teeth; it enhances the effect if you at the same time run around a table. Or, if you are completely exhausted, do stretches, especially with your right arm and then hit a door with your fingernails as hard as you can. It helps.

And by the way: my next job in Paris was remunerated. Now I had become the man who was indispensable when Nordic drama was on the bill. And for four years Gabrielle Réjane had thought about playing Nora.

No, you don't know her. You probably know Sarah Bernhardt. She was an international star. But in Paris la Réjane was the greatest, the most loved. She was la Parisienne.

Her first triumph was in the lightest of all the light plays. Playful and graceful, partly boyish and yet wholly a woman, cold and sentimental and ignorant of her own faults.

More than anything, perhaps one should observe her while she is working. Not at the theatre but at home – when she is learning a part. When she is sitting at the table in front of the open book, running her nervous hands through her reddish hair and gazing into space with her beautiful eyes as if she is making an effort, is listening to catch the author's tone.

Her face radiates willpower which the audience at the theatre will perhaps never see.

But while she is reading, line by line, it is as if the very essence of the character, the gaze and the smile and the voice gather to form a veil that sweeps across la Réjane's face. And across her entire body and soul.

Right then she barely realizes that the character has transformed her. But suddenly she makes a fist with her delicate hands as if she instinctively wants to hold on to something.

"Now I have it," she shouts.

At that point she can feel the character in her person.

And every detail to the very last is formed from inside – with an infinite amount of labour.

The willpower that doesn't cease until she has reached her goal is half of her genius.

No, she didn't spare herself. In the evening she played at the *Théâtre du Vaudeville* where her husband, M. Porel, was director. She played in *Madame Sans-Gêne* – a role in an elegant piece that Sardou had written especially for her. The theatre was packed every night, and she brought home a fortune for her children. She could have played that role for years to come. But instead she rehearsed *A Doll House* every day.

It was the dance that caused her particular problems. Mme Réjane had never been a dancer. But she had taken dance lessons for a couple of months to learn the steps of the tarantella and its many secrets. Now her dancing was simply too proficient.

She danced for an hour and a half, and I begged her to forget what she had learned and instead try to express fear and edginess. She started from the beginning over and over again.

Afterwards for the next three hours she acted the whole piece using her full voice and all the props that were used in an actual perfomance. I was impressed by her attentiveness and energy.

On the way back I visited Jonas Lie. I was deeply preoccupied with what I had seen and heard. The tarantella was still spinning in my brain and my body, and now I suddenly knew how it should be danced. Intensely, trembling, brutally, almost without grace. I ventured it, and two pictures fell off the wall during my attempt.

"Sorry, sorry. It wasn't really my fault, but Nora's."

We rehearsed every day, the great Gabrielle Réjane and I. She would laugh at my language. But she submitted to my will.

I cured her of the Gallic hand gestures. Nora is after all a nice little Norwegian wife, and Norwegian wives do not gesticulate like Parisian women.

"Yes, it was beautiful," I said when she had finished the first act. "It was extraordinary … but, Madame – your hands – "

"What!" she burst out.

"Your hands. Your hand movements."

Instinctively she stretched out her hands, staring at them. "What do you mean? My gestures – my highest accomplishment. They are famous, these hands of mine! Last year the applause lasted for two minutes because of them."

"I think it is terrible, and sometimes the gesticulation is false as well."

She looked stunned. "I see, you have been taking notes."

"Yes, and remember Madame, an actress' greatest assets are also her greatest perils, isn't it true?"

And she advances to the footlights and makes a deep curtsy. "Thank you," she says, smiling.

It is hard to believe that I had the audacity to speak like that to the great la Réjane, I must have forgotten who she was, and who I was.

Later I began to speak Helmer's lines to her, and I felt how her acting changed – how she became Nora.

"And now, Madame, the doll breaks apart," I said. "You must try to look like a doll with a square hole in her head."

She stared into space for a moment. "I will try."

Perhaps it was a childhood memory she recalled. The favourite doll that broke. For she really did succeed in looking like a doll with a square hole in her head.

Sophus Claussen noticed it too.

The day before the dress rehearsal Gabrielle Réjane wrote a letter to me:

"Dear Mr Bang!

Before I play Nora I wish to thank you with all my heart. If it is a success, it is because of you, and if it is a fiasco I can only blame myself, and I will know that I haven't completely assimilated all your good advice and instructions.

You have seen my fear, you know that I have despaired and also hoped that you at least would be able to say to Ibsen that if he has been interpreted incorrectly, I have only sinned because of my fierce enthusiasm.

My deep gratitude to you will always remain, as will my friendship.

Nora Réjane."

After the premiere she pulled me on to the stage. We stood there in the *Théâtre du Vaudeville* bathed in light, caressed by the applause from the audience.

Only Mr Sardou was somewhat reserved. And a critic mentioned that the play itself was an odd construction. A French woman would simply have blown up the postbox and grabbed the fatal letter.

But I had won a victory in Paris, and I left. Not right away, however. First I directed Strindberg's *The Creditors* and then two Bjørnson performances at Mme Adam's private theatre. It was an assignment that I had been looking forward to, for in that theatre there are princesses both on and off the stage.

Still, the great joy had faded away.

My good friend Sophus Claussen had left for Italy to recover after an unhappy love affair.

The little journalist Bigeon had committed suicide. Every time he had heard about someone who had ended his life this way, he would say in his lisping voice: "But it is so sensible. How wise."

In reality I didn't know him very well. But now that he was gone, I missed him.

But the reason I left was that I experienced time and again that unreserved warmth would change to coolness or that people would regard me with suspicion.

It was because of the letters. All the anonymous letters that followed me step by step after my success and often reached my destination before I did.

One day I was invited for lunch at Mme Réjane's. She welcomed me, chuckling. She held the letters in her hand and spread them out like an open fan. "Here are enough to put ten men behind bars," she said.

Every day while I had instructed her either she or her husband had received an anonymous letter about me: "Sex offender, pornographic writer, embezzler, deportee." There was no end to it.

Nearly all my French colleagues, friends and business associates had received letters like these.

In the last article I wrote to *Aftenbladet* before leaving Paris, I allowed myself to acknowledge having received them: "Several of these missives have passed directly from the hands of the addressees to mine. There they will remain – as a remembrance of home."

This was one of the reasons that I stayed far away from Copenhagen and my friends. I left for Norway, and at Jenny Bjørnson's pension in Sandviken I wrote about a little blond nurse.

One day Lugné-Poë came to visit. The whole theatre company was touring in the Nordic countries. He practically yanked at my arm. "We need you in Paris." But still, I stayed in the cold.

Shortly after this Claude Monet came to paint snow. I was the one in the pension most proficient in French, so at the meals we sat next to each other.

I saw how he painted the mountain top wrapped in snow like a young girl in an ermine coat. In the next painting the mountain looked like an old woman. There was something Japanese about these paintings, and I was full of admiration for the master.

One day he asked me if I thought he was a great impressionist painter.

"Yes, absolutely, yes."

"Good." In return he wanted to tell me that he had just read my novel *Tine* that he had sent for from Paris. "That book," he said, "is the first impressionist novel I have read. Why haven't you mentioned that you write?"

"Oh, I didn't think it would interest you any more than the neighbour's cat."

Imagine that people read Herman Bang in Paris while I was sitting there in Sandviken.'

*

He gives a short dry laugh that turns into a cough. He presses the handkerchief against his mouth, and his whole body is shaking. Finally, when the fit is over, he looks at the woman across from him.

She is leaning forward a little as if she wants to protect the boy who is lying with his head in her lap. She has dark, patient eyes and a slightly downy upper lip, she is not young, not particularly beautiful, a woman from the South and maybe not French at all.

'Do you think anybody is reading me now, Madame? Do you think I am in the wrong place?'

She smiles: 'May I see your hand?'

It is with hesitation that he extends his hands to her. But she indicates that she wants him to move over next to her so she can see the lines in his hand clearly.

He obeys if only to have some company and listen to her not so very beautiful French: 'Grief and fame, Monsieur – that's what I see. You can write and direct theatre. You can make people do a lot for you. If you should lie, people will usually believe you. Your heart line shows that you are sensitive and idealistic in matters of love. You have a tendency to worship your partner, and you try to turn a blind eye to the faults of the person in question. You will not be particularly happy.'

'No, happy. I have only been happy for two hours in my life at the most. That is my fate. But the life line, what do you see there? How much time do I have left?'

The woman bends over to look carefully at his palms. He can feel her warm breath against his skin. Then she folds his hands together as if she wants them to hide a secret or offer a prayer.

And there is a sound of metal. Iron reinforcements on the train conductor's boots and the shiny, dangling scissors. And the woman jumps up and pulls the boy with her. The child rubs the sleep from his eyes, and the two of them are gone as quickly as startled wild game.

He wants to follow them. But he has to lean on the table with the result that the rest of the red drink sloshes around in the glasses. He wants to look at his watch. But it slips off the chain and rolls on to the floor. And it is not the conductor but the waiter who comes. The waiter who bends down and picks up the watch and helps him fasten it to the chain and assists him down the corridor to the confounded door with the number eight. The door slides open for him and closes behind him.

And he can still feel the warmth from the waiter's hand on his elbow long after the young man has left.

14.

His face in the mirror is only a blur, just as it was in his childhood when he frightened himself by covering his good eye with his hand.

He puts on his glasses and sits down. For a moment he thinks that he is still aboard the steamer. It seems that waves are beating against the window. But the dizziness comes from inside himself as if the sea has entered his body. He must stay calm. Completely calm. Surely, there has to be a remedy in his lacquer box. Doctor Wasbutzki promised him that there were remedies for everything.

And as far as seasickness is concerned, the doctor was right. He lived through the storm without whimpering, without fainting. Of course, he had to be assisted back to his cabin. But everybody else had the same problem. And no sooner had he sat down than one of his fellow travellers knocked and practically fell into the cabin.

'May I stay here a little while?'

'Yes, certainly.'

'But I am not able to speak.'

'Nor am I.'

And then they sat down on the sofa side by side, trembling and silent, in front of the large mirror.

Afterwards he wrote to Betty Nansen:

'It is immense. But isn't it strange that sometimes the rough sea suddenly seems to solidify – and then it looks exactly like a lunar landscape. Remarkable. Great passion has such solidified moments too where it is dormant – like lava before the next eruption – – '

The sea reminds him of her strong vigorous features. And when he returns, he wants to work with her again, finding the right parts for her, teasing out nuances in her acting – maybe precisely this kind of solidification before the passionate eruptions.

Granted, the lady has said that she cannot allow herself to be just a pearl on the string of his achievements. It hurt him and created a distance between them.

But once he returns to Copenhagen, he will have regained all the energy of his youth. It will be just like the spring of 1896 when Herman Bang was strolling on Strøget and was famous. *Ludvigsbakke* had come out. His success in Paris had given his person a certain cosmopolitan aura. And his new close-fitting suit was flattering.

Right there in the bright sun a gentleman heads straight for him, and he stops, uncertain, when he sees that it is Gustav Wied.

Wied grabs him and pulls him into the nearest doorway.

'Kneel,' he commands.

And there is nothing else he can do than obey although he is thinking of his trousers. And of his hat which Wied snatches off his head before he lifts his cane up high and lowers it slowly towards the crown of the kneeling man. Once. Twice.

'Excuse me, but are we soon done?'

And a third time. And Wied says very solemnly: 'I have been weeping with Ida Brandt for three days and three nights.' And then he disappears.

And then it is just a question of brushing the dust off his knees and returning to the light and being happy that everybody loves Ida Brandt. *Ludvigsbakke* has been well received. Ida, the nurse, with her pretty step and her generous, modest character has walked right into the hearts and homes of the readers. *By the Road* and *Tine* didn't get that far. They were read, of course. Sometimes twenty ladies would read the same copy. But they didn't end up in the family bookcase.

It is an entirely new chapter in his life, and he also takes it as an acknowledgement of his success in Paris when Peter Nansen asks him to look after his young fiancée when she starts playing the role of Marguerite.

In fact, he met Miss Betty Müller in Paris where he admired her metallic laughter and her appetite. After lunch she was able to put away ten delicate little confectionary cakes.[40]

If only the young lady will remember to exercise her voice at least once a day and develop softer nuances. Nothing sentimental and saccharine, but rather something more vulnerable. Blasting the lines out doesn't work if she is supposed to play a pathetic, dying prostitute.

He himself has made preparations. He has asked Peter to provide both the novel and the script so he can immerse himself in the material. But a few things are still missing.

He needs a single camellia in bloom for his hotel room and a bouquet that will wither in the hands of Marguerite in the same way that the divine Duse can make the flowers wither right in front of the audience without anybody knowing how. And he must also get a large soft fan.

Fortunately he makes it back to the hotel in Hovedvagtsgade before Miss Müller arrives. And the flowers – they almost bankrupt him.

Betty Müller sniffs at them and seems slightly disappointed: 'But they have no fragrance.'

'No, Miss. That is the advantage. A camellia goes with any perfume. Try touching the leaves, it is a very chaste and yet a very erotic flower.'

'Dear Bang, I have a good grasp of my role. It is just all the coughing and the long death scene that cause problems.'

'Yes, Miss. We cough and we die.' And he throws himself on the sofa and coughs and coughs and presses the handkerchief against his lips.

Somebody knocks on the wall, and a deep male voice shouts: 'Are you ill, Bang.'

'We are rehearsing. Couldn't you go for a walk in the meantime.'
– – 'Dear Miss Müller, Marguerite is a sinner but an innocent sinner. She is deathly ill, but she radiates life. She loves her Armand, and therefore she must leave him.'

Miss Betty Müller repeated with an ironic smile: 'She loves her Armand, and therefore she must leave him.'

'No, no. You are not there yet, Miss. She leaves her lover, but she does it out of love. She sacrifices herself. Think about it. Put on your hat and shawl while thinking lovingly about Peter and sacrificing yourself for him.'

She tries, but so sloppily that she appears to be somewhere else.

'For goodness sake, please button those gloves. Marguerite doesn't forget to button her gloves. She is a whore but a decent whore. Not even on her deathbed does she forget to button her gloves.'

And the future 'Dame aux Camélias' buttons her gloves, very slowly like in a trance.

'That is good, Miss. Now you are getting it. Weep – just weep!'

She weeps – Peter's talented fiancée weeps. She weeps wonderfully with her back turned towards him. And he asks for more.

But she turns around, lifts the veil, blows her nose with a blast: 'Bang, can you lend me one hundred kroner?'

'But Miss, what are you saying?'

'You heard me, I think.'

'Why don't you ask your fiancé?'

'We are arguing. I have to leave. I thought you at least would understand it. You who have directed *A Doll House*.'

'But you are not even married.'

'But Peter wants to. And Peter wants to start a company. And then I will be the wife of the company director. And we will have a little director's son. And dinner parties. And what about me, then? My work is not as important. What I do is just entertainment. Light, powder and face paint. It is just something fleeting – like an insect. But you cannot demand that much of an insect. She will eventually fly away. Or she will sting and die.'

'Miss, you are not at all yourself.'

'Yes, I am. But you didn't answer my question.'

He searches his pockets nervously not knowing whether he is doing the right thing.

'I don't have very much at all, Miss. This is all I have.'

She looks kindly at the amount and asks him to call a taxi.

'But you will be so unhappy – and so lonely.'

'Yes, Bang. Do you think it will pass?'

'Yes, in your case I am convinced that it will pass.'

But now the rehearsal was ruined. And he is still sitting there, weeping, with an open fan and a bouquet of completely useless camellia flowers in his hands when Peter arrives to pick up his fiancée.

'Peter, I have no idea where she is. But you are a scoundrel. Don't you know that the theatre means everything to her? Now and at least for the next twenty years, it will be her triumphs that count.'

'Betty makes a drama of her life. Besides, I have discovered that she is a career woman.'

'But you must learn to understand it. Otherwise nothing will change.'

'Well, you would know from experience. You have enjoyed great success in Paris. And here you are in a rented room with your hardboiled eggs in eau de cologne.'

'I don't know what you mean.'

'Then take a look in the mirror, my friend.'

But in actual fact he is just sitting there, crying behind a white fan that goes exceedingly well with his complexion. And with his tears, too.

But in the same instant that Peter appeared, the camellias withered the right way. The unfortunate white petals now lie on the floor, and he is holding a bouquet of naked stalks. How it happened is beyond comprehension, and it never repeated itself.

But Miss Betty Müller returned to her role as well as to her wedding. And he actually managed to teach her how to die. She who radiated youth and life and defiance became devoted and sensitive. The entire audience at *Dagmarteatret* wept with Marguerite.

But admittedly, Herman Bang had spent much time playing the death scene for her and taught her to think back to an unfortunate afternoon to make her tears run more freely.

'It is life that has made me a poet – but I was born to be a theatre director,' he says, dreaming of having his own theatre some day. And then Jørgen Frederik Boesen walks into his room and his life. A fatherless boy of eighteen who wants to be given an audition like so many others. But Mr Boesen is special. Tall and blond and with beautiful, clean features. A student in the navy's quartermaster corps. No, a lieutenant in the guard corps.

'Yes, which role have you studied, Mr Boesen?'

'Aladdin – I was thinking of Aladdin.'[41]

'The beautiful scene at his mother's grave?'

'I was thinking of waking up in the cave and glimpsing the two mountain nymphs.'

'Yes, Mr Boesen, please begin.'

'Now? – '

'Wasn't that what you wanted?'

And the boy begins to recite, standing ramrod straight. You would think they sleep standing in the navy. But it helps when he finds a saucer with raisins and asks him to imagine that the raisins are fruits made of fine gems. The young man is naive and at the same time manly. He is a hero.

'Yes, Fritz. Of course you are an actor.'

'Fritz? My name is Jørgen Frederik.'

'Yes, Fritz. Fritz is my favourite name.'

He has baptised him. He has given him the name of his elegant father and the handsome acrobat. And he also has to feed and dress him.

He wants to give him roles to act. And new clothes so they can frequent restaurants together. And money so Fritz can finally enjoy a little holiday. And a small apartment so he can rehearse without being disturbed. And in the spring and summer months he will try out the big heroic roles with Fritz.

Sometimes they rehearse in the open air. In the courtyard the fuzzy leaves of the chestnut tree cover them. And the foliage grows thicker and darker. And he takes Fritz's hand and moves it. A gesture becomes more dramatic. And he whispers the words of love of all the heroines, and Fritz feels awkward and says that all the women are hanging out the windows gawking at them.

Five-fingered leaves brush against Fritz's forehead. And he assures him that the tree is a dense cover. And as far as an audience is concerned, he had better get used to it.

'I want to get you in *Folketeatret*, Fritz. I am going to be permanent director there. I will be working especially with young people. There are many real talents: Anna Larssen, Fjeldstrup, Albrecht Schmidt and Alma – Alma Ahlstrøm – the daughter of the caretaker. She came for an audition – precisely like you did.'

'Is she beautiful?'

'Beautiful – I don't know. Perhaps she is as plain as the spout on a watering can. But I think she has talent. Right now it is Anna Larssen I am working with. She has a certain sexual magnetism about her. Something that can turn into art. I doubt that she will have a long career. Perhaps she will end in a madhouse or in a prayer tent. – But at the moment she is a moving, poetic Mimi. It is going to be a breakthrough – I know it.'[42]

'How do you know that?'

'I teach her to work, Fritz. Simply, to work. To create a role effectively without being affected.'

And he jumps up and hits the door forcefully with his fingernails. Because he wants to act one of Mimi's scenes for Fritz. But this must have been the moment when he faints. And Fritz must have picked him up and put him on the bed and emptied all the ashtrays and opened the window, letting in the fresh air. Fritz is sitting bolt upright in the chair. Fritz is watching over him.

But other pictures pop up.

Fritz who says that he is so happy, so grateful that his life's dream has finally come true. And at the same time he reaches for the glass and for the bottle. He pours himself some of the dry champagne and especially some of the heavy, sweet liqueur. He drinks as if he needs to anaesthetize himself. Fritz, the reluctant lover. He never did see his eyes up close, for Fritz didn't love him. Behind Fritz's young, smooth lids were pictures of women.

Fritz in his white officer's uniform and with a golden rapier standing in the middle of the stage at *Folketeatret*. And Herman Bang, the director, captivated by the sight, shouting: 'Light! Light! More light on Fritz!'

The technicians obey. They direct the light towards Fritz who is standing among a group of women dressed in silk. Because of the great value of the robes, the women are not permitted to sit down.

And 'Light! Light on Fritz!' The echo comes from the wings. Only a joke but enough to spoil the joy of creating that stage lighting.

And now Fritz arm-in-arm with one of those girls in silk, their faces turned towards each other. On their way out to freedom, perhaps to a patisserie or a café.

'Fritz, I beg you to stay. There is a scene that I would like to go through with you.'

And Fritz who still has makeup in the corner of his eyes, turns to Bang: 'Now remember, this is my life. Not yours.'

And he cannot contain himself. He yells after the two of them: 'Yes, that's how life is. Lies! Deceptions! Desire! One thing life has taught me is that in this world there is only one governing principle. Which is desire! – Desire again and again – – Instead of the statue of the staggering horse on Kongens Nytorv, they should erect a monstrous column on the square and on the base inscribe in bronze: "Desire!" And then they would be most welcome to sign it with my name!'

And what if Fritz has invited the young lady to either Hotel d'Angleterre or À Porta restaurant by the square. What will they think at the sight of that horse?

He must apologize to Fritz for all the silly talk:

'It is my deepest wish that you shall live your life without any misfortunes, and the following advice comes from your best friend: live your life intensely and fiercely. It is in your nature to do so, and only by emptying out all your sensuality once and for all will you experience renewed joy in your life followed by the building of a strong will.

And then we won't speak of this again until the happy day when you might be able to talk to me in confidence – about this matter, too.

Au revoir,
Your friend
Herman'

He had known it would end this way. But he needed to be in love. He longed for the state of longing. Because the language of longing was the language he had shared with his mother. And he wrote about her again in the novel *The White House*. He made her as vulnerable as a flower. The toothache was a worm that was nibbling away at the white enamel. And love was just as necessary as the sun and the rain.[43]

> Like the plant that withers
> because its root lacks moisture;
> like the flower that pales
> because it's hidden from the sun,
> so I pale and I wither
> because you love me not.

Fritz could not help knowing that the words were meant for him. For the book was dedicated to a friend. And besides, he inserted yet another poem in the book that was dedicated personally to Fritz:

> Days of childhood
> to you I have fled,
> if only you could ease the ache in my heart.
> No one counts the tears
> that our dried-up eyes want to shed –
> Days of my childhood,
> soothe the sadness in my heart.

And Fritz thanked him. It was a good book, a wonderful book, he said. And almost all the reviewers fell for the idyll. Even Georg Brandes was kind enough to say that if genius was a neurosis, Herman Bang was a genius. That he was a neurotic was without question. Sophus Claussen was even of the opinion that several scenes seemed Homeric – especially the activities of the housewife and the girls in the kitchen and the pantry.

If only the reviewers had been as kind to Fritz when he got onto the stage. But to them the light didn't enhance his beauty. It disclosed his flaws. He could neither walk nor stand on a stage. You could barely hear what he was saying. Why had he of all people been selected to play the main role? There were so many other actors.

Abrahams, the theatre owner, spread out the reviews on his desk. 'Isn't it somewhat risky, Bang? I noticed that you have given this fellow Boesen the part of Elias in Bjørnson's *Beyond Human Power*.'

'I know that piece inside out. I directed it in Paris.'

'Yes, I know that. But do you know Boesen as well? It seems that you are giving him preferential treatment.'

'He is the right person for that role. Apart from that I don't know him.'

'Well, people are talking.' The theatre owner collected up his reviews.

And Fritz on the street. Only a glimpse. Fritz's young, open face is turned in his direction. But Bang cannot get away from a talkative gentleman of his acquaintance and rush across the street. And Fritz. Fritz looks down and turns quickly around the corner in his thin shoes and last year's hat. And the coat. That coat is ragged.

'*Tuesday, 5 o'clock.*

Dear Fritz

I cannot pretend – if you did indeed notice me – that I didn't see you on the street today. But I wasn't able to talk to you, my friend, in the presence of Sigurd Schou. Please, forgive me.

Apropos – you need clothes, a lot of clothes for the season. So, you might as well start buying some now. Don't you agree?

Herman.'

He finds some banknotes in his drawer. Ten-krone notes, fifty-krone notes and a solitary hundred-krone note. He crumples them thoroughly before enclosing them with the letter so that Fritz will think that they are casual notes from his pocket.

The first rehearsal is a pleasure. He bids them welcome and hands out cigarettes. For in Paris they smoke during rehearsals.

'Messieur, Mesdames, commençons!'

Fritz has really practised his lines. He knows his role by heart already. But he is tense. And if he could only make use of that insecurity and all that energy. If only the director Herman Bang had the courage to walk up to him, to put his arm around his shoulder and say: 'Relax, my friend. Calm down. You have no reason to be worried. You who are loved. You who are handsome. Stay so I can teach you how to do the monologue.'

But Fritz has adopted the impertinent ways of the street urchins when there are other people present. So, all he manages to say is: 'Excellent, Boesen. But the diction – a more relaxed diction.'

Miss Alma Ahlstrøm is much more nervous than Fritz. Her cheeks glow feverishly, and her big eyes sparkle. She won't need any makeup when acting a sick character. Her trembling hands. Her pathetic anxiety. He can make use of all that.

'Yes!!! – Good, hold it there – ' And the caretaker's daughter plays Mrs Sang in Bjørnson's *Beyond Human Power* so well that everyone thinks she is the new actress of the century, and the press applauds her as a genius.

The whole play is cohesive and moving. Only one role is unsuccessful: that of Elias. Mr Boesen knocks almost everything over when he comes on stage. How many roles will this untalented young man be permitted to mangle?

He didn't press Fritz's hand in the wings before the monologue. Fritz didn't seek him out privately. Neither did he have a chance to talk with him at the party after the première. He only had the opportunity to see from a distance how beautifully his new clothes suited him.

Everybody crowded around Alma Ahlstrøm who cried at the curtain call and afterwards laughed and drank wine and practised smoking cigarettes. Two blue clouds of smoke blew out of her nose like on a small dragon. And Fritz was her teacher.

Of course he had noticed it during the rehearsals. They looked like a fine couple. Her aura of vulnerability and nervousness, and Fritz's figure exuding nobility and masculinity.

Now he noticed very clearly how she devoured Fritz with her eyes while puffing smoke out of her nose. And Fritz took care of her in a protective, affectionate manner as if he wanted to lift her in his arms and carry her all the way home to his little apartment in Ny Vestergade.

Of course they had to show up at the theatre to act their parts. But otherwise they did little else than lie in each other's arms. In just two days Miss Ahlstrøm looked even more hollow-cheeked, and her eyes seemed unnaturally large which was an advantage for her role.

As far as he was concerned, there was only work to do. In a way it was as if he had created this romantic couple. People now compared Alma Ahlstrøm with Eleonora Duse. Sure, he understood Fritz. Understood that Fritz couldn't help losing himself in those eyes and that he wanted to watch the euphoria in her face and hear her sighing from happiness. And Miss Ahlstrøm, yes, he understood her more than anyone.

'*Wednesday. Night.*

My dear Fritz

You have to believe that now, as I am writing this, I am completely calm. As calm as I always am after having made irrevocable decisions. To spare both of us we must – and I have known this for a long time – personally part ways. It will be best for you if we don't see each other any longer because in reality I am just a hindrance to your happiness and your youthful sense of *joie de vivre*, a hindrance to everything that I wish with all my heart could satisfy you completely. It will be best for me too because I was never allowed to be a brother to you, which has been my life's greatest wish. You have been saying lately that I don't understand a joke. Well, my boy, I do understand, but your jokes were sometimes a little distressing; they tore at my heart.'

No, he didn't want to see Fritz all summer. Of course they will meet up again when the season begins. Fritz is going to study at his theatre. And he wants to help him as much as he can – at a distance.

He cried at the thought of the distance. But then he took lodgings at Klampenborg Beach Hotel for a week and had massages and ate eggs and drank cream to build up strength to face the summer's reading tour.

Every evening a reading and every day a travel article with illustrations by the young artist Christian Beck. Beck admires him and will consider it an honour to receive Herman Bang's dictation.

Beck will carry his suitcase and cover his legs with the traveller's blanket, and incidentally the fine young man is going to illustrate a new edition of *Tine*. He doesn't want to draw the novel's characters, only its landscapes and houses.

The reader's imagination has to remain as unfettered as possible. By the way, he virtually knows the book by heart.

There are all kinds of reasons to be happy and to write to his women friends in the provincial towns and announce that he, Herman Bang, is coming, and that he is actually famous enough now for them to do promotions and decorate the halls with flowers and festoons and monograms without being ridiculed. 'Use every trick in the book,' he writes and drinks the last mouthful of his pint of cream.

And a letter arrives from Fritz who is sending a stack of photographs of himself and is concerned about his health. And he has to reply:

'You don't have to worry that I am ill. On the contrary, I look so well that in the morning when I am bathing I can truly say that I haven't looked like this in ten years – so proud and so handsome. But it doesn't matter in any case. Thank you for the pictures. It is strange, but in the one where you are sitting down, you look like me when I was young. I was given a beautiful bouquet of flowers here by the mayor's wife which I sent to Miss Ahlstrøm.

Have you received a box with some candlesticks, et cetera. At Kähler's I selected some things for you. Soon I will send some chartreuse and champagne.

Herman.'

They are not going to lack anything, those two. And there is a certain bittersweet joy in imagining that they are intoxicated with each other and the expensive champagne.

And the child, Alma, bends over the generous bouquet and thinks perhaps for a moment that her director is a little bit in love with her. Perhaps she is whispering to Fritz: 'Do you think he is wealthy? Or maybe crazy?'

And the child, Fritz, closes her lips with a kiss or some wine: 'Don't worry your pretty little head. There is so much you cannot understand.'

Perhaps they will see him at the première of his reading series in Tivoli's concert hall. Perhaps the two of them will be sitting somewhere in the full hall, listening to him reading from *Ludvigsbakke* and *Irene Holm*. He is hoping that they will. For *Aftenbladet* writes: 'Mr Bang performed wearing an unpretentious suit, top hat and cane. He was evidently in great spirits and therefore more witty than ever both in his gesticulation and emphasis.'

The proceeds only amount to sixty kroner unfortunately. He sends fifteen to the children. And in addition they are going to get a rather large quantity of wine, some confiture, chocolate and pottery.

'See to it that Alma eats a lot and drinks heavily from the wine that Mr Sørensen has expedited today. A shipment of cigarettes will follow.'

The provinces, Zealand, Funen and Jutland, will yield a profit. He will read wherever people want to hear Herman Bang. Organizing committees welcome him. And he reads to packed houses. He performs with a magician in a community hall just because somebody happened to put them on the same programme. In one place he reads under the open sky, having changed into full evening dress in a pavilion in the garden with a little flock of curious sailors as onlookers. Later on it turns out that the lively young men are also his audience. They are friends of the maids, and no one else could be persuaded to show up at such short notice.

He doesn't show any misgivings. And his self-deprecating irony keeps him afloat. And an experience like that can easily be turned into a travel piece, and the young Beck is a perfect travel companion who amuses himself by acting as the celebrity's valet. And afterwards they both laugh about it. And yet another admirer joins them, a young actor Fritz Petersen.

But then suddenly on the ferry to Nyborg. Cold sweat and pain. Perhaps it is his heart and perhaps it isn't his heart.

In Nyborg he sees a doctor. An elderly military doctor who says precisely what the Royal Physician Oluf Lundt Bang would have said. 'Get out of bed. Your muscles need to exercise. Using only your head is not enough. There is no reason for you to drive to Kerteminde. Just walk briskly along the road.'

The doctor walks part of the way with him. And thank God that Beck is there to lean on and Fritz Petersen to carry his suitcase.

The fresh air feels sharp in his lungs, his shoes rub his feet, and there is no time to light a cigarette. As soon as the doctor has left, the poet collapses on the nearest pile of stones: 'Leave me, both of you. My final hour has arrived. Now the poet is dying. This bloodhound has killed me.'

Beck stays with him by the pile of stones. Fritz Petersen runs to Kerteminde and returns after having secured a landau and a duvet. So now Herman Bang is lying under the duvet in his unpretentious suit, top hat and cane. And the young and efficient Fritz Petersen says that if he had been the poet's impressario that kind of thing would never have happened.

But Herman Bang did the reading in Kerteminde, for nothing is worse than a cancellation. And besides, he needs the money.

'The money,' he thinks when he opens his eyes and sees that everything is white. The sky is white. His heart is white, and it feels as if he is drowning. His white heart has broken and his mouth is full of blood.

Darkness is better than light.

But they wake him up again, the white-clad people. They say that he has suffered an attack of neuralgia as well as a haemorrhage.

Why are they letting him lie in the ocean?

They smile. They smile gently and explain to him that he is so emaciated that they had to place him on a waterbed.

When he asks for an ordinary bed, they lift him and put cotton wool under his shoulderblades that are like small, hard wings.

He wants to write, he says.

White heads of bellflowers sway gently above him. And his words are lacking direction like fluffy dandelion seeds.

But he needs money. Money for Fritz.

They give him some white paper and a pen. Just to calm him down, he thinks. He closes his eyes and wakes up to the sight of lilies and roses. The smell is suffocating.

I love jam, but everybody sends me flowers.

Jam arrives in abundance. Jars of grape jelly tied with silk ribbons, red currants, raspberries, preserves from mixed berries, kilos of the sweetest blackberries from the island of Als. And after the jam there are sonnets. The Swedish poet Snoilsky, who hasn't written a line in years, is moved by Herman Bang's illness and sends a poem.

He reads that sonnet over and over again, and he learns it by heart. And understands that he has been close to dying and asks to have his medical record published in the newspaper. They won't allow it at the hospital. On the other hand, the illustrator N. V. Dorph arrives to immortalize him on his deathbed. And this happens exactly at the moment when he is out on his first walk in the hospital garden. But he jumps back into bed. There he is in his hospital gown, putting on the saddest expression the world has ever seen. Head bent forward on its chalky stem, eyes unnaturally large, nose long and narrow. And his bony hand with its protruding veins is dangling limply. Shouldn't he be able to pose as a dying man? He who has taught more than a dozen actresses how to die?

The drawing is truly captivating, and he is looking forward to seeing it publicized.

And then – finally. Finally. Fritz's footsteps on the stairs. Unexpected and longed for. Fritz takes two steps at a time. A drum roll. A fanfare. His light, young step.

A woman's small, sharp heels. Coquettish pitter-pattering. A little harp.

Alma, my sweet child. Wait a moment. Let Fritz and me have just two minutes alone.

Fritz is waiting. Fritz is waiting for her.

The lovers step into the sickroom together.

'Fritz!'

And then the most astonishing thing happens. Altogether in bad taste. Fritz introduces his new fiancée to him.

And this tart won't let them have just a minute together. She has travelled with Fritz all the way to the town of Assens.

'And Alma Ahlstrøm?'

Fritz smiles: 'She stayed with my brother in Jutland. The two of them have become quite besotted with each other.'

The girl, the new girl, squeezes Fritz's hand and covers his lips and forehead with kisses. And in Bang's presence to boot. Just as he was near death.

There is nothing to be done but to say that he is not well enough to receive two visitors.

And then. Then they take their leave. Although Fritz promises to come back.

If he had only died he would have been spared this scene.

That's what he says to Beck: 'Here I am, dying in the back of beyond. And then Boesen is fleecing me, travelling around on vacation with a girl I don't know. Someone who doesn't have enough tact to leave us alone – just so we could say goodbye properly.'

Beck is appalled. Beck will watch over him. Read to him. Or ask the nurse to bring him something to calm him.

But the only thing he wants is permission to use a telephone. Even though he hates speaking on the phone.

They humour him. Probably because they are worried he will suffer another haemorrhage.

Very briefly he informs Ritzau's Bureau that the poet Herman Bang will soon be discharged, and that the actor Fritz Boesen is now engaged to the actress Alma Ahlstrøm.

Then he sneaks back to his bed confident that Fritz will buy the paper at the station in the morning. And the new girl will make a scene.

And he, Herman Bang, will be as innocent and feverishly warm as a cat sleeping in the sun.

But a furious letter arrives from Fritz Boesen: 'You have, as is very clear to me now – done me much harm for several years.' He calls him simply a pest and a nobody.

Fritz hates him.

And what is the advantage of being discharged now? What good will sonnets and blackberries and money do if Fritz really hates him?

'*Behrendt's Hotel. Middelfart, 31–8–99*

If you would only write to me and tell me what I have done. I assure you that you wouldn't let an animal suffer as much as I do now. After all, once upon a time you were fond of me. Please, try to remember and tell me what I have done. Do you think it is right that I am not allowed to defend myself?

I cannot bear it, Fritz. I cannot – you must believe me.

And surely you must feel compassion for someone who – even if he has thousands of faults – was a good friend at one time. Do you think that you have the right to completely devastate me? But this way I will perish. And it would cost you so little to tell me what my crime is.

But what is the use of begging.

I haven't slept, nor eaten, nor existed these past eight days. You must have known how much I would suffer. Surely, you must have. If only you would feel a little compassion for me. But you won't.

Herman.'

And he left for Copenhagen and summoned Fritz to meet him at Hotel d'Angleterre. But Fritz didn't come. Or the waiter had said that Herman Bang wasn't there.

And Fritz wrote once again to the 'pest' Herman Bang and claimed that he just wanted to have him married to Miss Ahlstrøm so that he would discover how silly she was and end up being unhappy as a result. And that he, the director Herman Bang, was biased and had refused to give the future Mrs Boesen the same opportunities as he had given Alma Ahlstrøm.

And then he should know that he wasn't the only one suffering – the way things had turned out.

Once more he wanted to explain himself:

'You showed me the past couple of months a new side of yourself which I hadn't seen before – or perhaps you have changed: have become more bold, harder, less considerate. And I didn't understand this new side of you. I was waiting for just one single, gentle word from the man I knew; a single message from the softer, more thoughtful person who had vanished … Then I thought: Fritz must be happy … now he is happy. Therefore he has become his own person and is showing his true nature … And now you are saying that you have suffered. Have

I misunderstood you? And would you have been pleased to receive a friendly nod now and then, which I didn't give you? ... '

Suddenly Fritz walked into the living room. Fritz sat down in a chair, bent his head slightly and wept. And just seeing him was enough to forget everything else in the world. He had suffered too – a lot more than words could express.

At the theatre Fritz Boesen and Miss Alma Ahlstrøm were going to act together again, now in *Beyond Human Power II*.

Making a convincing Elias out of Fritz was not an easy task. Theatre owner Abrahams had several other suggestions. But the director Herman Bang was unyielding.

He looked forward to the rehearsals. But they were not lighthearted and fun.

And then the première came and the reviews followed. The play and the direction were commended, but 'Mr Boesen who plays Elias was awful. Bjørnson ought to have been spared an affected hermaphroditic comedy like that,' wrote *Forposten*. The other newspapers were not as direct, but in agreement with the verdict.

There had been other fiascoes. For instance, Sophus Claussen's *The Working Woman* was taken off the bill after the first performance.[44]

But this time he just let the reviews fall on the floor among the ashes and the cigarette butts, sighing and screaming: 'These people will not understand that I am the only one. The only one who can bring new energy to the dramatic arts of this nation. – In Paris I was understood. But here. No! Oh, this country, this tribe, this little duck pond!'

And he got up once again, stubborn and self-assured.

But after the words 'hermaphroditic comedy', there was only one thing to do. Give notice.

Fritz had to be informed:

'The words that I read in *Forposten* struck my brain with such horror that I find myself repeating them all day long – –

  It is all over. Oh, what misery,

Herman.'

But it was fortunate that Fritz was fully employed for the next year. He was going to do his military service in the navy.

As far as he himself was concerned, he wanted to write the novel that had been buzzing in his head for years. *The Grey House* – the novel about the hardships of old age.[45]

15.

Fritz. The idea of him running around shooting off canons or whatever is demanded of the young people in the summer …

Beloved Fritz. If only he could protect him the way an older brother protects a younger one. But the only thing he can do is send him food and letters.

'I sent yesterday whatever food I could get hold of. Roast beef was not available. Today, however, I picked up something from Købmagergade and sent it along with a pigeon et cetera with "Adam"… . On Saturday I will send something again.[46] It is a bit difficult finding a variety of cold luncheon meats, but I will do my best … . nothing has happened here. Scantily clad women are these days welcoming the spring, looking like tarts.'

He wondered if he has given Fritz adequate warning should he go ashore. Probably not. But the letter has to be posted. And then he must try to find a tin can so he can send some butter. The last time it spilled out all over the parcel. It is really strange that you cannot find proper packaging to transport butter in a country known for its butter.

And in the delicatessen they slice the meat much too thinly. It will probably dry up before Fritz gets it. And then he must make yet another trip to the Swan Pharmacy where they might be wondering at his consumption of cough medicine. But they sell the dreadful medicine in wonderful black bottles. And when he has emptied the content in the washbasin and rinsed the bottle thoroughly, there is in fact room for half a litre of the finest D.O.M. liqueur. If the navy folks discover it, Fritz will most likely end up in the hole. And now Fritz is sleeping next to a canon. You wonder how the food will keep there. The coolness of the metal might be an advantage. Oh, Fritz!

' … . I have now started working on *The Grey House* again. Oh, hopefully it will turn out the way I want, God willing. That grief will be transformed into marble and scorn into the great man's lifelong suffering. I wish more than anything that everything in this book might convey pride and peace. We will see. I fear the day when you will read it. I am always thinking about it, and I ought to. For you must constantly consider the person who demands the most from you … :

Fritz. The fine, dry champagne says: 'Fritz.' 'But I myself don't drink any longer, my friend, not since the days at *Folketeatret* – no more of this momentary stupor.'

However, there ought to be a regulation in the navy that would allow for Fritz's favourite drink, Pommery champagne, to be considered non-alcoholic and that would permit certain marines to wear socks of the latest fashion.

Six Swiss handkerchiefs. – 'They are nice and marked with the initial B. This letter spelled immediately the name Boesen in my mind, and I put them away. Yes, where will you get your flasks filled once you are home? If you could only, when the time comes, let me know at what time the delivery boy can bring them out. You could probably do with a cleansing of your pores with Maria Farina – :

Nini knocks on his door. One hard knock and two light taps. 'Are you working, Herman?'

'Yes.' He slides the letter under the blotting paper.

'Sorry to disturb you. But would you mind holding the ladder for the nimble little one, please?'

'Yes, Nini. Yes. But you know that I am writing.'

'I don't ask you to do very much. And we are in the middle of spring cleaning.'

Of course he will have to hold the ladder while the maid makes the feather duster dance around the crystal chandelier and polishes it afterwards with water and solvent.

It is fate and his editor and Nini who have contrived that the two of them now live together on Gammel Kongevej. Since the estate manager Holst's death, he has been boarding with his sister. All meals are consumed at the sororal table. Today it is milk toast and meat patties with caramelized onions. His expenses for room and board, for the doctor and occasionally for a nurse are deducted from his regular monthly salary which the publisher Hirschsprung has agreed to pay out while he himself sculpts his grief into marble and Nini tries to keep him at it.

But it is unbearable to be alone with one's sister. To sit at the shiny white tablecloth with the plates and candelabra of one's childhood.

On the days where cousin Margrethe joins them, it is easier. Or when the youngsters are at home. Little Bertha with her birdlike movements and shiny hair and her girlfriend Adelgunde von Scholten who travels from one boarding school to another to learn languages and, in particular, manners. Nini hopes that Adelgunde will have an educational influence on Bertha. And maybe she is also hoping that the young, gentle Jens Peter von Scholten with his promising military career would be a suitable match one day.

'And if Bertha would only settle down,' Nini sighs. 'And perhaps we did her wrong by adopting her – but when I think of our family – and you, Herman, are not of much help.'

'Nini, dear Nini. We are a bit odd both of us, but eventually we will learn to fall into step with each other like two horses past their prime.'

'Maybe – however, I wish you would keep a different kind of company. And that you wouldn't have all those student actors over. – It disturbs the peace and quiet in the house, which cannot be good for your health.'

'I will soon be going to Hørsholm, Nini. I need the money.'

'Yes, of course. It costs money to live in two or three different places.'

And does Nini know how close she is to the truth? Gammel Kongevej, Ny Vestergade and Hørsholm.

Something suggests that she does, for she tosses her head and slams the door.

And then they arrive – the women. Both the new students and the dear ones who have endured and studied with him for years. The well-groomed Mrs Neergaard who burns for the theatre and works seriously and with determination. He has recommended her to several theatres as the perfect countess. And one day she will surely succeed.

The tall, pale Miss Ville Christiansen receives lessons in exchange for a little secretarial help. By now he has written many recommendations citing her exemplary nature, her manners and dramatic talent. And this in spite of the fact that she can be rude and so completely unreasonable that he must take a sedative in the middle of the day. And he has scolded her, and she has shed tears onto her manuscript and he has repented:

'*Dear friend*

I am so sorry if I have been too impatient today and only added to all your suffering and difficulties. But dear friend, what can I do? Other than trying with all my might to make you pull yourself together. It will soon be the only solution, as far as I can see. And what a shame it would be if all your talent should go to waste.'

There is more hope in store for the young, beautiful Miss Causse who dresses more elegantly than most and from time to time feels the need to travel to Paris. That lady pays for her lessons, and 'lessons' translates into parcels to Fritz:

'This is a real parcel, Fritz. Danish strawberries picked this morning; sardines and mushrooms; and dragée candy; and salmon and everything. Today I had to have a delivery boy carry it home. It was too much for me … . I didn't meet a soul on the street. There were only Germans and Swedes … .

Bon appétit.
There is also some Henry Clay.
Herman.'

Even in the heat of the summer he runs around like a housewife. And Nini is right. The door doesn't close the entire afternoon. Ladies and gentlemen with writing ambitions come and go with manuscripts to be read. Actors come and ask for assistance. Mrs Betty Nansen comes to ask him to help out with Mrs Sang. Since he has directed *Beyond Human Power* so many times, he must be a specialist in that particular role, she claims. And on her way down, she meets the closely veiled Anna Larssen on her way up. For Martinius Nielsen, her good and sympathetic director, looks none too kindly on actors from *Dagmarteatret* who solicit help from Herman Bang.

The pretty lady takes off her hat and veil and snickers a bit after the meeting with Betty Nansen. 'Mrs Sang – she should drop that role; I think she will be extremely boring.'

And then she opens her own script.

'Anna,' he sighs. 'How can you! Demanding my lifeblood in such a harrowing scene.'

But he does what she asks for. He plays the role of Dina for her. And she is watching, and he knows that she is watching him: his pauses, his acting around the props, his movements, tone and expression.

'Was it good, Anna?'

'Yes. But you can do it better yet, Mr Bang.'

And he acts it again until the role is clearly imprinted on her visual memory. And she takes what she can use.

And they talk about the good times at *Folketeatret* where she was rehearsing happily, full of expectations. And he knew that her talent covered a much wider scope than she was aware of. Kätschen in *The Trial by Fire*.[47] Oscar Wilde's *Salome*.

'I am athirst for thy beauty; I am hungry for thy body; and neither wine nor fruits can appease my desire. Neither the floods nor the great waters can quench my passion.' He enjoyed directing *Salome*. Even if he didn't want to be lumped in with Oscar Wilde – he takes every opportunity to mention that he despises Oscar Wilde – or that he is completely uninterested in him.

The writer that he admires the most is the young Johannes V. Jensen from Himmerland in Northern Jutland. He has followed him since his first publication and encouraged friends and acquaintances to read him.

And one day the man himself is standing in his living room at Gammel Kongevej.

He has a funny little moustache and nice white teeth. But the most peculiar thing about him is his hands. Slender wrists and broad, red hands that he clenches into fists so that they look like mallet heads. You can't take your eyes off those hands.

Not even happiness seems to make him relax. But he notices a slight quiver in the young narrow face when he tells him how much he admires his writing: *The Fall of the King* that he has read over and over again like confessions of beautiful souls.[48] And the very language seems to grow spontaneously from some primal bedrock like nature itself.

'You,' he concludes, 'are Denmark's greatest writer. Your language is not refinement but revolution, no less.'

'Perhaps I could ask you to speak with Dr Edvard Brandes at *Politiken*, then.'

'Yes – of course. I assume you will write about literature?'

'I want to travel. Preferably to India. Or I want to see the Chinese railroad. Somebody will have to see it.'

'I don't think it will be easy. But I will try.'

'Actually, I have never read anything by you, Mr Bang. What do you recommend yourself?'

'*Ludvigsbakke* – perhaps you should read that one.'

He could hear it himself. His voice was weak and dry. But he laughed after Johannes V. Jensen left.

Those hands and that self-confidence. But, of course, the man was the son of a veterinarian. At least he, himself, had physicians in the family. He might as well go by *Politiken*'s editorial office right away and speak with Edvard Brandes.

Dr Brandes shook his head when Bang recommended that he send the man from Himmerland to China just because the man very much wanted to go. 'It appears that Mr Jensen has delusions of grandeur. But needless to say, he is most welcome to write to us.'

And now, after he had done what he could, he wanted to relax and read from Paludan-Müller's *The Dancing Girl*, mother's book that was kept in Nini's bookcase.[49]

> 'You fail me –the gaze of my eyes you flee.
> Though tenderly I call, I am not heard,
> your ear has shut out my every word,
> and you hand me the bitter drink while shunning me.
> My sun has set – it fades away undeterred
> and no one can return to me
> the rays in which my joy was born.
> Only this remains: It is over, you I mourn.'

And those lines are framed in fine pencil lines. Everything about love is underlined. It is like looking straight into his mother's soul. And it is not at all moralistic.

'Nini,' he shouts. 'Nini, have you seen this. Mother has underlined exactly the same lines that I love.'

'I have never seen any pencil lines.'

'But is it you, then?'

'Me?'

Nini puts on her hat and coat and runs out the door. And returns late in the evening from one of their mother's younger women friends. 'Yes, it is true. Those lines were added by Mama.'

'I knew it. But now I will take the book.'

And it is no wonder that he faints the following day. In the middle of a lesson with a male student. And the doctor arrives and sends him immediately to Hørsholm.

He leaves with nurse Astrid Pålsson. He has longed to see her beautiful face and listen to her not quite so beautiful mixture of Danish and Swedish. And they walk arm-in-arm across the wide lawns, and he takes her in to dinner and looks after her. For after her broken-off engagement, the young lady is somewhat unstable. She bursts into tears. She charms everybody and seems quite confused to the point where he doesn't trust her with the purchases for the food parcels. He sends canned rabbit and duck until Fritz writes back, disgruntled, that he is tired of canned food. Each day is like the last, consumed by tears, fainting spells, massages and cream. And he meets old friends and acquaintances who are also at the health spa. Karl Larsen, a friend of his youth, is there with his wife Mimi who admires Herman Bang and in an overly excited voice calls him 'child, dotard, man and woman', believing it to be flattering. Barrister Heise and his wife, Mrs Inger, who writes a diary and is delighted that she can add Herman Bang to its pages. And of course Christian Houmark comes to ask about his health and his novel and even gives him a bath robe as a present. And Ville Christiansen offers to read for him and take him for walks in the forest. And Miss Causse takes lodgings at the expensive Rungsted Hotel just to be nearby.

And there is the daily letter to Fritz:

'... The dog belonging to the professor's wife Mimi set the whole neighbourhood in motion yesterday. In a fit of less than proper behaviour he bit Mrs Ernst von der Recke on her upper lip. Naturally Mimi sided with the dog. "Good God, Bang," she said, "Mrs Recke has a horrid way of sneaking up on people and must surely have aroused the dog's suspicion ..." Regardless of how she walks the other woman's lip was damn well torn; and the doctor had to repair it with eight stitches.

Farewell for today, dear Fritz.

Herman'

And it is a lovely afternoon; the dog is stretching out, the lacy border of the table cloth gently brushing against his muzzle. And Mrs Ernst von der Recke is seated bolt upright with white gauze and a pink bandage under her nose and, much to her annoyance, is prevented from laughing. For Herman Bang has invited women friends and admirers for coffee, chocolate, wine, liqueur and the most wonderful cakes and sweets.

There they are, women of all ages, sitting around the table, enjoying the flower centrepiece, eating their cakes with fine little forks, sipping their drinks and devouring Herman Bang.

He is talking about his life. About how he failed to recognize Sardou that time in Paris. And he really should have. For just when the curtain closed after *A Doll House* and he and Gabrielle

Réjane came out on the stage, a short man approached la Réjane and whispered so loudly that everyone could hear it: 'What rubbish, Gabrielle.' Since then he truly never succeeded in recognizing Sardou – although they were introduced to each other on at least three occasions.

And once in Sorø where he stayed at Hotel Postgården with his good friend Christian Houmark, he hadn't slept for several nights. He was completely exhausted. His only wish was to be able to sleep even if it meant that he would never wake up again. But as soon as he lay down, he was wide awake.

One evening, late, he and Houmark dragged themselves down to the local doctor and asked for a prescription for a sedative. Houmark had even very obligingly borrowed the money – which is not an easy thing to do in Sorø.

Houmark knocked on the doctor's door and then on his window and asked for a prescription for Herman Bang.

'Herman Bang? Who is he?' the doctor shouted.

'Oh no,' the poet moaned. 'If the man cannot read, he probably cannot write either. Come, let's go.'

And then he fainted.

The ladies are laughing in the sun. They laugh and laugh – are cheerful and sympathetic. Mimi forgets all about the embarassing episode with the dog that she usually tries to keep on a short leash. She simply beams at him.

Professor Karl Larsen comes by and joins the company. 'Strange,' the professor says. 'Extremely strange. None of those stories will be told the same way again.'

The idyllic scene vanishes into thin air although the ladies look at their Herman Bang with adoration and at the professor with disapproval.

Being a poet, shouldn't he be permitted some experimentation? But nevertheless – he rises to his feet and says that he has to catch a train.

But already the next day eight people are admiring him at a lunch. 'Oh, how tired I am of being admired. I would gladly strike admiration squarely in its face. You, whose fate it is to be loved in life, cannot, no, will never be able to comprehend how cold and sad it is always to have to be satisfied with being admired or held in esteem,' he writes to Fritz and encloses some chocolates that he has sneaked into his pocket.

Time passes too quickly. Much too quickly. Not a lot of his novel gets written. And in October Fritz is coming home. The first coolness of the season will be in the air. And the glowing colours. October can be such a beautiful month. When Fritz returns home, he will finally be able to appreciate everything he has. The apartment is going to be filled with flowers, perfumes and champagne. But Fritz is going to spend the first night with the girl he currently loves. And there is no end to what one has heard about this woman. In the summer she loved a forest ranger who became outraged when she was also seeing his groom. And saying something to Fritz about it would just have the opposite of the desired effect. But the young woman's clothes – those he will have to do something about when he is free once again:

'I don't know how it is that she dresses herself. But it won't do. It is much too conspicuous and colourful. I saw her on the street yesterday and was astonished. Previously she has always been so elegant and discreet … . Please, don't be angry because of my comment, but it is damn well true … . The past two hours I have been rehearsing "The Flight from Sønderborg".[50] Oh, what energy I must put on display during the half hour it lasts … .'

Yes, another reading in Tivoli. Dionine injections, new summer clothes and the hairdresser. For he is to drive through Copenhagen in an open carriage with the royal actors to advertise the reading and the subsequent charity party that he has been chosen to arrange. In the first row sit Nini and Bertha and Miss Pålsson and Jens Peter von Scholten. And he can see on the children's faces that they are captivated.

Once again Herman Bang's name rings out like a fanfare through the city. And the next day he takes to his bed. And Miss Causse cries because he cannot come to the dinner that she has arranged in his honour. And Miss Ville Christiansen cries because she is not allowed to watch over him.

But he manages to send off a parcel to Fritz. And two hundred kroner – fifty of these he has to borrow. For the party cost him a great deal. And while he is lying there wondering how it would be financially possible to go back to Hørsholm, a telegram arrives for Jens Peter von Scholten. His father was killed when he plummeted down a mountain by the Rhine.

The boy cries and cries. He doesn't even think of the fact that he is rich now. And he is not at all suited to be poor. In the midst of all the grieving, the doctor discovers that the boy suffers from consumption. Nini falls ill from all this wretchedness. Miss Pålsson consoles the boy and cries and consoles him again.

'Oh yes, Fritz, how near you are in my thoughts … . By the way, it is all sheer misery here. I didn't get to go to Hørsholm and I am now feeling so dismal that I practically find myself incapable of working … . Miss Christiansen said: "You could open doors in Tivoli. But you cannot make it to Hørsholm." How right she was. It is ridiculous. But I cannot travel alone – for the sake of my heart – and there is no one who can accompany me … . And when you go ashore, you must present yourself at the theatre. Just imagine, if you weren't an actor but wrote poetry. Then it would be so much easier. And I am convinced that now it would be easier for the two of us to spend many days together without you being bored. The thought that you should be bored has always been the most dreadful of all possible thoughts. And it has haunted me ever since that Easter when we were in Frederiksværk, or wherever it was … . It is depressing here. I am ill, and Scholten who cannot endure any kind of emotional turmoil must take to his bed where he stays for the better part of the day. Then he cries. An odd officer to have in the King's Guards, I would think. There is still not a soul who knows how his father died, and every half an hour the boy asks: "How do you think it happened?" I constantly think about that time when you fell off your bicycle … .'

And in his mind's eye he saw Fritz in his bicycle uniform, athletic and glowingly young. And he also saw Clasen's Hotel. And the summer guests invading the hotel and the town. The posh, the pretentious, the droll and those with a good heart. And he saw Mrs Clasen in particular. A small person running in panic through hallways and rooms. She is wearing herself down not out of perfectionism but out of goodness. She never thinks of the cost connected with the meals and tables she prepares. She cannot mention the bill without blushing, and she is even less prepared to dismiss any of the staff.

Late in the evening she has often collapsed in a chair in Herman Bang's room and confided her problems to him. All that hard work is in vain when the purse remains empty.

And that story is so easy, so easy to write. As if he himself were on vacation away from it all. And he is paid an advance. Plenty of money.

And he was very pleased with the reviews. Right up to the moment when he read in a paper that Brasen's Hotel was Clasen's Hotel and that the hosts were Herman Bang's models.

Letters of indignation poured in. Some of them he dropped into the waste basket. But one of them he read: 'Mrs Clasen shut herself in and cried for an entire day. You must write to her.'

He tried. He tried to explain that he never intended to hurt her. He begged her to forgive him for having exaggerated a good deal.

But she didn't answer. She who had believed that she was the poet's close friend, she was just his model, a small clumsy woman whose washing-up was stacked up on the kitchen floor.

He began writing *The Grey House* again – lucky for him that the protagonist, his own grandfather, had long since died. And while writing, he felt very clearly the pain of old age. Like a chrysalis bursting under his skin. Even his handwriting changed. The graceful and wispy style of his youth transformed into the ragged scrawl of old age. When no one was looking he would use a magnifying glass on the sly. But his heart was still restless.

And Fritz returned home to flowers, money and a welcome letter: 'Dine with Miss S. and drink to my health – to poor old me.'

He went to lie down and covered himself with the duvet like an animal hiding in its den. And of course, luckily there is a nurse in the house though she mostly has to take care of Scholten.

And a Sunday letter came from Fritz who says that he has truly missed him. 'And perhaps it upset you that my fiancée was also here? Hurting you was not my intention.'

'No, you didn't hurt me – on the contrary. But this you know: in this life love, and love alone, has been everything and the only thing to me. That alone is worth every breath taken and bestows both life and death – I believe. All the rest is – and isn't. Because where love is, everything is: and all the rest is difficult and unnecessary. For that reason I have never had friends. Those who pretended to believe that they were my friends knew very well that they weren't. Friendship had always seemed just a word to me. What did it mean? What was it? I knew that I would be willing to stomp with my heels on my friends' faces just to receive a smile from the one I love. But now I believe that friendship is something attainable in life. For I know, Fritz, that we are friends and I know that the two of us mean something to each other. I know for certain that we can grant each other many good hours together and that we will never hurt one another … . But – and that is why I wrote as I did – there are truly hours, hours of exaltation in life where even your best friend is a stranger – a stranger who has no place being there because that moment and that hour alone belong to you and the one you love. How often have I not longed for that instant when this or that "stranger" would leave. In your eyes I will also be "a stranger" the first evening after such a long time.'

And he could have walked all the way out to Ny Vestergade with that letter. He could have paused in a doorway for a moment and watched two profiles in the window, Fritz and the woman leaning against each other, glowing like an icon.

But he put it in the postbox and just went for a short walk along the lake until he let himself in at Gammel Kongevej.

And right there in the sofa sits little Miss Astrid Pålsson facing the young, pale Jens Peter von Scholten. Her lips are full, deep pink and probably very soft. And the young man is a knight who lives off kisses.

The next day Fritz calls on him. He hadn't at all intended to pester the theatre directors with visits, he said. Perhaps he would be better suited to becoming a writer. And his love affair has given him plenty of material. The novel was going to be about his beloved.

'Yes, of course, Fritz. The woman. A little more showing, and a little less telling,' he says after having read the first draft.

'Yes, but what do you think mother will say?'

'What your mother will say, I really have no idea. But don't you think that she is aware of most of it?'

And unfortunately the novel is rejected. And Fritz looks at him as though he, Herman, could do something about it. As though he could have it accepted as easily as in those days when he was able to obtain roles for Fritz. And this expectation is like a bow where the tension gets tighter and tighter between them. And one day the arrow will fly.

He notices Fritz looking impatient and anguished and remembers himself as a young man.

'You have the ability. I know it. Don't ever forget it, Fritz.'

'And if I become one of those you never hear about. Then what?'

And he wants to put his arm round his shoulder. He wants to say that he is loved.

But Fritz pushes him away and shouts: 'I don't understand your feelings. Friendship it isn't. And the other thing is revolting to me.'

'After I had heard those words – after those long fights – I knew that we had to part ways, for my sake. I couldn't and wouldn't allow misunderstandings of this kind.

Since then, I have understood that we had to separate – and even more so – for your sake. After the woman you love had flung the word "perverse" at me during two conversations in which the context was my relationship to you, I realized that you will never be able to know a complete and free way of life as long as we know each other. I don't blame her in the slightest. She must have meant what she said and felt miserable before speaking like that about me and the one she loves. So I don't reproach her at all. But her words brought home to me the necessity of us having to separate forever so your life can finally be free and clear of all doubt in other people's minds.'

Fritz didn't come. Fritz announced by letter that he was leaving for

Paris now in order to develop as a writer.

He, for his part, let himself be admitted to a clinic for nervous disorders in Aalborg.

'But Bang, this will not end well if you continue to compromise your health and constantly think about death. Do think of something positive,' says the doctor, shaking his head.

But apart from death he is only thinking about how he can provide money for Fritz in Paris and how he can finish writing his novel.

Then suddenly flowers arrive from Princess Marie. And he is astonished that he has almost forgotten the princess. A chic Frenchwoman with an oval face and cheerful eyes under her curly fringe.

They met each other in front of a toy shop. Or more precisely, he met her sons who were standing there with their noses pressed against the window arguing and pushing each other, wishing for this and that. And he joined them in the game. Together they looted the window.

'The steam engine.'

'The lion.'

'The whole zoo. – Without the lion.'

'The train.'

'All the tin soldiers.'

'The golden helmet and the sword.'

'I want the sword.'

'The doll in the sailorsuit.'

'The rocking horse.'

'The fire engine.'

She laughed when she extended her hand to him. The children's mother. Marie. Princess of Orléans. And she invited him. It would please her if he would visit her in her atelier at the Yellow Palace. She did a little painting as a hobby.[51]

He sent her a copy of *Quiet Lives*.[52] And already the next day he received a letter.

'The story "Son Altesse" delights me, it appeals to me very much; unfortunately most princesses are brought up in the irresponsible

325

manner that you describe so well; fortunately it does not apply to one and all. I believe that people regardless of their position in the world should be allowed to be themselves and not let others diminish them – Once again I thank you for the book and apologize for my poor Danish.

I remain yours sincerely
Marie.'

He was proud. He began to appreciate his own story more. And he wrote in tiny letters on the princess's missive:

'Don't you think this is amusing? I will explain the circumstances tomorrow.

Your Herman.'

And he sent it to Fritz who pretended that he was not in the least impressed.

Now he wants to demand the return of his letter when Fritz comes home. And he will pay the princess a visit again at the Yellow Palace.

The first time she let him wait in the atelier where he was immersed in a thick, greasy smell of oil and turpentine. Meanwhile the waiter served cognac to him and Houmark whom he had brought to act as secretary. And it was actually something of an insult to serve cognac before noon. It ought to have been champagne.

But then she arrived. She showed her paintings. Talked about her charity work and about politics. Unfortunately she couldn't write for the newspapers herself. But perhaps Mr Bang could if they occasionally were of the same opinion. And she talked about her connections to Paris, Russia and Siam.

When he was ready to take his leave, he emptied his glass to the last drop as though he wanted to celebrate the completion of a deal.

The princess only moistened her lips.

'Why,' he suddenly asked, 'are royals never completely natural.'

'Do you think,' she said and offered him her cool fingertips on parting, 'that you are completely natural towards me?'

It was a tiny little sting, not a stab. And in that instant he felt affection for her.

The princess would read the book about his grandfather, the Royal Physician. He was certain of that.

And Fritz will read it and perhaps finally understand. 'It is so difficult for someone who loves to walk side by side with a person who merely feels fondness for one. For that reason I couldn't even accept your kindness. And one more thing. Humans, Fritz, will always turn their charitable gaze towards the person who has sunk the lowest although no one knows which one of the two has suffered the most.'

Poor Fritz was lonely and depressed in Paris. He had moved to the street of the deaf-mutes where Bang himself had stayed. Didn't succeed in writing a single line and was without money.

And his own book. Old age, pain, contempt and resignation – loss of the beloved. The cold in the grey house crept into his own bones and made his hand shake. When he lugged the manuscript off to Hirschsprung, he felt as if his heart was suddenly going to burst like a spring in a watch. And his lungs could suddenly let out every breath of air and refuse to take any in. And his brain. Fritz would have to understand that this brain of his would not be able to procure money for a journey to Paris:

'I thought that I had suffered a great deal. And yet, it is only now that I understand what hopeless suffering means. Fighting against your own disintegrating mind is the horror of all horrors. Summoning up all your willpower every day in order to hide the struggle from the world makes it even worse.

I cannot get you any more money because I am not able to do any readings. Soon it will be a year since the first time I felt this way, and ever since, every single minute of each new performance has been a walk along the edge of the abyss.

I cannot do it any longer.

And taking a vacation is not permitted me. From where would the money then come? In other words, you must return in February. After all, you will be in a position to live much more cheaply in

Skørping than in Paris. And at least I will be spared the daily torment of knowing that you are in Paris without fully "living" in Paris. Oh, that Paris trip. I haven't had a calm moment since the day you wrote that you had decided to travel. But when you return home at the end of February you will in fact have stayed down there for nearly half a year. That you haven't learned anything is no one's business.'

The Grey House came out. And the book was admired very much. But not loved – not at all like *Ludvigsbakke* or *The White House*. But thanks to Mrs Amalie Skram, he received a notice from the Ministry of Church and Education on the 24th of April, 1903, stating that he had been granted a subsidy of four hundred kroner for the financial year 1903-04 in support of his continuing literary production. She had taken the book under her arm and gone to the minister saying that she found it embarrassing that Herman Bang still hadn't been considered worthy of receiving state subsidy.

Fritz came home as a perfectly ordinary human being. An attractive, slightly plump young man. Fritz went to Skørping. For his part he stayed in Copenhagen. He told Peter Nansen, who was now Gyldendal's chief editor, that his next book would deal with the irremediable loneliness of the genius. Therefore he must go to Paris immediately. He had to see the Luxembourg Garden and the light above Rue de Rivoli.

He hired a manservant. A decent-looking fellow, a little jowly. And he ordered a livery with silver cords and a dark servant's coat lined with crimson wool and with the Hvide family's coat of arms on all the silver buttons.

The tailor's bill was overwhelming. He had to seek out the various editorial offices in Copenhagen and promise them articles from Paris and ask them for an advance. 'I will spend about ten days in Paris.' 'The trip will result in my transfer to the publisher Gyldendal.' 'I am not so ill that I am afraid of travelling.' 'I don't own an overcoat, last winter I gave my spring coat to a poor fellow.'

He was off along with his manservant Ernst whom he called 'the Estimable'.

'The Estimable' who carried the suitcase ended up on the wrong train to Hamburg. As a result he spent the first night at the hotel alone. But he could watch the light from his balcony.

It wasn't until the next day that he could wear his spring clothes and go out. He ate cakes and looked at a pair of grey gloves that he couldn't afford.

Unfortunately Fritz Thaulow and Mrs Alexandra were out of town. But the maid invited him for lunch with the children and the Norwegian painter Christian Krohg. Krohg interviewed him, and they talked about the light.

After that neither his health nor his money would last. He went back home.

'Paris was wonderful,' he wrote to Fritz. 'I wonder if a person who no longer loves any living beings can still love a place? It must be, for the feeling I have for Paris must be love, I think. It possesses a sense of joy that fills me entirely … .'

Fritz was interested in hearing about his book. He knew that he could find himself in its pages.

'Have I begun working on my book? Oh no, my poor brain is not in very good condition. Have I told you that it is entitled *Mikaël* and is named after Saint Michael with the flaming sword? The flaming sword stands for triumphant love … . If I weren't ill I would lock up my entire soul in this book like a precious ornament in a jewellery box – an ornament of rubies.'

*

Mikaël, Fritz – that was then. He still has the beautiful picture of Fritz as a young man. Fritz, his head slightly inclined, dreamy and melancholic. It is in the lacquer box together with the picture of his mother. Both are in silver frames that are so heavy that a burglar or maybe just a pauper would be tempted to scoop them up. Not that he would blame anyone for doing so. But he would rather not lose the pictures.

He opens the box. There are birds and flowers of mother-of-pearl inlaid in the lacquer. Perhaps he will see precisely those kinds of birds and flowers in Japan. And he still has his beautiful blood-red fan.

He has heard about plays over there where elderly men act as the most ravishing young women, their faces covered by carved wooden masks. And they have big, heavy braids of black silk threads for hair, and their costumes are all silk and gold and embroidery. In Japan, he thinks, he could perhaps have been an actor. And for an instant he feels as excited as when he was twenty years old.

He pulls out the two pictures. Mother and Fritz. The two most beautiful people he has ever encountered. Those two photographs are his church.

Calmness unfolds inside him like a silent, white wing. And then finally: sleep.

16.

It is a waltz in light and darkness. A very erotic waltz. The lovers are enfolded in each other's arms. And light. Shadow. Shadow. Light. He has choreographed that waltz himself. Now he whirls the lovers around – they are embracing, kissing. And when they are hidden in the dark the audience will imagine all sorts of things. That waltz – it is a mating dance. And quite indecent, actually. But indecency played out between a young man and a young woman is considered charming – that is how these things go.

He must have torn himself from his sleep and entered the wrong train carriage by mistake. For he finds himself among people who are sitting bolt upright in their seats, their eyes closed, their faces relaxed, young and old, men and women. Maybe they are dead, maybe asleep.

There is a young sailor, his lips slightly apart and with eyelashes that cast shadows on his cheeks like on a child. And a young woman in a beige travelling outfit stretches out a small foot dressed in a boot. Perhaps she is dreaming of a ball. She is smiling. Then she opens her eyes and meets his gaze. Long, silky lashes frame her clear and alert eyes, and she looks like Miss Anna, Astrid or Bertha.

He remembers a happy waltz. The wedding waltz at Astrid and Jens Peter von Scholten's wedding. They were glowing with happiness, resting in each other's arms – the first lieutenant and Astrid. She, swathed in silk. And he wished that she would have many children without losing the innocence in her eyes. She was already preoccupied with the furnishing of a mansion in Odense with nurseries and servant quarters and parlours. A white house where the doors are left open.

For his part, he danced with cousin Margrethe. With her bony back she carried herself straight as a poker and danced as if she were talking a stroll in the street, all the while talking about the new literature from England. Later on he danced with Bertha who was as light as a bird in his arms. Small drops of perspiration had collected like dew drops by her temples. They had to sit down, and he went to get champagne and ice cream. How pretty she had become.

And then he couldn't even stay with her the day the doctor examined her and established that she, too, had tuberculosis. He was on one of his usual reading tours when he received a letter from Nini that the girl was going away to recuperate. Otherwise Nini took it calmly. She figured it was the Lord's punishment because the child had been especially lippy of late.

There wasn't much he could do. But he still managed to send off an express letter to Mrs Inger, wife of Barrister Heise, and ask her to pay a visit to Salomonsen's Delicatessen & Game Meat and buy two jars of peach preserves as well as two bunches of purple grapes of the best to be had in Copenhagen and send it all to Miss Bertha Holst right away.

The child ought to have everything that tastes of the sun. And eau de cologne and flowers and books and money and letters. And a nurse more than anything.

When he visited her, she would run to meet him and put her slender arms around his neck. He warned her to be careful, ever so careful. To avoid sudden movements and preferably all emotional outbursts. It didn't help to worry too much: 'My own Bertha. People, dear friend, will always be walking on either side of a river and barely be able to reach each other with their wretched hands. Dearest friend, even elephants will weep over life, and yet we say that they are thick-skinned.'

And then, like a bolt from the blue, a short tear-stained letter arrives from Bertha who admits that she has been rather wilful. Nini has let her know that it would probably be best for both parties to break off all communication.

'*My own Bertha,*

Your letter stunned me. I, who have been very ill, haven't heard a word about all this. What happened? Yes, Heaven knows the ways of Nini, but I don't recognize her myself. A complete break – how is it possible or even conceivable in our social circles? Nini is forever a stickler for etiquette. Dear little Bertha – little unwell creature – how sad you must be … . No one, no one in the whole world except for Jens Peter and me.

Write immediately to your faithful friend
Herman.'

Subsequently he travels back and forth trying to mediate in the dispute. He tries to explain Nini's stubbornness by her frail constitution and difficult age, and the young girl's defiance by her illness. He employs all of his diplomatic sense, his resourcefulness and loyalty. He lies and uses his acting skills. And finally he is able to write a postcard to Nini: 'Please, do pay Bertha a visit. Both of you need it.'

Perhaps they embraced each other. Perhaps they just sat each in a rocking chair with a tired smile on their lips, rocking quietly, exhausted from the quarrel like two overly tired children.

Nini didn't give an account. And apparently Bertha didn't remember his birthday until several days past the day. But finally her greeting arrived.

'*My own Bertha*

Thank you very much for the violets you sent me, and thank you for your birthday greeting. I missed hearing from you on my birthday – I cannot deny it. On that day I feel more helpless than on any other day of the year. Sofie writes that you are studying Latin and weigh 52 kilos. I think both are too much. What do you want with Latin and with 52 kilos?

Now that Adelgunde and Miss Andersen are leaving, only Nini and I, two old ruffled crows, remain in the house. Nini is feeling much better now but she has been quite ill for some time. It is evident that she enjoys hearing any kind of news about you. To be sure, you are turning into a tremendously competent and steady little rascal.

I wouldn't be surprised if you end up founding a girls' school like Miss Lang's in Silkeborg. It would be a good thing, for in that case I wouldn't have to end up in the poorhouse but instead find refuge in the building's attic. Then I wouldn't dye my hair any longer but be a really nice old man with white hair.

A thousand greetings from your friend
Herman.'

One day Herman Bang received a very thick envelope from Miss Bertha Holst. The child had written a novel. And after having read only half of it he was able to say: 'You have the gift that one cannot secure for oneself nor labour to obtain, you have "the streak" in you which is a great sign of talent.'

He was certain that the book would be published. 'But my dear, don't think that I have any influence. I think that the fleas in the fur coat belonging to the Devil's grandmother, or what have you, have more to say than I do.'

'Yes, my very own friend, now we are colleagues,' he wrote after Peter Nansen had accepted the book. And he could assure Nini with good conscience that there was no mention of the family in Bertha's book.

But he was uncertain about his own work. His novel *Mikaël* was problematic. He was still at the beginning. And there were only tiny splinters of Herman Bang in the character of Master Claude Zoret, while there was too much of Fritz in Mikaël.

What is the use of changing the nationality and appearance of his characters if one could read between the lines and recognize Fritz in the master painter's handsome nude model?

Houmark, who makes fair copies for him or takes dictation while he himself plays out the plot, addresses him suddenly with a look of reproach. 'Couldn't you just for once show solidarity with your fellow human beings – and defend them.'

'Defend. – There are people in whose soul gratitude is transformed into hatred because they cannot cope with it!' he shouts. And he curses his ungrateful beloved and his own love which Fritz considers a sickness.

Houmark is writing and writing. And finally he says: 'It is the best and the truest thing you have ever written, Mr Bang.'

And he looks at Houmark who is impeccably dressed and has lately taken to pulling on his teeth and striking the door with his fingernails. Houmark who will do anything for him, lend him money, decipher his handwriting and make fair copies for a symbolic amount. Houmark who is an actor, a journalist and a writer. If he could only fall in love with Houmark.

But Houmark is barely out the door when he has second thoughts. It is necessary that Fritz be heard: 'If you insult a friend with as much as a glance, then you turn him away and out of your life without a word, without batting an eyelid, out on the street like the scum he is. He has been honoured by playing a role in your life. He no longer has that privilege. He can leave now. For you there are no ties to cut since none existed.' This is what he lets Mikaël say to the master.

And he must write to Fritz: 'You, my friend, you were the one who gave my life meaning. Like the higher powers, the pleasures and sorrows in my life washed over everything and seeped into my very being and what was and is mine. We had to separate, and perhaps we will never meet again. But as long as I live, you – my one and only friend – will remain in my thoughts.'

This novel is still too close to his life. He needs to put it aside, and in an almost euphoric feeling of relief he writes 'The Ravens' about an old, hunchbacked, rich aunt who sells her antiques and spends her fortune on parties.[53] She enjoys watching her family of ravens devour their inheritance. 'For what has life given me? Now I want to see them dance until they weep at my grave.' Once again his quick repartee flies across the dinner tables – wittily and brilliantly.

But the novel. The great novel.

There are so many distractions.

Herman Bang sells water from Ophelia's Spring and signs postcards in aid of Princess Marie's charity work.[54] And all those organizations that he usually helps out by doing readings gratis. And all those envelopes that he fills with money without ever investigating whether the recipients are of 'the deserving poor'. He even helps out with the funeral expenses for his old delivery man when the widow shows up with a tear-stained face.

And three days later he lets out a scream during an otherwise unexceptional walk. For right there on his usual corner is the 'old fellow', the delivery man, chatting with his friends.

And a much worse shock: a letter from America states that William Bang has shot himself, presumably due to his imminent bankruptcy. William Bang leaves behind his wife and six children.

The image of William as an adult had melted away from his consciousness. William was just a little boy who played with paper boats and petted the dog – an easy, placid child who hardly ever cried. And that little boy William had married on the other side of the ocean and fathered six children before lifting a gun to his head.

'Nini, dear Nini. What about all those he left behind? We don't know anything about them. Don't know what will happen to them. Nothing.'

'Take it easy, calm down, Herman. Let's see what the future brings. You are much too anxious.'

'*Marienlyst Thursday 1903*

Nini, dear Nini.

I am far from being anxious or nervous. I am working every day and keep to my schedule. But I have only faced – as I usually do – the harsh truth: that in all probability the unhappy people will have to go where their misfortune is most likely to be lessened. So, we must share their lot as they must share ours. It is clear to me that William would never had done it if he hadn't been facing disaster – – and now there is no one else but me to take it upon myself, even if this will also completely change my material life. Those are the kinds of ups and downs that life brings us, and we must accept the challenge courageously.

It is of no use whatsoever conjuring up solutions that later turn out to be illusions without any basis.

Your
Herman'

Nini was right once again. They never heard from William's widow. And if he thought about his own age and William's age and then about the children of his friends, perhaps not all the descendants of the little boy William would be small and unprovided for.

The thought of the six children had been a daydream and a nightmare. He himself would never have any other children than his books. And to *Mikaël* he would give everything. No more providing of meals or virtuosity. 'This book must be written. At some point it becomes one's duty to make a supreme effort.'

A whole year flew out of his life and into those pages. And when he delivered the manuscript, he begged Peter Nansen to read it and write immediately. If the book failed, it would be a terrible blow. But better to find out right away.

Peter Nansen was moved and impressed. And it was with great relief that he was able to write back to him:

'*Dear Nansen*

You have made me very happy – and not just the artist in me. I can only thank you. My books come into existence under a strain so great – and *Mikaël* embodies so much of myself and my bitter experiences and my self-knowledge – that it naturally would have hurt me deeply if I had failed this time. And from reading your letter I now know that the book is not altogether a failure.

Thank you
Herman B.'

Fritz was now travelling and performing in the provinces, and Herman Bang could advise him:

'Engelke must be given festive costumes and death scenes. And her husband wants plays cheaply.'

Or: 'Can't you let go of some of the costumes? Nudity, as far as it is possible, is always an attraction in the provinces where detailed knowledge of the artists is what they like the best … .'

But he didn't miss Fritz. When he strolled along the fashionable street Strøget it was with Christian Houmark and the young lieutenant Stellan Rye who wrote poetry and who had read his first play to him. He encouraged Nansen to publish it. And he himself certainly wanted to direct it. For in it were the most beautiful gems.

Finally *Mikaël* came out. And it was as though the book at first paralyzed the reviewers. No one wanted to utter the first word. But then the book was described as 'a deep, human work, shuddering with suspense and trembling with suffering, powerful and monumental.' Herman Bang's pathos was compared to that in Shakespeare's *King Lear*, and even Michelangelo and the Old Testament were mentioned.

In other words, he had finally succeeded.

'What happened to the essential chapter?' asked Houmark.

'Burnt. Time is not ripe for that yet.'

And then Harald Nielsen's review in *Tilskueren* appeared. And his words swept away all the other ones:

'Herman Bang is not endowed with that which is the source of mental richness – a deep fundamental feeling, a few seemingly simple ideas that coupled with experience will constantly breed new ones.

The significance of willpower is missing in his characterizations. There are no conflicts that can stir our souls. You are not being told what compels these characters in their actions – they seem to be unresisting prey. Therefore, frequently Bang's portrayals do not give an impression any more shocking than can be observed in a chicken coop where the hen without any objection lies down and her mate covers her in a blind, solemn act of necessity.

In *Mikaël* the depiction of Paris is lifeless. The passion is suited to nuns, or spinsters working at rural telephone exchanges. And: as far as Mikaël and the Master are concerned, they are not faced with the kind of opposition that would show the power of their feelings more clearly.

Mikaël is mannerism, scaffolding in all its barrenness. The bare ribs that remain after the green flesh of the leaves is removed.'

'You should have been more brave,' Christian Houmark said and confided to him that he himself was now writing about love between young men.

'Write a new *By the Road* or a new *Ludvigsbakke*,' Peter Nansen said. 'You could do it so easily.'

And he used his state subsidy as security to borrow money from Gyldendal for a journey to gather inspiration.

Along with his manservant Ernst he travels to Vienna, Prague, Budapest and Bucharest.

They stay at the best hotels and ride in the most comfortable trains. But Ernst is becoming increasingly gloomy since he doesn't hear from his girl who perhaps cannot spell all the strange addresses correctly. He, for his part, sits every day chained to his desk, writing journalism. 'We are throwing money out the window,' he tells Houmark with a sigh. And the journey does not lead to rebirth but to 'a farewell to life with all its splendour.'

Prague and the mountains are not shrouded in a blue spring haze but in dark winter coldness. They attend the theatre. And for an instant he believes he recognizes Max. He is playing Pierrot in a wonderfully talented manner and with a God-given face of beauty.

But he knows that it cannot be true. For Max Eisfeld does not play cameos any more. He is a star now. John the Baptist in Oscar Wilde's *Salome* was his breakthrough.

After the performance he asks the manager of the theatre who the young Pierrot was.

'Ivo de Raic-Lonja. And he has read several of your books, and his greatest wish is to meet you.'

And they meet. And the young man is wearing a flattering, close-fitting suit. And he talks about his loneliness, and tells him that he sleeps in Russian silk. He dedicates a picture of himself as Romeo to Herman Bang. And then they part ways. Like father and son.

Friendly and easily, overbearing and ironic.

And if he could only fall in love again. He longs for the pain, for the anxiety that accompanies the longing. And he takes his leave. Hurries along. And he sees a river that splits in two, brutally and with a roar. And over there near Bucharest is a grey stony island that doesn't exist on the map. A barren, cursed island. And this island burns an image in his brain. That is where he belongs – he, who grew old and weak in the blink of an eye.

He wants to go home. Now he has seen his island. And he and Ernst catch the first train that comes along. In the train he writes two sketches about de Lonja. 'Pierrot from Agram' and 'Beaten.'[55] For 'beaten' – is something that he himself feels. And he jots down on yet another sheet of paper: 'Leonardo da Vinci gave humanity a Jesus Christ with the body of a man and the face of a woman. I wonder if he wasn't right?'

But it is the stony island and the word 'beaten' that form the image and the situation in his head.

Love – being two together and being happy – is not meant for him. The divinity with a woman's face and a man's body – what if he wrote about that kind of love, that kind of erotic instinct. No, he hides behind that virtuosity for which he is admired and at the same time reproached. But Johannes V. Jensen – he writes completely freely. He gives generously from the vast fountain of language, he seeks the source. He creates a new style utterly ruthlessly and harmoniously.

He wants to write about himself and Johannes V. Jensen. The virtuoso who is defeated by a natural talent.

The two of them will meet on the Orient Express. And they will be musicians. Violinists – which is something he knows about.

And if he is going to be able to afford to write that book, he will have to look up his impresario Fritz Petersen – a few appointments directing plays as well as a reading tour will be necessary.

He wonders if all handsome men are called Fritz. For a moment he almost feels envious, for Fritz Petersen appears ten years younger than the last time they met. He is on tour with *The Merry Widow*.

And the widow is a young and very pretty blonde who is in love with him in spite of the fact that she is married to the hero in the operetta. A difficult life for the threesome. Much sneaking around on creaky stairs. Heady rendezvous in small hotels. Reconciliations. A few fist fights in the wings. And: 'Now let us behave like adults.' And 'Now we really have to act professionally.' And every evening the husband, the Count, takes her – the pretty waltzing widow – in his arms.

But when his deep breathing has become what most women would call snoring, then the pretty one in her melon-hued négligée runs off on her little feet. At night she belongs to her lover, Fritz Petersen.

And why is it that the three of them have to perform the most upsetting melodrama at the exact moment when Herman Bang arrives to talk about financial matters.

He implores her to show some consideration for her husband.

And she gazes at him remorsefully with her big eyes wide open as though she were a little girl.

And those eyes, he thinks – that gaze leads directly to the heart of Fritz Petersen.

And sadly, he is right on the mark.

For she is not there, not in the hotel's conjugal bed where she ought to be. And yet, her husband, Count Danilo, is a rather fine-looking man.

But had the Count only remained satisfied with the script instead of buying a revolver … .

Just before the curtain opens two shots are heard. And nothing is worse than having to cancel a show. But it proves necessary, for the hero, the husband, has shot the heroine, his wife, and afterwards himself. He aimed for the heart in both cases. But the damage was nothing more than a couple of flesh wounds.

And there she lies, the merry widow with her pretty, clean flower-face. With a look of surprise, she stares at the ceiling and resembles a little girl who has been sent to bed. And there he lies, the hero, and bellows that he would rather lose an arm or a leg than be separated from her. And Fritz Petersen finds himself repeating over and over: 'There she lies, the little one. The poor little thing.'

Only one person retains his composure. Herman Bang sends a telegram to Mrs Fritz Petersen who arrives – her face lacklustre and grey, her silk likewise – in order to quell all rumours.

Where do all the revolvers come from? All this passion? All those shots?

One day Esmann, a friend of his youth, was shot by his bright and beautiful mistress. The fact that he had spent the young woman's entire fortune was not a problem. But because he didn't want to divorce his wife with whom he had a friendly relationship, the young woman pulled out a revolver from her little theatre purse. She shocked the entire fashionable part of Copenhagen by showing her demanding character and her precise aim. In a matter of a few seconds she had been able to create a frozen image of two lovers in a hotel room, as if love was an illness she had cured.

And he, Herman Bang, spoke at Esmann's funeral. The friend from his youth with his divided soul and caustic remarks that frequently had been aimed at him too. Sometimes he had simply taken flight when he saw him on the street. Esmann, the leader of the pranksters. All that was forgotten now; only grief and loss remained – and the mourners who wept with him.

*

He wipes a few tears away at the thought of all the dead. And he wished that he could find his way back for he is in the wrong place, both in his story and in real life. Or as the satirical magazines used to write:

'Dear Bang – you are always providing us with material. You are always where you have no business being.

This time you have stirred our compassion and inspired us to put pen to paper. We have seen you strolling down Strøget, and we have taken the utmost pity on you. You were dressed in pitch black – top hat and mourning crepe and black suit. Your head was bowed, and you looked despondent. Grief – on display in the middle of Strøget. For you cannot help yourself. You have painted rings of Indian ink around your eyes and rubbed walnut sap on your face to darken it further.'

'Why,' he asked, 'do you always write about me?'

'You are so easy to do, Bang. We know you inside out.'

He began to dream of another identity. He could have been a diplomat. After all, he has given public lectures on national defence. He has written articles about foreign affairs and economics. He has met Tietgen on the street, and the great financier commended him and added that there is not a single incorrect word in his articles, oddly enough.

With the help of Princess Marie's character reference he applies for the position of envoy to Iceland. There, on the island of sagas, he will walk through sulphur fumes and snow storms. And he will be infinitely sad and full of longing, but rich and respected.

He delivers his application to a government offical who casts a quick glance at him and immediately begins to write a very long letter. With the letter in his hand he is sent to see the minister who opens it in his presence. The letter's great length is merely due to the foreign minister's many titles. Regarding the applicant Herman Bang, the letter only contains one single word: 'Impossible'.

How clever and polite he was, that government official. Only, he hadn't counted on the applicant's curiosity and slightly squinting eye.

'Impossible!' He laughed and dressed that evening in white tie and tails. He looked exactly like an aristocratic envoy, and with an honorarium from a reading in his pocket, he invited Houmark to dine at À Porta. They walked arm in arm and breathed a kind of carefree extravagance and understated intoxication that might have seemed provocative. A couple of young louts, bulging with muscles and aggression, approached them. He and Houmark quickly retreated to a dark passageway. It would be the easiest thing in the world to flatten those two.

The young men came closer. But instead of retreating further, Bang walked suddenly towards them and cocked his head with a pleading look: 'Please, spare us. We are from the provinces.'

The two fellows howled with laughter and went on their way.

'And me,' he said, shaking his head. 'ME they rejected – as a DIPLOMAT.'

The following day he was interviewed to promote his reading

tour. Positively the last one.

'Why?'

'There are many reasons. First of all my health which no longer can tolerate the anxiety that overpowers me for hours, sometimes for days, before each reading. I cannot endure this dreadful sensation any more. Moreover, I want to quit for artistic reasons. My performance style requires a supple and youthful body. If I were to continue and at the same time avoid the discrepancy between my type of delivery and my ageing appearance, I would have to alter my reading or lecturing technique. This I cannot do. Therefore I must give it up.'

He did readings for eighty full houses and travelled once again through the Danish provincial towns. That's where he belonged, his friends and most severe critics said. There in the quiet, melancholic provincial idyll. And all of sudden he agreed with them. In a town near the border he met a young girl who was like a character in one of his books. And he, Bang, was already playing a part in her life as well. She had read everything he had written; she even collected portraits of him and had arranged for the reading. She could serve as the protagonist in the popular novel Peter Nansen had advised him to write.

'I dropped by her home and met her and her father, a rich country grocer, and was shown the house. There was gipsy blood in those people. The family portraits had rather peculiar features. But every time I have thought about this little Miss Kaja, I have felt oddly emotional ... She had a sister who had drowned herself, and now Kaja was alone in the house – – So now you know this much, Sir.'

He moved into a hotel in Hillerød to write his book. He drank. He drank away days and nights. Bottles piled up in the wardrobe and in his suitcase. But it wasn't little Miss Kaja who stood out most clearly in his mind. It was Johannes V. Jensen with his little moustache and his clenched fists, the man who in a very forthright manner had said that he had never read anything by Herman Bang.

Yes, the two of them were going to be violin virtuosos. He himself is Count Ujhazi from the stony island. He meets his vanquisher Jens Lund: 'I have never heard you play, so I cannot compliment you,' says Jens Lund. 'I never read. I have no need for books. I have enough in myself.' And perhaps he also says: 'I have a homeland. That is my name, Sir.'

He gets up to make some notes. He feels dizzy. And nauseous. He is close to fainting. And then someone knocks on the door. And Mrs Betty Nansen seems shaken when she sees him and the room in such terrible condition. Especially when she finds an empty soya bottle among the empty wine and liquor bottles – thinking that he must have consumed that as well. She had hoped for a cozy, civilized dinner along with a little theatre gossip, but she gives up.

The next day he receives a deplorable letter from his tailor's lawyer. Apparently the publisher is still withdrawing funds from his government subsidy, meaning that the debt incurred on his travels abroad is still outstanding. And he has arranged for the tailor to be paid out of his subsidy money.

And he leaves without paying his bills although he knows it is despicable. He abandons his room and his clothes and all the empty bottles and travels to Randers and moves into a small hotel where he starts writing with burning intensity. For it is crucial that he finishes it before he has to direct Stellan Rye's play *The Faces of Deception*.[56]

He didn't quite finish it. But how wonderful it is being able to travel to Copenhagen with most of the manuscript completed and then being given the opportunity to direct again. And it is a success. On 23 September, 1906, he reads in the journal *Verdens-Spejlet* that the play at *Dagmarteatret* is a completely unexpected success.

Evidently people had feared that Bang himself was the author behind the play. Or that the young Rye had been influenced too much by Bang. The scent of patchouli favoured by Bang practically wafted from his clothes. And Bang's 'inner Virgin', journalist Christian Houmark, interviewed the dear boy with his pleasant manners worthy of a devout nun, the kind of friendliness that comes naturally to journalism's very own Auntie Christina.'

But these were only pinpricks. The most important thing was that the performance itself was described as being masterly and dramatically effective.

Finally he was able to send off his most gloomy book to date, *Those Without a Native Land*, to Peter and Betty Nansen.[57] And on

26 November, 1906, he could draw a sigh of relief. They were both enthusiastic about the book.

Until the book came out he only had to think about the theatre and his journalism. He made himself comfortable in a small apartment in Lille Strandstræde with his housekeeper Miss Thune and his estimable manservant Ernst. The actress Gerda Christophersen who lived next door was on occasion invited to partake in simple, elegant dinners. And she for her part would serve her famous yellow pea soup prepared with brined goose.

Then one day he reads in the smutty tabloid *Middagsposten* that a couple of young men have been arrested in an inner courtyard in Tordenskjoldsgade where they were about to engage in indecent behaviour in the outside privy, one of them holding a bouquet of carnations in his hand.

He reads about the 'brothers of the night' and about repulsive youths with enormous bills incurred at second-rate and third-rate perfumeries. Readers are told that a 'men's club' exists in Nørregade and that a number of well-known personalities – 'as well as some artistocrats' – will be reported to the police by some young actors and shop clerks. A dentist has already handed over names of sixty homosexual persons.

He faints. And when he finally opens his eyes due to the most disgusting smell on earth – concentrated ammonia water – he sees in a fog Miss Thune run out of the room. And he can hear her footsteps down the stairs.

When he later reproaches her for doing this, she explains that she tried first with cold rags, camomile and eau de cologne. And when she finally managed to revive him with a little ammonia, he had the wildest look in his eyes. He looked as if he was going to be violent.

He shakes his head.

And he leaves for the theatre, for he is first and foremost an actor and a director. 'Messieurs, mesdames, commençons!'

He gives the extras lines to practise: 'Miss, please shout from the top of both your lungs while clapping your hands: "Today is Bang's birthday. Today is Bang's birthday!" And you, Miss, would you be kind enough to jump up and down while saying "We had fruit soup for dinner!"'

The sixty extras are to appear as a crowd of several hundred. It is necessary to keep them, as well as himself, under control.

As soon as the rehearsal is finished, he collapses. Gerda Christophersen accompanies him to the car. Ernst or Miss Thune is waiting for him in the car. The newspapers he will read when he comes home.

Every day new arrests. Every day new attacks.

One day Johannes V. Jensen makes a statement.[58] He shouldn't really be reading in his dark room without proper lighting. But he is compelled to read everything that Johannes V. Jensen writes. He picks up his magnifying glass.

'*30.11.1906*

Let them come, one and all, to try me personally. I will be ready with a stick or with my bare hands.'

Bang looks briefly at the article. The man from Himmerland, Johannes V. Jensen, is afraid as well, it seems.

There is something about newspapers and theatres. He peers through the magnifying glass to read the passage:

'For reasons other than purely sociological ones, it is about time to let the gentlemen who have a distaste for woman's incompleteness know that they have been discovered; and that the authorities are fully justified in arresting them precisely because these gentlemen are convinced that they are normal. They have lately made themselves known in the city in a rather provocative manner, they have formed circles and secured their presence in papers and theatres, everywhere people are gathered to the point where you get the impression that there is no one else. They have written books and entered the literary scene as priests of "beauty", "the superman ideal" and whatever else they prettify their disgusting sickness with. They have in their public lectures succeeded in advocating unnatural relations as if these were the single most refined thing in the world. A very well-known writer who, in addition to being abnormal, also has a certain talent, has lately gone as far as standing up to speak about the nation's defence! The poor devil, who has probably never held a weapon in his hand, is presumably at the moment suffering from a bout of platonic love for a lieutenant. Instead of making themselves scarce when some common sexual criminals were arrested here in the city, this gang of writers, these highly cultured sinners, show their inclination and take the opportunity to foment a united attack. *Now* the time has come. *Now* we are all going to be told at once how simple and very human we are. *Now* Hellas and the entire classical world of the aesthete is going to be resurrected. Let them withdraw quietly! The time has not come. Let them run their private lives as hitherto, let them be in charge of their own persons and let them find each other in secret. But they have no mission. Their filthy sexual madness only bores ordinary people. Keep them and their madness away from the light of day.

The criminal code takes care of the rest. Crimes committed by sexual deviants against children are punishable like other kinds of misdeeds committed amongst persons of the same sex, and there is no reason to change that. However, it is not entirely right that men who have relations with other men should be punished; they ought to be handed over to the medical profession. If the insanity cannot be cured, and it seems that it is unlikely in most cases, it is worth considering that the unyielding patient should be taken into custody for life by the authorities. Since the man does not suffer any other ailment, it would be unreasonable to lock him up in an ordinary insane asylum. But since there are sanatoriums for nearly every other illness these days, would it not be conceivable to arrange for mandatory confinement at designated hospitals for these sexually miserable creatures? Moreover, apart from their unfortunate anomaly, these madmen often demonstrate exceptional talents that ought to be utilized and for which favourable conditions ought to be arranged. Many, remarkably many, have artistic talent and seem only to be in need of a patron; let the state take care of that. To everyone concerned it appears that with all their feminine tendencies they lack woman's inefficiency. Couldn't something be done about that? Confine them and give them some needlework to do! That is my opinion. They could be trained to be excellent seamstresses, and they would be able to remember every last thing. They are also suitable for library work; lock some of them up in there! Society is obliged to get the most and the best possible out of its citizens.'

So, Johannes V. Jensen had him in mind as well.

Christian Houmark came by. 'The Authors' Association has called a meeting. Jensen will be barred.'

He went into his study and wrote to Nansen:

'*My dear friend*

I implore you urgently and from the bottom of my heart that you will do everything in your power to prevent anything untoward happening to Johannes V. Jensen at the Authors' Association. It will only harm me, and all I wish is peace.

For I cannot bear it any longer.

I have used up all my strength.'

Herman Bang is called in for questioning and confronted with four rent boys.

'Do you know this man?' asks the young police advocate Wilcke, who is notorious for his rudeness and brutality.

A boy with a beautiful, narrow face shakes his head: 'We don't know that gentleman, do we?'

He politely bids the boys farewell and drives to the theatre.

The newspapers write that his name ought to be taken off the government subsidy.

One day he sees a headline printed in red type – red as blood: Herman Bang a murderer. The paper reports that a young apprentice clerk has hanged himself after having confessed to having sex with Herman Bang.

Journalists have gathered on his stairs. They are falling over each other, trying to get a statement from him.

'Please, report that I am not charged with anything,' he says. 'That's what you can write in your paper.'

He is busy. He has to choreograph a waltz. A waltz in light and darkness. The lovers in each others' arms. A very erotic waltz.

He whirls the lovers around on the stage.

'Kiss!' he shouts. 'Let it rain with kisses. Remember that you are young and beautiful.'

And then she suddenly tears herself away from her partner and from the waltz. Gerda Christophersen walks towards him as if the two of them are in somebody's living room. Her face has become heavier. Perhaps she is drinking. Perhaps she has difficulties sleeping. Her hands are very beautiful. And with these hands she reaches out to him.

'We,' she says. 'You and I. We could get married if that would kill all the stupid rumours.'

'No, Gerda. In that case you would never be anything but my nurse.'

And then she went back to the waltz.

In the daily news he read: 'After an interrogation in which he lately took part, and after all the world has renounced this man of letters, it appears that this time he is finally determined to stand by his anathema. If he manages to flee this time, it will give rise to extreme anger against police and judges.'

He received a letter from Karin Michaëlis: 'You have given your country and your people so many rich and wonderful gifts that there is no reason you shouldn't hold your head high even if all of the riffraff point fingers. – Never before has anything made me feel so heartbroken as Johannes V. Jensen's dreadful attack, and mostly because he is not at all the way he seems. He has all his life been a divided soul, his sensitivity has made his life miserable to the point where he has shut it out and created a false, hard shell to protect himself.'

Houmark came and wanted to give a report of the meeting at the Authors' Association.

'Would you mind being silent, Houmark?'

'Only one thing. I got up and declared in front of the whole assembly that I am homosexual.'

'Why? Why did you do that?'

'Because of you.'

'I begged you not to attend.'

'We have many allies, Bang. In fact, only Mrs Thit Jensen sided with her brother. She stormed out in protest and knocked over two rows of chairs.'

'How long has this been going on?'

'The case has lasted almost a year.'

'When it is over, I am leaving.'

The first of October, 1907, fourteen people were convicted.

But no acquittals. No retractions from the papers.

The only good thing was that now he could travel freely to Berlin again and start over.

His greatest concern was Ernst. For how would he be able to keep a manservant when starting from scratch? He asked Nansen:

'Then there is Ernst. I should have talked to you about him a long time ago – and he believes that I already have – but I would rather not have to bother you. But what shall we do? The thing is that he is a treasure as far as discretion, neatness, thriftiness and dependability go. As I have often said: I haven't met anybody who can measure up to his pure character. And if a new theatre were to start presently, he would be indispensable as a factotum or private secretary. But what can we do about it now? Isn't there some place – an opening – somewhere in one of the many enterprises associated with the publishing house where he could be placed as a matter of form until another postition is found for him? Your wife, who otherwise has difficulties showing her sympathy, is fond of him as well, as you know.'

Unfortunately Nansen was unable to help out. Ernst would have to come along to Berlin. 'Dear Bang, do you really have to leave?' Gerda Christophersen threw her arms round him and held on to him tightly. She was a strong woman with talent, temperament and theatre in her veins and the kind of human extravagance that made her sacrifice herself completely for an acting part.

'Yes, it is unavoidable. I have been been spat at and flogged. I must leave Denmark.'

*

He cried and thought of the title of his book: *Those Without a Native Land*. He had almost forgotten it, and so had his former readers. He was just a name in a trial now.

He gets up and presses his forehead against the window.

The entire landscape is covered in a wonderful golden haze. Like in the early mornings of his youth when he woke up and wrote with his finger on the misty window pane.

Perhaps there are mountains beyond the mist, cliffs that he will never climb, rocks that will make the train yield and move in graceful curves. Or, perhaps cities with tall buildings and bitter, salty air. And why is he here, exactly? Where he doesn't know a single human being?

He glances at the passengers who are slumped in their seats, looking listless. Only a young girl is standing – a girl in a light suit. She looks as if she is searching for something out there in the fog. As if she is in the theatre and has forgotten her opera glasses. Or perhaps she is looking for a face. A young man she doesn't know but has never forgotten.

Suddenly the train jerks, and the girl smiles at him when he lets out a scream and covers his mouth with his hand, frightened. She looks at him precisely as if he were an exotic bird in a cage. He wants to get away. Away from her childish, prying eyes.

Luckily a young man in uniform comes along. He bears a vague resemblance to Ernst but only a touch because this one is taller, his expression is verging on cocky and his buttons are nothing to boast of. He opens the door, and it is so easy just to follow him and return to his own berth.

But as soon as he is alone, he shakes uncontrollably from the coldness that always sets in when sleep escapes him.

Tall, thin glasses break and turn to diamond dust that swirl around the dancers' heels. And winter's ice needles, white ferns and lilies form under his skin.

He presses his face and hands against the window for a moment. If only he were out there – in the pale golden mist –

*

How cold he was the first few months in Berlin while setting up a home with the help of his pen. 58 Fasanenstrasse, the most beautiful apartment that he has ever lived in, overlooking a piazza and a balcony where vines creep up and hang on tight with their tiny feet. There is room for two bird cages on the balcony, and in the summer he keeps his birds there. Otherwise they fly around the pinewood bookcases he has bought in instalments. And much to his delight, two of them are building a nest between some silk cushions in the sofa.

'But my God,' says a woman who is visiting, 'you really don't need this much space, Bang.'

In actual fact he only has the study and the bedroom at his disposal. The dining room is shared. Ernst and Miss Thune have each their own room. And there are other concerns as well. Because Miss Thune cannot speak a word of German, he had to hire a German girl for three weeks to teach Miss Thune how to do the shopping. And Ernst needs a German tutor, for how else will he manage to get around in Berlin? And every day Herman Bang's good friend Ossip Melnik comes for dinner at seven. Melnik is Russian and a journalist at *Berliner Tageblatt*. And not very industrious at that. It takes Melnik a year to write what Herman Bang can write in a week. But this young man with his beautiful resonant voice spends his evenings reading out loud to his older friend who cannot read by artificial light any longer. The kind, gentle Ossip reads Chekhov's short stories and plays without reproaching his listener for lounging on the sofa generally looking tired and depressed. And to prevent any misinterpretations of this situation, Melnik sometimes brings a lady: Mrs Frihling who is very proper and wealthy and who doesn't at all mind being referred to as Melnik's fiancée although there is no suggestion of any erotic sparks between the two.

He looks at himself from the outside. For he knows very well how they talk about him in Copenhagen. That he lives beyond his means and has practically surrounded himself with a court. But he hardly makes any new acquaintances. He is isolating himself. And it is as if the cities that embraced him in his youth are now grey and buttoned up. His work on *Strange Tales* is progressing at a sluggish pace.[59] He approaches it in the sweet state of mind on the edge of fainting. 'Are we the only ones who cannot see it, and is it possible that death was as multifarious as life?'

He lives in the borderland between sleep and wakefulness, between life and death. He doesn't believe in an afterlife. But the soul must be somewhere.

'From the soul's unknown regions we hear from time to time whispers of strange and mysterious tales.

They are secret and sinister, and they lead us to half-dark places, to where we can only grope our way forward with tentative steps and arms outstretched.

But at the same time they light erratic and flickering candles that allow us glimpses into the deep spaces that we otherwise never see – the deep secrets of our own souls.

For that reason I have written these tales.'

And he dedicated the stories to three friends from abroad: Ossip Melnik, Madame Bertha Wasbutzki and Count Maurice Prozor.

Denmark had become a source of agony. 'I would rather be burnt alive than to ever return – were it only for a day – to that country,' he wrote to Nini after his first serial had appeared in *Berliner Tageblatt*.

Peter Nansen's letters he barely dares to open. Sometimes he lets them lie around unopened for a fortnight in fear of them perhaps containing notices that his monthly payments have been suspended.

Sometimes he writes 'Nansen' and uses the formal address – as if they had never known each other in spite of the fact that the painting of Princess Marie above his desk is flanked by Peter and Betty.

In reality he only keeps company with, especially, Doctor Wasbutzki since the doctors who know his 'true face' always become his friends. And then Mrs Wasbutzki who on their first meeting was somewhat reserved because she found him much too tense and his laughter joyless, hysterical and full of sadness. This woman he felt compelled to charm, and now she actually takes care of his translations. He couldn't bear that his doctor's wife scrutinized him with a frosty look in her eyes. But now they see each other almost too much – he and the wife.

At his first reading, organized by Wasbutzki and wife, his entire home is filled with flowers. But to his credit, he had worked on his language. And it was necessary. It is imperative that he speaks without an accent. If for no other reason than to please his German publisher Sammy Fischer. Sammy who publishes him at a loss and always makes his accountant write on the negative statements: 'For your information only' – often accompanied by a friendly letter inviting him to the palatial villa or for a ride in Sammy's large comfortable automobile.

But it puzzles him to remember he once enjoyed being sociable. He writes to Peter Nansen:

' … Otherwise I have little desire to live most days. Johannes V. Jensen hit the bullseye when he hit me. At home I would still laugh once in a while. In this place you never hear anyone laughing.'

But when on a rare occasion he is out at a party and overhears people talking about the odd Mr Jensen who has come to Berlin, he just says: 'He is Denmark's greatest writer.' And one day he receives a letter that shakes him to the core:

'Berlin 13/12 08

Dear Mr Herman Bang

I was here to see you after Mr Fischer had told me that you were ill and alone. If you are still giving the unfortunate incident any thought – in which it was too easy for me to throw my weight around – I assure you that I wasn't aiming at you personally but at certain political power centres whose influence I had a bias against at that time. I wish you could forget about it. Bjørnson passed a greeting on to me from you the other day. If you will accept a hand from me – not because you or I believe that we can help or can be helped, and not in the hope either of being able to improve the miserable conditions at home through such a gesture – I mean, if you would stop counting me as your primary adversary when unhappy memories surface, I, too, would be very relieved. When abroad you would rather not be ashamed of being Danish; at home it doesn't matter. I hope you will soon be well again and able to revisit people and places that mean something to you.

Sincerely yours
Johannes V. Jensen.'

He stared at the signature. He looked around the room. He looked at his birds, his green plants, the wicker chairs, the silk cushions, Ernst in his handsome livery, Miss Thune – a kind and rather unshapely woman. He looked at it all through the eyes of Johannes V. Jensen. He was not going to let that man into his home. It took him a long time to reply:

'*An Johannes V. Jensen*

11.1.09

Herzkrankheit verhinderte mich, früher zu schreiben. Ich danke Ihnen voller Aufrichtigkeit für Ihren Besuch.'[60]

He realized to his own surprise that he had begun the letter in German. Yes, he thought. No 'Dear', no 'Truly yours'. From now on they were going to communicate each in his own language. He continued his letter.

Thanking him for paying him a visit was reasonable enough. But he had to admit that under no circumstances did he want to receive Johannes V. Jensen. It was not due to personal ill will, but it was still preferable if they didn't see each other any more:

'You have acted in a way that I cannot fathom. And the reason I cannot understand it, I will try to explain as well as I possibly can.

You see: I know very well that you would never, and possibly rightly so, compare yourself with me. But it must still have occurred to you when you look at contemporary Danish and European literature that, after yourself, I am one of the few worth mentioning.

And for that reason alone you ought to be the last person – no, rather, you shouldn't have allowed yourself at all to take up arms against me. I don't know if you can understand how I feel – but the feeling itself is unalterable. Therefore it is best if we don't meet or visit each other again.

I thank you once again for wanting to pay me a visit. You should also know that few people wish you success with your life's work as profoundly as I do.

Herman Bang.'

A letter in German. The writing clear but cutting. He asked Ernst to put it in an envelope and post it. He was relieved to think that the veterinarian's son was not going to cross his threshold. Nini was the person he particularly wished would come to see his home.

Fritz Boesen had visited him and had even advanced him a loan. Fritz had become a very able tour leader.

Christian Houmark had been in Berlin for three days. And during those three days he had repeated several times: 'I would never have thought it possible – – dear Herman Bang, I would die living here …' That is how much social life there was in the house.

But if Nini could come along with her best friend, Mrs Bauditz, then Nini could have Ernst's room. And he would rent a room for Ernst somewhere in the city. And if Houmark could come at the same time and show the ladies around. Houmark had made a charming impression on Nini. Sometimes she missed him outright. And he himself was both hard at work and bone-tired.

'Shall I bring some silverware?' Nini asked.

'Nini, my dear Nini. Don't bring any silver. It will look odd with what I have here. The only thing you might invest in is a bed. A proper bed. Mine is not very good. Perhaps you could rent one.'

Nini didn't come. Perhaps it was better that way. She would probably be horrified, like Houmark, to discover a household with eighteen towels and eight tea cloths.

But the 'children' came. Astrid and Jens Peter von Scholten had decided to come to Berlin to visit him.

'*My dear Astrid*

How happy I was to receive your letter and to know that you are coming. You can stay in a place a couple of streets from here – it is cheap and clean – and you will of course eat here. It will be wonderful to see you and hear you talk and to watch Jens over in the corner sitting comfortably in the best chair the house can offer … It will be like a fairy tale. That said, you will have to take it as it is. The food is good enough – Miss Thune makes sure of that – but the tableware is plain and everything is as you would expect to find in a worker's cottage. It is not so easy to build up a household without money … But you will be going to the theatre and Jens to a real circus where there are a hundred thoroughbreds to watch. Oh yes, I am looking forward to seeing you very much.

Your
Herman.'

And he also asked Astrid to do him a favour – a very big favour:

'Speak with Ernst and ask him in a cheerful and natural way where he intends to seek employment once he has finished his training – the first of July – and say that it is about time to think about it … You understand what I mean. This situation must come to an end. Even the clothes are becoming too expensive (Wages ninety marks. Instruction one hundred marks – both amounts are monthly), and at some point he has to get out in the world and fight for a position.'

Ernst had thought about it. He wanted to go home. And it was both a relief and a loss when the 'Estimable' left.

Betty Nansen came fluttering by on a tour. She was looking forward to the season. She now had that giant bitch Macbeth by the tail, she said.

He for his part laboured his way through a German reading tour. And he had a moment of intense longing: 'There is no sky like the one above the fatherland,' he sighed when Princess Marie sent him a linden flower.

And then Fritz Petersen wrote and asked if he would like to come to Copenhagen and take up a permanent position as director at *Casino*.

Wouldn't he just –

17.

The summer of 1909 he left Berlin. He was once again working as a theatre director and moved back into Lille Strandstræde. Every morning at six o'clock Miss Thune brings coffee, cigarettes and the script. He reads until eight o'clock and learns the scenes for the day by heart. But he only makes a few notes. He wants to leave space for the actors to express themselves. He bathes, gets dressed, makes himself look beautiful and steps into the car that is waiting in front of his door precisely at nine. A quarter past nine Doctor Abrahamsen stabs him in the shoulder with the small syringe containing dionine, almost like a morning greeting, and he continues to the theatre to take possession of the stage before the actors arrive.

And it is neither Shakespeare, Ibsen, nor the much coveted play *Three Sisters* by Chekhov that is on the bill. Herman Bang has become a director of operettas. Herman Bang swaddles dancers in gossamer costumes, and Herman Bang teaches the chorus to do a rustic clog dance in *King for a Day.*

'The things he demands, this king of the cats,' he complains to Peter Nansen when rehearsing the operetta *Prince Incognito.*[61]

And he buys flutes and noisemakers for the children among the extras and instructs them in playing and simulating a carnival mood.

He indulges himself with a short lunch break and a tea break at the Dagmar Café and continues working with the actors until half past six. Then the car waits for him in front of the theatre, and he is driven home to Miss Thune's dinner and a German servant who is not only respectable but also totally silent. It happens that he brings colleagues with him, and they eat and talk and drink wine, and the ladies blush from cheek to plunging neckline. But between half past eight and nine, he retires to his room. He has exerted all his strength.

There is one première after another. Fritz Petersen manages both theatres – *Casino* and *Dagmarteatret* – and Herman Bang, the director, labours like a nice workhorse that is fed gold and flowers. The money goes to the doctor, the chauffeur and the tailor. When Sarah Bernhardt comes to Copenhagen, he has to show her around. And the money flies in all directions to buy shirts, eau de cologne, dinners, cabs and bouquets of flowers. He writes about her. He loves her Hamlet – the neurasthenic's Hamlet.

He collects his portraits of actors in the book *Masks and People.*[62] He analyses the actors and actresses he admires: Betty Borchsenius, Josef Kainz, Gabrielle Réjane, Gerda Christophersen, Betty Nansen.

'The novel,' Peter Nansen asks. 'What happened to the great novel?'

He doesn't know but asks shamelessly for an advance of a hundred kroner nevertheless.

' – And all this is because of Mrs Wasbutzki. The woman came this evening. I thought it was early – and at the end of the month. By God, everything was in order and furnished and prepared and sorted out, so I was safe. But then the woman arrives two days before payday.'

In fact, the woman, his soulful friend with her dark eyes and swishy silk dress, causes him nothing but inconvenience. There is no room for anything else but the theatre.

'I don't belong to anyone any longer,' he writes to Bertha Holst, ' – and least of all to myself. I belong to two theatres which is nothing but one big deception, and I am constantly anxious about the livelihood of 150 people. The theatres consume all of my willpower which I have to conjure up every day artificially, and all of my strength which I also have to arouse every day artificially. – When my life one day is over, it will not be possible to list a hundred hours when

I truly lived – and not two when I was happy. The other day when I was involved in a car accident and blood poured from my face, I had only two thoughts. One was to get away from the rabble that stared at me – the other: why wasn't I allowed to be ejected from the car and lie dead on the street.'

A stay at a nerve clinic would perhaps be a possibility. But the prima donna at *Dagmarteatret* beats him to it; she suffers religious scruples and lets herself be admitted to an institution.

'You will have to sort this out, Bang,' Fritz Petersen says. 'You said once yourself that she would perhaps end up in a madhouse or in a house of prayer. Turns out it is both at once. But if Anna Larssen stops acting, we will most likely go bankrupt.'

Yes, if anyone can fix things, he is the one. He buys a beautiful bouquet of flowers as if she has just had her debut, and he asks Albrecht Schmidt to accompany him to Doctor Jacobsen's nerve clinic on the pretext of congratulating her on her birthday.

She is turning thirty-four and is sitting in the sofa looking so healthy and rested that she could be taken for a twenty-five-year-old. She smiles, puts the flowers in a vase and serves hot chocolate with whipped cream as is the traditional birthday treat. Then she sits down again, waiting politely, her knees properly together while a little white kitten nibbles at her lace and turns somersaults in her lap.

He throws himself on the sofa and begins to act Hamlet. He is certain that she will get caught up in it. She will not be able to contain herself and will act along with him. And then he and Albrecht will tell Doctor Jacobsen: 'Mrs Anna Larssen is exactly the way she usually is. She must be discharged immediately.'

He puts his heart and soul into the acting.

But the lady has no desire whatsoever to act a mad woman. She is at a nerve clinic and wants to play with her cat.

'But Anna – your talent. Aren't you thinking of the theatre?'

'Yes, all last night I was on my knees praying to God to provide me with seven hundred kroner so I could be released from my contract. But now I think I will sell all that I own instead.'

'But my dearest Anna, think of everything we will lose.'

Yes, she had been thinking whether it would be possible to run a theatre that offered a decent, religious repertoire. 'But,' she concluded. 'It would probably be too boring.'

Her smile was subtle, reserved and a bit ironic.

And many thoughts went through his head that very instant.

Her shyness when in general company. Her sarcasm when Mrs Nansen took on a role she perhaps wasn't suited for. And her cheerfulness in a vacation letter from Spain where she had just cured her lover's stomach trouble by throwing his medicine in the chamber pot and feeding him fresh fruit.

And he remembered a young man who was practically brought to ruin after having acquired blood-red azaleas that he threw at her feet. He cut them out of the flowerpot, and they landed on the stage with a thump.

Now she was just sitting there calmly and scratching a kitten behind the ears.

His Hamlet had been of no use whatsoever.

'Yes,' he said when he and Albrecht stepped into the street, 'here is nothing to be done. There is no hope for the future.'

From now on her sexual magnetism and delicate, breaking voice belonged to the mission.

Shortly thereafter Fritz Petersen had to take his leave. He had used his position as manager to abuse the young women at the theatre.

And it was with a great relief that Bang could finally give notice to quit his job as director. He was thoroughly tired of choruses and rustic clog dances.

And then the thought of travelling came back. The inspirational journey round the world. In the beginning it was only a dream. But Ossip Melnik is now publicity consultant for the Hamburg American Line to New York. Ossip speaks in favour of it. Peter Nansen speaks in favour of it.

Perhaps it is in Japan that he belongs. The cherry trees' delicate clouds of pink blooms. Lakes covered in lotus blossoms. Secretive moss gardens and ponds where the carps play trustingly with his shadow. And he will get to see the mirror of the sun goddess and Buddhist temples with hundreds of golden statues. And Mount Fuji covered in blood-red azaleas and eternal snow.

He dreams and lets the others take care of the practical things.

In any case, he has enough to worry about.

Suddenly first lieutenant Jens Peter von Scholten shows up in his living room. Deathly pale and very quietly he tells him that he has gone bankrupt. The big villa will be rented out or preferably sold. The servants have already been dismissed. And Astrid, whom he had wanted to carry in his arms and spoil like a princess, she cries and cries.

The children who now have two children of their own can stay and eat at his place. Miss Thune cooks every day anyway. It will be like having a family:

'*My dear Astrid*

Jens Peter was here and told me that you are devastated to have to leave Odense. Dear child, don't take it so greatly to heart. It will all turn out well in time. Get going with the packing and the renting of your house – as quickly as possible. I am very much looking forward to having you stay here. You will have two adjacent rooms with a connecting door and have it all to yourselves.

Just come as soon as you can.

Your old
Herman.'

They came – the children. His young charming nurse who was easily moved to tears had become a handsome, dignified wife, still with her winning smile. And she and Jens Peter still looked at each other like a couple in love.

While he directed the season's last three performances, his friends made arrangements for his journey.

One day a young man came by and inconvenienced him, wanting to buy the film rights to 'The Four Devils.'[63] He didn't have much faith in that project and sold it cheaply for a hundred kroner. The man was both sympathetic and young.

He was busy. He negotiated with editors at weeklies and dailies.

As soon as he gets away, he will be able to write. Write about everything. But in order to finance his journey, he needs an advance.

Moreover, he will have to do another reading tour: Gothenburg where he has good friends, Stockholm, Helsinki, St. Petersburg and finally Moscow, the city he has never seen but where he is now being read. Being an admirer of Russian literature, he longs to meet the Russian people.

Miss Thune is coming too. She deserves to see the world. She is as suited to travelling as a chicken is to swimming, and she shows her gratitude by staying in the hotel equipped with a small pair of embroidery scissors, cutting out everything that the newspapers write about Herman Bang. By virtue of her profession she carefully samples all the dishes at lunch and dinner.

Gothenburg is a joy. Here he is received by friends who know about his nervousness before a performance. His program is:

Wednesday: 1) The Master from *Mikaël* dies. 2) *Pastors*.

Friday: 1) The mother from *Those Without a Native Land* dies. 2) The dancer Irene Holm. 3) The guests arrive (*Joys of Summer*).

And the reviews that Miss Thune cuts out are excellent.

In Stockholm he makes a supreme effort with the dying Master. But he doesn't know precisely what impression he has made. After Miss Thune has gone through all the papers with her scissors, he reads in *Svenska Dagbladet* that he is an author who acts and displays himself like a work of art that can be admired from all sides. But he is still celebrated, and even Nini will have to admit that his program is no vacation:

'*My dear Nini*

Forgive me that I never write. But I will show you my schedule for two days so that you will understand my silence:

Saturday	9.15	the doctor
–	9.30	bath
–	10	hairdresser
–	12.30	lunch with the Danish envoy
–	2.15 – 3	write an article for a large paper

	6.30	dinner
–	8	supper and reading at the Danish Society.
Sunday	9.15	the doctor
–	9.30	bath
–	10	hairdresser
–	12.30	lunch with the Norwegian minister
–	2	matinées at a theatre
–	6.30	dinner at my place
–	8	attending The Royal Theatre

There you are – many thoughts to you from
your Herman.'

And he must write to Astrid, but not a letter that requires an answer.
The child is probably busy. Just a casual note:

'*Stockholm 3.11.1911*

My friend. I am only here for seven hours. But one thing I will steal
the time to tell you. From the depths of my heart: I am delighted
that you became Jens Peter's wife.

This you must believe,
Herman.'

And then he is going to travel with a dance troupe through Sweden.
Two ladies and a gentleman are dancing. The gentleman is of noble
stock and one of the ladies is engaged to a pastor. This is what he
explains to Miss Thune when she raises an eyebrow all the way to
her hairline.

'It is perfectly decent.'

He is not dancing himself but will be reading elegant, witty texts
while the dancers change costumes.

The unfortunate thing is, however, that he is obliged to pay for
the meals consumed by Miss Thune and himself. Miss Thune eats
for two grown men and insists it must be the air.

And the troupe gets stuck in Norrköping for financial reasons.

He has to telegraph Gothenburg and ask for an advance payment on his travel pieces. And at the same time he begs them not to spread any rumours that he, who is soon to embark on a world tour, is stranded in Sweden.

But he is looking forward to Helsinki. The city of his youth where he was celebrated as an actor.

What meets him, however, is a half-empty theatre. Herman Bang is completely forgotten. Polite applause and only a couple of bouquets, and from the impresario: nothing.

By the time they board the ferry to St. Petersburg, Miss Thune's coat is tight and reveals the contours of her figure, while his clothes practically droop around his frame.

The seagulls' long, narrow wings and their annoying screams fill the air above the grey sea. He thinks he can hear the disdain in those screams. But fortunately he is received by the Norwegian legation as a dear and eagerly awaited guest.

There is post waiting for him at the hotel. He opens his impresario's letter that rather matter-of-factly informs him that the business has gone bankrupt and all payments have been stopped. He must telegraph Ossip Melnik and ask him for help; he doesn't even have enough to get back to Berlin. And dear, kind Ossip who demands so little for himself sends him what he can. And it is enough for him and Miss Thune to be able to keep up a facade in the beautiful, fashionable city where they are constantly invited out – although no one has made arrangements for any readings to take place. And to that end many formalities are required.

In the end he sends a telegram to the Empress herself. And suddenly his problems cease. A Parisian, they call him, and a tragic actor. He receives the most beautiful bouquets. The mother's song from *The White House* is attached to one of them. And the laurel wreath is large. He tears a couple of leaves off and sends them to Olga Dahl; he tells her the tragicomic story about the dance troupe and Herman Bang. Just prior to his departure he had heard that she was sick, but hadn't been able to visit her. Now he will send her letters – one every day. 'My very own friend, just imagine that you would be the one to be sick.'

He must keep on going. He hastens to reach Moscow. He longs

for the city and its people, plain and simple.

'There must be a kinship between me and those people. Otherwise I wouldn't have so many readers in Russia. At least, it is not my story-telling technique that has won them over. I am not so conceited that I will compare myself to the great masters. But to speak in Russia – to advocate for one's own work personally. That is worth all one's efforts,' he said to Miss Thune who was asleep, leaning on his shoulder and making small, raspy snoring sounds.

When they reached Moscow he had to wake her up. In a joint effort they threw their suitcases out of the train. Nobody was there to welcome them. He rushed off in the bitter cold to find a driver who could take them to the hotel.

Perhaps they had simply forgotten him. But he showed up at the appointed hour for his reading, formally attired, his hair brushed, all sleek and shiny. The hall was just bare hospital walls, and on a rough-hewn box covered in blue oilcloth stood a table and a chair.

On a slack rope hung a brown velvet door curtain. And through the curtain's rather wide slit he eyed his very small audience.

He didn't welcome them and began telling about his novel as if he was called in for questioning. After that he read 'The Master dies'. He threw himself down across the wooden table and sobbingly declared that the only person he loved had deserted him.

At first not a sound could be heard. But then the whole room shook with applause from the audience. He was given bouquets and was carried off to a salon where the hostess had arranged a party for him.

He sat down in an armchair and sighed: 'I have thought a great deal about Russia and always loved it – this mythological country. And now see what has happened, a terrible fiasco!'

'A success,' the hostess gushed. 'You will see for yourself the next time you come to do a reading in Moscow.' And she told him about young people who were reading his books and would give years of their lives to have experienced meeting him.

'Oh, you are probably just making up all these young people to comfort me,' he laughed. 'But I am not really so devastated. In New York or Chicago, in those cities I will be able to forget it all.'

Now he had offended her, he thought: 'Yes, of course I am sad.

Terribly sad. It just feels so ridiculous when you consider that it is about a person who every day for the past thirty years has known that everything in the world is a matter of vanity.'

But the worst thing was, after all, that nobody had thought of anything that looked like an honorarium – and that it was mentioned in the review that he was cross-eyed.

Moscow itself was wonderful. He went to the opera with Miss Thune. And a pretty young woman told him that you could always find rubies, topazes or diamonds on the floor here. The settings were so fragile that the precious stones fell out.

To the Russians' surprise, Bang had to return to Berlin.

The European tour was over. And it didn't yield any profit.

He wrote to Heise, the barrister:

'*Dear friend*!

My suffering never stops. In Russia I was defrauded of everything I had earned. In fear I returned to Berlin where my fear only increased: three of my papers had abandoned me!'

To Nini he wrote: 'Moscow is a fairy tale that transcends reason. A white dream of splendour and misery. But he who hasn't seen the Kremlin hasn't seen anything … Miss Thune walked around in the palatial halls as if in her own living room and said they were "pretty". This adjective she also used to describe Ivan the Terrible's tower.[64] I stood one evening in the Kremlin overlooking a snow-white city. That hour I will remember until my dying day … .

The pension here is very elegant with scores of white-painted parlours where ladies in dresses with trains constantly drink tea and eat pound cake.

After having filled herself with six-course meals (that were wonderful) in Moscow, Miss Th. finds that four courses are not much. Besides, the French chefs in Russia make better mayonnaise.'

And he concluded with: 'In Russia they love me very very much.'

But he couldn't stay. The sixth of January, 1912, he had to be in Hamburg to board the steamer *Moltke* that was expected to be in

New York on the seventeenth of January. And in Berlin a doctor was waiting. Doctor Wasbutzki wanted to examine him before the long journey, and he, for his part, wanted to write his testament. Not regarding assets, although he had often mentioned this to Fritz when he couldn't raise any money. His real testament was not about finances but about sexuality.

He was sitting in the living room of his doctor and friend, dictating. The lady of the house served coffee and disappeared quietly. The doctor's pen flew across the yellow notepaper. They didn't make eye contact. Herman Bang spoke after a lifelong silence about his problems with his sexuality. He saw it as his duty to do so. He spoke soberly and quietly as if he wished to approximate a physician's clinical language.[65]

'The problem of homosexuality is a question that concerns the welfare of millions of people,' he said. 'Any step forward in the general understanding of the problem is therefore a step forward in the understanding of humanity.'

'There is no doubt in my mind whatsoever that pronounced homosexuality is innate. And I, who admittedly am only a layman, see it this way. Nature (or whatever you would call the driving force in Creation) that pursues her mighty and for us unknown purpose is in a hurry to take care of every detail, and in her hurry makes mistakes everywhere. A perfect plant hardly exists; neither does a perfect animal.

Nature makes mistakes and creates crooked leaves or a crooked ear. It seems to me that nature also makes errors when completing the human organism and that she creates in the otherwise externally masculine organism a so-called feminine psyche. Through an error in nature or the creator himself, an imperfect human organism is created without a uniform character.

One homosexual literally recognizes another before they have seen each other's faces. This fact I don't understand myself at all. It is as if they are instinctively connected through an electric current. A homosexual can identify another homosexual even if he only sees this other person's back from a great distance. The easiest way of recognizing homosexuality is by the person's eyes, which almost always reflect a certain melancholic yearning. And a deep and from time to time restless mournfulness is most likely the main trait of his personality. Mournfulness and restlessness. Most homosexuals travel a lot – as tourists if they are wealthy. Among the lower classes homosexuals are attracted to professions that allow them to change residence; probably because they to a certain degree feel safer this way, but also because through travelling they can curb their inner restlessness.

But if a poet really is homosexual, exceptional conditions will affect his art. He is by nature Janus-faced and has the ability to study the life of the psyche in two directions, if you will allow me to formulate it this way. Shakespeare's greatness would not have been possible without the Earl of Pembroke. The homosexual poet would be able to express something greater should the time come when he is brave enough to express his feelings directly. Not until such time as he can abandon the disguise that is currently necessary – not until then will he be able to show his talent's full originality and strength. In order to avoid a perpetual masquerade, he turns away from himself and his own emotions and as an artist becomes first and foremost an observer of his fellow human beings – and in most cases a great storyteller because he can see with four eyes, as it were.'

He paused for a moment. He saw himself in a not too distant future. It would be like breaking a window. Being released from a prison.

He then continued his dictation. They didn't finish it in one day. Not until the next day, late in the afternoon, did he watch his doctor carefully seal his testament and lock it up in a drawer. Not even Mrs Wasbutzki knew about the drawer's existence, and the testament could not be opened until after his death.

The doctor gave him capsules of morphine that would ensure peaceful nights on the journey and some drops that would magically wake him up and make him feel cheerful and animated.

He laughed at the thought of being able to switch himself on and off. On the entire journey he could now stage himself as though he were a theatre. His laughter turned into a cough. And the doctor gave him even more bottles and powders so he didn't have to call on some unknown doctor on the other side of the globe.

They shook hands. Mrs Wasbutzki wept. He bowed his head to comfort her and he brushed her cheeks with kisses that were as insubstantial as onion skins. But she wouldn't let go of his hands. She suddenly leaned forward and inhaled the smell of cigarettes and eau de cologne. She kissed his hands greedily until they were wet.

Miss Thune was waiting for him. She accompanied him to Hamburg where Ossip had arrived with his ticket. Ossip was going to meet him on the return trip. They were going to visit Naples and sail on the canals in Venice.

Right now he desperately wanted a big coat for travelling. It would protect him against the wind and the cold on board and make him look like a man who was accustomed to crossing the ocean.

Ossip smiled, and he was too nervous to thank him properly.

Miss Thune was emotional. For just an instant he wanted to say to her that she was a wonderful woman, a handsome, determined female and expensive to keep supplied with mayonnaise. She hugged him; his head rested on her bosom – a bosom where a cat would be happy to take her afternoon nap.

*

If only she had been here now.

He presses his forehead against the window. The train's speed is preposterous. He can barely make sense of the landscape. It is deserted. Sulphur-yellow, yellow, golden. There is not a soul to be seen. It might have been on the moon. Salt lakes, rocks, plateaus. As if everything is petrified and lifeless. It is a silent, dry landscape. Perhaps there are only snakes out there, sleeping in their dens, serpents with heads too small to know of love or hatred.

His fingertips touch the lacquer box. But there is probably no medicine to combat the landscape. No medicine for loneliness or for the feeling of being as fragile as a dry leaf.

The red fan has fallen on the floor. He picks it up, and it crumbles between his fingers like wings on a moth.

He wants to lie down although it is still daylight.

And there is another landscape. A field with white flowers. Camomile and dandelions gone to seed. A young woman dressed in white is going for a stroll, flowers and blades of grass brush against her white skirt. She bends down and picks one of the white seed heads. She blows, and all the downy tufts fly straight up to heaven.

He runs after her. He can see the back of her head and her thick dark hair gathered in a bun. But the wind loosens it, and in a little while it will spread out and cover her shoulders.

He runs. His legs are very short. And his heart is pounding and he has a stitch in his side.

He falls down and stays there, falls asleep in a bed of straw and wild flowers.

Coda

M rs Nini Holst, Mrs Sofie Göttsche, Peter Nansen and Ossip Melnik were waiting at the quay in Copenhagen. Because of a storm, the steamer had been delayed a couple of days, and the passengers had passed the time waltzing to the melodies from *The Merry Widow* and *The Dollar Princess*. In Kristiania they had felt a bit awkward when an enormous laurel wreath with long ribbons had been brought on board. But they blocked it out. They were excited from the journey, they laughed when they disembarked and brushed snow flakes off their clothes.

The snow settled on Mrs Holst's and Mrs Göttsche's collars. The wind lifted their long black veils while they huddled together and tried to wipe away their tears.

Ossip Melnik wept openly and blew his nose noisily. He was supposed to meet his friend in Naples. And Herman Bang had said jokingly that he would probably die before seeing Naples. But maybe he would make it to Honolulu. He had begun playing with the word and pronounced it with different intonations. His laughter was much too loud. He could be playful like a boy and depressed immediately after. And his last letter had been a reproach: 'My dear, good Ossip, for the first time in my life I am angry with you. It is entirely your fault that I have undertaken this journey. In Hamburg I implored you to ask just one single question: Are the meals in America included in the price? But either you didn't ask or else you were lied to. For I have to pay for everything myself. And I begged you earnestly. Oh, Ossip.'

Peter Nansen held the freight documents close to his body to protect them against the snow. Without those papers he wouldn't be able to have the casket handed over. 'One piece of freight,' he said. 'One piece of freight – that is Herman Bang. More than a thirty-year friendship.' He saw him suddenly as a boy, a young prince who wanted to see the world and conquer it with his language, his sensitivity, stubbornness and boundless generosity.

He wanted to write about him: 'A strange child. A boy who didn't look much like the practical men of his family line, a boy of almost womanly grace and refinement. Of an odd, exotic beauty.

He was born to triumph and yet never to experience the joys of triumph.

He was born to be doomed, and he possessed like no one else a streak of fanaticism which made him want to appear strong, want to be strong.

He understood his fate already as a very young man. He knew that he wouldn't leave any progeny behind.

The good fairies of his line had endowed him with all sorts of talents. But the Weariness Fairy had touched him with her barren hand and condemned him to be cursed by other fertile clans.'

Perhaps he had spoken out loud for it seemed to him that Mrs Holst gave him a disapproving look.

But suddenly it was as though a whistling sound cut through the air. A piercing sound of metal chains.

The four who were dressed in mourning looked up, and Mrs Holst covered her mouth with her hand to stifle a scream.

The coffin was being lowered. Or rather, it floated in the air, small, elegant and exhibitionistic while a cheerful swinging melody could be heard from one of the cabins.

He quickly handed over the freight documents, and when they were sitting in the carriage, Mrs Holst placed her hand on his arm.

'Are you sure that my brother will be buried properly?'

He nodded.

'I have read all the obituaries and haven't seen the name Bang.'

'Your brother wants his funeral to be private. No speeches, no headstone, and only his close relatives will be present.'

She cried piteously and was practically shaking him.

'I had wanted Pastor Fenger to officiate. But he declined. I had imagined that the funeral would be held in Holmens Kirke. My brother truly deserved that. But the pastor rejected it. And he was even born on the island of Als himself.'

'It will reflect badly on Fenger.'

'Holmens Kirke would have been packed with people. The church would have been filled with flowers. And now it will be Valby.'[66]

'Dear Mrs Holst, we are following the wishes of your brother as far as possible.'

'I am not sure it is the right thing to do. There is a difference between a private ceremony and one that is virtually secret. And dying is hardly a crime after all.'

'I promise you that it will be a beautiful ceremony. And I will write a tribute to him.'

'Yes, do that. I will read every single word.'

He hurried home to write. And he couldn't stop writing about Herman Bang. After the article he added a poem:

'You gave incessantly.
No one has ever been as generous as you.
You yearned to receive in return.
To meet someone who would be as devoted as you
was your dream of happiness.
You wished happiness and peace for those you loved.
You have now found the friend who gave in return – Death.
You forbade us to speak at your grave
and we are not the ones who speak.
It is death who speaks.
It is death that taught your friends
what we owed you as your friend.'

Perhaps Betty could read it. At the funeral he will see her again. After the divorce they were able to meet as friends just as they could when they were married, as friends. Herman had grieved deeply and tried to comfort both of them.

He put the poem in his pocket before he drove to the funeral, and naturally it had to snow just that day.

A small group of actors was waiting outside the church. Betty looked fabulous in her silver fox, and as soon as he had greeted her, she led her colleagues into the sanctuary.

The families Holst, Göttsche and von Scholten sat in the front pews. The young author Bertha Holst wept quietly, her eyes fixed on the coffin that was covered with the Danish flag *Dannebrog* and a bouquet of white roses.

Jens Peter von Scholten hid his face in his hands.

Peter Nansen stayed outside.

Two men in immaculate black suits approached each other. They took off their hats and before greeting each other, they wiped their brows as if to wipe off their agony.

'Imagine that it should happen so soon,' Fritz Boesen sighed.

'I knew it,' said Christian Houmark. 'I received a card from him. It said: "Have all of you forgotten me?" I read it to people exactly on the day he died, and everyone said that I sounded just like Bang. For a minute the lights went out. After that the telephone rang. It was the news of his death. 29 January, 1912. – I will never forget that day. He died all alone in Utah. But they found a photograph of me in a silver frame with his belongings.'

'I thought it was my picture Herman carried with him on his journey.'

'Have you seen him?'

'No – no, I didn't think of it. Have you?'

'Nansen advised me not to. – He was presumably murdered. Robbed and murdered.'

Peter Nansen walked over to the two men. On an impulse he handed his poem to Christian Houmark who glanced at the many deletions concerning friendship and death. He smoothed it out and put it in his inside pocket. Then he turned to Fritz Boesen.

'Your letters, Boesen, have you burnt them?'

'No, my son is going to inherit those letters.'

When they walked into the church, both of them suddenly noticed how much the other person resembled Herman Bang in terms of dress, gestures and tone of voice.

The actual ceremony was moving. The pastor, Oscar Geismar, thanked Herman Bang for his loyalty to Denmark. He thanked him for being the Good Samaritan to so many people. And he also thanked him for all his literary work. Only one thing surprised him: that a poet for whom love was everything, could have done without a relationship with the God of love.

The coffin was transported to the Western Cemetery which looked like a park in all the snow. The dark soil and the top layer of yellow clay at the grave site contrasted sharply with all the whiteness.

The mourners were weighed down by the cold and their grief. White faces framed in black and a certain heaviness pressing down from their bowed heads all the way to their feet.

But suddenly the silence was broken by agitated whispering. The solemn calm dissolved in frantic movements.

Mrs Nina Holst stepped away from the other mourners. As if pulled by a magnet, her sister Sofie Göttsche, Bertha Holst and Mrs Astrid von Scholten followed her.

'It is not the right place. It is not the burial plot we chose for my brother.' Mrs Holst's voice trembled like a thin branch covered with frost.

The pastor apparently attempted to mediate between the grave and the tall, handsome woman who insisted on her rights. She didn't move. She simply barred the way for the coffin.

Oscar Geismar took himself off. The first steps at a dignified pace, subsequently at a run on the slippery paths.

He returned with the grave digger who looked stupefied. The fellow took off his cap, put it on again, left and came back with a pair of workers who waved a piece of paper that should prove that the grave was indeed the one ordered.

Mrs Holst shook her head and asked them to follow her. The ostrich feather on her hat collapsed under the snow. But she held her head high, walked down the white path and turned around the corner with the grave digger and the workmen behind her.

The mourners waited, with their eyes fixed on the embarrassed pastor and the small coffin adorned with bronze handles.

Snow settled on the pastor's ruffed collar and melted on the gentlemen's uncovered heads. The dampness seeped into boots and shoes. The ladies' black veils got heavy. Mrs Betty Nansen pulled her silver fox up to cover her ears.

Finally Mrs Holst came back. And her cheeks were red from indignation. A whispered exchange ensued between the pastor and her, after which she withdrew.

Oscar Geismar finished the burial rite and announced: 'Due to an error the coffin has been placed at a grave site that is not the right one. Mr Bang will now be lowered into this grave but will, as soon as the other grave is ready, be moved to his final resting place.'

Which was section B, row 9, number 8.

*

In Copenhagen's cinemas the film *The Four Devils* was playing. Thereafter it was shown on five continents.[67] In Berlin it ran for half a year in nine theatres, and Kaiser Wilhelm watched it several times.

Herman Bang's only legal will was written at Valkendorf's Student Residence, and his heirs were the porter's two sons. One of them had become a barber, and the other had emigrated to America.

Acknowledgements

Quotations from letters in this book are taken from the The Royal Library of Denmark's collection of letters to and from Herman Bang, from Anna Levin's publication *Fra Herman Bangs journalistår* (From Herman Bang's Years as a Journalist) and from *Breve til Fritz* (Letters to Fritz).

The letter to Anna Ferslew is fiction. Unfortunately, only a thin, blue envelope remains intact. But like the rest of the book, it is built on Herman Bang's writing, journalism and interviews.

Harry Jacobsen's four-volume biography – *Den unge Herman Bang* (The Young Herman Bang), *Resignationens digter* (The Poet of Resignation), *Årene, der svandt* (The Years That Passed), and *Den tragiske Herman Bang* (The Tragic Herman Bang) – have been a great help to me as have Mette Borg's *Sceneinstruktøren Herman Bang* (Herman Bang as Theatre Director), Wilhelm von Rosen's *Månens kulør* (The Colour of the Moon) and Vivian Greene-Gantzberg's *Herman Bang og det fremmede* (Herman Bang Abroad).

Of memoirs I have found the following very useful: Anna Levin's *Fra Herman Bangs journalistår* (From Herman Bang's Years as a Journalist), Albrecht Schmidt's *I liv og kunst* (In Life and in Art), P. A. Rosenberg's *Herman Bang*, Octavia Sperati's *Fra det gamle komediehus* (From the Old Playhouse), Gerda Christophersen's *Memoirer* (Memoirs), Inger Heise's *Min skitsebog* (My Sketch Book), Anna Larssen's *Teater og tempel* (Theatre and Temple), Agnes Henningsen's *Letsindighedens gave* (The Gift of Being Carefree), Christian Houmark's *Timer, der blev dage* (Hours That Became

Days) and *Når jeg er død* (When I Am Dead).

Thank you to Erik Rasmussen for sharing his knowledge about Herman Bang and his books with me. Also many thanks to the staff at The Royal Library's reading room.

19.6.1996
Dorrit Willumsen

Notes

1   'Den, Gud giver et embede, giver han også forstand' (To those God gives a vocation, he also gives brains) is a common saying in Denmark and Sweden.

2   The Danish word is 'Karlsvognen' (Karl's Wagon or Karl's Carriage), the popular name for a seven-star constellation that forms part of the constellation The Great Bear (Ursa Major). In the USA, the seven-star constellation is called The Big Dipper; in the UK, it is named The Plough.

3   Dionine is an opiate narcotic analgesic also known as ethyl morphine and codethyline; it was invented in Germany in 1884 as a weaker alternative to heroin.

4   Anne Marie Mangor (1781-1865) was a popular Danish author of cookery books.

5   The original pun is too complicated to convey in English: Miss Kall asks for three roasts (Danish: 'stege') to be placed on her body, a gesture which should illustrate 'Stege på Møn' (Stege is the name of a town on the island of Møn, and 'møn' can also mean 'the maiden'. Hence 'Stege på Møn' refers to 'roasts on the maiden' as well as to the town Stege on the island of Møn. The English pun 'Made/Maid in Denmark' is only an approximation of the original.

6   N. F. S. Grundtvig's hymn 'Det er så yndigt at følges ad' (How Sweetly Beckons the Path Ahead) translated into English by Paula Hostrup-Jessen (1988).

7   'Slægterne' (The Generations) was the working title of Herman Bang's novel *Håbløse slægter* (Hopeless Generations, 1880). In his letters, Bang often referred to the novel as 'Slægterne', even after the publication of the novel.

8   Johan Ludvig Heiberg's one-act vaudeville *Nej* (1836) was performed at The Royal Theatre in 1886, featuring Oda Nielsen.

9   Erik Bøgh's one-act vaudeville *Alle mulige roller* (All Sorts of Roles)

premiered at *Dagmarteatret* in May 1886, featuring Martinius Nielsen and Oda Nielsen.

10   The medal for Arts and Science was bestowed on Arma Senkrah by Count von Sachsen-Altenburg. The name is misspelled 'Attenbourg' in the Danish text.

11   Herman Bang had booked passage aboard the steamship *Cleveland* from San Francisco to Japan.

12   Edvard Brandes' two-act play *En forlovelse* (An Engagement, 1884), Peter Nansen's one-act play *Kammerater* (Friends, 1884) and Herman Bang's one-act play *Inden fire vægge* (Within Four Walls, 1881).

13   Gefle is the older name for modern day Gävle in Sweden.

14   In the letter dated Gefle 21.5.85, the words 'Ved Stranden' refer to the address of the newspaper *Nationaltidende* in Copenhagen. The newspaper baron J. C. Ferslew bought the former Hotel Royal at no.18 Ved Stranden in 1876 and established the editorial offices and his family's private quarters in the building.
See (http://bangsbreve.dk/dokument/18850521001.
The address 'Ved Stranden' is misspelled 'ved skranken' in the Danish text.

15   Jens Christian Hostrup's comedy *Gjenboerne* (The Neighbours, 1844).

16   Herman Bang's short stories 'Kærlighed' (Love) and 'Præsten' (The Pastor) were published in the volume *Præster* (Pastors, 1883).

17   'Solen – Giv mig solen' (The sun – Give me the sun), Osvald Alving's famous line at the end of Henrik Ibsen's play *Gengangere* (Ghosts, 1881).

18   The country railway station referred to is Skørping station in North Jutland which becomes the model for the setting in the novel *Ved vejen* (By the Road, 1886), publ. in the collection *Stille eksistenser* (Quiet Lives, 1886).

19   The short story was originally titled 'Son altesse' and later 'Hendes højhed' (Her Highness), publ. in *Stille eksistenser*.

20   The publishing firm Salomon & Riemenschneider collapsed in 1883 when Benedikt Salomon and Adolf Riemenschneider were arrested for counterfeiting hundred-krone bills. Herman Bang describes the scandal in his novel *Stuk* (Stucco, 1887).

21   There are two different English translations of the novel *Ved vejen*: Tiina Nunnally's *Katinka* (Fjord Press, 1990) and W. Glyn Jones' *As the Trains Pass* (Dedalus Books, 2014). For the sake of clarity, the more literal translation of the Danish title has been used in the present text: *By the Road*.

22   Until December 1886, 'Bernhard Hoff' was the working title of the novel *Stuk*. Bernhard Hoff is a character, a journalist, in the earlier novel *Håbløse slægter*. Initially Bang intended to use the same character as the protagonist in *Stuk* but ultimately chose Herluf Berg.

23   'Facades': The Danish word used by Dorrit Willumsen is 'stuk' which

alludes to the novel *Stuk* that Herman Bang was working on intermittently while living in Vienna and Prague in 1886-87. 'Stuk' means stucco or plaster, a building material used to embellish interiors or exteriors, in particular in the construction of the fictitious Victoria Theatre in the novel. Figuratively, 'stuk' connotes a facade or fake ornamentation that conceals a false or tainted reality.

24 Herman Bang stayed at Hotel Skandinavien in the town of Nakskov in 1889 when he was completing the novel *Tine* (1889). The hotel is named Hotel Harmonien in the original Danish text, which is an error that Dorrit Willumsen made me aware of.

25 The retreat at Dannevirke during the Second Schleswig War, February-October 1864 is featured in the novel *Tine*.

26 Irene Holm, an itinerant dance teacher, is the protagonist in the short story of the same name, published in the collection *Under åget* (Under the Yoke, 1890).

27 The poem 'Der vaagnede den Morgen et Lig' (That Morning a Corpse Woke up) is from Bang's *Digte* (Poems, 1889).

28 The small town of Laurvig is now called Larvik.

29 The daily paper *København* was founded by the writer Ove Rode in July 1889. It was politically independent, considered literary and in opposition to the status quo. Johan Knudsen was editor from 1889-91.

30 The four flying trapeze artists are the inspiration for the novella 'Les Quatre diables' (1890).

31 The name of the estate 'Bangsbo' has no relation to Herman Bang's family. The name originates from 'Bangsboodh' (noted in 1334), meaning Bang's store or booth.

32 The hospital Kommunehospitalet (The City Hospital) is the main setting for the novel *Ludvigsbakke* (1896) where the protagonist Ida Brandt is a nurse.

33 'Skumringshistorie' (Twilight Tale) refers to the short story 'Fortællinger fra Skumringen' (Tales from the Twilight) in Herman Bang's earliest literary publication *Tunge Melodier* (Heavy Melodies, 1880), a collection of short stories.

34 The tragedy *Brødre* (Brothers) was published in 1891 along with the tragedy *Når Kærligheden dør* (When Love Dies).

35 'Den sidste dansker' (The Last Dane) was meant to be a sequel to *Tine*, but the novel was never completed.

36 The town of Sæby and Clasen's Hotel become the setting for Bang's short novel *Sommerglæder* (Joys of Summer, 1902).

37 The estate Rodvigsballe is the model for the fictional estate Ludvigsbakke in the novel of the same name.

38 The reference is to the 1893 student uprising in Paris that nearly ended in revolution.

39 Bjørnstjerne Bjørnson's plays *Over Ævne* (Beyond Human Power, I [1883], II [1895]).

40 Betty Müller married Peter Nansen in 1896. They divorced in 1912.
In 1917 Betty Nansen bought *Alexandrateatret* and changed its name
to *Betty Nansen Teatret*. She managed the theatre until her death in
1943 and introduced many old and new classics as well as a modern
repertoirc to the theatregoers of Copenhagen. The theatre is still one of
the most popular in the capital city.

41 *Aladdin eller den forunderlige lampe* (Aladdin or the Wonderful Lamp,
1805) by the Danish Romantic poet and playwright Adam
Oehlenschläger.

42 Mimi is the protagonist in the play *Frie fugle* (Free Spirits) translated
into Danish from the French *La Vie de Bohème*, a play (and originally a
novel) by Henri Murger. The French play was later adopted by Giacomo
Puccini in his opera *La Bohème* (1896).

43 *Det hvide hus* (The White House, 1898), a fictional memoir of Herman
Bang's childhood.

44 *Arbejdersken* (The Working Woman, 1898), a tragedy by Sophus
Claussen, directed by Herman Bang at *Folketeatret*.

45 *Det grå Hus* (The Grey House, 1901) is a fictionalized memoir dealing
with Herman Bang's early years in Copenhagen (1875-1877) while
residing at his paternal grandfather's home in Amaliegade near the
royal palace. Oluf Lundt Bang was then employed as the royal
physician.

46 'Adam' refers to a moving and transport firm established in 1884.

47 Heinrich von Kleist's drama *Das Kätschen von Heilbronn, oder die
Feuerprobe* (Katie of Heilbronn, or The Trial by Fire, 1808).

48 Johannes V. Jensen's historical novel *Kongens fald* (The Fall of the King,
1900-1901) is set in the sixteenth century during the reign of the
Danish king Christian II.

49 *Danserinden* (The Dancing Girl, 1833), a narrative poem by Frederik
Paludan-Müller.

50 The flight from the town Sønderborg on the island of Als during the
Second Schleswig War in 1864 is featured in the novel *Tine*.

51 Marie d'Orléans (1865-1909) was a descendant of the House of
Bourbon. Both her parents were grandchildren of Louis-Philippe
I, the last king of France. Marie married the Danish Prince Valdemar in
1885 and lived with him and their children in 'Det gule palæ' (The
Yellow Palace) in Copenhagen. She was known for her political and
artistic interests and her liberal upbringing of her children.

52 *Stille Eksistenser* (Quiet Lives, 1886), an anthology of four narratives:
Ved Vejen (By the Road), 'Min gamle kammerat' (My Old Friend),
'Enkens Søn' (The Widow's Son) and 'Son Altesse' (aka 'Hendes
Højhed,' [Her Highness]).

53 *Ravnene. To fortællinger* (The Ravens. Two Tales, 1902).

54 In 1858 J. S. Nathanson opened Hotel Marienlyst (then known as
Marienlyst Kur- og Søbadeanstalt [Marienlyst Spa and Baths]) in the

town of Elsinore, and as an attraction he had 'Ophelia Kilde' (Ophelia's Spring) and 'Hamlets Grav' (Hamlet's Grave) built on the property. Herman Bang was a frequent guest at the hotel.
See: http://www.helsingorleksikon.dk/index.php/Ophelia_Kilde

55 The intial title of the story 'Slagen' (Beaten, 1905) was the German 'Geschlagen.'

56 Stellan Rye (1880-1914) was a Danish playwright and film director born in Randers. He was Herman Bang's protégé, and *Løgnens ansigter* (The Faces of Deception, 1906) was his dramatic debut. After having served a three-month prison sentence in Denmark for homosexual activities, he left for Germany in 1912 and became instrumental in early German film-making that anticipated the expressionist revolution. *Der Student von Prag* (The Student from Prague, 1913) is his best-known film. During WWI he joined the German army and died in France as a prisoner-of-war.

57 *De uden fædreland* (Those Without a Native Land, 1906).

58 Johannes V. Jensen's article 'Samfundet og sædelighedsforbryderen' (Society and the Sex Offender) appeared in *Politiken*, 30.11.1906.

59 *Sælsomme fortællinger* (Strange Tales, 1907), an anthology of three stories: 'Barchan er død' (Barchan Is Dead), 'Men du skal mindes mig' (But You Shall Remember Me) and 'Stærkest' (Strongest) inspired by the gothic themes of Edgar Allan Poe's fiction.

60 '*To Johannes V. Jensen*. Heart problems have prevented me from writing to you sooner. I thank you sincerely for paying me a visit.'

61 The 'king of the cats' appears in *Prince Incognito,* not in *King for a Day.* Although not stated in Dorrit Willumsen's novel, Herman Bang is referring to two different plays that he directed: 1) *Si j'étais roi* (King for a Day; in Danish: *Konge for en dag*), a popular French 'opéra comique' by Adolphe Charles Adam and 2) *Prince Incognito* (in Danish: Prins Incognito) a Danish operetta by Frederik Richard and Axel Breidahl. The former opera was staged at *Dagmarteatret* in 1910; the latter premiered at *Casino* 14.8.1909.

62 *Masker og mennesker* (Masks and People, 1910).

63 Herman Bang's novella, originally entitled 'Les quatre diables' and published as a serial in the paper *København* in August–September 1890, was later renamed with the Danish title 'De fire djævle' (The Four Devils, 1895) which is also the title given to the silent film by Robert Dinesen and Alfred Lind in 1911.

64 Herman Bang was mistaken. The famous tower is called Ivan the Great's Bell Tower and was completed in 1508. It was not built by Ivan the Terrible who reigned from 1530–1584.

65 The following excerpt is from Herman Bang's so-called 'Erotic Testament' that was published with the title 'Gedanken zum Sexualitätsproblem' in *Zeitschrift für Sexualwissenschaft* (Bonn, 1922). Herman Bang had mandated that the treatise not be published until

five years after his death, but due to the intervention of WWI, the publication was delayed. The first Danish translation, 'Mine Tanker om det sexuelle Problem,' appeared in the weekly *K. T. Smart* in 1927. Peter Nansen had unsuccessfully tried to prevent the publication.

66 Herman Bang's coffin was moved for one night to Jesuskirken, a church in Valby in the southwest part of Copenhagen and a short distance from the cemetery Vestre Kirkegård (The Western Cemetery) where Herman Bang's body was put to rest. Holmens Kirke in central Copenhagen is a much older and more prestigious church than Jesuskirken.

67 By the end of 1912, the silent film *De fire Djævle* (1911) by Robert Dinesen and Alfred Lind had been shown in Europe, America, Asia, Australia and Africa. Three other film versions based on the novella have since been made. In Germany: *Die Benefiz-Vorstellung der vier Teufel* by A. W. Sandberg (1920); in USA: *4 Devils* by F. W. Murnau (1929); and in Denmark: *De flyvende djævle* (The Flying Devils) by Anders Refn (1985).

Postscript

'Yes, that was a happy time …
But then I got married …'
Herman Bang: *By the Roadside*

Danish writer Herman Bang (1857-1912) was a true master of understatement. The old cliché about reading between the lines – or in his case the ellipses – could have been written with his best works in mind. Although a flamboyant, media seeking, drama queen himself, Bang's major novels and some of his most successful short stories focus on quiet, unobtrusive, often downtrodden characters whose downplayed existential tragedies they keep to themselves; the famous depictions of 'stille Eksistenser' ('quiet lives') made Herman Bang one of the most loved authors in Denmark in his time. Even today he is not only canonized but actually read by all generations.

In the above quote from the short novel, *By the Roadside* (1886), the kind, introvert, somewhat passive and fragile Katinka Bai, wife of the boisterous railway manager Mathias Bai who loves not only food and drink, but also women, falls in love with another quiet person, the enigmatic Huus who has been sent to manage a farm in a backwater of Jutland. The two develop a fragile, understated romance based on mutual interests in flowers and music and all the little details that Bai has no interest in.

Whilst Bai fathers at least two children outside his barren marriage, Huus and Katinka, despite their mutual attraction, never 'consummate' their love - if that is what it is. Huus leaves and Katinka dies of consumption like an unspectacular 'lady of the camellias', the heroine of the 1848 novel by French romantic writer Alexandre Dumas (1824-1895), by whom Bang was inspired. No one knows about Katinka's and Huus' secret love and suffering but the narrator and the reader, who become complicit in this tale of impossible, extramarital love and death.

Love and death are recurrent themes in Herman Bang's works, but more often than not surprisingly undramatically depicted. Katinka is no great tragedienne but an ordinary, somewhat fragile woman with a little too much sensitivity and a hint of angelic sacrifice. She is one of the many quiet everyday female martyrs that Bang based on his beloved mother who passed away when he was only fourteen, a relationship that is beautifully captured in Dorrit Willumsen's novel.

*

Katinka was to have many 'sisters' in Bang's later works. Perhaps Dorrit Willumsen considers herself one of them. Although a century apart, both writers produce proto-feminist stories about vulnerable women who suffer disastrously in their marriages and relationships. And neither Bang nor Willumsen have many illusions about love and happiness. Relationships more often than not fail or go terribly wrong. But Willumsen adds a discreet modernist absurdism to her writing that is absent in Bang's texts.

A famous 'sister' to Katinka is *Tine*. This novel from 1889 is set in the era of the disastrous Danish defeat in 1864, when the country lost more than a third of its territory to Germany. *Tine*'s protagonist is a more robust and practical woman than Katinka. 1889 marked the twenty-fifth anniversary of the Second Slesvig War, the catastrophe that forced Bang's family to leave their home on the island of Als in Northern Schleswig. Als remained in German hands until 1920 and Bang did not live to see the region as Danish territory again (Northern Schleswig was returned to Denmark after a plebiscite in 1920).

But *Tine* is no patriotic war novel celebrating the lost greatness of Old Denmark. Although Bang levels harsh criticism against the recklessly chauvinistic, megalomaniac and delusional Danish politicians who were responsible for the defeat, his main focus is what happens to desire when normal barriers disappear. The handsome and happily married forester, Henrik Berg, experiences the horrors of war while his beautiful wife and little son are shipped off to Copenhagen. Tine, the neighbour's young daughter, becomes his interim housekeeper and ends up in bed with Berg on whom she has always had an innocent crush. Tine's downfall is interwoven with her country's defeat. Mismanagement on the personal level is paralleled with national, political blunders. The girl's body becomes a symbol for the 'rape' of Als and, in the bigger picture, Denmark, by Austrians and Prussians.

Beware of the dogs in this novel! Berg's hunting dogs accompany the sad love affair between the decent man and the young, inexperienced girl who mistakes desperate desire for true love. When Berg is mortally wounded in battle, Tine seeks him out on his deathbed where he no longer recognises her. But he does recognise his dogs... Thus, realising that Berg never loved her, Tine drowns herself in the pond like Antinous in the Nile. Like Katinka, her first experience with love and sex is not only tragic, but fatal.

*

The third female martyr to love is the altruistic nurse, Ida Brandt, in the last major masterpiece from Herman Bang's workshop: the novel *Ludvigsbakke* (1896). Ida is the victim of a tyrannical mother who leaves her a substantial inheritance. As she has been brought up to serve and live for others, she takes on a position as a nurse in a Copenhagen hospital, the very hospital to which Bang himself committed himself in 1891 suffering from depression and suicidal thoughts.

At the hospital, Ida meets a childhood friend from the manor house Ludvigsbakke in Jutland and falls in love. But the long-legged beau, Karl von Eichbaum, is a lazy good for nothing who gets a better offer from a wealthy merchant's daughter, Kate Mourier. In this world of ruthless capitalism and queer gender trouble, money *can* buy you love – or at least sex – and the prize of the attractive gentleman is handed over to the richest female buyer. Ida probably does not kill herself literally, but it is clear that for the most part, her life is over.

All of these female martyrs to love can, of course, be read as Bang's way of criticising and demonising patriarchy, heterosexuality and the institution of marriage. 'We are all here to reproduce', sighs Katinka Bai's exhausted childhood friend, Thora Berg, who herself is slave to a grumpy husband and a handful of sons. Thora was actually Katinka's first love and the novel plays with more lesbian subthemes than this one. The manly Agnes Linde, the local vicar's daughter, also seems to have more than a crush on Katinka.

As a subtle, almost coded way of deconstructing the marriage institution, Bang names Thora's husband 'Dahl', and thus, the typical pattern is hinted at. Miss Berg ('mountain') becomes Mrs. Dahl ('valley') and marriage is a one-directional journey 'downhill'. Marriage and reproduction are depicted as the iron laws of heteronormativity that rule the world, but it is the barren outsiders like the childless Katinka and the marriage-shy bachelor Huus who get the sympathy even though there is, fundamentally, no room for them, neither in the text nor in the world. Katinka dies and Huus leaves and the 'little life' ('Smaa-Livet') lingers on.

*

There is an uncanny continuity between Bang's fiction and the famous German essay *Gedanken zum Sexualitätsproblem* ('Reflections on the sexual problem') that he dictated to his Berlin doctor Max Wasbutzki. When Willumsen dates this text to Bang's departure for his last journey, she applies poetic licence. In reality, the essay was produced in 1909, right before Bang left Berlin after his two year exile as a sexual refugee. In 1906 and 1907 he had been a victim of the first large public homosexual scandal in Denmark when he was hounded by the press and by colleagues, most infamously the young Johannes V. Jensen (1873-1950). Bang never forgave Jensen this, but he nevertheless always recognised the younger colleague's literary genius. This Bang describes in his last novel, *Those without a Fatherland* (1906). The novel has also been read as an allegory for homosexual men who are homeless 'aliens' or permanent 'sexual refugees' in this world, and particularly Denmark.

In the Gedanken-essay, which was not published until 1922, Bang writes about the trials and tribulations of the typical homosexual man who represents nothing but a harmless mistake in nature: a woman's soul trapped in a man's body. Bang's homosexual is a self hating, altruistic, almost pathologically generous and misunderstood man who only tries to do good but is unjustly persecuted because of superstition, prejudice, ignorance and misconceptions. He is a victim of blackmailers and misguided public opinion. The salvation, according to Bang, is science and medicine.

Here Bang is in perfect accordance with the early German advocates of homosexual emancipation like the doctor and sexology pioneer, Magnus Hirschfeld (1868-1935), whom Bang actually met during his Berlin stay. Bang ends his essay by hoping that one day future doctors will be able not to cure, but to prevent homosexuality altogether: 'This is needed for the sake of reproduction'.

In his fiction Bang himself uses the same technique that he hopes the doctors of the future will apply: he gets rid of all the unproductive people, all those who for some reason or another will not or cannot propagate the species. The normal heterosexuals are more often than not depicted as vulgar beasts but they are still granted existence while the noble, barren, often refined martyrs suffer sentimental deaths. In that respect Bang does not represent queer sexual politics but is a firm believer in heteronormativity.

*

Bang's critique is instead expressed by the way he distributes his sympathies. There is little doubt that he regards himself to be, if not doomed, then cursed by his sexuality. His essay leaves little room for love and life for homosexuals, who are described as prone to suicide, tragedy and unhappiness. The homosexual is born with an enormous 'debt' that he works his whole life to 'repay'; his existence is compared to that of a hotel guest who knows he can not pay his bill, a situation that Bang himself certainly was acquainted with.

Herman Bang's first novel, based on his own person, was consequently called *Hopeless Generations*, describing the tragic fate of a degenerative, sensitive young man who is doomed to fail because of his family history with a tubercular mother and an insane vicar as a father. This pattern — inspired by his own childhood — Bang kept reproducing and rewriting in his work, especially the biographically inspired novels, *The White House* (1899) and *The Grey House* (1902). The settings are respectively the childhood parsonage on Als and the wealthy grandfather's house in Copenhagen which the orphaned Herman often visited in his youth.

When publishing *Hopeless Generations* in 1880 Bang was an upcoming media celebrity working as a journalist, a playwright, a critic and a writer. He was omnipresent in the cultural life of Copenhagen where he often shocked the conservative public with outrageous fashion statements. From early on he was ridiculed in the satirical journals, especially the Danish version of the weekly *Punch*, where he was almost the 'protagonist' for over thirty years.

This 'career' capsized when his first novel was confiscated and deemed 'immoral', a verdict that was just as much aimed at the text as at its flamboyant author whose homosexuality was soon to be an open secret. Interestingly, the text was revised in 1884 and reissued in a version that more than hints at the degenerate protagonist's suicide in the end. Perhaps the only way to make 'moral' a novel about a homosexual was to kill him off, thus confirming the assumption that a good homosexual is a dead homosexual. Heteronormativity in Bang's time always also required 'heteronarrativity'.

*

Homosexuals are prone to be artists, Bang claims in his Gedanken-essay, and often very good ones because of their 'androgyny', the fact that they can see the world with the eyes of both sexes. But because of the impossibility of mentioning homosexuality they have to disguise themselves and become masters of literary masquerades. For instance, William Shakespeare would have been an even greater writer if he could freely express his love for men.

Thus, all of Bang's romantically suffering women are perhaps not just versions of his mother but can be read, also, as allegories of homosexual men whose love is from the outset doomed; for these characters love can bring nothing but sorrow, disappointment, pain, disaster and often death. And the connection between love (or sex) and money is a given.

There are clear connections to be made between Herman Bang's outline of a certain homosexual poetics in his essay and his own development of what was to become the impressionistic style in Danish and Nordic literature. The hidden or very discreet narrator who dares not speak in his own voice but hides behind the characters and can only hint at things represents the homosexual artist's role in a society where his love dare not speak its name.

Today, it is rather difficult to characterise Bang's art as a 'style', for over the last century, Bang's impressionist technique has been seen less as a time-bound style of literary expression and more as simply a measure of quality. To write like Bang is today less a description and more simple praise. One can almost say that in Denmark today it simply means to write well.

'You tell us nothing but show us everything', Bang wrote about the Norwegian writer Jonas Lie (1833-1908) and the same goes for Bang's best works. His first novel, *Hopeless Generations*, is way too long and too detailed in the naturalist tradition and his last tragic and pessimistic works — *Mikaël* and *Those without a Fatherland* — are somewhat sentimental and melodramatic, leaving too little to the imagination of the reader. In contrast, Bang's novels and short stories from 1886 to the end of the century are masterpieces of literary minimalism, tight, economical and seemingly 'sketches' where the careful reader has to 'finish' the works and fill in the blanks herself. Unfortunately, Bang seems to have lost confidence in the reader in his last works, which explain too much.

*

'Many homosexuals travel if they are wealthy', Bang states in his Gedanken-essay. This was certainly true in his own case, although he suffered from financial problems all of his life. From the very start of his career, Bang was focused on the European continent, spending long periods of time in Paris, and particularly the German-speaking world. Many of his works were translated into German in his lifetime but they did not sell substantially until after Bang's death, when his reputation continued to grow. The interwar period is characterised by a veritable boom in the German reception of Bang, including numerous translations and editions.

Many great writers, including Thomas Mann (1875-1955) and, especially, his son Klaus Mann (1906-1949), state their great admiration for the Danish writer whose name in Germany became almost synonymous with homosexuality, perhaps comparable to the role that Oscar Wilde played in the English-speaking world. Dorrit Willumsen is not the first to produce fiction about Bang. In 1939 Klaus Mann wrote a short story based on Bang's visit to the United States and his death on the train in Utah: 'Journey to the End of the Night. Herman Bang'. The essay was part of a substantial manuscript entitled 'Distinguished Visitors', about famous Europeans in the USA. The English original of Mann's text on Bang remains unpublished but German, Danish and Italian translations have appeared in the last twenty years.

Bang had no knowledge of English and experienced no reception in the English speaking world but my hope is that Willumsen's exquisite novel will spark an interest in Herman Bang and pave the way for many more translations of his major works, including the Gedanken-essay, a fascinating document both in the field of literary history and in the history of sexuality.

Dag Heede
Lektor, mag.art., ph.d.
University of Southern Denmark

CPSIA information can be obtained
at www.ICGtesting.com
Printed in the USA
LVHW012034050220
645949LV00011B/733